From the Extreme

From the Extreme

Renea Collins

www.urbanchristianonline.net

URBAN CHRISTIAN is published by

Urban Books
11199 Straight Path
Deer Park, NY 11729

ISBN-13: 978-1-60162-955-5
ISBN-10: 1-60162-955-9

First Printing February 2008
Printed in the United States of America

10 9 8 7 6 5 4 3 2 1

This is a work of fiction. Any references or similarities to actual events, real people, living, or dead, or to real locales are intended to give the novel a sense of reality. Any similarity in other names, characters, places, and incidents is entirely coincidental.

Submit Wholesale Orders to:
Kensington Publishing Corp.
C/O Penguin Group (USA) Inc.
Attention: Order Processing
405 Murray Hill Parkway
East Rutherford, NJ 07073-2316
Phone: 1-800-526-0275
Fax: 1-800-227-9604

From the Extreme

Renea Collins

URBAN
CHRISTIAN

www.urbanchristianonline.net

URBAN CHRISTIAN is published by

Urban Books
11199 Straight Path
Deer Park, NY 11729

ISBN-13: 978-1-60162-955-5
ISBN-10: 1-60162-955-9

First Printing February 2008
Printed in the United States of America

10 9 8 7 6 5 4 3 2 1

This is a work of fiction. Any references or similarities to actual events, real people, living, or dead, or to real locales are intended to give the novel a sense of reality. Any similarity in other names, characters, places, and incidents is entirely coincidental.

Submit Wholesale Orders to:
Kensington Publishing Corp.
C/O Penguin Group (USA) Inc.
Attention: Order Processing
405 Murray Hill Parkway
East Rutherford, NJ 07073-2316
Phone: 1-800-526-0275
Fax: 1-800-227-9604

Acknowledgments

I thank Jesus Christ my Lord and Savior for having mercy on my life and Who lives inside me. I thank Him for making me clean.

I want to thank my Apostle Maurice Broomfield who has ministered to me and showed me that God does give us a new life if we live for Him and surrender to His will. I thank God for him!

I want to thank my Pastor, Pastor Sherry Broomfield, who has shown me what it really means to be a virtuous woman. I admire you; you are a beautiful woman inside out and I love you and your Apostle for being my spiritual parents and for guiding me on all of my many ideas and adventures. You have supported me and have given me faith that I can do whatever I think I can do! I thank God for the God in you.

To my daughters, you are spectacular women of God. Keep growing and keep God first in your lives.

I thank my sister, you are my strength, and you have supported me and helped me when I couldn't help myself. You are truly a diamond. Don't ever lose sight of Jesus; He will and has rewarded you for your obedience. I love you!

I love you, Momma, and I hope you understand this is something that will help others. I know it was tough for you, and I know that you love me. I love you too.

Special, special thanks to Joylynn Jossel for inspiring me to write in the spirit of excellence.

I also want to acknowledge my cousin, Toni Goff, for working with me and helping me make the necessary changes I needed to make.

Also, a special thank you to Ms. Shatoya Wilson for being patient and sitting with me and reading.

Thank you to everyone else that has helped me and those that have hurt me along the way. I know now that God had you in my life for a purpose and time, even if it was just to see the transformation in me. God has received the glory in my life. My family and friends and my church Power and Glory Ministries, I love you! God bless you!

From the Extreme

From the Extreme

Introduction

"Wow" is how I would describe the sequence of events in my life. It wouldn't be right if I didn't start from the beginning. Nowhere is where I literally came from. The gutter, the ghetto, roach-infested, mice-infested nowhere. Most will have to understand that for me to share my life, only the Almighty God in Heaven has given me this strength. God has ministered to me to keep faith always, and to help others to receive that, through divine revelations, it takes faith to turn your life around. 1 Peter 1:4-7 says: "To an inheritance incorruptible and undefiled and that does not fade away, reserved in heaven for you, ⁵who are kept by the power of God through faith for salvation ready to be revealed in the last time, ⁶In this greatly rejoice, though now for a little while, if need be, you have been grieved by various trials ⁷that the genuineness of your faith, being much more precious than gold that perishes, though it is tested by fire, may be found to praise, honor, and glory at the revelation of Jesus Christ."

You have to understand God has a purpose for your life, but it takes faith and obedience to find that purpose, and trust God to do the rest. Ecclesiastes 3:1 states: "To everything there is a season, a time for every purpose under heaven."

Chapter 1

Innocence Forsaken

As we drove down Miami Chapel Avenue, Aunt Angel shouted, "Oh, look. That's the house you girls lived in when you were babies!"

Aunt Angel was a dark-skinned woman with long, thick hair. Her hair was almost in the middle of her back. Voluptuously built and somewhat short, she was so pretty. She smiled at me with those deep dimples through the rearview mirror.

I smiled back at her then looked over at Crystal, my big sister, as she slept while we rode in the Volkswagen bug. I thought, *How can she sleep through the yelling and the music on the radio?* The DJ was playing "Family Reunion" by the O'Jays. *She's so pretty.* I couldn't help but wonder why we didn't look alike. Crystal looked as if she was mixed with white, with her nice soft, long hair and beautiful grey eyes. I didn't. I had nappy hair and was darker than her and Momma. Again, I wondered why.

I rose out of the black leather seat of the car that was sticking to my pink Pleather coat. I'd been chewing on the collar before Aunt Angel screamed. I pressed my face and hands against the car's cold window while we drove past the old house that was abandoned now. It was boarded up, and the paint was coming off the sides.

Aunt Angel startled me again. "Rachael, you girls were so precious back then. So innocent and beautiful," she said.

I smiled at her the entire time she spoke, but remembered the pain of the things that took place in both of those houses, our house and the Hestleys' home across the street. She had no idea the torture we experienced in the prison across the street from our house. I never spoke of the things that went on in that house.

I hated even riding down that street in little old Dayton, Ohio. The memories would haunt me for years. I would always look over at the now-empty lot and just thank God that the house was torn down. In some kind of way, that made me feel a little better, knowing that house wasn't standing any longer. Too bad I couldn't say the same about my pain.

I remember being around four years old and Crystal being around six and Momma would take us across the street to Mrs. Hestley's house. We hated going over there. It was terrible. I don't remember every little detail of what took place. After all, I was only about four, but what I did remember haunted me for years.

"Crystal, Rachael," Momma would holler. I could hear her high heels walking on the wood floors downstairs while Crystal and I played with dolls upstairs.

Crystal looked up at me and sighed. "Momma's going out." She held her head down, dropped the Barbie from her hand and said, "Come on." Crystal's grey eyes told it all. It was as if someone else took over her body. She became a walking zombie. She wouldn't come back to being herself until we came back from across the street.

I can't really remember her doing or saying much of anything over at that old rundown house across the street.

"Come down here. I need to take you across the street for a little bit," Momma said.

I stood at the top of the steps, looking at Momma in the living room, putting on makeup in the mirror over the fireplace. She never turned around and looked at us standing there. Just told us what we needed to do.

"Grab your coats. Crystal, help your sister put hers on, please." She was in a rush, trying to get out of the house before Paul got home from work. "Let's go." She then turned around and said, "How I look?"

Momma was light-skinned and had the prettiest hair you ever wanted to see. It was jet-black without dye, wavy and long, down to her bottom. Her eyes changed colors like a cat. Sometimes they were grey, and sometimes they were green or blue. She always dressed as if she had just come from a photo shoot. Momma was lovely.

We walked down the steps slowly, holding hands. Crystal looked at me, squeezed my hand tight, as if to say, "We'll be all right."

I still hear the steps squeaking, especially the one that was halfway along, and the last two.

Ring, ring, ring!

Momma ran in the kitchen to get the phone that was hanging up right beside the white medicine cabinet I had sneaked in a few weeks earlier. I'd used my red tricycle to climb up on to see if her pills were candy. I found out a few hours later that they weren't when Momma had to rush me to the emergency room to get my stomach pumped.

"Hello," Momma said into the receiver. "I said I'll be there in a minute, Calvin. Shoot, don't call here!" She slammed the phone down.

I wondered who Calvin was but never asked. Crystal and I stood there watching her every move.

"Hey, girls." She would smile and put her hands on her

hips, walking toward us. "When I come back, let's do something fun."

We didn't react the way she thought we should have. We just stood there looking sad.

"Why you both standing there like you lost your best friend or something? Huh?"

I finally decided to speak up. I only had a few minutes to convince her not to take us over there. "No, Momma, please don't take us over there. I hate it over there. They mean to us."

"Girl, stop all that yelling. Shoot, I gotta go run some errands. I'll be right back." She looked down at the beautiful watch that Paul, my stepfather, had given her for her birthday.

As Crystal struggled to put on my coat, I wasn't helping her. I was standing there being difficult because I didn't want to go. Looking for a way to escape, I cried, "Can you call Grandma? She'll come and get us."

Momma bent down to my level and said, "No, I don't want to call Grandma, and don't tell her you been across the street." She squinted her eyes at me and continued, "You better not tell her either," and put her finger to my lips. "Now come on." She held the door as we walked under her arm, feeling the fur from her mink on our faces.

She locked the door tight and said, "Wait a minute." She turned her back away from the cold wind that was blowing and lit her Kool cigarette. She took a long puff. "Crystal, grab Rachael's hand."

I was wrapped up tight with my red boots, gloves, scarf, and hat. My eyes were watering from the cold air, but other than that, I didn't feel a thing.

"Slow down. Watch the cars. Crystal, hold her hand. Shoot!"

Beep, beep! That's all I heard from men driving by, looking at Momma.

She smiled and said, "Hey, baby," and kept stepping. She was in such a rush and wanted us to hurry up, but we were walking as slow as possible, dreading going in that house. That might possibly have been be the longest walk I ever took.

I cried and stopped halfway over there. "Momma, no! Don't, Momma, don't! Don't make us go, please! They mean to us. Momma, please!"

She grabbed my hand from Crystal. "Come on, girl. Stop all of this. You hear me?"

I got louder and louder until I was screaming.

"I know you hear me, Rachael. Crystal ain't crying. Look at your big sister. She's okay. You gonna have fun with Steven and Michael and everybody else. They love you."

Momma was bent over with her hands wrapped tight around my upper arms. I felt so secure right then. It was time for me to tell her what was happening over there. She was ready to listen, I thought.

As she held me by my arms, I reached up and wiped my eyes. I glanced past Momma into Crystal's face and saw the fear of what would happen if I told.

Momma interrupted my thought and said, "It's like you have big sisters and brothers over here." She was smiling. "Now stop all of this nonsense before they think I been beating you, girl."

I looked up to that scary house as I walked up the cracked concrete steps to the porch. The house was grey, and the shutters were black. They had no grass in the yard; just dirt from all the kids playing. On the side of the house was Tiger, their scary pit bull, foaming at the mouth, held by a chain used to tow cars. I knew he was waiting to eat me. I hated that place.

I did everything I could think of to show Momma that there was something wrong when she dropped us off. I kicked, I screamed, I fought so that I didn't have to enter that place, but nothing worked. Momma walked over those signs as if I was laughing and running toward the house, not away from it. The house was a prison cell to me and my sister, but to Momma, it was the village that was helping her to raise her children.

There were eight children at the Hestleys' house, all of them older than Crystal and me. To give you an idea of this family, I recall Michael, the oldest son, catching a mouse in his bedroom. The mouse had babies, and he kept them all as house pets.

Momma would drop us off, tell us we would be there for a little while, but then not come back for days. I believed her when she said she would be right back. I loved my mother. I trusted her every time. I dreamed of the things she said before she left.

"When I come back, we'll have a picnic," she'd say. "I'll take you girls to the park so you can play. I'll be back before you miss me."

Momma was tall and slender with long legs, and always looked classy. She looked like a black Jackie Kennedy. Beautiful! Everywhere Momma went, she would get attention. She had a glow all around her. I would look at her when she was on the other side of the glass door, looking like an angel, saying good-bye to me with fear in my eyes, knowing we were in the house of the devil himself.

Momma didn't know the hell her little girls faced in that house. She thought we cried because we missed her. The truth was, she had no idea what we went through from the moment she left.

Momma would tell Mrs. Hestley, "I'll be right back. I just need to make a few runs, girl. You know how it is."

I looked at Mrs. Hestley's face as she listened to my Momma. She didn't believe her. I could tell she didn't even like Momma, but Momma would give her money for watching us, and that's all she wanted. She didn't care about us; just the money.

Mrs. Hestley would turn her lips up and say, "Uh-huh, Janice, I know how it is." Mrs. Hestley was a gray-haired, older, stocky woman, and she was mean and bitter. She never did much besides sit on the couch with a cigarette in one hand, a Pepsi in the other, while watching the soaps and screaming at the top of her lungs at all the kids.

When Momma would leave, I would stand at the front door crying, trying to open the door by turning the gold doorknob to flee and escape the prison—escape the molesting, the beatings, the emotional abuse, and starvation. I would stand at the front door, holding the gold doorknob for what seemed like hours.

Kathy, Mrs. Hestley's baby girl, would say, "Stop turning our doorknob. You gonna break it. You stupid. You can't get out, dummy."

I turned around and looked at her. Her teeth were sitting out of her mouth from sucking her thumb. She was lighter than the rest of the kids, but had the very same features as her other brothers and sisters.

"Leave me alone. I want my momma."

"Yo' Momma ain't coming back today." She was leaning on Jimmy, her brother. Maybe because they were twins, they were inseparable.

Jimmy never said anything. He just watched everything that would happen. However, if I got into a fight with Kathy, he would jump in every time. So, fighting with her was always fighting two.

Kathy sat on the steps and watched me, laughing and snickering.

Eventually, Mrs. Hestley would tell me, as she puffed on her cigarette, "Now, little girl, no sense in you crying. Get over here and sit down." She pointed to the orange-green-

and-yellow striped loveseat beside the matching couch she was sitting on. "Get in here and sit down, or get out of my house with all that crying. You stand there every time yo' momma drop you off, and you still too stupid to realize she don't care about you girls. Sit down, with your nappy hair."

I would cry louder and louder. I knew what was to come. Mrs. Hestley didn't, but I did. So did Crystal. Mrs. Hestley's sons were molesting us. Her daughter would beat us. She had no idea that when she told them to give us something to eat, they wouldn't. She was too busy on the phone, running Momma into the ground with the other neighbors.

"That whore ain't coming back no time soon," she'd say into the receiver, and then she would laugh.

I walked over to the living room, looking at Mrs. Hestley and on guard to make sure she wasn't going to haul off and smack me. I waited in the front room for hours, sitting there biting my nails and shaking my leg like Momma did whenever she was upset. I watched the roaches go from the kitchen to the living room with food on their backs from the floor.

I sat there watching Mrs. Hestley talk on the phone with whoever would listen. "Girl, Janice done dropped her babies over here again. And you know it ain't no telling when she coming back for them. Shoot, Greg gonna be mad when he get off work and they here. We barely got enough over here for our own kids, and this tramp drops her kids off."

She watched me watch her as she talked on the phone, never giving the other person time to say a word. She didn't even care that I heard her talk about us. Now, that's mean.

"She better be glad I care about her kids. You know when her and Paul start fighting and he black one of her eyes or bust her nose, she run out on him for a few days. She needs to stay there and work it out. That's what I do when Greg starts fighting with me. Sometimes you have to take the beatings so your kids can eat. She ain't never gonna learn. She stupid."

Mrs. Hestley's face was so drab, like she had been in a war or battle. She acted as if she had no feelings about anything at anytime. Looking back, I understand it was because of the abuse she endured. She hated her own life. I heard Momma and Paul talking about the many beatings, and the other women and kids Mr. Hestley had. I even remember looking out my bedroom window one night at all the police and ambulance lights flashing. The police were pulling Mr. Hestley off, and the paramedics were taking Mrs. Hestley to the hospital. The kids were standing on the porch in their underwear, looking at their father, enraged, fighting and screaming at their mother as they dragged him off.

Once night fell and I realized we wouldn't be going home, I asked Crystal, "What happened to Momma? Why she ain't back?"

"She'll be back in a little while." Crystal didn't have an answer for me. Only a couple of years older than I was, she herself was confused, terrified, and afraid. She didn't know why Momma left us.

As I think back, Crystal took more of the abuse than I did because she was trying to protect me. Those kids would pick on her bad. They would kick her, pinch her, and make fun of her because she had very light skin. She would stand there, take the abuse, and never fight back.

I would always scream out, "Leave her alone! She doesn't wanna fight!" I hated them picking on her even more than when they picked on me. Crystal's gentleness, meekness, and intelligence were what made her special.

"Momma," Michael would holler from the kitchen, "we going to the park. You want us to take them with us?" He was speaking of Crystal and me. "We gonna play basketball. They can play at the park while we're there."

Michael was tall and dark-skinned. He played basketball in high school, and his little brother, Steven, wanted to be just like him. He went everywhere Michael went and did everything he did. He dressed liked him and bounced the ball like him. Whatever Michael did, Steven wanted to do too.

Mrs. Hestley would mute her television remote and holler back at Michael, "Okay, take them to the park, but don't go anywhere else. You hear me?"

"Yes, ma'am, I hear you," Michael would respond.

Their mother believed that they really were taking us to park, but instead, they would take us into abandoned houses and molest us. The boys would walk us down the street, holding our hands, and take us into this old yellow house down the street from ours.

The first time they claimed they were taking us to the park, I looked up at Steven with a big smile on my face and said, "I can't wait to get to the park." He looked down at me and just smiled.

Steven and Michael looked so much alike. Steven was just a smaller version of Michael. He was dark-skinned with a huge afro, and they both wore Chuck Taylor gym shoes. They always wore gym clothes, like jogging pants, and I never saw them without a basketball in their hands. Steven had long eyelashes and bad acne, and always, always held his hands over his face when he talked.

I looked around the front room of the yellow house. It was cold. Someone had pulled the green plush carpet back, so I could see the wood floors. The front room was painted black and the kitchen was red. There was mouse poison in the kitchen, but there wasn't a stove or refrigerator anywhere.

Steven led me into another room upstairs. I looked back at Crystal in the living room. I walked up the stairs and listened to them squeak all the way up.

Steven went in the pink room first, grabbed my hand, and

said, "Come on. We playin' house. You the momma, and I'm the daddy, okay?"

"I wanna go to the park. You promised you would push me on the swings."

"I'm gonna take you to the park when we leave here." He looked at me. "So shut up!" He pushed me on the dirty, cold wooden floor and pulled my pants down.

I fell back and bumped my head, but that didn't stop him. I screamed, "I'm gonna tell on you! Stop that! I want my momma!"

I remember Steven lying on top of me, yelling in my ear, "You better not tell! I'll kick your butt if you do! I'll bash your face in then I'll tell Kathy to beat you up!"

My holler reached a pitch that was so high, but it still didn't stop him. He smelled so sour. I got so mad, I closed my eyes and began to kick my legs and hit him with all my might in his back, but nothing stopped him. He just got angrier.

Steven was older and stronger than I was. He was fourteen or fifteen. His voice was much louder than mine, and scarier. "Shut up! Stop crying! I'm the daddy. We just playing house."

"Crystal, Crystal, Crystal!" I'd cry out to my sister, who was downstairs enduring the same thing with Michael.

"Leave me alone, Steven. I hate you! Leave me alone. I want to go home. Please take me home!"

I don't remember much after that. I'd rather forget it altogether. The molesting went on for the next two or three years. As time went on, Steven would take me to different places; anywhere he could sneak in such as garages, alleys, bushes, abandoned houses, and empty trains. I soon learned to take myself out of the situation as he forced himself upon me, so I would dream. Whenever it happened, I wasn't there. I was somewhere else. At the park on the swings, on the monkey bars, riding my bike, or at home with Momma.

Oftentimes, he would take me to the yellow house at the end of our street. I soon knew that screaming and hollering wouldn't work, so I stared at the pink ceiling in the house as I lay on the dirty floor. I could hear the kids outside playing, not too far away, laughing, having fun, while I was inside the abandoned house, losing my innocence.

The boys told us we had better not tell, so I never said a word. Back then, I was afraid of them and believed every threat they made. I truly believed they would hurt us. I acted as if nothing happened.

As I got older, I somehow convinced myself that I agreed with what he did to me. I stopped remembering the things from my past until I gave my life to Christ and God, started digging up those painful memories so I could truly be free. I realize now that not exposing those demons made room for many more to come in. If I had told someone when I was older or even acknowledged that it happened, healing and deliverance could have taken place long ago, but it kept me in bondage for years. The devil tricked me and made me think that it was my fault and that I wanted it to happen because I never told. The devil is a liar!

Psalms 10:7-10 says: "His mouth is full of deceit and oppression; under his tongue is trouble and iniquity. He sits in the lurking places of the villages; In the secret places he murders the innocent; His eyes are secretly fixed on the helpless. He lies in wait secretly, as a lion in his den; He lies in wait to catch the poor; He catches the poor when he draws him into his net. So he crouches, he lies low, that the helpless may fall by his strength."

Remember, the truth will make you free. The mistreatment that took place in my life had a crippling effect on every decision and every relationship I would have in the years to come, opening up doors that allowed me to accept any treatment I received, as long as someone would pay attention to me.

After we returned from "playing house" with her sons, Mrs. Hestley, hand on her hip, said to Michael and Steven,

"Where you been? Why were you gone so long? I told your sister to go down to the court. She said she didn't see you."

"No, Ma, we were there. She lying! We lost track of the time playing basketball. Rachael and Crystal were busy on the swings and monkey bars."

I wanted to holler out, "They had us in a house doing the nasty to us!" Nothing ever came out of my mouth, though. I was too afraid.

Mrs. Hestley stared at her sons for a few more seconds then dismissed them. It was as if she knew they were doing something to us, but she wouldn't acknowledge it. She stood there, hands on hips, looking at Crystal and I as we stood at attention, then hollered, "Stacey, come get these girls and feed them dinner!"

I thought to myself, *Oh no. Here comes the monster.*

Stacey was about eighteen years old. She was very dark with short hair, and I never saw her smile. She wasn't very excited when her mother made her look after us. Actually, she was pretty upset. She didn't like being around my sister or me.

Before we even saw her come downstairs, we could hear her walking across the floor upstairs. She sounded like a thousand elephants running in the wilderness. She was furious. She came downstairs with a big frown on her face and holding her nose, as if to say we stank. I couldn't stand her. Every time she turned her back, I would roll my eyes at her. She was mean and ugly.

"Your momma is a whore! She's not coming back to get you. She hates having you around. That's why she left you. Ya dirty. Ugh, you dirty!" Stacey's face would be frowned up when she spoke, and she rolled her eyes the whole time. "Your momma didn't even leave you clothes to change into. She so nasty. She don't care about you. Ha, ha, ha! That's messy. Yo' momma so messy."

I wanted to reach up and pull out the little bit of nappy

hair she had and knock her in the mouth for talking about my momma like that. What did she know? They didn't have very much themselves, but here she was, almost grown, putting down a little girl's momma right in her face.

Mrs. Hestley interjected, "Stacey, quit telling them that. You so mean wit' yo' ugly self. Shoot, girl, don't make me get up and beat you. Feed those kids like I said."

She would roll her eyes at her momma and suck her teeth and say under her breath, "Shut up, you witch."

She looked down at me and said, "Come on, go up the steps."

I started crying because I knew she was going to kick one of us in the back on the way upstairs. She always did that. I looked upstairs in the hall and saw Kathy standing there with her pants down, bent over, saying, "Ha, ha! She gonna beat yo' butt."

Crystal said, "Rachael, you go first."

I looked at her and knew she meant she was going to take the kicks. The stairway was dark with a wooden railing and a tall ceiling, kind of like the ceiling at church. I looked at it all the way up the stairs, and heard Stacey counting and laughing at how many times she kicked Crystal in the back.

At first, Crystal tried not to cry. She'd moan a little, but it seemed like Stacey kicked her harder and harder each time. Stacey would hold onto the wall with one hand and the rail with the other then pick herself up and push with all her might. Crystal started falling down some of the steps.

Michael appeared at the top of the steps to see what was happening. He laughed. "Stacey, stop doing that. That's wrong."

"Shut up, Michael. You want me to tell Momma what you were doing with them?"

On that note, he disappeared as quickly as he appeared. Stacey knew what the boys were doing to us because she caught Michael pulling down Crystal's pants in her bedroom and screamed out to Mrs. Hestley. Michael told her he would never do it again, and that was the end of that.

Crystal was crying, and so was I. I could hear Mrs. Hestley from a distance, hollering, "What's wrong with them now? Did you feed them? Shoot, I be glad when they momma come get them. Hell, I can't take all this crying they do."

"Yes, ma'am. They got their hot dogs in my room. They eatin' now," Stacey said.

I went in Stacey's room and looked around. She had a big brass bed with no sheets, an old dresser that had red crayon writing all over it, and a window with no curtains over them.

She pointed. "Come in here and sit right there and eat yo' hot dog.

Kathy stood in the doorway. "Can I come in?"

"No!" Stacey slammed her door. "Now, stay right here on the floor, Rachael. Don't move till I say so. You hear me?"

I nodded. I sat on the floor Indian-style, scratching my arms and legs and hitting myself. That's really what I wanted to do to them. Hurt them. I thought if I did things like that to myself, it would make them feel sorry for me, grab me, and hug me.

"Why are you doing that? Why are you hitting yourself?" Stacey asked. "You so stupid."

By nighttime, I was crying myself to sleep, wondering where my momma was, and praying nobody came in there to mess with us. When would she come for me?

Jesus was always there comforting me when I was on that cold floor, crying. Psalms 10:14 says: "But You have seen, for You observe trouble, and grief, to repay it by Your hand. The helpless commits himself to You; You are the helper of the fatherless."

By the time I'd convinced myself that Momma wasn't ever coming back, she came walking through the door. I ran and gave her the biggest hug and kiss. I whispered in her ear right there in front of Mrs. Hestley and her fake smile and said, "Momma, promise we don't have to come back."

She rubbed my back and kissed me on the forehead. "I promise, baby." However, within a few days, we went back across the street, into our prison.

Isaiah 49:15,16: "Can a woman forget her nursing child, and not have compassion on the son in her womb? Surely they may forget, yet I will not forget you. I have inscribed you on the palm of my hands; Your walls are continually before me."

Momma was twenty-seven when I was born. Her name is Janice Ann Bradley. I was the youngest of four children. Sally was the first. Then there was Johnny, Crystal and I. Sally passed before I was ever born. She was two when it happened. Momma said she believed she had gotten into some mouse poison. The pictures that Momma had of her were beautiful. She was a beautiful baby—curly black hair and light brown, oval eyes with colorful cheeks with dimples and caramel skin. I would daydream of having her around. Momma didn't speak of Sally that often. I assume it hurt her too bad.

Johnny and Sally looked alike. They had the same father. Johnny was eight years older than I and was raised with his father, so we didn't see him much as kids.

One day, I said, "Momma, why Johnny don't live with us? When is he going to come stay with us?"

She turned her head to the side and said, "I'm gonna get him soon." Then she puffed her cigarette.

I looked at her standing in the kitchen, frying potatoes and onions, and thought, *It sure would be nice to have him around. Nobody would pick on me with my Johnny here.* I stood there daydreaming and smiling, thinking about it.

Momma said, "Girl, go sit down somewhere, standing there smiling, looking silly. Sit down!"

I ran upstairs to my room and thought, *She's so mean.* I wanted my big brother

home. *If he was here, I would be okay, and kids wouldn't pick on us or make fun of us.*

Now that we're older, Johnny and I have a close relationship, and I praise God for it. A truck driver driving the big rigs back and forth across the country, he called me while he was on the road and said, "Hey, baby sis, what you up to?

"Nothing. Just doing hair. What's up?"

His voice screamed out desperation and loneliness, and I could tell he'd been drinking. He said, "You know what? I wonder why Momma didn't come and get me when I was a kid. I could see if she was in a different city, but she was in the same city I was in and she never came for me."

I could hear the pain and anguish in his voice. He was trying to keep it together, but at the same time looking for some answers. But I didn't have one for him.

"My daddy's wife would beat me when I lived with them. I mean real bad. She said I didn't belong there with them but my momma didn't want me. She said Momma was a whore and couldn't take care of me. Daddy would stand there and watch her. He never said a word. He let that woman beat me and kick me like I was a dog." He began to cry.

He cried so hard that I couldn't understand him any more. I know now that it really affected his life, not knowing or feeling like he had the love of his mother. Johnny was now battling with alcohol and didn't have a place to call home. He didn't spend a lot of time with his two children or family. His excuse was that he had to work, but I believe it was a cover-up from the pain he was feeling from his childhood.

"Johnny, I can't understand what you're saying. Call me when you're sober. Please quit drinking like this, Johnny. It's not gonna solve nothing." I was getting impatient and frustrated with him. After all, I felt like I went through hell as a child. I was thinking that at least somebody came and put him someplace where he didn't have to look at roaches or worry about if he was gonna eat or have a place to sleep. I was bitter myself and couldn't help him with anything at this point. Shoot, I couldn't even help myself. God was gonna have to do this for me, for him, and Crystal.

Johnny said, "I used to dream that Momma was coming for me. I cried myself to sleep every night hoping she was coming. I couldn't understand why she had you and Crystal, but didn't want me."

By this time, he was touching areas inside me that I didn't want to deal with, so I snapped on him. "You know what? You should be glad she didn't come and get you, all the trouble we went through being with her." I was smacking my lips and everything, talking to him. "I wish I had a father that could come and get me, but I had to stay there with her. Shoot, you had it better where you was at."

Crystal was the third-born, and the only sibling that I grew up with. Crystal and I had a very strong bond. Growing up, we had God and each other. We were taught about Jesus Christ at an early age. Our grandparents made sure of that. At the ages of six and eight respectively, we were baptized and became active in the church. I've been baptized again since then. We ushered and were in the children's choir.

While facing my pain and revisiting my life, I needed to remember how I came to know Christ. When did my love for Him start? I prayed and asked the Lord to show me. He showed me my mother; who first introduced me to Jesus. I had to be about four, maybe three. I was lying in her bed watching cartoons, when I asked her, "Momma, do you love me more than anything in the world?"

She said, "Of course I do, baby."

"More than anything?"

She stared straight ahead for a moment and thought. "Well, I do love someone more than you."

"Who? Crystal?"

"No, I love you both the same."

"Who then, Momma?"

"Jesus Christ." She smiled.

I knew the name, but I didn't know who He was. When my mother said she loved Him more than us, I wanted to know more about Him. I asked her who He was and why she loved Him more than her own children.

She told me, "Jesus died so that we can live. He's God's son. You can't see God, but He is there. And if you need Him, call Him and He will help you."

After she introduced me to Jesus, she taught me this prayer: Now I lay me down to sleep, I pray to the Lord my soul to keep. If I should die before I wake, I pray to the Lord my soul to take.

Crystal and I prayed that prayer every night for years. I started talking to Jesus daily after that. I praise God for us knowing Him at an early age.

I never knew who my father was. Crystal knew who hers was, but I never knew mine. Momma never told me. When I was a little girl, I would say, "Momma, where's my daddy? Who is he and why he don't come and see me?"

She always looked at me like I was aggravating her. She said, "I told you he was in the Army when I had you." Her eyes always let me know when she was telling the truth or telling me something to make me leave her alone. "He came to the hospital when you were born and brought you some clothes. Then he went to Vietnam, and I never heard from him again."

I loved hearing that. I wanted her to tell me over and over again how he came and brought me clothes when I was a baby. "Momma, couldn't you find him?" I said, wondering what he looked like.

"Girl, leave me alone."

"Okay, Momma. Do I look like him? Tell me, please." I watched her face to see what she was going to say.

"Well, you look a little like him. You have his hair, that's for sure." She laughed.

Momma never told me the same name twice or the same story twice. Once she told me he was in the Air Force and was sent to Vietnam. Then she told me it was a man who was married with a family and lived in Dayton, in the suburbs.

As I got older, I stopped asking. I realized I would never find out the truth because she didn't want me to know who he was. I knew she wasn't going to ever tell me. It has been discouraging, but now, I know God is my Father, and He has filled the emptiness.

"Do not call anyone on Earth your father; for One is your Father, He who is in heaven."—Matthew 23:9.

My stepfather, Paul, wasn't around very much. I don't remember a lot about him, except the drinking and fighting he and Momma would do. Paul worked at the post office as a mail carrier. He would go straight to the bar after work, get drunk, then come home and fight with Momma.

I remember Momma taking us on his mail route one day to get his check. She dressed us up so pretty to go. She said, "Come on, we going to get Paul's check before he spends it at the bar. If he gets to the bar, we won't eat this week."

She put Crystal and me in the car. Then she got in the front and looked in the mirror. Putting on her lipstick, she said, "I'm tired of him." She sighed aloud, like she didn't know how she got herself in this mess.

One night, she put us to bed, and I remember awakening to screaming and yelling. I rose straight up in the bed and looked over at Crystal's bed. She wasn't there. I was scared. I tiptoed to the steps.

Crystal was sitting there. She looked at me, and put her finger over her lips. "Shhh. Be quiet, or they will hear us."

Paul was shouting, "You're a whore, Janice. Why do you go to the bars and embarrass me? Why, Janice? I take care of you and your two kids." He beat his chest. "I don't deserve this." He was crying, and his speech was slurred.

Momma said, "I can do better than you. You are a sorry excuse for a man. Look at you. You're a drunk." She motioned her hands at him, like he was pathetic.

Paul said, "I love you, Janice. You're so beautiful. Why you treat me this way? Why you treat me like this, huh? Why?" He started throwing furniture across the room. He shouted, "Yeah," nodding his head and smirking, "that's what you want me to do. Hit you. You like that."

Paul turned around and hit her in the face, and she grabbed her nose and started screaming once she saw the blood flowing down her hand.

I began shouting and crying, "Stop! Don't fight! You're scaring me!"

Crystal had gone next door, over Aunt Hildred's house, to call Grandpa.

Paul picked me up and said while smiling, "Don't worry, baby girl. We okay. Everything gonna be okay. Isn't it, Janice?"

I could feel his heart beating fast as he held me close, looking at Momma for her approval.

She stood there looking at him and holding her nose, the blood still running down her hands. "Give me my baby." She reached out her hands for me.

By the time Grandpa got there, neighbors were outside, and the police were pulling up in front of the house. My Grandpa told Momma, "I'm taking the girls with me. You coming?"

"Take the girls. I'll be there after I pack." She never looked at her father; she would hold her head down when she talked to him.

Momma never came.

I can still see her standing there with blood coming out of her nose down her face. It hurt my heart to see her hurting.

I cried and held on to her as she carried me to Grandpa's car. I didn't want to leave her there. I was scared for her. I held her so tight and stroked her hair as she put me in the car. I thought Paul was going to kill her, and we were never going to see her again.

Momma kissed me on the cheek. She smiled. "Don't worry about a thing. I'll be there in a little bit."

I would calm down, and before we would reach my grand-parents' house, I would be fast asleep. Grandpa would carry me into the house, not saying a word on the ride over. But his silence was felt. I know it had to hurt him to see his daughter going through the abuse.

After a couple more years of fighting and loving, Paul and Momma got a divorce. I was six when Momma divorced Paul and we moved. For a while, things were looking up for us. Paul was gone, and so were Mrs. Hestley and her kids.

The house we moved into was Momma's best friend's. She had moved to Philadelphia and needed someone to pay her house note, and we needed a new house, so it worked out perfectly.

The house was beautiful. It was a red brick, two-story house with a big maple tree in the front yard. The neighborhood was quiet, and everyone's yard was manicured. Our house had a huge front porch. Momma put a swing chair and some flowers on it. It was lovely, and I was so excited! The bad was over with!

I walked in the front door, and the first thing I saw was the fireplace, then the big picture window in the living room across from the fireplace. The stairs were over to the right, and there was a window halfway up the stairs, but if you went past the fireplace, you would make a quick right and be in the dining room.

There was carpet on the floors and beautiful wood borders everywhere. After exiting the dining room and hanging another right, there was the kitchen. It had a new refrigerator and stove there. Momma bought all new furniture for the move too. We even had new beds!

Momma ran through the house and screamed, "Girls, come and look!"

We ran through the house, laughing and saying, "What, Momma?"

She was standing in the middle of the backyard, smiling with her dimples showing. "We gonna invite everybody in the family over for a barbecue. Daddy is going to love it!" Her eyes darted around the whole backyard. "I'm going to put you girls a swing set right here." She pointed to a spot. "We can have a barbecue pit built over there."

Crystal and I were so happy. We ran around the whole backyard playing for hours while Momma unpacked.

My mother loved that house. Every time she entered it, she had the biggest smile you ever wanted to see on her face. She was classy. Momma always had herself together. Whatever she wore was beautiful. If she had a dress on, her shoes, purse, and hat went with it. In today's time, she would be referred to as a real diva! That was the happiest I ever saw her.

I did miss my Great Aunt Hildred, though. The house we moved out of was hers. It was a duplex, and we lived on the other side of her. I would knock on her door often to talk. She loved to see me coming. She sat in her rocking chair and told me stories about Jesus. She gave me and Crystal children's Bibles when we were five and seven. She'd tell us to bring our Bibles when we came over there, so she could teach us how to study. So, when we went knocking on her door, we had our Bibles with us.

Aunt Hildred would pray with us. She told me often to believe God and He would guide me all of my life. That's true.

I don't remember seeing Aunt Hildred after we moved. I don't think I ever saw her alive after that, but I do remember her. I can even remember what she looked like. She had long, black-and-gray wavy hair, and wore glasses when she read to us. Her skin was flawless and was butterscotch in color. She would sit in her rocking chair and knit as she talked to us.

I don't even think she owned a television, but when we were there, we never thought about watching one. She kept us entertained. She was an awesome woman.

Things were great for a while in the new neighborhood. After the move, Momma started looking for a job. She hadn't worked when she was married to Paul, so she had to start from scratch. Momma would sit and look at the newspaper and circle all the waitressing jobs and barmaid jobs she could find.

"What's wrong, Momma?" I would ask while climbing on her lap, moving the newspaper out of my way.

"Oh, nothing." She would smile. "Just trying to find something. It's hard when you don't finish school."

"Rub my back, Momma." I was so comforted, wrapped in the arms of my momma, that I went right to sleep.

Momma got me ready for school the next day and decided to come in with me. "Let me park, Rachael. I'll walk you to your classroom, baby."

"Okay," I said. I was excited. My teacher, Mr. Greg, could tell her how good I had been doing.

"Hey, Janice." The secretary came running out the office after us. Momma turned around and said, "Hey, girl."

"I know you been looking for a job, and we have something you might be interested in."

"Girl, I don't care what it is. I need it. Thank you, Celeste. Thank you." She looked as if she was going to cry right there in the hallway.

"Go to the gym and tell Mrs. Smith I sent you." She smiled at Momma and looked at me and smiled, then went back in the office.

Momma bent down to me and said, "Go to your class, baby. I'm going to check on this job then I'm going to Crystal's class, okay?"

I said, "I thought you were coming to my class, Momma." I didn't understand.

"Go ahead, girl. Go to class. This is important."

I stomped my feet and ran to class.

The position started off being a volunteer service, but eventually the school gave Momma an opportunity to take some classes and become an assistant to the gym teacher. Momma was good with the kids. She knew how to make them laugh, and she would study in the evenings and have new ideas when we went back to school. I could tell she was enjoying what she did, and I really liked her being at school with me all day. It felt good! Momma had time for us now, and her mind wasn't distracted by anything. The only thing she wanted was to take care of her kids. I was secure.

About a year or so after the move, Momma started dating. She started having parties at the house and hanging out with new people. Eventually, she was going out to the bars with her friends and missing work and us. We were either over at the neighbor's house or Grandma's and Grandpa's. It didn't bother me at first because we were being taken care of correctly, not like how it was at the Hestleys' house, but I started missing Momma. Where was she?

Momma started complaining of severe back pain. She quit her job at the school and decided to work at a bar not too far from our house.

We stayed in that beautiful house on Frazil Avenue for two years. Momma couldn't afford it any longer, though. First, the telephone went; then the lights and gas were turned off. Eventually she went down to the welfare department for assistance and food stamps so we could eat. Finally, she said we needed to move. Living in the house on Frazil Avenue was the closest I have ever been to my mother.

We moved from the house two years after we moved in. I was now eight and Crystal was ten years old. We moved to a little two-bedroom apartment in the projects. When I first saw them, I didn't know what to think. Where were the trees and the grass? I didn't understand. All I saw was concrete and dirt. It was a big difference from living in the house.

Momma tried to make the best of the situation, but I could tell she wasn't pleased with the apartments we moved into. It wasn't far from the house on Frazil, but it was so different. It wasn't a good neighborhood. Our apartment had cold concrete floors, a living room, kitchen, bathroom and two bedrooms. You could stand in the center of the living room and see all the other rooms.

The front windows had bars on them, so no one could break into the apartment or get out of them. The walls were cold and concrete too. I could hear people walking upstairs and their conversations. I could hear music playing outside, and there were plenty of people outside all hours of the day and night.

I watched Momma when we moved in. She was trying to make me and Crystal feel safe, but her look said it all. She looked scared herself and unhappy with herself, like she let us down or something. I caught her a couple of times coming out of the bathroom crying.

I said, "What's wrong, Momma?"

"Nothing," she replied.

I ran to her and hugged her.

"Hey, girls, we're not going to be here for long. I promise!" She was looking around at the surroundings and hearing the music of the people upstairs. She looked at the ceiling and smiled at us with tears coming down her face. I now know she didn't ever expect to come out from living like that. She had decided to settle for the lemons in her life. She didn't believe she could ever get out of the poverty we were faced with. She gave up hope.

Never give up hope!

I liked living there. I had plenty of friends to play with. There were kids everywhere! I stayed outside constantly and played kickball and tag, hide and seek, and raced up and down the middle of the street.

Every weekend, we would go over to Aunt Sue and Uncle Nate's house. I believed it was to get us out of those projects to a nice neighborhood.

Aunt Sue had a strong, raspy voice, short curly hair, and she always told jokes. She always helped Momma with food, clothes and sometimes even shelter for Crystal and me. Their house reminded me of a dollhouse. It was yellow, with pretty bay windows and many flowers in the yard. She loved animals. She had two poodles and a cat.

Aunt Sue's husband, Uncle Nate, would come by our house sometimes and see Momma. We would see him leaving as we rode home on the school bus. I would look at Crystal when we saw his car leaving before we got off the bus. Momma would stand there in her bathrobe in the door, her cigarette in her hand, puffing and blowing smoke out.

We didn't understand why Uncle Nate was at our house. By the time the bus let us off, she would be back in the house with the door closed, as if we didn't see him leave. It made both of us furious.

We raced to the door to find out what was going on. I ran up the three steps to the door, and shoved it opened. "Momma, what was Uncle Nate doing here? Where is Aunt Sue?"

"Uncle Nate is letting me borrow some money." She was so calm and cool, not ever looking at me when I questioned her. She sat there smoking her cigarette with her legs crossed, looking at the soap operas in her nightgown.

"Don't tell Aunt Sue. If you do, I'll beat your butt!"

Crystal came in the house, walked straight to the bedroom

and slammed the door. She didn't say anything, but I knew she felt the same way I did.

I was confused. I started questioning Momma, and it made me look at her in a completely different light. Why would she have him over? What was really going on? Did I really want to know?

I always thought of Uncle Nate as a soft-spoken man who loved Aunt Sue, but now I was looking at him and thinking not-so-nice thoughts of him. I can't say anything inappropriate happened because I never witnessed it, but it didn't feel right. Why was it a secret?

We would go over Aunt Sue's house for every occasion. Momma and Aunt Sue would sit, drink, and laugh all day long, giggling and talking nonstop. I was eight years old and on an investigation. My Momma was the case. I wanted to know if everything I was hearing my grandma, aunts and uncles say about her was true. I was seeing Momma in a completely new light. She was fake. She sat in that house and smiled right in front of my aunt, and my aunt had no idea what she was doing behind her back. Uncle Nate, too! He acted as if he hadn't seen us the day before.

Momma was watching me, her grey eyes shifting back and forth as she drank her vodka and laughed with everybody. I was devastated. My forehead had wrinkles in it as I stared at Momma.

One time, she caught me and Crystal whispering. She came over to us. "You better shut your mouths. Uncle Nate gave me money for you girls, that's all." She was getting nervous and edgy.

Aunt Sue said, "Janice, is everything all right? Why you fussing at those angels?"

Momma said, "Girl, these kids got too much mouth. They need to go outside and play." She turned to us. "Go outside!"

We both stood and looked at her for a minute like she was crazy, then she put her hands on her tiny waist, moved her head to the side and hollered, "Now!" She turned and walked back to the front room, looked back at us in the hallway where we were standing, and with piercing eyes, whispered, "I'll kill you if you open your mouth."

We both ran outside. We knew not to ever say a word.

That incident left me resenting my mother. I was eight years old then, and thirty-eight now, and can remember it like it happened yesterday. That was one of the reasons I despised my own momma. I begged God to help me with my feelings for her, but it was hard for me to respect her.

Over the years, the anger and bitterness grew stronger for her. I couldn't be in a room with her longer than ten minutes. I tried to talk to her. I asked her, as I got older and when I became an adult, why were there so many hidden secrets and so many dark times.

She always stuck to the same answer: "That never happened."

What can you say to somebody who won't even admit the past? I despised her. I hated when people said I was going to be just like her. They couldn't possibly know what I knew, or they wouldn't say such a thing.

I know things had to happen so I could share my testimonies and help others. I mean, it hurt me and affected my life, but God has prevailed in my life! He is all that! I can now sit and look at old pictures of Momma and only hope I am as beautiful in appearance as she was. She was a beautiful woman, no doubt; she just made bad choices and decisions, and she really didn't know how much God loved her. The devil will get a lot of us with problems like that.

As for my mother, I realize now that once you fall into deceit and lying, if you don't get delivered from it, it gets worse! There are some stories I wouldn't dare tell about some of the behaviors or things I've seen my mother do, because it would hurt too many people, but once you start in the pattern of deception, it grows. It's hard to get delivered from pain like that, but possible. First thing you have to do is forgive.

"But if you don't forgive, neither will your Father in Heaven forgive your trespasses."—Mark 11:26. Get free from the bondage, and then let God show you how to help the other person.

"Stand fast therefore in the liberty by which Christ has made us free, and do not be entangled again with the yoke of bondage."—Galatians 5:1. The devil tries to deceive us so no one can get the victory. You have to be obedient to God's Word. When I gave my life to Christ, He showed me you can't fight people for their behavior; you have to pray for them.

"For we do not wrestle against flesh and blood, but against principalities, against powers, against the rulers of the darkness of this age."—Ephesians 6:12.

Before I was truly saved, I thought it was okay to feel bitterness toward my mother; after all, she hurt me. But God shows us that we have to forgive people. Regardless of whom it is or what they did, you need to get over it and move on. You will never go any further in your life if you don't understand how to forgive. I'm not saying it's easy, because it's not, but you can do all things through Christ Jesus that strengthens you. You may be the person that God sends to help that individual. God has a way to turn the whole situation around.

"Let love without hypocrisy. Abhor what is evil; cleave to that which is good."—Romans 12:9.

The abuse, misunderstandings and way of life for me went on. I can remember being over Aunt Sue's for a barbecue and being manipulated into going into a doghouse way in the backyard of her house. The doghouse sat behind the garage. It was in an odd place, now that I think about it. It sat behind the backyard, behind the trees. The doghouse was grey with a black top on it.

One day we were all outside playing jacks; me, Crystal, my cousins, Shawn, Aunt Sue's grandson, Tracey, and Lamar. The other kids were a lot older than Shawn and me.

Lamar said, "Hey, Shawn," and whispered in his ear.

Shawn smiled and began looking at me.

"What? Why ya looking at me?"

Lamar gathered the rest of the kids up in a huddle and said, "Rachael, we gonna play dare." He was looking sneaky and I was feeling uneasy.

"What you mean?"

He said, "I dare you to go in the doghouse with Shawn and kiss. We all gonna do it. It's just your turn. Do it, Rachael. Kiss him."

"He's my cousin. You don't s'pose to kiss each other. That's nasty." My face was frowned up. I looked at Crystal, but she never said a word.

I did it. I kissed him, and everybody laughed.

Lamar then ordered, "Take Rachael in the doghouse and get on top of her."

"No! I'm not going to do that!" I shouted. I put the jacks down. "I'm tellin'!"

Lamar, with his buck teeth, looked at me, bounced the basketball, shot it in the net, smiled and said, "If you don't, we gonna say you did it and you will get a butt-whupping."

Everybody else was standing around laughing and giggling.

I went in the doghouse with Shawn, and Lamar pulled my pants down and told Shawn to get on top of me. I was eight years old, and Shawn was seven when this happened.

Crystal stood there for a moment then ran in the house to get Momma and Aunt Sue. Next thing I knew, Momma pulled me out of the doghouse and beat me. "What's wrong with you? You so fast with your hot butt!"

She never said anything to me about what we were doing or why we were doing it. Who showed me about sex? She just came out there, took a switch, and beat me.

"Momma, they made us do it!" I cried, but she wouldn't listen to me.

As soon as we went home, Momma and Aunt Sue got on the phone and told everybody they knew what had happened. I could hear her on the phone, talking about me, saying, "Girl, she so fast. That child is going to have a baby before she turns sixteen. I don't know what's wrong with her."

After the doghouse incident, I remember relatives looking at me like I was dirty. I never forgot the looks. Every time we went somewhere with the family, I knew they were going to stare. I was the fast one, the one that was like her momma—hot to trot! I started feeling out of place everywhere we went. They would watch me around the other kids. I hated that! I wanted to be looked at as they looked at the others, not thought of as a perverted kid. It was terrible.

I remember being at a funeral. I was ten years old. When my cousin Toy and I went to the bathroom, her father, my uncle Bill, came busting in the door, shouting, "What you doing in here?" He was furious! I was sitting on the toilet and Toy was washing her hands. He said, "Toy, get out of here! You girls don't need to be in here together!" He kept screaming from the top of his lungs, "What you doing in here?"

We both were looking at him like, "Using the bathroom." Toy didn't get it, but I knew why he was acting that way. That hurt my feelings so bad. I acted as though it didn't, but it hurt me.

I looked at him with tears welling in my eyes as he pulled Toy out of the restroom. I stayed in the bathroom for a little longer, crying and punching the air, wanting it to be the people that hurt me. They made people think I was a freak!

I talked to myself in the bathroom that day. "I hate myself! I wish I was never born! Everybody thinks I am a freak or something. I hate myself!"

I cried and sat against the cold, damp wall on the bathroom floor, bent over like a human pretzel. I stayed there until I heard Crystal come to the door and say, "Rachael, is everything okay?"

I looked up, wiped my face with my hands and said, "I'll be out in a minute. I'm okay." I got up off the floor in my floral dress, white tights and black patent leather shoes, discouraged and beaten. I looked in the mirror at myself and said, "You aren't what they say. You're going to show them one day." I left the bathroom and never shared that moment with anyone.

Toy was my favorite cousin, and I thought the world of her father. Toy's dad and my mother were brother and sisters. I admired the life Uncle Bill and Aunt May created for Toy. They were awesome parents. A picture-perfect family, they were.

Uncle Bill was tall, about 6'2" and handsome. He had black, short, curly hair and strong facial features. His face looked like God carved it to perfection. I can remember when we celebrated him coming home from Vietnam. He was a soldier in the Air Force. I wasn't that old, maybe five or six at the time, but I remember.

Aunt May was beautiful. She was very dark and her skin was flawless and smooth. She kept her hair shoulder length and had a pretty smile with the whitest teeth I ever saw. I loved everything about their family; one girl, one boy, a nice tan-and-brown split level house and one dog; two cars, two-car garage and many groceries in the house.

Aunt May cooked every day. I mean every day. Their house was immaculate. Their living room furniture had plastic coverings on it so if you sat down, you couldn't harm it. It was gold velvet and colonial in style. They had a 25-inch color TV with the stereo component on the other side of it in the family room, and a navy blue sectional couch with the two La-Z-Boy chairs on both sides of it, a wooden coffee table and plenty of toys on the floor.

Toy's room was for a princess. She had baby dolls all over her bed and stuffed animals. There were pictures from her dance recitals and basketball games hanging on the wall. Her bedroom furniture was white, with a canopy bed; I always wanted to sleep on a bed like that. Her sheets, pillowcases and comforter matched. The curtains even matched. It all seemed perfect, like a fairytale.

Toy was in every dance class, karate class and swim class imaginable. She was dark-skinned with long ponytails. She had her mother's complexion and her dad's facial structure. I had so much fun when we would see each other. We liked doing the same things. We would dance, ride bikes and talk about the boys at our schools. We liked the same things on television and liked the same foods; pizza and hamburgers.

We were best friends. I always wanted to take dance classes too, but we couldn't afford to, so when we went to Atlanta to visit them for the summer and holidays, Toy would teach me everything she had learned from her classes.

That's why Uncle Bill's perception of me was so devastating. I wanted to scream back at him, "What are you talking about? Don't treat me like that! I'm tired of you guys thinking badly about me! Ask me what's going on!" I just wanted somebody to talk to me, not assume things about me. I really hated what they thought of me.

Of course, I never said a word. I just smiled and pretended that I didn't understand what they were saying about me. They didn't know all of the things I was going through. They didn't know of all the different times we were at cookouts and family functions, older cousins taking me in bathrooms and bedrooms, doing what they wanted to me. But I was the one they thought needed to be watched! I was the one that was singled out.

"Thus says your Lord, the Lord and your God, Who pleads the cause of His people; See, I have taken out of your hand the cup of trembling, the dregs of the cup of My fury; You shall no longer drink it. 23But I will put it in the hand of those who afflict you, who have said to you lie down, that we may walk over you; And you have laid your body like the ground, And as the street, for those who walk over."—Isaiah 51:22, 23.

I often thought of what Uncle Bill said. It wasn't the first time he insinuated something like that. My sister and I went over their house one summer for two weeks. I was so excited because we didn't see them that much. I couldn't wait to go down there. I knew that my uncle and aunt would have activities for us to stay busy. The first night, I soon found out that the nice thoughts I had for them, they didn't have for me.

When it was time for bed, they separated me from the rest of the children. I knew without a doubt that they thought I was going to do something to Toy. It hurt me deeply. Toy and I wanted to sleep together so we could talk all night, but I wasn't allowed. Aunt May and Uncle Bill made excuses for me to stay in another room. I knew what they were thinking, but I never said anything. I went to the other room, lay in bed, crying and listening to the other kids laughing and playing all night.

People don't realize the things they do and say. It could plant a seed in a child. If a child as young as I was is promiscuous, most likely they have been abused. Children just don't start having sex. I didn't wake up one day and say, "I'm going to go and have sex today." No! Not at the age of four! Somebody has to molest you to put the seed of lust and perversion into your spirit at that young age. A child is innocent. Someone has to show a child how to have sex. I was a young child, and I had different relatives accusing me of being a lesbian! I don't know if they really understood how serious that accusation was. I was a child and I knew what they were thinking and saying, and it hurt! Kids are not stupid! They understand when they are talked about, mistreated, or lied to. They understand.

What they thought of me left me confused. I couldn't understand why people I loved and thought the world of thought so little of me. I never told anyone what happened when I was down there. I was too embarrassed. I talked myself into believing I was overreacting. They didn't mean anything by it, I would reason.

Over the years, I remembered every harsh word that was said to me. I wish that before people assumed a child was just bad to the bone, they would find out the problem. Something could be wrong with that child. Get to the root of the problem so the kid can be free, or they will become adults with that hurt in their hearts. I know, because I did. Only Jesus could heal me of that pain.

"And a servant of the Lord must not quarrel but be gentle to all, able to teach, patient."—2 Timothy 2:24.

I never said a word to anyone in my family about how I felt. I smiled and laughed when I was around them. I wanted my aunts and uncles to look at me and think I was successful. I wanted them to talk to me the way they talked to Crystal. Truth is, when I get looks like that now that I'm an adult, I stand with confidence. Through all the pain, although I might have felt as a child that my life was worthless, there was still someone left who didn't . . . I gave my life to Christ.

"At first defense no one stood with me, but all forsook me. Let it not be charged against him."—2 Timothy 4:16.

Chapter 2

Leave Momma Alone or I'll Kill You!

O ver the years from six to eighteen, we moved into and out of almost every project in Dayton, Ohio. We moved either voluntarily or involuntarily (evicted!). I remember some of the places and incidents, but a lot I don't recall.

I can remember this one like it happened yesterday. I was ten and Crystal was twelve. Crystal was into schoolwork and reading books. She didn't talk very much. She also watched a lot of television to escape the reality that we went through as little girls. I, on the other hand, was outside constantly. I loved being outside and I loved to play.

I was a chameleon. I could interact with any kid. I was tall and very skinny, mostly legs. I wore my hair parted down the middle, with two nappy ponytails. I would play basketball with the boys, then turn around and jump rope and do somersaults with the girls. I would lie in the grass, look up at the sky for hours and daydream. I talked to myself about having a different life and what I would do when I was all grown up.

When I was in the house, I was in my bedroom listening to the radio and talking to my imaginary friends and family. I dreamed for the majority of the day, even when I was with other kids or at school. I was always talking to myself inside my head. I believe that's what kept my mind free from what my reality was.

Momma was working at the bar, and still received government assistance and food stamps. My mother's sisters, Lisa and Angel, were now home from college. They were both teachers at Dayton public schools. My aunts would take turns coming to get us on the weekends. They were a blessing to Crystal and me. I loved going with them.

Aunt Angel was the funniest. "Okay, girls, what you want to do this weekend?"

We were so excited, talking at the same time, trying to tell her what we wanted to do.

"Okay, okay, I can't hear you both at the same time." She would smile with those dimples of hers. Aunt Angel would take us to the movies and Wendy's restaurant. "You can order anything you want." I can smile just thinking about those times with her. She really saved us. God used her to keep our spirits up.

"Oh, I know what I want. Let me have a triple with everything on it!" I hollered. Crystal would do the same. We never could finish our whole hamburger, but it was nice trying.

Aunt Lisa was a little more serious, but she always had something planned for us. She taught us how to cook and tried to teach us how to sew and knit. Lisa also took us to the garden to plant vegetables.

Everyone thought I looked just like her when she was a little girl. She was pretty. She had long, thick, black hair, and a light brown complexion. She was very shapely and always liked sports. She married her one true love, Uncle Earl, when I was around six years old. They were high-school sweethearts. I always wanted them to take me so I'd be their little girl.

We never were home on the weekends. Whether we were

at Grandma and Grandpa's house or with Lisa or Angel, we went to church every Sunday. When Aunt Angel and Aunt Lisa graduated from college, our lives changed. They were a lot younger than Momma. They showed us a life that we wouldn't have ever known if they weren't around. Both of them had spectacular apartments with central air, swimming pools, dishwashers, and plush carpet. Aunt Lisa's apartment had a balcony. I thought I was a movie star when I was over her house. I would get a blanket, go out, and lay for hours. I daydreamed that I lived in her apartment. I told Crystal I was going to have an apartment like that when I grew up. I would ask God, "Why didn't you let one of them be my mother?"

My aunts were the ones who got us through. I know them being there instilled success into me. Any time you can make a difference in a child's life, do it! It might not look big to you when you do it, but it could change their whole direction. Crystal and I never would have experienced some of the things we did growing up if it wasn't for them. They took us horseback riding, roller skating, ice skating, bowling, to the movies, restaurants, and many church functions. Momma knew when we were with them she didn't have to worry.

Momma started seeing a man named Champ, who she met at the bar. They were together constantly. Soon enough, he was living with us. I didn't like him. He looked sneaky and slimy.

"Momma, why he got to stay here?"

"Girl, if you don't get out of my face . . ."

Ever since we moved from Frazil Avenue, Momma was different. She was at the bar constantly. It was like she forgot about us. I felt alone, abandoned by her, like she didn't love us anymore. She left us all the time to survive for ourselves.

It didn't feel good with her not being around. I worried about her a lot. I would lie in the bed and wonder where she was and when she was going to come back. The only difference was that I was no longer being molested, but the thoughts of not having my mother return were still there.

Crystal was old enough to watch us now, so we stayed home alone. No food, no clean clothes, sometimes no lights and heat. We were abandoned. Sometimes she would leave on Monday and we wouldn't see her till Friday. We knew the phone numbers to at least three of her favorite bars. Using the next door neighbor's phone, we would often call them. We would have to eat and be full at school or hope one of our aunts would come by to check on us.

I thank God for my grandparents and my aunts coming for us on the weekends. My grandma and Momma didn't get along. Momma would tell us, "Don't tell her what's going on over here, you understand?" She would look serious at us, like we better not say a word or else.

"Yes, Momma, we understand."

See, Momma didn't want Grandma to find out nothing—stuff like the lights being disconnected or no food, or how she wouldn't come home for days.

Momma would ask the neighbors if they could help us out, letting her run an extension cord from their apartment so we wouldn't sit in the dark. She'd say, "Not for me, but my kids." She looked so desperate. She definitely didn't want Grandma to know that Champ was there and he was beating her just like Paul used to—no, worse.

Grandma would tell us to pack our clothes for the weekend. I can't ever remember her coming inside one of our houses or apartments. Grandma was a half-white, half-black, stocky woman. That's where Momma got her looks from and her pretty hair. Grandma had gray hair with a few black strands in between. She was a funny grandma, always making someone smile.

The summer I turned twelve was the summer Grandma

died. Grandma showed me what a mother and a wife truly was, cooking, cleaning, and watching over her family.

Momma did not want to be without Champ. At least that's what it seemed like. He was tall, about 6'2" and maybe 195 pounds. He was dark chocolate, with short hair, and a lot older than Momma. I thought she really loved him. It was the first man I saw her bring home for more than one night in a long time.

He received his name because he was a fighter. Well, that's all I ever saw him do—fight my Momma. He was always quiet around me and my sister, but when he got angry, his whole demeanor changed.

One day, Champ came in our house as if he owned the place. "Crystal, where your momma at?"

That day was different than the other days he beat her. I felt like something terrible was going to take place from the moment he came in the door. He had a sly look on his face, like he was a cat and he had caught the mouse.

Momma never let us know what happened or why things went the way they went in our lives. It was like we just fell into evil.

Crystal looked up at Champ and pointed her finger toward Momma's room with her head hanging to the ground. We never got used to him beating her; however, this time it was different. I was tired of him. I started breathing heavy and staring into space, thinking to myself, *This has to end today.* I wanted to kill him myself.

Crystal and I always talked about him and Momma when we were walking to school or lying in the bed at night, trying to figure out a way in our little lives to get rid of this monster. He had to go or somebody was going to die, and most likely, it would be Momma. We prayed that God would take him away.

Crystal would say, "Rachael, we have to ask God to take

him away. That's the only way we are going to get rid of him."

"I want him to get run over by a car!" I'd say. "I hate what he does to Momma. He making her look ugly! I'm tired of hearing everybody in the neighborhood talking about her." I was in tears by now.

Crystal took my hand and said, "Come on, let's pray."

We bowed our heads and asked God to let that be Champ's last time in our house and around Momma and us. In the middle of our prayer, we heard commotion coming from Momma's room. She ran through the house, and he was behind her. Everything seemed to be moving in slow motion. There was blood everywhere in the house. I couldn't believe he was doing this. He had never beaten her out in the open like this. We only saw the results from the beatings in the past; the black eyes and the bruised faced or busted lips and limbs, but this day, he didn't care. He did it right in front of us. Right in front of the whole neighborhood. He didn't care at all.

Momma had been peeling potatoes and onions in the living room before he showed up. When she heard Champ at the door, she jumped up and ran into her bedroom. "Crystal, tell Champ I'm in my room." She looked so scared. "Um, I'll be right back, girls."

I think she was trying to stop us from seeing what he was going to do, but he beat her from the back of the house to the front that day. He was drunk when he came in the house. I mean, this animal beat her so bad, he hit her in the face like he was fighting Mike Tyson or somebody.

I watched him kick her in the stomach and hit her in her side with a closed fist. I was screaming, "Stop!" but he didn't hear me. It was like he was in a trance.

Momma ran outside to try to get away from him. She stumbled in the street, almost getting hit by the cars going by. Champ ran after her, not caring if they were hit by the cars. He walked up to her and kicked her in the stomach, picked her up by her hair, then spat in her face. Her hair was soaked with blood, and her orange robe was dirty, torn, and wet from blood and urine. She fell to the ground, and he started stomping her with his foot.

I cried so hard. "Help, please help! He going to kill my momma! Please stop him!"

Crystal was standing there crying with her hands on top of her head. She didn't know what to do. She couldn't even speak. She was in shock.

Nobody helped us. They stood there and watched. Mrs. Greenlee from the corner, who had given us food before and said if we ever needed anything we could just walk down to her house to use the phone, just stood in her screen door watching. Cars kept going by and people kept watching. I couldn't believe it. Why didn't someone stop him?

I ran up to Mr. Thornton, who lived in the big green house on the corner. He was in his backyard barbequing with a couple of his buddies, listening to Marvin Gaye and drinking. He was my friend's father, so I knew he would help. But he didn't. No one wanted to get involved. If I were big enough, I would have done it myself.

Momma got up out of the street and ran back into the house. She screamed out, "Crystal, shut the door!"

Champ overpowered Crystal and kicked the door in. I had run in the house right after Momma. By the time Champ came in the house, I had grabbed the knife Momma was peeling potatoes with, picked it up and shouted as loud as I could, "Leave Momma alone or I will kill you!"

Momma looked at me. "Rachael, baby, put the knife down." She had so much blood coming from her face, her arms and legs, her head. It was everywhere.

"No, Momma!" I said, crying and looking Champ straight

in the eyes. "Get out of our house! Leave my momma alone! We hate you!" If he moved, I would have cut him. I wasn't playing with him. I was only a child when this happened, but I will never forget it.

I forgive Champ for this, and I pray to God he is delivered and healed of his rage. I believe he would have killed Momma if I didn't pick up that knife. He was enraged. He didn't see anyone else there, and his eyes were just on Momma. Champ's eyes were different than I ever saw them before. His eyes were beady and real dark. She was his target. He didn't look normal until he saw me with the knife.

"I'm so sorry," he said. "I don't want to hurt you, Rachael. I will leave."

He left and never came back again. Our prayers were answered that day.

Momma was black and blue all over her body. Her lip was busted and swollen. She had two black eyes, and her face was unrecognizable.

"Rachael, we have to take care of her. We need to be strong, okay?" Crystal told me.

"Okay."

Crystal had it together. She was and has been my mother ever since we were little.

Momma could hardly stand up. Her body looked like she was run over by a car. I felt sorry for her. The whole time we were putting her in the bed, she was asking us if we were okay. We put ice on her bruises for days.

"Momma, you need to go to the hospital. Please, Momma, let us go down the street to call Grandpa."

"No! Don't do that! I'll be all right."

I said to Crystal that day, "I will never let anyone do that to me."

"Me neither," Crystal stated.

That was our vow. I could hear Momma moaning in her bedroom for nights because of all the pain she was in. I cried myself to sleep every night until she was better. Prayers got us through my mother's relationship with Champ.

"We are hard-pressed on every side, yet not crushed; we are perplexed, but not in despair. [9]Persecuted, but not forsaken; struck down, but not destroyed."—2 Corinthians 4: 8, 9.

Chapter 3

Growing Pains

Ever since I was a little girl, I can remember God being there. His comfort was always there. I prayed every day that prayer I was taught as a child. Prayer is what helped me. I knew to call on the Lord when I was in trouble. He was truly all I had. God sees it all, and I felt Him. I talked to Him and could often feel His presences near me, with me, around me.

The summer after Champ left, Momma sent Crystal and me to Virginia to stay with our cousins, Tanya and Felicia, for the whole summer. They were the same ages as Crystal and I. Tanya was my age. She was a basketball superstar then. She always wore jeans and a T-shirt. I guess you could say she was a tomboy. She had very long braids in her hair, but kept a baseball hat turned to the back on her head. Tanya was pretty. She favored her momma, but she was very tall and skinny like her dad.

Felicia was prissy, but she looked like their father. She liked to cook and read romance books. Felicia talked about being married and having many children when she grew up.

I often thought, *It must be nice to live like this*. They had no worries, no concerns. They never had to worry about food or clean clothes. They didn't worry about their momma not coming home or being beat. They slept at night. I had the best time in Virginia. Everyone was so nice and pleasant.

When we woke up in the mornings, there would be breakfast waiting for us. Their home was so pleasant. They lived in a ranch on a farm, a brick house that sat on a hill. Everything in their house was new or appeared to be new. They had five bedrooms. It was huge.

The girls had their own bedrooms and bathrooms. Everything was decorated so nice with pastel décor in each of their bedrooms. Their dining room was formal, with place settings and china in the hutch, and there was an eat-in kitchen. I thought they were rich. I had never seen a house that big or been on the inside of one.

In the mornings, Cousin Wanda would fix pancakes, waffles, sausage, gravy, bacon, eggs, and French toast. They even put ice in their orange juice. We never drank orange juice except at school. They treated us as if we were their kids.

Cousin Wanda would say, "You girls are getting so big! I remember when your momma was pregnant with you, Rachael! Now look at you. You're a beautiful young lady." She was smiling while she was talking, and I was smiling back at her. "Turn around." She turned me around like I was dancing with her.

Cousin Wanda reminded me of a TV mother, like JJ's mom from *Good Times* or somebody. I didn't want to go back home. I enjoyed myself so much, but I did want to see Momma. My cousins were funny, and we all would talk for hours. The farm was so big, we walked around all day. We played tag and hide-and-seek when it got dark outside.

The last night we were there, Cousin Mike took all us horseback riding. He took us to parts of their farm we never walked. That night when we came back, Momma was supposed to come get us, but she didn't show. It got later and later, and she wasn't there. I worried a little but thought it would be nice if she left us here. I started dreaming that she asked them if they would keep us. I shared my thoughts with Tanya.

"Tanya, wouldn't it be nice if nobody came to get us?" I was smiling and excited.

She said, "Yes, we would be sisters."

We were giggling. We grabbed hands as we went around and around in circles, laughing. Then we saw a car pull up to the long circular driveway. We stopped and looked at each other. I thought Momma was gonna get out of the car, but it wasn't her. It was Uncle Al, Momma's baby brother.

"I'm here to pick you up," he said, furious, as if Momma made him come and pick us up.

I frowned, thinking he sounded drunk. "When we leaving? In the morning?"

"No, get your stuff now. I got to get back. I have things to do. Hurry up, girl. Quit looking at me like that."

Uncle Al was the youngest of Momma's brothers and sisters. There were six of them in all. Momma was the oldest. He was spoiled. Uncle Al was big, about 270 pounds and 6'3". He looked as if he needed to be out on a football field tackling somebody. He was so busy getting into mischief that he was always in trouble with somebody. Everyone treated him like he was still a child, and so he did whatever he wanted to. He knew that one of his big sisters or brothers would come and get him out of any mess he had gotten himself into.

"Don't be looking at me like that," Uncle Al mumbled. "Shoot, yo' momma wouldn't come."

"He gets on my nerves." Tanya put her arm around me. "Don't sweat it, cuz. We have next summer."

I said, "Yeah, I know."

When Uncle Al was ready to go, Cousin Mike and Wanda tried to convince him to leave in the morning. They said,

"Al, you been drinking. Don't get on that road with those girls."

Al was stumbling back and swaying from side to side, trying to keep his balance, looking at them as if they were talking to him in a foreign language.

"I'm fine!" he said, his speech slurred. "I don't want to wait. We leaving now."

Mike put his arm around him. "Listen, man, take off in the morning. You been drinking and it ain't safe."

He broke through his arm, flung it off, and said, "No, I'm leaving now."

He tried to fight Cousin Mike. They scuffled and held each other tight in headlocks. Uncle Al knocked over their patio chairs and tables. Mike's face was blood red. He was angry but didn't want to fight.

Eventually, after an hour or so, we left.

On the freeway, Uncle Al was swerving and hitting the divider and guardrails. I sat in the back seat and talked to God. He was driving Aunt Lisa's new red convertible Ford Mustang with the uncomfortable leather seats. I could hear cars passing us by, blowing their horns at Uncle Al. He was cussing and fussing at everybody driving by. He had the radio so loud, I couldn't hear myself think. He kept playing the Commodores and saying, "Ya know they from Dayton?"

"Yes!" we replied with a sassy attitude.

It was so cold in the car. He had the top down to try to stay awake, but it wasn't helping. My heart was beating so fast. I looked at him and Crystal in the front. Crystal was shifting her eyes from him to the road and looked terrified. I closed my eyes and put my feet in the seat. I put my hands together and bowed my head and said, "God, please get us home safe. I'm scared, God. I don't want to die. Please stay with us in this car. Thank you, Jesus."

I looked at Crystal in the front seat. She was praying. I

could see her lips moving and tears running down her cheeks. I knew she was scared too.

Crystal kept saying, "Uncle Al, watch that car. Uncle Al, get in your own lane. Uncle Al, wake up!" She was his eyes, keeping him awake, making sure he didn't run off the road.

I closed my eyes in desperation and said, "Jesus, please help us." I was crying softly under my breath.

Uncle Al said, "Girl, quit all that whining. I'll get you home safe. You always whining, you big baby. Shut up back there!" He continued his rant. "Yo' mammy wouldn't come and get you, so shut up!"

I continued to pray as he kept nodding off while driving. A few miles later, he wiped his eyes. He realized he couldn't go any farther, so he pulled over to get some sleep and sober up. When he pulled over, the back part of the car was still in the driving lane, and all night the car would shake when a car or truck went by. But God didn't let one car hit us. It was as if He had His hand cuffed around our car that night.

"Again I say to you that if two agree on earth concerning anything that they ask, it will be done for them by my Father in Heaven; 20For where two or three are gathered together in My name, I am there in the midst of them."—Matthew 18:19-20.

God shielded us, and He was there with us. He heard Crystal's and my prayers.

We returned from Virginia to an empty apartment. Momma was nowhere to be found. Crystal opened the door and I went inside. I said, "I'm going outside." I dropped my bag on the floor in the living room and went out the door, headed to my friend Jennifer's house. I was mad Momma wasn't there because school started tomorrow.

She makes me sick. Where is she? She knows we were coming back. She don't care. All she thinks about is herself. I walked down the street furious.

Jennifer and I had been in class together since the first

grade, and it just so happened that the projects we lived in were down the street from her house. Jennifer's house was so nice. She had three sisters and two brothers, and they lived in a big white house on the corner. I always asked God why we didn't live like this. Why was it so hard for my family? I hated being poor.

Jennifer's little brother opened the door for me.

When I went in, her mother said, "Hey, Rachael. I see you made it back from your summer vacation." She was smiling. "Did you have a nice trip? You ready to go back to school tomorrow?" She had an apron on and was in the kitchen cooking. It smelled good.

I smiled and said, "Yes, ma'am." What I really loved about Jennifer and her family was they never treated me like they had more than me or were better than me.

"Well, Jennifer's in her room. Go ahead back there, baby."

I was looking at her momma getting dinner ready for her family and I thought, *Where is my momma? I'm hungry.* It smelled so good in there. She had corn, mashed potatoes, fried chicken, and tossed salad.

She hollered, "Hey, Rachael. You gonna eat dinner with us?"

I grinned. "Yes, ma'am."

As I passed through the house to Jennifer's room, I noticed the walls were filled with pictures of Jennifer and her brothers and sisters from babies until now. My eyes looked at the many pictures from their vacations and holidays. I could see on their faces all the good times they shared as a family and hoped one day I would have that for myself.

As I got closer to Jennifer's room, I could hear the loud music playing before I even got there. I opened the door and hollered, "Hey, what's up?" The radio was blasting and Jennifer was lying on her back with her arms folded under her head, singing from the top of her lungs. She sounded like a chicken getting plucked.

She jumped up and grabbed her heart, and screamed, "Oh, shoot! You scared me." She was so excited to see me she couldn't stop talking and asking me questions. "I'm so glad you back. What you wearing to school tomorrow? Did you have fun?"

I said, frowning and looking down, "I don't know. Momma ain't home and I don't know if she got something for us to wear or not."

Jennifer walked over to her closet and opened it. She looked through her clothes and grabbed a pair of jeans with the tags still on them and a T-shirt to match and said, "Here, take this. My mom and dad won't even notice it missing." She put the clothes in a book bag and opened the window and set it outside. She turned and looked at me. "Grab them out the backyard when you leave. I got plenty of stuff." She pointed toward the closet. "Daddy took me shopping last weekend."

"Dang, Jennifer! You have everything." I walked toward her clothes, wishing it was my stuff.

She looked at my braids that Momma had done at the beginning of the summer, almost three months ago.

"Rachael, you should let my sister braid yo' hair for school tomorrow, okay?"

"Okay." I was happy somebody was gonna do my hair because I knew it looked terrible.

She called her older sister, Tracey, in her room and said, "Will you do Rachael's hair?"

Tracey smiled and said, "Yeah, I'll do her nappy hair."

We laughed.

After hanging out with Jennifer, getting my hair done, and eating dinner, I headed home around 11:30 P.M., and Momma still wasn't there.

Crystal was washing out some clean underwear for herself and me in the bathtub with a bar of soap. "Where you been?"

"I was at Jennifer's house. Here, I brought you some food." I set the wrapped-up plate of food down beside her.

She smiled. "Thank you."

I smiled back. "It's cool. Look what Jennifer gave me to wear." I took the book bag off my back and pulled out the clothes. I held them up so Crystal could see.

Crystal smiled and said, "Good. All I have to do is wash me something now. Go to bed."

I walked back toward our bedroom and smiled. I felt good inside. I had taken care of Crystal. "Goodnight, Crystal. I love you," I hollered from the room. I looked down the hall into the bathroom.

She was still on her knees washing clothes. She didn't look back, but just yelled, "I love you too."

I woke to somebody knocking on the door. I got out of bed and looked over and saw Crystal fast asleep. I could hear the water dripping from the clothes Crystal had washed that were hanging from the shower rod. I walked through the dark hallway. I got to the front door, rubbed my eyes, and said, "Who is it?"

"It's Momma. Let me in."

I looked at the watch Grandma had given me for Christmas. *It's four in the morning. Where she been?*

I opened the door, and she was standing there all dressed up, her makeup expired on her face. She looked so tired, but still beautiful. I noticed she had cut her hair while we were gone. It was still pretty; short, with the front hanging down in her eyes, the back tapered close to her head.

"Hey, baby. You happy to see me?"

I looked at her and wished I could hurt her the way she hurt me. "No. Why you ain't come get us? Why weren't you here when we got home?"

Before she could answer me, I said, "Where you been? It's not like you work or something," I added under my breath.

She grabbed me and tried to put her arms around me, but I backed away. I looked at her with one eyebrow raised and said, "I'm going to bed." I knew I had hurt her feelings, but that's what I wanted to do. I thought if I acted mean, she wouldn't do the things she did to us, and it would perhaps change her.

I plopped down in the bed and lay there for the next few minutes, staring at the ceiling, thinking to myself, *This apartment looks just like all the other ones.* There were no differences except for the neighborhoods, but the inside was identical to the last few places. Momma put the couch in the same place. The TV, kitchen table, and our beds were in the same place. Where could she have been? And what was so important that she wasn't there anymore?

Then I said aloud, "I will never do my kids like that! OOH, she makes me sick!"

I looked over at Crystal. She was 'sleep. I whispered, "Crystal, Crystal."

She opened her eyes and slowly looked at me. "Huh?"

"Momma here." She looked at me with her grey eyes for a minute then she turned over toward the wall and never said a word.

Crystal woke me up that morning. "Get up! You gonna be late! Rachael, come on, so we can eat breakfast at school." Crystal knew that was the only way we were going to eat breakfast. She was rushing me.

I turned over, looked at the poster of Michael Jackson I had hanging on the wall, touched my lips, closed my eyes, touched his lips and jumped out of bed. "All right, I'm getting up."

I was excited to go. Jennifer had given me an outfit for the first day. I looked in the mirror and smiled. Tracey had put some fancy braids in my hair, so I was cute.

Momma was still 'sleep when we left for school that day.

* * *

My sixth grade year was full of sexual experiences. I didn't have intercourse, but the boys would grab on my body parts. That was a game we played while standing in line, waiting to go from one class to the next. Don't get me wrong; I allowed them to do it, and so did the other girls. In the fifth grade, we raced, played tag or kick ball, but now one year later, we were pairing up with boyfriends.

One boy in class said, "Hey, look."

When we looked back at him, he had his penis out, holding it in his hand. The teacher was right there and never noticed what he was doing. We thought it was funny. I didn't see anything wrong with it—besides getting caught.

By the time I was ten, my body was built like a woman's, and men were looking at me, making me feel uncomfortable. I was walking home from school one day. It was nice out. The sky was soft blue, and the birds were chirping. I saw a man in the window looking at me. He was leaning out the apartment window, his shirt off, his jeans below his belly button, and a beer in his hand.

"Hey, baby. How old are you?" he shouted. "You know you fine."

I looked at him and turned my nose up. I thought, *Ugh! He's gross!* I never said a word. I was uncomfortable and scared, so I stood there facing the direction he was in with my hands crossed across my chest in a daze. I snapped out of it after a few seconds and started walking faster toward the back of the apartments where we lived.

"Hey, baby, don't run away. What's yo' name? I don't bite."

I looked back to see what he was doing. A young woman with a black eye holding a baby came to the window and looked at me and then screamed out, "Leave that baby alone!" She smacked him in the face, and then they started arguing.

I started running down the sidewalk and turned the corner, shouting, "That's what you get, you freak!"

One man that lived behind our apartments would stand in his front door naked, when me, Crystal, Jennifer and Tracey walked by. We ignored him, but I wish now we'd told someone. We were scared that if we told, we'd be in trouble, because they looked like the perfect family. He lived in a nice house and had a little girl with long, wavy pigtails, a little boy, and a pretty wife.

At the time, I would say, "Jennifer, act like you don't see the pervert. He's in the door again naked." Our eyes would go toward his front door anyway. I felt embarrassed, ashamed even, whenever I saw him. I felt dirty and violated.

I know now that things I experienced growing up were there to plant bad seeds. God had the ultimate plan to come and destroy those awful times that I went through. The man in the door was being used by Satan. A man in his right mind would never do such a thing to children.

A few years went by, and it was the same ole life; moving, Momma, her issues and mine. I was fourteen years old and going to the ninth grade. I had slowed down quite a bit from the sixth grade. I hadn't had sex since then. I was active in school with volleyball and basketball. I was pretty good, too, making most valuable player in both sports. My future was looking brighter, with talks about college sports from the coaches.

Aunt Angel headed the youth department at church, and Crystal and I were active in it. Momma was still working in the bars sometimes. We didn't see her often. We traveled a lot that summer with the youth choir at church. Our choir sang all across Ohio that summer, so we really had an awesome time with Christ.

That summer was the first time I received the Holy Ghost. I remember singing in Kentucky at some church when I couldn't control myself. I felt so warm, and my heart was only thinking about my Savior, Jesus Christ. I couldn't contain my mouth or my actions. I was filled right there with the Holy Ghost. One thing I can say is I felt so good. God Himself had come down out of Heaven and given me a gift.

In the middle of that summer, we moved again. These projects were the worst so far. We were in the heart of the hood, and there was a lot going on. Maybe because I was older, I noticed more than I did when I was younger, but it was a hot mess. There was an after-hours spot next door to my apartment, and people were there day and night. It was never quiet. Momma even frequented the place.

Moreover, I knew the boys that stood on the corner weren't out there selling candy. I stepped out of the U-Haul truck that day we moved in and could smell the weed in the air. I looked to my left and saw a group of young ladies sitting on the steps of their building smoking weed, laughing, dancing, and listening to the radio that was in the window of the upstairs apartment. Across the street from them was a group of older women sitting on flowered lawn chairs, playing cards in the dirt yard of their building, fussing and cussing at each other.

And there were plenty of kids running up and down the street and back and forth across the street to the park directly in front of our apartments. The park was filled with guys playing basketball. Females with their faces made up and lips glossed leaned into the fences, their fingers holding on for dear life, it seemed.

I thought I'd just walked into a block party or something, but no, this was the everyday routine in The Bass.

The Bass was the largest project in Dayton, housing at least 250 tenants. It was also the roughest project in Dayton, Ohio, with more murders, rapes, and drugs sold out of these apartments than the entire city put together.

I stepped out of the truck, looked around, and felt Uncle Al pop me in the neck with his raggedy towel.

"Uncle Al, stop playin'! Momma, tell him to quit hitting me."

"Al, leave that girl alone. Shoot, I don't want to be movin' all night. We going to the bar," she said, a cigarette in one hand and a plant in the other. "I told you I'll buy the drinks. Al, come on now."

Uncle Al and Momma were partners in crime. They went to the bars together and ran with the same crowd. Uncle Al kept hitting me in the back of my head when we were moving. He was a big kid. He always played around and aggravated us, but I loved him. He was like a big brother.

The only difference between this apartment and the others was that Crystal wasn't there. Crystal decided that she wanted to stay with Aunt Angel permanently. It was smooth how she moved, because she knew Momma would never let her go if she knew that's what they were going to do. I didn't know either. Crystal never said a word to me.

When Crystal turned sixteen, Aunt Angel came and picked her up for the weekend. I didn't go because I was busy with friends now that I was older. Momma had gotten a check for a lump sum of money because Crystal's father had died. I think it was for ten thousand.

Well, Crystal and Momma got into an argument because Momma spent all the money and didn't give Crystal any of it or buy her anything. Crystal was at the end of her rope with Momma after that, and decided she couldn't be there anymore. Aunt Angel told her she could stay with her. So, when Momma came to pick her up, she never returned. She was tired of Momma leaving us home alone, and said I was old enough to take care of myself now. It bothered me, but I would have done the same thing if someone came for me.

I walked out of the apartment then looked at the park directly across the street. We lived at the end of twelve apartments, but there were apartments behind us, beside us, and up and down the street as far as my eyes could see.

I walked toward the U-Haul to grab some more stuff. *We just gonna move again in a few months. Why even bother?*

I was frustrated with Momma and all her many "next times."

"Next time, it's gonna be better. Next time, I'll do things different. Next time, we gonna be fine," she would say. I hated those words, *next time.*

I thought, *This is the last time. Then I'm running away.* I wasn't watching where I was going and bumped right into a cutie pie.

"Oh, I'm sorry. I didn't mean to bump into you," I said to him. I know my mouth was wide open because he was fine.

The first thing I noticed when I looked at him was his beautiful smile and his white teeth. He was dark-skinned with a short haircut faded out with a sweet edge up around his face. He had waves in his hair that would make you seasick. His eyes were nice, kind of oval. When he looked at me, my heart melted. He looked as if he played some type of ball because he was athletic in build. He had his sleeves rolled up, so I could see his muscles. On top of all of this, he was tall. Well, at least taller than I was.

"It's all good. How you doing?" he said, looking me up and down.

I looked at him and smiled. "Okay."

"Rachael, get yo' fast tail over here and get these lamps!" Uncle Al said.

I ran to the truck and grabbed the lamps from him.

"Stay away from them boys, you hear me? They ain't no good. You hear me, nappy head?" he said, pushing me in the back of my head. "Huh?"

I smacked my lips. "Yeah, I hear you." I looked at the cutie pie still standing there.

"Look at me, Rachael—They ain't no good."

I ain't never seen Uncle Al so serious. I took the lamps into the house and then stood in the doorway.

"What's your name?" the cutie pie asked me.

"Rachael." I looked him in the eyes like women do in the movies. I even batted my light browns at him. I liked the fact that he was fine, but another thing that caught my eye was his clothes. He was clean and didn't look as if he lived in the hood because he was dressed so fly. His tennis shoes were clean and white, and his gear was fresh to death.

"Ya need some help?"

"No, young man. We are fine," Momma said in passing.

"Momma, can he help?"

"No, Rachael. We'll be fine. Besides, we're almost finished. You can go in the house now. You hear me? Go in the house," Momma said.

I rolled my eyes at her as soon as she turned her head. Then I smiled at the cutie and said, "Okay, well, I guess I'll see you around."

"No doubt. I'll be back," he said. He smiled at me with that beautiful smile he had and walked toward the back of the apartments.

I ran back in the house and screamed, "Oh-wee!" *He was so nice*, I thought. Momma scared me because I didn't know she was standing there watching me.

Momma lit a cigarette, shook her head, and said, "You so silly. You don't even know what to do wit' a boyfriend. I'll be back. I'm going out wit' Al real quick. Get some rest."

"All right. See you in the morning," I said, real smart.

She turned, made eye contact with me, but never said a word, just shut the door.

I was so happy we were finally through moving. I hoped this was the last time for a while, but knew in my heart it wasn't.

I was excited about my new friend. I knew he was the one for me down deep in my heart. I felt that we had a connection. I felt it. Shoot, I was a woman now. It was time for me to have a real man, and he looked like he might be a real man.

I couldn't quit thinking about him. I remember everything about him; his smile, his lips, his eyes. I thought it was love at first sight.

I took a bath and decided to watch TV when I heard a knock at the door. I went to the big, ugly, lime-green steel door and I whispered, "Who is it?"

"TJ," a male voice called from the other side of the door.

"Who's TJ?" My heart was beating fast and fluttering. *Could this be the cutie I met earlier?* I thought.

"I met you earlier, when you were movin' in." His voice was so deep, not like the boys at school.

I couldn't believe it. I had just been thinking about him, and now he was at my door. My heart was beating so fast. I stood there a moment before saying, "Just a minute." I went to my room, biting my nails, and put on a T-shirt and pair of shorts. I then went to the door and opened it.

"Oh, my," he said when he looked at me. "You distracted me when you opened the door. You so fine and all."

I blushed.

"I was out here with my boys and seen yo' momma and them leave, so I thought it would be okay to come and talk to you."

"What you mean? You can't come in here. I don't know you," I said, all the while rolling my eyes and frowning at him. *What does he think? I'm easy like that?*

"Oh, I ain't mean it like that, baby." His hands were moving back and forth as he tried to explain what he meant. "I just want to talk to you, get to know you." He laughed. "Don't be so uptight. Dang! I didn't mean nothin' to upset you. That's the last thing I want to do." He smiled again.

"Oh, okay," I said, putting my hand in my hair and fidgeting around. I thought to myself, *Mm-mmm, he's so gorgeous.* I couldn't help but look him up and down. I had to catch my breath looking at that brother. I was nervous talking to him, not because I thought Momma was coming anytime soon, but I had never talked to a real boy like this before.

He said, "I got an idea. Why don't we go to the back window? You can talk to me through your window."

"That's cool." I nodded my head. I shut the door, locked it, and ran to the back window. He was already there.

"So, my name is TJ. I just graduated, and I'm going to Central State University."

He was so confident. I liked that. When he said he was out of high school, I got nervous. I hadn't ever had a relationship with a boy, let alone a grown man on his way to a university. I liked him, though. He made me feel warm inside from the moment I met him.

At first, I was scared to tell him the truth that I was fourteen on my way to high school. But if I lied, he would've found out. "Well, I'm fourteen, and I'm going to the ninth grade."

"I don't care how old you are. I want you in my life. Can you roll wit' that?"

He knew all the right things to say. I wasn't ready for him at all.

He looked at me and shook his head. "I can't believe you only fourteen. Mm-mm-mmm." He laughed. "You look at least eighteen with that body of yours." He shook his head again. "Come on, now. You playin' wit' me, Rachael." His head was leaning to the side and he was grinning. "Tell the truth—You eighteen?"

I was so nervous that I was biting my lip. "No, I'm not playin'. I'm fourteen. I won't be fifteen till November." *He gonna leave now for sure.*

He didn't leave, though. He just stood there half the night talking to me, holding on to the gated window while he watched me and just listened to me. We talked through the window until four o'clock in the morning. He kept telling me that he didn't want to leave me there by myself.

"I'll be fine. I'm used to it." I smiled.

He took a piece of paper out of his pocket with a number on it. I guess he must have written it down before he knocked on the door. "Here's my number. Call me anytime. I want to see you tomorrow. Maybe we can go to the movies or something, okay?"

"Okay," I replied. My eyes lit up. I had never been to the movies with a boy. No one had ever talked to me, looked at me, or adored me the way TJ did.

He lived in one of the houses on the next street over from all the apartments. His house was a little red brick house with a white fence around it. He lived with his mother and his three sisters and their dog, Cleo. From that day on, until he went off to school, anyway, he would stand at my bedroom window and say everything I wanted to hear.

"Rachael, when I get out of school, I'm going to get you out of these apartments. I'm going to marry you."

I would smile and reply, "I love you, TJ."

"You so beautiful. You need to be on a runway somewhere like Paris or Italy, not trapped in yo' momma's house." He would rub my cheek and look into my eyes. "Rachael, you a diamond. All you need is me to polish you. Stick wit' me and watch where I take you, baby. To the top." He would walk up real close to me, kiss me on the cheek, and whisper in my ear, "You gonna be my wife someday."

I closed my eyes and imagined him doing everything he said he was gonna do, sweeping me away from all the mess Momma had done. I was gonna be happy with the man of my dreams.

That's all I ever wanted; someone to love me, talk to me, and notice me. He was there doing and saying everything I had seen men say and do for women on television. The only problem was that no one let me know that fourteen-year-old little girls do not need to have nineteen-year-old boyfriends.

Momma didn't care that I dated him. She invited him in and allowed us to be at the apartment alone. It wasn't a big deal to her—or his family, for that matter. She acted as though it bothered her when Uncle Al was there when I first met him, but after that day, she never said a word, never cared what time he left or anything—just as long as she didn't have to be there. It was kind of like he took the place of Crystal being there with me.

TJ taught me many things, like how to drink, smoke weed, and skip school. One day at his house, he said, "Rachael, you ever smoke weed before?"

I looked at him. *He's gonna think I'm a baby if I say no.* My heart was beating fast, then faster, and I looked at him sitting there leaned back in his favorite chair, smoking on his weed, waiting to hear what I was gonna say.

"No, but I'll try it." I wanted him to think I was a woman, mature, like he'd been saying I was the last eight months of our relationship.

"Take a hit of this." He got out of his chair and walked slowly toward me, looking at me the whole time.

My heart was beating so fast because I was scared of drugs. I always thought the first time I took them I was going to be hooked forever.

When he reached my chair, he stopped in front of me and took a long hit of the weed. He bent down over me with his hands on the arms of the chair and said, "Close your eyes." He blew the smoke up my nose and into my mouth, looking at me the whole time.

I pulled my head back and started coughing.

He handed me the joint and started laughing. "Smoke this."

I put the joint to my lips and started puffing. I'd seen him smoke too many times not to know what to do, but what I didn't know was how I was going to feel when I did it. The first hit put everything in slow motion. I didn't care about nothing but just hitting it again. All my troubles and worries were gone. I didn't care where Momma was; or Crystal, for that matter. All I wanted to do was keep hitting the joint.

Everything TJ said or did became funny. His momma up-stairs hollering at him to turn the music down and quit smoking in her basement became funny. I became relaxed. All the tension I usually had was gone. I just didn't care. All I wanted to do was keep puffing. Every time I puffed, another one of my problems disappeared. I felt like I was out of my body.

I looked at TJ sitting there as if he was the king of the world, watching me with those sexy eyes. I thought, *I never noticed how sexy he really was until now.* My body was tingling all over, and the room became extremely hot.

Every time I tried to pass the joint to him, he would smile real slick and say, "Go ahead."

After that experience, it was over. I started smoking weed regularly with him. Shoot, he supplied it, and I smoked it.

After I started smoking, skipping school with TJ followed. He'd quit college after the first two quarters and came back home. He wasn't working, just sitting at home supplying the neighborhood with the weed he sold.

Most of the time when I left for school, Momma wasn't there or she was passed out in her room. TJ's momma worked, so we were there alone. Sex appeared shortly after the weed and skipping school.

What really was attractive about him was how polite he was. He never talked about sex with me for months. He knew when we first met that I loved God, and he even attended church with me sometimes. I told TJ early how important it was for me to wait until I got married to have sex. He knew everything about my past. He told me that was fine with him and how it made him love me more. So, for months, he kissed me, hugged me, and was affectionate, but he never tried to rush me into having sex with him—until one day.

I skipped school and was at his house. He sat across from me and puffed on the joint he had rolled and watched me and said, "Rachael, you know I love you, right?" He took a long hit of the weed then blew it out slow. "You know I don't want anybody but you." He looked so sly, like he was up to no good, smiling with only half his mouth. "Don't you?" He put his hand on my knee and leaned over and blew smoke up my nose then started kissing me on the neck.

I said, "Yeah, I know, TJ."

"I want to make love to you, just one time. I know you want to wait, but I want you to know how I feel about you."

I was scared. I hadn't had sex for years. And this was different. This time it would be with somebody I loved and wanted to be with. This time it would be with a man. But it was important to me to save myself. I had made a promise to God that I wouldn't do this anymore until I was married. I was now big enough to defend myself and say no when I wanted to, and I wanted to say no.

"I know you ain't scared of me, Rachael, huh? You scared after all I do for you? I stay wit' you when you home alone, buy yo' food and clothes. Come on now, baby, you know I love you, don't you?"

If I don't do this, he will leave me alone. He'll think I'm a baby and be with someone his own age. I was high and I didn't want the way he felt about me to disappear. I was nervous and felt out of place. I was staring straight in space.

"Ain't nobody here but us. I know you young, but you a woman to me. Show me you a woman. Let me make love to you." He kept kissing me the whole time he whispered in my ear.

That was all it took, a good line, and I gave myself to this man. After that day, we didn't stop. We were having sex daily. I wasn't going to school, and I almost flunked the ninth grade. I was out of control. Falling fast. I thought I was an adult and could do whatever I wanted to do. I really thought I was in love with him. The truth is he was the only one paying attention to me, telling me how special and beautiful I was. Not even Momma was.

I no longer wanted to hang out at my grandparents' house. Crystal always went over there, but I was too busy with TJ. I did stay in the youth choir and ushered, I just wasn't listening to the minister when he spoke. He'd say, "You teenagers are responsible for the choices you make in life. If you don't make the right choices, you're going to pay for them!"

I thought, *Yeah, yeah, I hear you.* I continued making bad choices from that day forward. I thought I had all the answers. I felt like I wasn't responsible for the way I was acting. After all, I was always told I would be like Momma, so much wasn't expected from me anyhow.

I did hear the pastor say that Jesus died for our sins. I thought as long as I asked for forgiveness, I was okay. I could have sex, smoke marijuana, and drink all I wanted. All I had to do was ask for forgiveness afterwards. I didn't realize back then that I was crucifying Christ every time I did something that I knew was wrong.

When church got out, I would be dropped off at the apartment. I knew Momma was busy at the bar, so I spent time with TJ. He and his family fed me dinner, took me places with them, and he showed me how much he loved me.

TJ had plenty of money from selling weed, and he didn't mind spending it on me. He would drive me downtown and take me shopping. He bought me designer jeans and tennis shoes. TJ would pick out everything I wore. I had no say-so if he was buying it. I wore whatever he wanted.

At first, I liked that, but after a year or so, I wanted to wear what I wanted. I wanted to go visit my grandparents sometimes, but he didn't want me out of his sight. Everything I did, he wanted to be there or be a part of it. He never left my side. Even when I went to school, he came and got me and waited until I came out of the building then took me back to our neighborhood.

TJ always thought I was going to leave him or be with

somebody else. I kept assuring him that I wasn't and that he was the only one for me.

"You cheatin' on me, Rach? Huh? Tell me the truth."

I would roll my eyes in the air and think, *Here we go again*. I couldn't believe that as fine as this man was, as secure as he appeared to be in the neighborhood, and with all the respect everybody gave him, he was so insecure.

"TJ, why you so paranoid? You need to quit smokin' so much. You trippin'."

I was at his house more than my own. I felt like a motherless child. I felt alone at that apartment.

Crystal didn't approve of me and TJ. She would say, "Rachael, why you hanging around him? He's too old for you. What he want with a kid? You ever think about that? You too smart for that, Rachael. He's bad news, and you need to leave him alone before you get in trouble."

I flung my hand at her and yelled, "Leave me alone! You getting on my nerves. You don't even know what you talking about." I heard what she was saying to me, but I didn't care enough to stop seeing him.

Crystal was still talking. I could hear her from my bedroom with the door shut, saying, "I know you be smoking weed. You think I don't know, but I know you are."

I busted in the bedroom where she was at. "Shut up! You don't know what you talking about!" I was furious, but I didn't like it when Crystal and I fussed. It bothered me until we made up. After all, she was all that I had until TJ came along.

"He ain't even doing nothing with himself. He don't work or go to school. He sitting in his momma's house all day. Loser!" She motioned her fingers in an *L* shape.

I ignored her. I didn't care what she or anybody else said. I loved him.

I changed my clothes and went out the door, over to TJ's house. I never argued with Crystal again after that day. We were different. We went through many of the same things, but reacted differently. I dealt with the problems by being promiscuous and rebellious, but Crystal didn't. She kept everything inside. She tried to escape the pain inside by eating, reading, and watching television.

She and I both decided at early ages that we weren't going to do the things our mother did. I remember lying in bed across from each other and whispering in the dark about the things Momma would do. But now that Crystal wasn't living with us anymore, there was no one to whisper to. Nobody seemed to care that I was all by myself. Why didn't they take me?

Crystal had traveled everywhere with Aunt Angel. They had gone to Six Flags. It hurt me. That's when I stopped going around altogether. How could you take one child out of hell and leave the other one there to burn? Crystal would give me all the details of her trips, including the scenery. I wanted to know everything.

I was home one night watching TV when Momma came in after being at the bars. She walked past me and looked. She went toward her room and asked, "Why you laying on my couch like that? Get up and do something. The house look like hell."

I was halfway 'sleep when she walked in. I didn't say anything, but thought, *Oh, here she go. It's only so big in here. You can see every room if you stand in the middle of the living room. It ain't that much to clean. Dang, she get on my nerves.* I sucked my teeth.

"This couch raggedy anyway, old green couch with a hole in it."

She went toward the bathroom and shouted, "Get up!"

"Ma, it's twelve in the morning. Leave me alone! You always messing with somebody." I rolled my eyes at her.

How can she tell me anything? She ain't never here.

"Girl, you gonna get smacked if you don't quit talking crazy to me! That's why yo' aunt ain't take you too. You too

smart! Crystal out there livin' nice and they left you here."
She started laughing.

I couldn't believe she went there with her raggedy self. My
boyfriend was doing more for me than she ever did. Who
did she think she was?

She was standing there all dressed up, looking at me,
smirking with that cigarette in her hand. I don't know what
was wrong with her that night, but she kept picking with me.
I think that was the worst argument I ever had with Momma.

I got my covers off the couch and went in my bedroom. I
never said a word, but the rage was right in my throat.

She opened my door and said, "You and that boy been
having sex? I know you have, ya fast!" She was looking at me
like I was a woman in the streets she was beefin' wit'. I couldn't
believe it. She was trippin' like she was high or something.

"How would you know? You're never here!" I even used
my hands when I was talking.

"Little girl, you must want me to beat you tonight. I've
been taking care of you all these years all by myself with no
help. Hell, I did everything for you girls, and you running
around with that nappy-headed boy. You tramp! And your
sister, she just picked up and left. Now I ain't got nobody to
watch what you do." Momma walked back and forth, talking
crazy to me.

By now, it was one o'clock in the morning. I felt like I was
in a nightmare. I didn't want to stay there anymore with her.
I decided then I was going to do everything in my power not
to become her. I was going to prove her and everybody else
wrong about me. I became determined that night—determined not to be on welfare, determined not to have kids by
different men, determined not to be her. That was my ultimate goal in life from that point—not to become my
mother.

She was hollering at me, telling me that Crystal and I were
ungrateful, and how she did everything she could for us. She

stood there, took off her earrings, and laid them on the coffee table, and then she took her dress off and threw it on the loveseat.

Eventually she sat down on the old green couch with the hole in it and looked at me. She crossed her legs as she sat with her black slip still on. "You girls don't know what I did for you. You think I don't sacrifice for you, huh? You don't remember that Christmas when you was little and I left you and your sister at the neighbor's house?" She was looking out the window, smoking her cigarette and shaking her crossed legs. "You remember?" she shouted.

"No, you left us all the time. What made that time any different?" She couldn't get no brownie points with me. Her sad story wasn't gonna work. I was tired of all the lies, all the men, and all the times she left me.

"Well, this time I went out so you girls could get what you wanted for Christmas." She never looked at me, just out the window. "I wanted you to have everything you wanted. So when my friend called me—you remember my friend Angela, don't you?"

"No, Momma. What are you talking about?" I was confused and a little scared of what she was getting at.

She stared into space. "She offered me three hundred dollars if I would sleep with her." Then under her breath, she added, "I just wanted you girls to have a good Christmas." Her eyes were beady and black. She looked as if she'd lost her soul. Momma was empty inside. "I did it so you and your sister could have the best Christmas ever. And you said I don't love you."

I looked at Momma and said, "No, Momma, don't tell me that!" I covered my ears and began to cry. "No, Momma, don't say that! Why you say that? Why?" I shook my head and just looked at her.

Momma looked at me smugly. "Don't judge me. I did what I had to. I did it for you and your sister."

I looked at her with my face frowned up. "Momma, I didn't want Christmas that bad!" I jumped up out of the chair and ran out of the house. I didn't have on anything but my nightshirt and underwear. I ran barefoot down the dark alley to TJ's bedroom window and knocked.

He came to the window and looked out. "What's wrong?" he asked.

"Let me in." I was hurt, confused, and devastated.

He knew that something terrible had taken place between me and Momma, but I never told him what it was. Once inside, he made me feel loved. He cuddled me and cared for me, hugged and caressed me. I thought I needed that.

I stayed at his house for a few days, never leaving out once. Momma never came to get me, but TJ was there. That was the trick of the enemy—to make me feel a counterfeit love. I was looking for love, and that was the only love I felt.

I was too embarrassed to tell anyone what Momma had said to me that night. TJ asked me a couple of times what happened, but I never said a word. I never could get it out of my mind, though. What my mother said to me that day stayed in my mind and heart for years. It left me confused and grieved. I was ashamed of her.

I returned home a few days later. Momma never mentioned the incident to me again. I acted as though it never happened. She never said a word about where I went or anything. The tension in the house was bad between us. I would walk past her and not say a word. I didn't like her. Knowing what I knew, she was a freak to me.

How could she be with a woman? That's so nasty, I thought.

I hated Momma. I didn't want to eat food she cooked, use the bathroom after her or anything. I thought she was nasty. She was a disgrace to me. She was at the clubs and bars, and I was with TJ, being his human doll baby, doing whatever he wanted me to do—"Dress this way. Comb your hair like that." Whatever he wanted, I would do.

* * *

Shortly after, I found out some news about myself that made me ashamed of myself. I remember calling Crystal up to tell her.

"Hey, what you doing?" Crystal asked me.

"What up? What you up to?" I couldn't say anything else. I was scared. I just held the phone and cried.

"Rachael, you there? What's wrong?" She breathed aloud through the phone and asked, "What did she do now?"

I blurted out, "I messed up!"

I was crying hysterically. I was at the phone booth in front of IGA carryout around the corner from the apartment. I watched people go in the store whispering, "Is she all right?"

I looked down at the numbers on the phone so they couldn't see me. I was pregnant. All I worried about was what others would think. What they were going to say. I never once thought about the baby in my stomach; just me.

"Calm down, Rachael. What is it? What's wrong?"

I took a deep breath and blurted out, "I'm pregnant. I messed up!"

"Oh, man. Okay, okay, calm down. I'll figure out somethin'. You hear me? We'll figure out what to do, Rachael. Okay?"

"Yeah, okay," I said, crying and whimpering.

After I hung up the phone with Crystal, I felt a little relieved. I walked back to the house to wait for Momma to get home. I wanted to tell her I was pregnant. It took me about five minutes to get to the house from the corner store where the phone was. I went in, turned the television on, and waited. I didn't know when she would be there, but I wanted to be up when she came home. I needed to tell her now while I had the courage.

I waited about an hour before I heard a car pull up outside and heard Momma holler, "I'll be right back."

I peeked out the window. She was bent down, leaning in

the window of some ol' raggedy tan Cadillac, talking to some man. She started walking toward the apartment. I quickly sat back down on the couch.

Momma was rushing as soon as she stepped in the apartment.

"Hey, Ma. I got somethin' I need to talk to you about."

"What, Rachael? I need to hurry. I got a date tonight." She was in her room, changing her clothes as I talked, putting on her yellow suit with her tan-and-black stilettos.

"Why you standing in my door lookin' all crazy like that? What's wrong?" She was irritated. She walked by me and went into the bathroom and brushed her teeth. Momma looked in the mirror and put her lipstick on. She took a step back from the mirror and took a good look at herself then asked, "You gonna tell me or not?"

I was so nervous my stomach was turning somersaults. I closed my eyes. "Momma, I'm pregnant." I just blurted it out.

She didn't say anything for a few minutes, just kept getting ready for her date. She walked by me again, went back in her bedroom, and sat on the bed. "You keeping it?"

I looked at her sitting on her bed, pulling her stockings up in a rush, never missing a beat. It didn't bother her that I was pregnant; or if it did, I couldn't tell. She was much more interested in who waited for her outside than the child that was inside me.

Momma didn't wait or give me a chance to answer her. She just said, "I got to go. Let me know what you gonna do."

I was shocked because she was really going out the front door as if I told her I got a "C" on a test at school. She went to the front door, turned around, put her purse on her shoulder, and looked at me. "I got to go. We'll talk about it tomorrow, okay?" She shut the door.

I could hear her heels clicking down the sidewalk in a hurry to the car. I heard her get in the car, and then they pulled off.

I was standing there in the middle of the living room floor without a thought. I didn't know what she was thinking. I stayed up a few more hours trying to watch TV. Then I fell asleep on the couch.

I heard the front door open about five in the morning, and I opened my eyes and saw Momma and her friend from last night going in her bedroom. She was telling him to be quiet because I was 'sleep. I rolled over toward the wall on the couch then I took my cover in haste and went in my room. I slammed the door so hard because I knew Momma didn't know that man.

I woke up later that day about 1:00 P.M. I smelled breakfast cooking in the house. I thought to myself, *I can't believe she's cooking*. Momma was in the kitchen frying bacon and eggs. I had my nose frowned up. I didn't know what to think. Why was she cooking? And where was old dude from last night?

She turned around and looked at me. "Hey, Rachael, I was thinking . . . if you want, I'll sign the papers so you can get married. Shoot, you might as well."

I didn't know what she was really thinking. Was she trying to be funny because I was pregnant, or was she for real? I couldn't figure her out.

She was making her plate. "I told you this was gonna happen, didn't I? Huh? You think you got all the answers, runnin' around here wit' that grown man, trying to play house. Well, play house now. You got the baby. You so stupid. Just done messed yo' self up now for real." She shook her head and walked to her bedroom with two plates of food and shut the door.

Momma and I went over to Grandpa's house a few days later, and when I got there, I could tell everybody knew. Everybody was looking at me all funny, like I was infected or something.

I waited until Momma went upstairs to the bathroom, and I followed her. "Momma, you told them, didn't you?"

She smiled and said, "No. You know I wouldn't do that. Go ahead back downstairs, girl. I need to use the bathroom."

I knew she wasn't telling me the truth. I started walking down the stairs and saw Crystal at the bottom of them. She put her finger over her lips.

Crystal said, "Come upstairs with me."

I turned around and walked up the stairs to Momma's room when she was a little girl. Crystal shut the door and said, "I got something for you."

"What?" I asked.

She grabbed my hand. "Here, take this."

I looked in my hand and it was a wad of money for an abortion.

"Don't think about it. Just do it so you won't mess up your future," Crystal said to me. "You too young for a baby." She was passionate about what she spoke to me, and was sad that I had to make a choice like this. But at the same time, I knew she was sincere and only wanted what she thought was best for her little fifteen-year-old sister in a crisis.

I stopped Crystal from saying anything else because I knew she felt she was just as responsible for me being pregnant as I was. For some reason, she thought she was the blame because she wasn't living with us anymore. That was not true. It was my fault. I knew the consequences.

"Do you think I should do it? Momma said marry him."

"Don't do that. That's not smart. You too young!"

I didn't think I needed a child either, but I knew that in my spirit I was going against God if I got an abortion. It made my decision a very painful one, but it didn't stop me from having the abortion.

I fought with the decision for a while, but decided to have it done. The abortion was and has been the hardest thing I ever did. I worried about what everyone was going to say, and what they would think about me if I were to have a baby.

I heard people say, "Have an abortion. It's your right." But let me tell you from experience, it wasn't right for me.

It is wrong in the sight of God to kill your child. It is murder! The baby is alive inside of you. No matter how hard you try to forget, that will stay with you and you will know in your heart it wasn't the right thing to do. No matter what you say in your head, in your heart, you will know it was not right. Trust me; I know what I am talking about.

I had no idea of the torment I would deal with after I had the abortion. I knew the commandments, and I knew I was old enough to face God's judgment.

"For the Word of God is living and powerful, and sharper than a two-edged sword, piercing even to the division of soul and spirit, and joints and marrow and is discerner of the thoughts and intents of the heart; [13]And there is no creature hidden from his sight, but all things are naked and open to Him whom we must give account."—Hebrews 4:12-13.

I tried to fool myself and blame other people for the decision I made, but I felt guilty down inside because I knew the truth. The truth was that I didn't want a child. I knew I was too young, and I didn't know what I wanted to do with my own life. I took the easiest way out, but I knew I was wrong. I was having sex and smoking weed. What did I think was going to happen? I didn't care about the repercussions. I figured I would just cross that bridge when I came to it. I just didn't think that it would happen to me, and that's what a lot of other young ladies think.

"Do you not know that your bodies are members of Christ? Shall I then take the members of Christ and make them members of a harlot? God forbid."—1 Corinthians 6:15.

* * *

I always remembered everything about the day I went to the clinic for the abortion. I asked TJ if he would come with me, but he refused.

"Rachael, I won't have no part in killing my seed."

I needed to be strong and stay focused on what I was about to do. That was the only way I could get through this, so I blocked out what I felt or thought and what TJ said and thought. I had convinced myself that I wasn't pregnant and I was going to the doctor for just a simple check-up.

When I opened the door to go to the bus stop, Momma stopped me in my tracks.

"Wait, Rachael. I'm coming with you," she said.

Oh, no. I don't want her to come. She's going to drive me crazy.

"You gonna make me miss the bus. I'm okay." I tried to hurry out the front door.

"No, here I come. You won't be late." Softly, under her breath, she said, "I promise."

As we walked to the bus stop, the wind hit our faces. It was very cold and drab outside.

"Rachael, wait for me. Quit walking so fast." She was trying desperately to catch up.

Why she want to come? She don't ever be here. What she want to be around for now? I didn't understand why she was trying to be with me and show me she cared. I was cold to her. I had little love for her—on the outside, that is, but I was still a little girl myself and wanted my momma. I was trying to be hard, as if I had everything under control, but to be honest, everything was out of control.

The bus ride over to the clinic was long and quiet. I faced the window the entire ride. Momma sat beside me and tried to start a conversation.

"Hey, Rachael, you want me to cook you some stuffed peppers when we get back home?" She knew that was my favorite.

"I don't care what you cook."

Momma reached for my hand, and I pulled away. I reached up and grabbed the bell for our stop.

Once inside, we found out that I was the youngest girl in the building for the abortion. Soon as I got in there, I could no longer hear what anyone was saying to me. I would have to say constantly, "Excuse me. What did you say?"

I was terrified; not of the place or the people, but because I knew it was wrong. I was afraid—afraid God was going to get me.

I talked to God inside my head. I asked for forgiveness the whole time inside. *God, I'm so sorry. Please forgive me, please.* I tried to reason with Him and explain that I myself was just a child, but somehow I knew He wasn't buying it. *I'm scared, God. I don't know what else to do to get out of this.*

I cried the whole time I was in the place; for hours, it seemed, even though the abortion took about two minutes.

As the doctor did the procedure, the nurse told me, "Stop all that crying. We had a girl in here before, fourteen years old! Suck it up and quit whimpering."

Then the doctor said, "Open your legs."

I was ashamed. I covered my eyes with my hand and wanted to disappear, but I was in the room and it wasn't a nightmare that was going to end. It was my life, my bad choices and actions that got me to this place. It was me. When I took my hand off my eyes, it was my reality! My bad choices had come to the surface.

While lying in the procedure room, I kept saying, "I want my momma. Please get my momma."

"No, your momma wasn't there when you was with that boy, now, was she?" the nurse spat. "You'll be all right in a minute."

I couldn't believe she was talking to me like that, but I guess she thought I shouldn't have been there. That was the last thing said, and then it was over. No more baby, no more problems, so I thought. I told God I would never do that again.

Outside of the clinic, Momma said, "Now, Rachael, don't

be telling nobody what you did. You hear me? Don't tell your friends or nobody in the family. They just gonna talk about you. Keep your mouth shut. You hear me, girl?"

"Yeah, I hear you." I felt so horrible.

I thought once the baby was out my problems would be over, but to be honest, it was the guilt of having an abortion that had me bound the next fourteen years.

Momma never said another word to me about the abortion. She never told me, "It will be all right. Don't cry." She just got on the bus and acted as if we had been to the grocery store or something.

When we got back to the house, I wanted to go to bed. I went straight to my bedroom. I flopped on my bed and turned toward the wall. I began to repeat softly, "I'm sorry. I'm sorry." I said it with the wet pillow over my face until I fell asleep.

When I woke up, I went to the bathroom and I heard Momma on the phone talking to somebody. "Yeah, girl, Rachael had an abortion today. I went with her for support. Yeah, that child fast. She gonna have a baby. I wouldn't be surprised if she get right back pregnant."

She was in her pink nightgown with her legs crossed, smoking a cigarette and watching TV. I knew she was going to run her mouth even though she had told me not to say anything. I walked back in my room without her ever knowing I was standing there.

TJ came over later that night to find out if I went through with it. I was lying down in my room and I heard him come in.

"Rach?" he said quietly. "You all right?"

I could not look at him. I kept my face in the pillow. "Yeah, I'm okay."

TJ lay on my bed beside me and hugged me. "Rach, there will be other babies. We will get married and be happy. Okay?"

I felt bad because I knew it was over between us. TJ was in love with me, but I was young and I didn't want kids or to be married. Besides, he had quit school and became the local weed man in the neighborhood. That's not what I wanted. I could just picture myself getting pregnant again and not wanting to make a decision like the one I'd just made. The pregnancy made me realize I wasn't ready for a husband. I didn't want to pretend anymore. I wanted to turn my life around, start over.

"Even a child is known by his deed, whether it is pure and right."—Proverbs 20:11.

After the abortion and breaking up with TJ, we moved from the projects out to the suburbs. Momma was working at factory, packing bacon. I tried to put the past behind me. Don't get me wrong; the abortion continued to haunt me, but I tried to find other things to occupy my mind.

I became friends with the most popular girl at my school. Linda was the girl next door. She was preppy, and everything she wore matched. She was bright and had her head on straight, and her priorities were together—not to mention, she was beautiful. She had hair down to her shoulders and she went to the beauty salon weekly. She was dark-skinned, but didn't look all-the-way black. She looked mixed with Indian or something. She was small-framed, and never looked out of place. I mean nothing about her; her hair, her clothes, or attitude was out of place.

Linda's mother, Ms. Katie, and her sister, Yolanda, made me feel like I was a part of their family. I spent every weekend over their house. Ms. Katie would allow boys and girls to stay over. I thought it was cool how she had an open relationship with her daughters, maybe because I had no relationship with my mother. I didn't see anything wrong then with Ms. Katie allowing boys to spend the night with her daughters. I thought she treated them like they were grown, and that was cool to me. Ms. Katie was like a mother to me. She took me in and allowed me to stay over while my mother worked and played.

When I met Linda, I was still with TJ and pregnant, getting ready to have the abortion. But I never told her or anyone what I had done. Overall, Linda's family helped me get through some times of loneliness and low self-esteem.

We would go skating every weekend and to every dance our high school had. Their house was like the neighborhood house. Kids would be everywhere. Ms. Katie had a heart for kids. She made sure I had clean clothes and made sure I ate. If Linda or Yolanda went to any type of function, she made sure I was right alongside them.

We stayed near Linda for about two years then we moved again.

"Why we movin' again?" I asked Momma. "I like it here. I have a lot of friends, Ma."

Her reply was, "Girl, my back is acting up again, and I can't afford this house. We got to move where we can afford to pay. Shoot, girl, don't be questioning me. Can you pay for it?" She was packing up boxes in the kitchen and living room while on the phone and talking to me.

"Hold on a minute, Libby." She put her hand over the receiver of the phone so Libby couldn't hear her then said, "I didn't think so. So, you best to be packin'!" Her eyes were big as she stared at me for a few moments before she returned to her gossiping about *The Young and the Restless* on the telephone.

I rolled my eyes and said to myself, *Uuugh! She make me sick!*

I was so frustrated with her. I grabbed my coat and ran out the front door. I heard her calling my name, but I acted like I didn't. I kept going, never looking back. I went over to Linda's. Their house was so full; I mean, it felt like a home, loving and peaceful. At my house, I was always alone. There was never anyone there besides me, but her house was full with people all the time.

When Linda's mom answered the door, she could see there was something wrong. My face said it all. "What's wrong, Rachael?"

"Nothing," I said with a half smile.

"I know you. You've been around here now for a couple of years, child. I know when there's something wrong wit' ya. What's wrong, Rachael?"

I covered my eyes and said, "I'm tired of moving. Momma said we have to move again."

She grabbed me and hugged me. She was so thin. "It's all right, baby. You can stay here if you want. Stay as long or whenever you want."

I was relieved, but at the same time uneasy. I didn't understand why we moved so much. Why couldn't we get somewhere and stay? I hated that, not to mention having to explain to my friends why we moved every few years.

I stayed at Linda's house often. Momma said that would be fine. She was busy working at Uncle Al's bar, so being at Linda's house really saved me from being by myself.

My sister was now attending college, and she was away from Dayton. We didn't see each other that much. When she came home, she would go out to my aunt's house or my grandpa's. I really didn't see my family as much as I did when I was younger, and I wasn't attending church either.

I stayed at Linda's house all summer long, but went back to Momma's house when it was time for my eleventh grade year to start. It was time to revisit hell.

Chapter 4

Murder, Rape, Deception, and Suicide

Hanging around Linda made me feel important. I was popular, and everybody from all the high schools knew who I was. Linda showed me how to dress and keep myself up, and I figured out that I wasn't half bad. Matter of fact, I was really cute. I didn't need TJ to make me feel like I looked good. It was natural beauty that did it, not him. I was also becoming a little stuck on myself, with all the attention from the boys now. I had a nice shape and a pretty face, not to mention boys loved light-skinned females.

I watched Linda and learned from her attitude and confidence how she dealt with people and got them to like and respect her. She had it all together. I wanted to be just like her, so being around her rubbed off on me.

I was actually excited about starting a new school. Meadowdale High School was the school back then. Shoot, every star athlete was there. Dayton was big on football and basketball in its high schools. Dayton birthed some pretty famous star athletes.

I made up in my mind that nobody would know what Momma did for a living, which was now a barmaid. I decided that Momma was a nurse, and when anybody asked what she did for a living, I would tell them that.

I changed my whole image at Meadowdale. I had no problem getting new clothes or having money because Uncle Al and Momma had their own after-hours joint and it was boomin'! They raked in some money. I could go to the mall or downtown anytime I wanted and get clothes and my hair done. Momma didn't care. I don't even think she knew how much money she had in that four-foot jar she put in her room, filled with money. I would go in her room, grab money out, look in her dresser drawer and get some weed, get on the bus and go shopping.

I told everyone that Momma worked the night shift at the hospital. When I was younger, kids never asked questions about where my momma was, but now that I was older and they were coming by the apartment, they wondered why I was always there alone.

I was such an expert liar now that it didn't move me. I had myself convinced she was at the hospital working a double. I had to make up the story. I didn't want kids to think she didn't care. They wondered why she never came to a track meet or a volleyball game or basketball game.

They asked, "Why your·moms don't come to parent-teacher conferences?"

I felt bad when they would ask, because those questions brought me back to my reality, the one that I knew I had to face when I went home alone. I wanted to make her look perfect. I would always reply by saying, "She's a nurse and works all the time."

Nobody knew that when I left school, I was going home to an empty spot. It was just me. I had my own place at the age of sixteen. Momma came home and changed clothes, and sometimes she did come spend the night with the different guests she would bring home with her, accompanying her to her bedroom.

I would hear her in her bedroom. The walls were so thin. I would wake up, look around the dark room, grab my pillow from my head, and put it over my face to escape from all the noises that came out of her room.

Momma and I never talked. Whenever we had a conversation, it was an argument. She couldn't say anything to me without me going off like the Hiroshima bomb! I hated what she was making me become—a liar, a pretender. I didn't like her or her ways. I was still a little girl who had to grow up fast, and I didn't appreciate it. Why did everybody else have to take responsibility for me when I was her kid? I hated her.

I met this girl named Renee Palmer one day on the school bus. She was quiet and laid-back. The boys on the bus were all around her because of her beauty.

I got on the bus and sat right beside her. "Hey, how are you?" I asked.

She looked at me and scooted over and said, "Hey." She acted as if she didn't want me to sit with her, but I was determined to be nice to her for some reason. She looked as though she could use a friend. She was always by herself every time I saw her.

I looked over at her, and she was looking down at her freshly done nails. I knew she just had them done. I could tell. They were pretty, with a French-manicure polish.

"What's your name?"

"Renee. What's yours?"

"I'm Rachael. I came from Trotwood."

"I heard something like that in class. You friends with Linda, right?" She was looking in her compact mirror at herself. Renee was beautiful. She looked exotic, like she was from the Caribbean somewhere. The only way I could tell she was black was by her hair. She had black people's hair.

"Yeah, that's my girl," I said as I put on some lip-gloss.

She said under her breath, "Yeah, everybody knows her."

Renee was short, with a cute hairstyle, and she wore a lot of makeup. I never wore makeup, so I was impressed. She always had on cute shoes or clothes. I never saw her wear the same thing twice.

I thought that her family must be rich or something. *Everybody reruns sooner or later.*

By the time we got off the bus that day, we were laughing and talking. We were two peas in a pod from that day forward. I enjoyed being around her and her whole family.

I called Renee one day after school and told her I was coming by.

"Come on. Maybe we can walk down the block to Hooks Barbecue and get some burgers," she stated.

"Cool. I will be there in a minute," I told her.

As I walked, I wondered why she wasn't meeting me. *Usually she would meet me by now. Where is she?*

I reached her house and looked on their porch from the corner of the street. All of them—her mom, her brother Dwayne, and Renee—were huddled together, screaming and crying. I ran toward their house from across the street.

"What happened?" I screamed.

Everybody was there but her youngest brother, Tyrone. They were hysterical. The tears had already started falling from my eyes. I could feel their grief.

Renee said, "Tyrone is dead!"

I could barely understand her. Her voice sounded so desperate, like she would do anything to bring him back in that moment.

"What?" I didn't think I understood her correctly. "What did you say?"

She grabbed me and screamed, "He killed him! He killed him!"

I didn't know what to do or what to say. I just stood there hugging my friend and crying with her.

Renee's mother never said a word. She was in shock. She

looked as if she was a walking dead woman. No emotions; she was lost.

As I looked at her, it seemed she couldn't even hear what was going on, like everything was in slow motion for her. Dwayne was pounding the concrete and the side of the house with his fists. He was enraged. His hands were bloody from hitting the house.

Tyrone was shot in his eye, killed instantly. Tyrone was thirteen years old when he died. His friend had taken the gun to school earlier that day and hid it in a locker.

After Renee's brother died, her family's life never was the same. Dwayne got in some trouble with the law and went to prison for ten years. Renee had a baby, and her mother moved from the neighborhood.

Renee and I didn't see each other as often now that she had a son. She was working at a restaurant in the mall and trying to finish her last year in school. I did talk to her often, and she told me how tired she was from working and going to school. I really felt bad for her. I never saw her really laugh or hang out again. Having a child changed her whole life.

The summer break was over, and it was time to go back to school. I went to my first period class and saw Ronnie Swagner sitting there. I thought, *Oh, no. Bad news.*

I had met Ronnie at Linda's in the summertime. He and his friends were friends with Linda. They came over her house sometimes and hung out with us. Ronnie and them stayed in trouble, fighting with every bad boy in the city. They were headed for something bad.

"What's up, Rachael?" he said to me. "What you doing in here?"

I smiled and said, "What you think?" I thought I was being cute, but I was talking to a gangster.

Ronnie got up, walked over to me real close, and whispered, "Don't be scared."

I backed up from him, looking him in his eyes, and I thought back to the past summer and remembered how dangerous he was.

Everybody in school was impressed by the money, the clothes, the flashy jewelry, and cars he drove, but I knew how dangerous he was. I had experienced it firsthand that past summer.

Linda had said to me, "Rachael, you know Ronnie wanna take you out?"

"Yeah, I hear ya."

However, I knew he was trouble. Real trouble. So, I tried to stay away from him, but at the same time, I wanted to impress Linda and the females she hung with. Her friends didn't exactly welcome me into their social circle. Using Ronnie to impress them might not have been the brightest idea. Ronnie was crazy. I didn't trust him. Nevertheless, I felt that I had to prove myself; like the type of boys they liked.

And I did. I liked the bad boys as much as the next girl did. Ronnie was very popular. Every female in every high school would have jumped on the chance to ride in his car and hang out with him and his friends.

Linda and I went to a party one night and Ronnie and his friends were there. The whole night he watched everything I did, everywhere I went, and whoever I danced with or talked to. I was dancing with this dude from school when I saw Ronnie whispering in Linda's ear and looking toward me.

I wondered what was said, but never asked her. He had arranged to take me back to Linda's house. I didn't really want to go with him that night, but I did it anyway.

I told Linda, "I don't want to go with him."

"You'll be a'ight." Linda smiled and nodded her head.

I looked over at him, and he was watching us. He winked his eye at me and passed a joint to one of his friends. My hands were sweaty, and I was nervous.

Ronnie came over toward me and said, "You ready?"

I looked at him and smiled. "Yeah." I did not know what to expect, what he was going to do, or where he was taking me.

"Why you so scared, big head? I ain't gonna do nothin' to you. Dang, girl, loosen up." He bumped into my shoulder with his. "I'm gonna take you over Linda's. You act like I'm gonna kidnap you or somethin'. Girl, chill out."

We looked at each other and started laughing. He grabbed my hand and started walking toward his car. The closer we got to the chromed-out candy apple red Monte Carlo, the more I thought I was all that. I could hear his friends and mine laughing in the background. Truth is I didn't know where he was taking me. I just figured I would deal with that when he stopped the car.

Ronnie opened the car door for me and got on the driver's side.

He got the nerve to be a gentleman. Yeah, right! I smiled.

Once he got in the car, he turned the music up as loud as it could go.

I thought it was cute. I was special or something, I thought. All the chicks were gonna be mad when they heard I was in this nice whip, riding down Salem Avenue with the most popular dude in Dayton at the time.

I was silly. I had made a bad choice that night and didn't even know it. I was in the car with one of the biggest gangsters in Dayton. And I didn't know how much beef this brother really had in the streets.

Ronnie started the car and took off down the street, doing about eighty miles per hour, dipping back and forth in between cars. My eyes were big and I was startled. I had no idea he was gonna drive crazy like that. I couldn't let go of the seat. I was holding on for dear life.

He finally stopped at a gas station, got out of the car, and came over to the passenger's side where I was. He opened the door. I was so scared and nervous of the driving that when he opened the car door, I didn't even know he was right there. I had been praying the whole time he was driving. I knew I wasn't safe.

He bent down and said, "Don't move."

"What?" I felt cold, hard metal pressed against my thigh. I looked down and saw the gun against my skin. I started breathing heavily, wondering what he was going to do. Was he going to kill me? I couldn't understand why he would put a gun to me.

What did I do to him? He is crazy! I screamed out, "JESUS!" and started crying.

He looked at me and started laughing and said, "Aw, girl, I ain't gonna do nothing to you. I was just playing. It ain't even loaded and you doing all that crying." Ronnie looked around the gas station then kneeled down inside the car where I was sitting, put the gun on my lap, and pointed it up. "This right here is for the streets, not for you. You too pretty." He got up and winked his eye.

"You crazy," I said to him. "You need to quit all that gangster stuff before somebody gets hurt." I felt like smacking him, but I thought about it and figured he would smack me back.

He wouldn't listen to me. He was standing there outside the car, laughing at me.

I couldn't help but think that he didn't even look like he was capable of doing all the stuff he was doing. I tilted my head and watched him. Ronnie was clean-cut with manicured nails and a fresh haircut all the time, crisp edge up. He wasn't bad-looking. Just the stuff he represented made him unattractive. He dressed suave in linen and khakis. He was always clean with new sneakers daily. You never would know by looking at him standing there with a big gun in his back that he was a gangster.

I was so scared, I could have used the bathroom on myself. I was shaking and trembling. I hollered at him, "Take me home! Now!" I was furious.

No, he didn't pull a gun on me. He crazy. Wait till I tell Linda that. I knew from that moment that he wasn't in his right mind.

In class was the first time I had seen him since that incident. Ronnie whispered in my ear and said, "I'm sorry about the gun. You know I wouldn't hurt you." He was smiling and hugging me. "Remember what I told you? You too cute for that."

I smiled. I talked to him and even flirted with him in class, but I knew not to ever take it out of that class.

Ronnie was the first dude I knew that sold crack cocaine.

"Why you messing around with dope?" I would ask him.

He would say, "Girl, I get money." Then he would pull out a stack of money and start showing me. "You know what I can buy selling that stuff?"

I looked at him and shook my head.

Ronnie would come to class every day when school first started, but halfway through the semester, I barely saw him. We would sit together and talk all period when he came to class, and when I would see him in the halls, I would smile. He would smile back at me.

"I can buy you anything you want. Give me a chance, Rachael," he would say to me.

The guys in class looked up to Ronnie like he was a superstar, but he wasn't. He was an out-of-control teenager headed for danger.

"Ronnie, you too smart for drugs. You out there, fighting at all the parties. You too good for that."

Ronnie's father raised him and was a teacher with the

school system, so he didn't have to struggle. His dad was a good provider, but he still wanted to be in the streets. Eventually, he was only coming to school two or three times a week.

I sat and looked at his empty chair and wondered where he was, and hoped he was okay. I started hearing kids in the class talk about how Ronnie had a party this weekend and that weekend.

"You seen Ronnie's new car? You seen Ronnie's necklace?"

Every week it was something else. It got to the point where he never came back to school.

The next time I saw Ronnie, he was lying in a coffin. Ronnie was killed. He and his friends were arguing with a dude. Ronnie walked up to the guy's car, opened the door, and they shot him right in the head. Ronnie's friends were there to see the whole incident.

As tough as all those so-called gangsters were, they were broken down after his death. I was hurt from his death too. After talking to him, he really wasn't as tough as he seemed. I believe he wanted to be accepted by his friends, and in his mind, he had to be tough. As teenagers, we all were lost.

I can remember Ronnie and his friends showing up at Linda's house one day wearing ski masks and carrying guns. I was lying on the couch watching TV when I saw some masked men run up in the house. My heart was beating fast. I ran toward the bedroom and busted in Linda's door, screaming. She looked up, startled.

Ronnie and his crew ran in behind me, laughing. They took off their masks and said, "We got you good. Ha, ha!"

"Y'all play too much," I said and then started play-punching them.

Within a few seconds, we all were sitting in the front room of her house, laughing about what they had done.

There are so many different ways the devil can confuse us.

He gets in the heads of our young people and eventually destroys them. He tears down their self-esteem, making them think they have to be like someone else to be accepted, and that's deadly.

As for the dude that killed Ronnie, I heard he and Ronnie had beef and he was afraid that Ronnie and his crew was going to get him first, so when Ronnie opened the car door that night, dude took his father's pistol that he had stole and shot Ronnie. That is a sure sign that the enemy was upon him, because God doesn't give us the spirit of fear.

"And that they may come to their senses and escape the snare of the devil, having been taken captive by him to do his will."—2 Timothy 2:26.

Ronnie's death left me heartbroken. Renee went to his funeral with me. We watched all the gangsters, hustlers, and drug dealers come in and pay their respects for Ronnie, but the sad part was that no one learned a lesson from all this—not the females, not the gangsters, hustlers or drug dealers. Within a few weeks, everything went back to the norm, and there was a new "Ronnie" who was popular.

At the funeral, I remember saying to Renee, "I won't get involved with a dude like Ronnie again." I leaned my head on her shoulder and cried. I whispered, "This is for the birds." I got up, put on my shades and said, "Let's go."

Renee followed me out the door. We got in Renee's car and she said, "So, you won't talk to nobody who sells drugs?" She had her lips turned up as if she didn't believe me.

"No, it's too much drama. Besides, they either go to jail or die, and I don't want the grief."

Renee looked at me then turned the key in the ignition and pulled out of the church parking lot.

I stared out the car window for a few minutes then mumbled, "My next dude will be an athlete. He has to play sports."

She looked at me and said, "How you know that? You

might meet a nice guy, and you mean to tell me you won't holla at him if he ain't playing sports?"

"Yep, that's exactly what I'm saying."

"Okay, how you know that, Rachael?"

I never answered her. I sat back in the car seat and closed my eyes. I was serious. I had made up in my mind that I wanted an athlete. I had my own agenda. I wanted out of the ghetto, and a dude with a pro contract could make that happen. I wasn't thinking about what I could do to change my situation, or trying to go to college. I was busy figuring out what I could do to get some dude to take care of me. I didn't believe in myself enough to think I could make it on my own, so I needed a man to be there when I graduated. Most kids were thinking of going to college or getting a job. I was thinking of who was gonna go to college or work and take care of me.

I walked down the halls of Meadowdale, smiling and flirting with the boys of my choice, laughing and talking with Renee. I knew they hoped for a chance to get to know me, but I was too good for the average Joe at Meadowdale. He had to be somebody or be going somewhere to go out with me. I had become quit the little diva, with my hair done up and nails polished to perfection. I had been told one too many times that I was cute. It had gone completely to my head and created a monster.

"Renee, I'll see you after drama class," I said.

"All right, see you in a few," she responded.

I watched Renee run toward her class as the bell rang. I laughed to myself and turned around to walk into class when I bumped smack dab into Denny Calhoun. He was so huge that I fell back. He grabbed me by my waist and helped me up. We never said a word to each other, but our looks said it all—I was interested in him, and he was interested in me.

I locked eyes with the cute football player and watched him while he walked by. I was smiling and grinning, looking

so innocent, but I wasn't. I knew he played football and was
the best on the team—in the whole state, for that matter. At
the time, I had no idea that he was my future husband.

School let out for the summer, and I thought that would
be the end of seeing him, but I was wrong. Halfway through
the summer, a great depression came over me. All I thought
about was how lonely I was, sitting in my bedroom listening
to Prince's album *Purple Rain* and looking on my wall at all
the posters and album covers of him and Michael Jackson.
Crystal was in her second year at Wilberforce University and
decided to stay at school through the summer, so I didn't get
to see her at all now. And as far as Momma, who knew where
she was? All my friends had their own families, and they were
either on vacation or busy doing summer activities. I believed I was all alone; no one loved me or cared.

I had so many negative thoughts in my head. I never went
to church anymore. I missed God. I missed singing in the
youth choir. I sat at home, watched TV, and listened to
music. That was enough room for the devil to get in my
thoughts. I will never forget that summer. It was the start of
my spiraling out of control.

Knock, knock, knock!

I went in the living room and looked out the peephole. It
was Dayton Power and Light. I opened the door.

"May I help you?"

"Yes, ma'am. Your electric bill is past due, and I can collect
from you before I have to shut it off. Is there any way you can
pay now?"

I was just standing there. I didn't know what to do. I didn't
have the money to pay it, and the money Momma kept in
the jar was gone. I looked down at the brown carpet. "No, I
don't have it."

The white man with glasses and a baseball cap looked sad.
"I tell you what; call your mother and I'll come back in a little while. Will that help ya?"

"Yes, sir," I said, but I knew it wouldn't. It would give me a little time to get to Linda's house, though.

I was frustrated with Momma because she'd said earlier that day that she was going to pay the bills. She lied. I hurried and packed a few outfits and a pair of sneakers in my backpack, put it on my back, and headed for the door. I left the apartment to catch the bus when I saw Darrin, from school, driving down the street.

Beep, beep!

I turned, pushed my shades down with my finger, and smiled.

He looked at me and said, "Where you goin'?"

I looked in the small white Honda Civic and replied, "Oh, what's up? Over Linda's."

"I'll take you. I live down the street from them," he replied.

I said okay and got in the car with him.

Darrin graduated and was on his way to some major college on an athletic scholarship in football, but he just wasn't my type. First of all, he already had three kids and a baby's momma that would fight if she knew I was even in the car with him. That's all I knew about him. But I thought it was cool just to cop a ride from him. I wasn't worried about his girl. I didn't want him. I never thought anything different. I was safe. I hadn't heard anything negative about him before. He appeared to be a nice dude, helping me out.

The whole time he drove, he kept looking over at me.

Why he keep looking at me like that? And why is he licking his lips? I know I probably had wrinkles on my forehead.

When he got close to Linda's house, he turned right at the corner.

"That's the wrong way. She lives to the left," I told him. I never thought much of it. I thought he missed the turn.

"I just want to talk to you," he said.

I was confused.

"I've liked you for the last two years. Girl, you know you're fine."

I looked at him, but I was speechless. I didn't know what to say, so I shouted, "Stop the car! I want to get out!" I grabbed hold of the door. I started to panic. "I'll walk from here. Just let me get out the car!"

It was as if he couldn't hear me. Darrin was driving so fast, he drove up the sidewalk and through the playground at the elementary school. Then he went behind the elementary school where there was grass in the field. He drove through the grass, far away from the school, where I knew nobody could see us.

When he reached the field, I told myself that I was going to jump out and run, but he locked the doors. I quickly remembered the times when I was a little girl, trapped and helpless. Everything was happening so fast. I struggled and fought with him. I tried to reason with him.

"Darrin, what are you trying to do, huh? Don't do this. We friends."

His eyes looked piercing, like a madman or animal; a tiger looking at prey. He was breathing so heavy and hard. He reclined my seat and jumped on top of me.

I pushed him, but his strength was much greater than mine. I was 5'7" at 125 pounds, and he was 6'2" at 240-plus pounds. There was no comparison. I did everything I could possibly think of. I screamed, but it was after seven in the evening, and nobody was at the courts a few yards away. It was getting dark outside.

I tried to bite him and kick my legs, but there was no room. I hit him on his back, but it didn't bother him at all. I had all kinds of thoughts going through my mind. *Am I the cause of this? Was I asking for this?*

He never took my shorts off. He unzipped his pants and went up the side of my shorts, all the while shouting in my ear, "Don't fight! You know you wanted this to happen! You like this. I heard about you." He was breathing even harder than before and sweating.

"Darrin, stop. I don't want you! I hate you! I hate you!" I was reaching for the lock with one hand, while the other hand was on top of his hand, which was wrapped around my throat. I was so terrified, but I didn't want to give myself to him. I didn't want anyone else to have me that I didn't give permission to. I was tired of being someone's piece of meat.

I remember him whispering in my ear, "Shut up. You know you like this, teasing everybody all the time."

I kept reaching for the lock, ignoring what he was saying and looking for a way to escape. After a few minutes went by, I pulled up on the lock and opened the door. It startled him and made him back up a little. With the door opened, I slid out to the grass. I landed hard and cut my leg on his door. I didn't care; I was out of the car.

I got up off the ground and started running as fast as I could, never looking behind me. I ran and ran. I began to cry.

Why does this keep happening to me, God? Answer me! What did I do to deserve this, God? Tell me something, Jesus! Please! Why is my life so bad?

I looked a mess. My shorts were all dirty with grass stains and dirt everywhere. My hair was all over my head, and one of my shoes was missing—not to mention my thigh was cut up from the door scraping me as I fell out. I stopped running and started walking when I heard a horn blowing from the distance behind me. I looked back and saw Darrin and his white Honda coming. I rolled my eyes with fury and started running again.

He reached me and said, "You know you wanted me to do that, right?" Now he was thinking of the consequences. "I wasn't forcing you. You just was scared! You liked it. Don't act like you didn't! You were moving all around and stuff."

"Yeah, I was moving—trying to get out the car, you maniac!" I looked over at him with a frowned faced. "I want you dead!" I shouted.

"Rachael, you don't mean that." He had the nerve to be smiling at me.

"Yes, I do! I hate you!" I was screaming from the top of my lungs. I could have killed him with my bare hands, I thought.

He thought it was funny. He was actually laughing.

I was now walking in a neighborhood by the school, and people were looking out of their doors and turning on their porch lights to see what was going on.

Darrin was getting nervous. He looked around and said, "Get in the car. I'll take you."

"No, I ain't going nowhere with you! You are a rapist!" I picked up a rock off the sidewalk and threw it at him and his beat-up Honda.

He looked at me and got serious. "You better watch what you say out your mouth, you little slut. Don't make me get out this car. I'll show you who I am. Now, you wanted it too. Don't start acting silly. I said I'll take you home. Get in!" He stopped the car in front of me and threw out my backpack. I could see the anger on his face.

I darted across the street to Linda's house. I could hear him calling my name and his horn beeping in the distance, and then it was silent. He made me feel like I was nothing! I felt dirty. I hated myself and remembered the pain from my childhood. I was a little girl all over again. Defenseless! I was so embarrassed and afraid of what others might think or say about me that I never breathed a word of what happened that day.

I stopped at the bowling alley down the street from Linda's house and went in the bathroom to change my clothes and my shoes. When I went in the bowling alley, people were looking at me, asking me if I was okay.

I tried to pull myself together quickly. I put my hair back in a ponytail and stared at myself in the mirror, looking past my face at my own soul, trying to figure out what had really just happened to me and why. I left the bowling alley quickly because I knew that Linda was wondering where I was by now.

I pulled myself together when I saw Linda's house from the corner. I glanced around to see if Darrin was lurking, but he was gone. I walked in Linda's house two hours later than I told her I would be.

Linda said, "Girl, where you been? I was worried about you. You okay?" She was concerned. She looked at me and said, "What's wrong?"

I couldn't look her in the eyes. "No, I'm fine," I said with a phony smile on my face. I thought I was going to start crying right in front of her. "I need to use the bathroom. I'll be back." I walked past her and peeked in her bedroom on my way to the bathroom. I saw the other girls who hung with Linda.

Linda could tell that I didn't want to be bothered with anybody. After we talked, she decided to have a slumber party. She said, "You know, get everybody together again." She was excited.

I thought, *Great.* When I went in the bathroom, I shut the door, turned the water on, and began crying. There were so many thoughts in my head.

Why? Why is this my life; sex? Why did I have to go through this? Was I asking for it? I felt so dirty. I felt like Darrin was watching me. I was losing it quickly.

Darrin's semen was on my underwear. It was a disgusting feeling, and I wanted to die! I was so angry I wanted him to die! I stayed in the bathroom as long as I could before others started knocking to use the restroom. I wanted to get all traces of him off me, so I scrubbed my skin raw in some areas, trying to get his touch off me.

I had to pull myself together, act as though I was cool, like nothing happened. I knew if anyone found out, they would think I was lying. I thought nobody would believe me over him. They would ask why he would have to lie. I convinced myself it was a bad dream.

When I came out, it seemed like everyone knew what he had done. I took the clothes that I had on during the rape out of my backpack, and when all the other girls were busy laughing and talking, I threw them in the garbage outside the house.

As I came in from throwing the clothes away, I overheard Linda's other guest, Nae Nae, telling her, "She brought roaches in your house."

I stood by the door listening to them. They didn't know I was listening. I was hurt. They were all laughing and making fun of me, saying, "Her momma's a whore and she ain't never got nothing. She dirty."

That day crushed me like a ton of bricks. I turned around and went back outside so they could finish their conversation about my momma and me. I did hear Linda defending me, telling them that they needed to stop because I was her friend. But the words had already pierced my heart.

When I came back in the house, I went to the bathroom and began to cry. I wanted to punch Nae Nae in the mouth, but I knew it wouldn't change a thing. She would still feel the same way, and my reality was my reality. I wanted to go home, but I knew there was no food or lights at my house. Our electricity had probably been cut off by now. So, I knew the only option I had was to stay there. I knew I was safe at Linda's.

These girls had no idea the things I faced. Their lives seemed so perfect. With mothers and fathers at home to care for them, they didn't have the worries I did. I watched them as they sat there all stuck-up, looking at me like I was infected with a contagious disease.

I had a problem defending myself. I let so many people say what they wanted about me and I never stood up for myself. I would try to forget about them, pretending it never happened, acting as if I didn't hear them, or their statements didn't bother me. I kept their words inside, though, in my mind and heart.

"And be kind to one another, tenderhearted, forgiving one another, even as God in Christ forgave you."—Ephesians 4:3.

I stayed at Linda's house one more day and decided to call my aunt Lisa to see if I could come over her house for the rest of the weekend.

She said, "Yes, come over. I haven't seen you in a while. I need some help getting this house clean."

I smiled as I held my end of the phone and thought to myself, *That was just what I needed—a getaway to my auntie's house.*

She picked me up a couple of hours later. I smiled and sat back in her brand-new Audi. She had her music on, and the air was on blast.

"Rachael, you hungry?"

"Yep."

"I'll take you down here to Wendy's and get you something to eat."

"Thank you." I was okay now. With my aunt, everything was going to be fine. I sat back in the leather seat and folded my arms behind my head. I was relaxed.

We drove up to her suburban split-level home. I loved that house. I went in her house and walked down the stairs to the plush family room.

She said, "Hey, Rachael?"

"Yeah," I yelled, still sipping on my soda from Wendy's.

"Don't steal anything while you're down there!" she screamed from upstairs.

I had just picked up the remote to the television, sat down and was smiling before she called my name. I had been thinking, *I can sit in a beautiful house all weekend and watch cable.* Then what she said began to sink in my head, and I thought, *Why would she say that?* I was embarrassed that she thought that of me. I had never taken anything before. Why would she think that? What did my family really think about me and why? I always did what they asked me to. I didn't know how to react to what she'd said. I was hurt; I know that.

I left there feeling empty. I couldn't believe my aunt would think such a thing. I wondered, *What could make her think I would steal from her?* If I ever needed anything, I would ask. I had no problem asking her for something.

I was so upset with her that I hardly said anything on the way home. I just wanted out of her car. I wasn't mad, just hurt. I got out of the car and said good-bye. I walked through the crowd of men standing on the block smoking weed and selling dope, over to our apartment door. I thought, *I'm tired of this.*

I heard, "Hey, baby," about seven times from the men before I reached my door. I never responded. I turned the key and thought, *I hope Momma is here.* I didn't want to be alone.

I could see every room from the front door. I looked over to the left at her room, and saw her bed hadn't been slept in.

I put my bag on the floor and walked into my room. I looked around at the four walls and sighed. It was five o'clock in the evening. I stood in front of my bed and went backwards, falling onto the bed. *I hope the lights are on,* I said to myself.

I got off the bed and checked the light switch, and the light came on. "Thank You, Lord." I smiled and turned on my radio to listen to some jams, but all I got was commercials.

I went to the refrigerator to see that there was nothing to eat. I tried to put the past week in the back of my mind, forget about it like I forgot about the rest of the things I went through, but this was too much. I couldn't forget it. That statement had blown up to everything that had ever happened to me. I felt so sorry for myself; low, depressed, very empty. I didn't want to live anymore.

I sat on the floor of the apartment and cried for hours. I hated my life and myself. I had no one. I started thinking of the abortion I had when I was fifteen, blaming myself repeatedly for the rape and the molestation, and the abuse I had endured. I was pitiful, desperate, and alone. It was my fault—my fault for Momma not being there; my fault because I didn't have a father. It all was my fault.

I believe the devil was sitting right there in that apartment with me. He was saying in my ear, "Kill yourself. Do it. Do it. Nobody cares about you."

I was feeling sorry for myself, and the devil was happy. He tormented me with thoughts of suicide all night long.

The devil is a liar, and if a person doesn't guard their mind with the Word of God and know what authority they have over him, he will confuse them. John 8:4 says, "You are of your father the devil, and the desires of your father you want to do. He was a murderer from the beginning, and does not stand in the truth, because there is no truth in him. When he speaks a lie, he speaks from his own resources, for he is a liar and the father of it."

I prayed and told God I wanted to be with Him, with no idea it was a trick from the enemy for me to take my own life.

I began to talk to myself, but I was really talking to the devil and didn't know it. I said, "Why do people treat me so bad?"

It answered me. *You're nothing. You're pitiful. Kill yourself.* In a sleek but powerful voice, it spoke again. *God feels sorry for you. He will welcome you. Put His arms around you. He knows they all treat you bad. He will make an exception for you.*

"Yeah, I love Him. He will welcome me. He sees what I'm going through down here. He knows I made some mistakes." I nodded my head.

Besides, you're a kid, a teenager; you can't be accountable for killing yourself, can you?

"No, I can't," I said softly.

Look in the cabinet and get the pills. Tell God you're on your way. Let Him know you're sorry. He will forgive you.

I was crying and trying to figure out what was real and what was make-believe. Was I dreaming? Was I imagining this conversation?

I heard a voice again. *Grab those pills and take them. All of them!*

I went through the medicine cabinet looking for the right pills to take. I took every pill I could find in the medicine cabinet. I got a cup of water and took seventeen pills in all. I thought that would do the job.

I didn't write a note. For what? Momma didn't care about me.

I lay on the floor of our apartment, looking up at the ceiling. So many thoughts began to flow through my head. I wondered who my father was. *Where is he?* I remember everything getting blurry, and I kept saying, "Forgive me, God. Forgive me, God."

All of a sudden, I heard a loud banging on the door, but couldn't get up to answer it. I was almost 'sleep, like a baby in a cradle.

I heard the devil say, *Yeah, that's it. Go to sleep.*

I could remember everything bad or good that had happened in my life. I was dying. I could no longer sit up straight. I was leaning against the wall across from the door and the front window, but I couldn't move.

Renee and her boyfriend, Michael, were knocking at the door, yelling my name, and they were looking at me through the window. I couldn't answer them.

Renee said, "Rachael, you all right? What's wrong? Answer me!" She screamed, "She's not moving. I can see her, but she's not moving, Michael! Michael, kick the door down!"

I heard a loud bang and saw the door coming off the hinges. Michael picked me up, put me in his car, and took me to the hospital. In the car, Renee was asking me questions, trying to keep me focused and awake, but I couldn't respond.

When we reached the hospital, I was placed on a stretcher and taken in the back immediately. The doctor pumped my stomach, gave me charcoal to drink, and sent in a psychiatrist to talk to me. I was a head case, but I wasn't crazy. I was just a sixteen year old girl who had been through so much in a short lifetime and was fed up!

I knew to tell the doctors and psychiatrists what they wanted to hear. "I'm sorry. I won't ever do that again. I learned my lesson." I knew God would send me to hell.

After talking to the doctors, I knew that killing myself wasn't the answer. I don't know how to explain what I heard or felt earlier that day, but by the time I reached the hospital, the feeling was gone. I knew deep down in my heart that there was going to be a better life for me, and I felt there was a reason for my life, a purpose.

The only one that would have been happy was the stupid devil. He knows what your future holds, and if he can throw you far off, then his work is done. That is one of his ultimate plans, to fool someone into taking their own life. He knows we cannot repent for suicide. If you kill yourself, you cannot ask for forgiveness. That's the bottom line.

"Thou shalt not kill."—Exodus 20:13.

When I returned from the hospital, my relatives were calling, very concerned and upset. It wasn't my aunt's fault, me taking the pills and all. I was confused and emotionally wrecked. I had been raped, talked about, and ashamed all in one weekend.

I carried that pain around with me for my aunt for twenty years, all because I thought she said, "Don't steal." Now that

I know how deceitful the devil is, I may have imagined she said it. We truly do perish for lack of knowledge.

"Casting down arguments and every high thing that exalts itself against the knowledge of God, bringing every thought into captivity to the obedience of Christ."—2 Corinthians 10:5.

I wanted to live and enjoy life! I thank God that He gave me a second chance to live. He could have easily let me die in my self-pity stage, but because of His mercy, He gave me a new day. I love my God!

Chapter 5

First Love

August came around, and Linda and I decided to go to Sassy's, a nightclub that opened every Friday night for high school students on summer vacation. This was the last weekend it was open before school started again. It was stacked, people dancing and mingling with each other everywhere. Every high school in Dayton was represented at the club that night. The athletes, the cheerleaders, and of course, us—the "QTs." That was the name of our group.

Linda founded the QTs when she was a freshman at Trotwood High School. There were many groups, but we were the most popular, hands down. The QTs consisted of females that went to Trotwood High. Trotwood wasn't a city school. It was in the suburbs of Dayton, so that made the females at Trotwood hot commodities. There were so many females wanting to be a part of the QTs, but they had to be voted in.

We watched the different girls and how they looked and acted in school. If we liked what we saw, we asked the girl to join, not the other way around. There were only twelve members, but we were constantly being asked if we were ac-

cepting any new ones. Linda wanted to keep us elite. That
was one of the things that made us special—not to mention
we all dressed nice and kept our hair and nails done. We had
jackets, shirts, and wore them when we went to the clubs.
Everybody knew who we were.

We had so much power as teenage girls that nightclub
owners used to ask us to throw parties at their clubs so kids
would come. Of course, we had our haters thinking we were
stuck-up or sleeping with all the popular dudes in every high
school, but to keep it real, we weren't. We were just friends
who looked out for one another. We had each other's backs
and had a lot of fun hanging around each other. We went
everywhere together. Our name was so big that the radio station put us on to advertise for parties. That's big! I was the
only member that didn't go to Trotwood anymore because
when we moved, I had to transfer to Meadowdale High.

Sassy's would have the music bumpin', and everybody
would be dancing or conversing. As soon as I walked in, I saw
Denny, the football player from my school. My heart flut-
tered, I was so nervous. The football player I locked eyes
with every day before my drama class was there in Sassy's.

"I never seen him in here before," I said aloud, nodding
toward Denny.

"What you say?" Linda said over the loud music.

I was surprised she even heard my voice because while we
walked in, people were flocking around her like she was a
movie star.

I whispered in Linda's ear, telling her the story of Denny;
how he was my one true love.

She laughed and said, "Well, all right, you better get 'im
before somebody else do." Then she pointed her head toward him.

I looked and saw some chick in his face. I hit Linda in the
back. "I'll be right back." I made my way over to where he
was.

He was standing against the wall, talking to the girl, when I walked by. When he saw me, he turned and said, "Hey, don't I know you?"

I smiled and said, "No, you don't know me." I walked back over by Linda. I turned to see what he was doing.

He turned to the female and said, "Excuse me," and walked over closer to me.

I couldn't take my eyes off him. There was an instant connection at that moment.

Linda looked at me and said, "Here he comes, girl."

I looked up, and Denny was heading my way. He was tall, had a caramel skin color, with only a couple of pimples on his face, and he was beautiful. His eyes were slanted, and his hair was short and curly. He looked like the magazine-perfect superstar athlete, and when he smiled, I swear his teeth sparkled. Denny was huge, the biggest dude in the whole club, and everybody knew he was the next athlete to go to the pros out of Dayton.

My heart was pounding fast. I could see how big he really was. I guess that's why they called him "The Refrigerator."

"You want to dance?" he asked.

"Yes."

We talked while we moved to the dance floor. "What's your name?" he asked.

I could hardly hear him over the music, so I moved closer to him and stood on my tiptoes. I put my ear near his mouth so I could hear him.

"What's your name?" he repeated.

"Rachael," I said in his ear. "What's yours?" I already knew his name, but I didn't want him to know. I knew a lot of females were after him because he played ball, and I figured the less he thought I knew about him, the better my chances were to get close to him.

He smiled and said, "Denny."

We smiled and grinned at each other.

"Rachael, you want something to drink?"

"No, not right now."

Denny wasn't like the other dudes. He was genuine. Denny didn't have no game. Yes, he tried to act cool like he was all that, but I saw through it. Denny was a nice guy.

"Let's go talk for a minute," Denny said after we danced a couple of songs.

He took my hand, and I followed him off the dance floor, over to the corner away from the noise.

I knew I was looking good. I had my QTs wife-beater on and some Guess short-shorts. I, along with the other QTs, wore all-white Nikes so we could dance and be comfortable.

"I have to confess. I know who you are. Everybody knows you are a QT, right?"

I smiled, tugged at my QT shirt and said, "Right."

"I been asking around about you all summer, ever since I seen you in the hall that day," he said.

I stayed with Denny until the club closed, never paying attention to anybody or anything but him. I don't even think I heard the music.

"Last dance, last dance," the DJ said into the mike. "Okay, if you want to get yo' slow dance on, this is the last time until Christmas break. We won't be open for the high schools until then. This is the last dance."

I looked at Denny, and he was staring at me.

"Let's go." He held his hand out and led me to the crowded dance floor.

I felt as if we were the only two on the floor. The DJ was playing an oldie titled "Slow Jam." My eyes were closed tight, and my heart was melting for Denny. My stomach was turning somersaults.

After that dance, it was time to go. He walked me to Linda's mom's car, gave me his number on a napkin, and kissed me on the cheek.

I smiled and could hear Linda saying, "Come on, we got go." She was standing on the frame of the door, hollering, "We going to White Castle. Tell him to meet you there. I'm hungry."

Denny looked at me and reached for my hands. He took them inside of his and said, "Well, I have to go home." He looked down at his watch. "Supposed to be there now." He stepped in closer to me and leaned forward, grabbed me around the waist and gave me a big hug. "When you come from White Castle, give me a call. I wanna know you got home safe, okay?"

I could hear Linda and them saying, "Aw, that's so cute, but she better come on. I'm hungry, Rachael. Come on."

I heard her start the car. I backed up from Denny, still holding his hands, and said, "I gotta go. I'll call you." I walked backwards, watching him get in the car with his brother until they pulled off.

"Tonight."

All the way to White Castle, I talked about Denny. "Denny is so nice. He's so cute. He's a gentleman. He ain't like the rest of them."

Linda laughed at me. She said, "Girl, I ain't ever seen you this crazy about nobody." She turned her head toward me, looked me in my eyes, and said, "I think he might be the one, Rach."

I said, "Nah, I ain't taking it that far." I smiled. I looked out the window the rest of the way to White Castle in silence, thinking about Denny and my fairytale night.

As soon as we got to Linda's house, I took off my shoes and dialed Denny's number. The phone rang twice, but I hung up because it was so late and I thought maybe he was 'sleep by now. I told Linda I would call him when I woke in the morning. So, we went ahead and laid down to go to sleep.

No sooner than our heads hit the pillow, the phone rang.

We looked at each other and Linda said, "You know that's him."

I smiled and picked up the phone. "Hello."

"Hello, Rachael?"

"Yes."

That was beginning of many nights on the phone and falling asleep on the phone. Denny and I became close; best friends. We went everywhere together. When we weren't together, we were on the telephone, talking and giggling. Between our classes at school, we were writing notes to one another. We shared everything. We were in love. He was my first love.

What I loved about him was that he knew he was going to college on a football scholarship. He was so confident in what he wanted to do in life, but I didn't have a clue what I was going to do. I loved talking to and being with him. He was so excited about his football career and he loved the sport. His eyes would light up whenever he talked about football. Denny treated me so special, like royalty.

His plans were to go to college and play football. My plans involved whatever his plans were. I had no plans for life after high school. I was insecure, and I knew chicks were coming for him.

Once we were together, I was determined to hold on to him. Nobody was going to break him and me apart if I had anything to say about it. I thought that this was the first person going somewhere who loved me for me. I became manipulative, cunning, straight-up deceitful to hold on to him. I heard what people were saying around me about my boyfriend: "He's the next NFL star out of Dayton, Ohio. He's the million-dollar man."

I learned quickly how to hold on to Denny. I knew what to do to make him stay with me. A couple of times, he told me he wanted to take a break from our relationship before he went to college. To make him see things my way, I went into this story about how my mother was dying of cancer and I wouldn't have anyone. That was about six months after we were together. Another time, he tried to take a break, just for a while until the end of the summer. I pretended to take a bottle full of pills in front of him.

I wasn't happy with the schemes, but I didn't want him to let me go. In fact, I did everything I could to keep him interested in me.

Denny's father was a preacher in Dayton, Ohio. As I look back, the way I viewed his parents was the way a rebellious teenager would. I now know that it wasn't his parents who were out of line. It was me. I had their son on a short leash, and they knew it. Especially Denny's mom.

One time, we were over his house in the family room and had fallen asleep after lying together on their floor and watching television. She came downstairs and woke us up in a hysterical scream. Denny was lying there in the covers, and he still had his pants off. He talked me into having sex while his parents were upstairs in their bedroom. We fell asleep afterwards, and he never put his pants back on. I had my clothes on, but he didn't. His mother pulled the covers back while we were fast asleep, and she saw that.

After that, she hated me. Denny would tell me that his father had lectures with him almost daily about our relationship. They thought I was holding him back, and his mother tried to fix him up with a couple of good girls from the church. He told me they thought I was from a bad family and that I was going to eventually pull him down. They told him he would never amount to anything with someone like me by his side.

Once I was with Denny, any remote idea I may have had about starting a career went out the window. My career was marrying Denny. That was what I lived and breathed until the day we walked down the aisle and my dream came true.

A friend of mine told me about beauty school. She said

she was going, and it only took eleven months to finish. I figured I could be close to Denny and still start some type of career.

"So, Jennifer, how long did you say it took you?"

"It takes about nine months if you don't goof off. You can get through."

I was going to beauty school. I wasn't going to sit at home and do nothing; I wanted a job—for now, anyway. I had no idea where cosmetology would take me.

It's funny how God strategically put things into my path. I thought at the time that I was just going with the flow, but truthfully, God was setting me up for greatness. My God, He is so amazing!

"I know the thoughts I think toward you, says the Lord, thoughts of peace and not evil, to give you a hope."—Jeremiah 29:11.

When I turned eighteen, we moved in with Grandpa. My mother could no longer get public assistance to help with me, and she was no longer working at my uncle's bar. It had been closed down, raided by SWAT. They came in and took the money, drugs, alcohol, and everybody to jail. Momma and Uncle Al got out a few days later with fines, but no real trouble. After that, Momma left the clubs and bars alone for good. I never knew her to go back.

I loved Grandpa so much. He was a mighty man of God! There were terrible things that happened in my life, but believe me, he was definitely my hero. My granddad would always come to my rescue, always! Looking back, he definitely was a praying man. I know my grandpa prayed and asked God to watch over my life and Crystal's life. God loved him so much that He woke me up to understand the plan for my life based on the prayers of my grandfather.

All while in school, I stayed at Grandpa's house, but on the weekends, I was in Columbus with Denny. I bought myself a Ford Escort, blue and old, but it got me where I needed to go. I had a part-time job working with Linda at McDonald's after I came home from school in the evenings.

I loved going up to Columbus and being on Ohio State's campus. It always made me feel like I was in college, but at the same time, I had to face the truth. I didn't go to college. I enjoyed walking around campus and the idea of students living on their own, being free.

"Come on, Denny. Let's go out. Let's get out of this room and explore Ohio State!" I was so excited that I had forgotten he walked around the campus all day.

He put on his shoes and coat. "Let's go."

We walked around holding hands and hugged up while he showed me different sights. He held my hand and excitedly pointed with the other, sharing his new college experiences with me.

"What? Why you smiling?"

"Nothing." I held on to his arm tighter.

After seeing the sights, we would always end up at Tommy's Pizzeria on Lane Avenue. We went there so much that they knew us by our names. I loved everything about college life. And being a football player's girlfriend surely had its advantages. I went to every football game OSU played, with excellent seats. It was awesome; something I never would have experienced if I wasn't his girl.

By the time Denny was in his second year of college, I was pregnant. I wanted to be loved, and I thought sex was just that—love. I had always been under the impression that if I slept with someone, it showed that I loved him and he loved me. I guess that's what I wanted to believe; things that I had seen on television. That's the only time I really saw any type of affection growing up—TV shows and movies. That is what I wanted—a fairytale, the movies—but it was all a dream.

I was excited about having a child, even though I knew we hadn't planned for it and we weren't married. I was still happy. It was different than with TJ. Denny and I were truly in love, and I could make my own decisions. Now I wasn't confused. I knew I wanted this child with no doubt. I was ready. I thought the only reason Denny and I weren't married was because he wasn't finished with school. He was headed for a great career, and I was the woman he had by his side. We knew everything about each other. I could finish his sentences, and he could finish mine.

We had already been dating for four years when I became pregnant, so everything was under control. I only thought about me, Denny, and our love for each other. I didn't factor in my issues with his parents or his career as a football player. I believed him when he said we would be married when he finished school. I didn't know that all along he had been looking for someone better. I thought Denny was the perfect man; handsome, smart and talented. I thought I had everything under control.

He and I had always talked about having kids and getting married when he finished school or he went to the NFL. He knew about the abortion I had and how painful it was for me. He always assured me that I would never have to worry about him asking me to do that. "I would never let you do that. I would never let you kill my baby. I love you," he had told me.

I was safe with him. He told me that he loved me and that we would get married if I ever got pregnant before we got married. "That's murder," he had said adamantly. "Killing your baby is murder." He was so passionate about it, as if it hurt him when he watched me cry from talking about it.

I looked at him softly, with warmth on the inside, as he yelled and defended the unborn. That made me love him even more.

But when I became pregnant and I went to him and told him, he said, "Get an abortion." He explained, "I'm in school, and my parents would be outraged."

I was heartbroken! I couldn't believe this was the same man I loved five minutes ago. What was he saying? Who was this in front of me? Didn't he remember what I said I experienced? As Denny continued, I was speechless.

"I can't have any kids. Not right now."

Denny pleaded with me, but I wouldn't do it. I couldn't do it! I had promised God that I wouldn't do such a thing again. I was crushed that he wanted me to have an abortion. All the stuff he said he would do if I got pregnant went right out the window. After all, I thought Denny was the love of my life, and we were in love.

I thought back to the days when we were in high school and he told me he loved me and he wanted to marry me. The smile he had on his face and the kisses he had on his lips for me made me melt back then. I thought of the way he held my hand and told me he wanted me to be the mother of his children one day; how he hoped they would have my eyes and smile. I remember how we would look in the mirror together and picture our children. We used to sit on the phone and make up names for our make-believe children.

I snapped back to reality and heard Denny saying, "Get rid of it!"

I was devastated. My heart ached. What could I do to change his mind? I then realized I was alone and betrayed. I didn't know what to do or who to tell my problem to. Denny was standing there with his hands on top of his head, looking at me like I had the answer.

"Denny, the problem isn't the baby I'm carrying inside of me. It's you." I walked over to him and touched his chest.

He looked down at me and shook his head. "Come on, Rach. You know my folks gonna flip out."

"Denny, you know what's hurting me?" I cried and struggled to get the words out. "What hurts me is you. You lied to me. You told me you loved me and I could count on you, but I can't."

He grabbed me and hugged me. "I love you, Rach. I do, and you know this, but this is serious." He grabbed my face under my chin and made me look at him. "This is real, Rach. We in trouble." He stepped back away from me and said, "I'm in trouble."

"Okay, so you don't feel the way I do? You in this by yourself now? Huh, Denny? Is that what you're saying?" I walked up to him and touched him, and he pulled away. "You lied to me, Denny. You know what I've been through, and you're telling me your career and yourself is more important? I'm leavin'." I grabbed my coat and ran out of his dorm down the hall past all the screaming jocks in the hallway.

I went to the elevator and heard him hollering, "Rach!" while he was putting his shirt on and coming down the hall.

"Hold that elevator for me. Don't let it close, man," he said to one of the jocks.

I was crying as the guy that grabbed the elevator door stared at me. "You okay?"

"Yes, I'm okay."

"Bad fight wit yo' boy, huh? Here he comes."

Denny got on the elevator and grabbed my hands. "Come on, we need to talk, Rach. You can't leave; not like this."

I closed my eyes and tilted my head back. The pain I felt in my heart was unimaginable. Denny was the only person I trusted, and now that trust had been broken.

"I don't wanna talk right now, Denny," I said softly.

"I know you don't, but come on. We have to."

We walked back to his dorm room.

I sat on the bed in his room, and he sat on the desk across from me. He was leaning back on the desk with his hands over his face. I watched him with his legs crossed and his shirt open with his chest exposed.

"Were you lying to me when you said you loved me? That's all I want to know," I asked.

He took his hands off his face, looked at me and said,

"You serious? You know I love you, Rach. All the stuff we been through. Don't play me like that. Come on, Rachael. For real, that ain't cool."

"I don't know what's real and what's not anymore. As far as I know, you a fake." I was upset. I couldn't believe my fairy-tale was over. I didn't know what to think or say. I just knew I was in this by myself, and it wasn't going to be easy from this moment on.

My pregnancy became one of the hardest times in my life and one of the loneliest times. Denny and I couldn't come to any agreement, so I left. I decided I'd rather be alone than listen to him and look at him. I went back to Dayton. I kept thinking about everything and trying to figure out a way to tell him I wasn't having an abortion, not even to keep him.

Don't get me wrong; I told him time after time that I wasn't going to do it, but he wouldn't hear me. He kept asking me, no matter what I said or did. So, I needed him to understand and prepare himself for this child, because I was having it.

I decided the best way to deal with Denny was to tell him a lie. Denny called me from school, constantly pleading his case. "When are you going to the clinic? Rachael, you can't have that baby! Come on, now. We have to get rid of it."

He was stressing me, and on top of that, I was finishing beauty school and working two jobs.

"What about my parents?" he reasoned.

"Denny, I told you over and over, I can't do it. Please quit asking me."

I couldn't betray God this time. I promised Him I wouldn't do that to my body, to a living baby ever again. I was determined I wouldn't.

"I thought you loved me," I said.

Denny didn't hear anything I said to him. He just kept saying, "I can't have a baby now."

I screamed out, "You're makin' me feel like a fool!" I

blurted out from the top of my lungs, "I'll die if I go through the procedure! The doctor said I'll die!"

I couldn't believe I had just told him that. I grabbed the phone and covered the mouthpiece with my hand. What was I thinking, lying like that? I should have just told him I wasn't going to do it and left that at that.

I put the phone back to my ear, listened for a minute to the cold silence, then hung up. I sat in my bedroom for the rest of the night, looking at the telephone, hoping he'd call back after seeing things my way. He didn't call back. I picked up the phone a few times, but decided not to call him either. We needed time to think.

I fell asleep that night crying, but woke up and realized it didn't matter. It didn't matter if he ever called back. I was having my baby, a beautiful baby we made. I wanted someone to love me unconditionally, and I knew my baby would. All the while, I thought the baby would change Denny's feelings. I figured once the child was here, he would love it and see we would make a beautiful family. I didn't care what people would think about me having a baby. It was mine, and I would be the one that had to take care of the child.

I figured I was out of high school and just about through with beauty school, so I would be fine. I had two jobs; one working at McDonald's and the other at Lloyd's hair salon, Chateau Capree, as a shampoo girl.

At eighteen years old, I thought I had all the right answers. I knew it all and didn't think I would run into any obstacles. I tried to assure Denny that we would be fine. I would work until he finished school and went to the NFL.

I kept my word and worked five days a week at two jobs, and when I finished beauty school, I went to one job from 9:00 A.M. until 5:00 P.M., and the other job from 8:00 P.M. until 11:30 P.M. I told myself I wouldn't fail. I refused to! I went from thinking about how to prove others wrong about me to wanting a better life for my child and myself. I wanted more for my child than what I experienced growing up. My son or daughter would not come into this world and be on welfare until they were grown. I wanted my children to know I always worked hard for them, so they would appreciate their mom when they were old enough to understand.

I hadn't spoken to Denny since the day I told him I would die if I had an abortion. I watched the phone ring at night and picked it up with anticipation, hoping that it was him, but it never was. I was disappointed, but kept to my work routine.

"Rachael, somebody's up here for you!" I heard Mr. Lloyd calling me from the reception desk. If you wanted to be the best, you trained under Lloyd Richards in Dayton. You were guaranteed to be one of the best stylists in the whole city.

"Lean up," I said and wrapped a towel around the client's hair. I couldn't figure out who was up front for me. Nobody ever came there for me.

I grabbed my hurting back and walked through the wood-grain-and-marble salon. It was nice, first-class at Chateau Capree hair salon. I made my way to the front and saw Denny standing there.

He started walking toward me, saying, "I'm sorry. I don't care who know I love you. I'm sorry." He was crying right there in front of the clients, Lloyd and his wife.

I couldn't believe he was really there. I thought he'd left me. I started wiping his tears with my hand while we embraced. He grabbed me tight, picked me up, and hugged me. He whispered in my ear, "I'm sorry for everything. I love you, Rach. You forgive me?"

"Yes," I said.

We never discussed the abortion again. Denny and I decided not to tell his parents about the baby. We knew that we would have to tell them eventually, but not right now. We hid the pregnancy for seven months. Before we had a chance to sit them down and tell them, someone else told them.

Denny's parents were upset, to say the least. Who could really blame them? Denny's future was bright, very bright, and now he was stuck!

Of course, I didn't see it like that. I felt that we were getting married after he graduated, and we would be just fine.

First, we were in sin and God can't bless no mess. We were having a child and were not married. We were having premarital sex, which God does not honor. His commandments do not change. Even though we know them and try to get them to fit our needs and circumstances, they don't change. The only way I should have been having sex or children was in a marriage. Then I wouldn't have had to worry about if I was doing things the right way—God's way. He created us for marriage. He didn't create us to try each other out. If a person can't or won't get married for any reason or circumstances in their life, they should practice abstinence. It's a blessing in it. Do not get me wrong; I love my daughters, but our lives could have been easier if I had honored God and been obedient to what His plan was for my life.

I knew that the result of sex was children. I was living wrong, and it was displeasing in the sight of God. A woman cannot make a man love her based on pregnancy. All that does is bring a child into the world in the middle of confusion and pain. If a child is born under a condition of stress and rejection, it will feel rejected its whole life and make the same mistakes its parents have made or worse. Trust me; I know firsthand.

Chapter 6

A Mommy Now

I moved from Grandpa's house and found a real nice one-bedroom apartment. I loved it! I wanted to leave and be on my own before the baby came. I thank God Grandpa allowed us to stay with him, but it was crowded there. Uncle Al lived there, Momma, Grandpa and me. Crystal was living on University of Dayton's campus, where she was now doing the other part of her double major, and my grandma had died when I was thirteen, right before the relationship with TJ began.

I loved being around Grandpa, but I was ready to go. Grandpa's house was old and had mice. When I went to sleep, I would wrap the cover around me and tuck it under me all around my body. I was scared of them. It reminded me of when we lived in Philadelphia when I was twelve.

Momma had moved us there with her fiancé, Rockie. Crystal and I didn't meet him until we moved there. Rockie seemed like a nice person. He appeared to care for Momma. He was crazy about her. Whatever she wanted, he gave her—anything for Momma. By the time we were comfortable in

Philly, she was moving us back to Ohio. We were there for eight months, maybe nine.

I remember Rockie going to work one morning and Momma saying, "Get up and pack everything." She was frantic, looking around and out the windows as if she was frightened.

I said, "Why? Where we going? Why we got to leave? We like it here, Momma!"

"Get your butt out of that bed 'fore I knock you out of it! Get up 'fore I leave you here!" She mumbled under her breath, "We going home." She walked out of our bedroom back to hers. Her feet were padding loud across the wood floor.

I sat up and went in Momma's room after her. I wiped my crusty eyes and looked around her room. She had everything packed. I looked out the window and saw there was a U-Haul truck. "Momma, why you ain't tell us we were leaving? What's wrong?" A part of me wanted to go home. I missed Grandma and Grandpa and my aunts.

"I'll tell you on the road. Let's go." She was putting her clothes on as she talked.

Rockie's house in Philly had mice in the ceiling. We could hear them running back and forth above our head while we watched TV or ate dinner. That was disgusting to me. He had a nice home, but they all were connected like apartments. The houses in Dayton weren't like that. Outside was concrete—no trees, no grass, not even dirt; just concrete. His house was fairly big on the inside, though. It had a living room, dining room, full basement and kitchen. There were two bedrooms and one bathroom upstairs.

Rockie had black leather furniture and a nice dinette set. I could tell he was a bachelor before Momma. His ceiling was dropped, and that's why the mice could get in. It was a horrible sound. Hearing mice over the top of my head was disturbing. It gave me the creeps.

Years later, I found out that Rockie accused Momma of taking a large sum of money when we left. I don't know if she did or not. All I know is when she left that house, she didn't take anything that didn't belong to her. She told us he mistreated her, and she was tired and wanted to go home.

A few people she knew from Philly called and said Rockie was looking for her and he wanted his money. All she did was laugh. "He can't get blood from this turnip."

I would think about him sometimes. He was a big guy, kind of looked like a gorilla. Seriously, he did. I would think of the things he did for us. He treated her better than anyone I ever knew her to be with. Well, almost.

Years before Rockie, she dated Mr. George. He was a policeman, and he treated Crystal and me as if we were his own kids. Mr. George made sure Momma looked out for us. With Mr. George around, we would go to the park and go fishing regularly. Momma started dating him right after the incident with Champ.

Mr. George passed seven years after he and Momma were together. He had bone cancer. About a year or so after he passed, I saw his eldest daughter, Eva, on the city bus. I was coming from Grandpa's house for the weekend when she saw me get on the bus.

"Rachael?" she called out to me.

I looked over at her and thought, *Oh, no. Trouble.* I didn't like her very much because she had a smart mouth. She got smart with everybody she came in contact with. She was wearing a purple-and-pink scarf on her nappy head, and her outfit matched the scarf. She had so much lip-gloss on that I could have skated on her lips. She had huge gold hoop earrings with her name engraved on the inside. Eva was about seven or eight years older than I was. At the time I saw her on the bus, I might have been ten, and she was very vicious, like a python snake.

She called me over to her on the bus. "So, how have y'all

been?" she said, speaking of me, Momma and Crystal. She looked me up and down the whole time she talked. She was chewing some bubble gum and popping it loud on the bus. The other people riding were staring at her.

This older grey-haired man who was sitting directly in front of her turned and said, "Sweetheart, do you think you can lower your voice and stop popping that gum like that?"

She looked at him and rolled her eyes and said, "Anyway, how y'all been?"

"We all right," I said reluctantly. I stood the whole time she was talking, wondering what she was up to. She never liked Momma, so I'm assuming that's why she started directing her anger at me that afternoon on the bus.

"Rachael, my daddy told me before he died that he didn't love yo' momma. Yeah, he said she was a witch. She killed my Daddy." Her face looked disfigured as she talked to me. Her mouth and nose were all frowned up, waiting to see if she was going to get an argument out of me, but I didn't know what to do. She was so much bigger than me. I didn't say anything. I just stood there and took the hits for Momma.

"Yo' momma wouldn't even give him his medicine. He told us. She would listen to my daddy cry and beg for his medicine. He said she watched him and walked away. My daddy said he pleaded with her. She stole money from him and everything. Yo' momma is a mess. I hope she die! He begged her to bring him to my grandmother's, but she let him suffer instead."

I looked around at different people, and they were shaking their heads and whispering. I was embarrassed and ashamed. I wanted to go home and ask Momma if all the stuff Eva said was true. I was shocked. I couldn't believe she was saying such mean and vicious things about Momma. I knew Momma loved Mr. George. I saw her with my own two eyes taking care of him. She loved him.

My face and eyes said it all; red and swollen from the tears I was holding in. I didn't know else to do but pull the string on the bus and get off. I backed out the aisle, watching her scream at me from the top of her lungs.

"Yo' momma a witch. She a witch!" She was screaming and crying.

I never said another word to her. I just went to the front of the bus and jumped off when it stopped. I ran and ran. I cried all the way home. I could see the big, raggedy place we lived in from the bus stop, and that's all I had my eyes on. I ran in and shut the door behind me.

"Momma!" I screamed.

She hurried out of her bedroom. She was putting on her robe and looking at me, saying, "What's wrong? What happened?"

"Momma, I seen Eva and she said you killed Mr. George!" I was talking, but my voice had vanished from all the crying I was doing on the way there. Words were coming and going so fast that Momma couldn't understand me. I was so hurt and frightened at the same time. I didn't know what was going on.

"Why would she say that?" I looked at Momma to give me the answer. "You loved him, didn't you?"

She looked at me and held her head low. She thought for a moment then looked up at me and said, "Baby, that's not the truth. I wouldn't do anything to hurt him. You know I loved Mr. George, don't you?"

After that day, we never discussed Mr. George again. I put it in the back of my mind and acted as if I had only imagined Eva on the bus that afternoon. I was very good at hiding secrets, and I heard some of the meanest things people would ever say to a child. I would put those hurtful things in the back of my mind and lock it up, never to be heard, and I tried not to remember.

"Yes, I know." I held my head down and nodded. I felt horrible for Momma. She loved him and everyone thought she hurt him.

After she answered me, she turned back around, ran her fingers through her beautiful wavy hair, and walked back to her bedroom.

I moved into my apartment a couple of months before the baby was due. The apartment was cozy. It was a flat on the second floor. I had a terrace, which led to the living room area of the apartment with beautiful hardwood floors throughout the place and a fireplace too. My first apartment reminded me of a brownstone in New York. It was lovely, and the rent was reasonable too. I always loved my aunt's apartments, and wanted a place like theirs when I became an adult. When I visited them, I would fantasize about living in an apartment like theirs, with central air conditioning and plush carpet, and a community swimming pool for hot summer days. That was my dream; my way of thinking that I had made it out of the hood.

With Denny home for the summer, his school hooked him up with a nice summer job, making pretty good money so he could help with the baby.

Ring, ring, ring!

"Chateau Capree, may I help you?"

"Hey, Rachael, meet me for lunch around the corner from my job at Red Lobster."

"Okay, what's up? What's so important, Denny?" I could tell by his voice he was up to no good. I didn't have time for his mess right now, so I decided to go. I was eight months pregnant and tired, but Red Lobster did sound good right about then.

He came in Red Lobster a minute or so after I was seated. I had seen him at the front looking for me. He was smiling at the greeter, trying to describe me to her. He was motioning his hands, telling her my height and explaining to her that I was pregnant.

I smiled and watched him. He was so cute. I saw the greeter smiling at him and touching her long dreads, flirting with him. Then she said, "She's this way, sir."

I laughed. I didn't think Denny wanted anyone but me, so it was funny. After all, I was his boo.

He bent down toward me, put his hand on my stomach, and then gave me a kiss.

I smiled and said, "Hey." My eyes lit up every time I saw him. I loved this man with my whole heart.

"Rach, I found a way to make some extra money."

"What, Denny?" I didn't get a good feeling from the moment he opened his mouth, but I listened.

He sat down across the table from me and looked around the place. He leaned in closer to me and said, "I just cashed a four-hundred-dollar check, no question asked."

I didn't know what he was talking about and I didn't know if I wanted to. "What you mean, Denny?" I had my elbow on the table and my fist under my chin, looking at him.

"I found a stack of blank checks in the building where I work. I went home, took the typewriter and wrote the checks out to me."

I bombarded him with questions. As bad as we needed money, I didn't want him to get in any trouble. Besides, I was on the bottom of the friends list in his parents' eyes, and I knew when this scheme fell, I was going to be the one that was blamed.

"Nobody gonna know."

I sat there and just looked at him like he was stupid, thinking, *You know they gonna find out, and besides that, it's wrong!*

"What's wrong with you? You can't take that money. Them people gave you a job and trusted you and you gonna steal from them?"

"They ain't even gonna know it's gone. They rich, Rach. They ain't gonna miss it."

I was shaking my head the whole time I listened to him. "Denny, you gonna get caught. You shouldn't do that. It's stealing. Don't do that again." I wanted to smack him in the head. I couldn't believe he did something so stupid like this.

Then he turned and said, "I want to do it just a few more times. We need to get the stuff for the baby and you can't hardly work one job anymore, let alone two. Rachael, we need the money."

As he talked, I started listening to him more and more. Eventually, I stopped shaking my head.

"I don't see any other way, Rach. I tried to tell you this would be hard, us havin' a baby, but you didn't listen. Who gonna pay the rent when you have the baby? Huh? Who? I'll be back at school, and ain't nobody else gonna help you."

He was right, but this wasn't the right way. I looked at him with my head tilted and begged him not to do it.

"Baby, I'm going to do it a few more times." He grabbed my hands, looked me in the eyes, and said, "We can use it for the baby." He was smiling—the smile that kept me captive to what he wanted from me.

"Okay."

See, that was my mistake, agreeing with someone's mess. I should have stood for what I believed. I knew the difference between right and wrong. I should not have settled for someone else's bad decisions and choices. Some of the decisions and agreements I have made in my life, I am still cleaning them up. I should have been more responsible for my choices. The only love that should have allowed me to make a life decision should have been one I know was ordained by God. Nothing else is worth it!

Denny cashed four of the checks before his job caught on to what he was doing. He never was allowed to work while in school again. He paid the money back with the rest of the checks he worked for during the summer, and tried to convince his parents that it wasn't my idea.

"Rach, I told 'em I was under stress and we didn't have everything we needed for the baby."

I held my head down at this point in his conversation. I already knew they thought I made him do it, even though I hadn't. I had done everything in my power to stop him from cashing those checks, but he wouldn't listen to me. I went along with him so he wouldn't get in any real trouble, and when his father and boss came to my apartment, I said I told him to do it for the baby.

When summer ended, Denny was back at school for football practice. I was going to miss him, but I knew he wouldn't be out at the clubs and bars because they had him on lockdown when the season first started.

Everything seemed to be working out. I thought I was living in a perfect world. Denny and I were still in love and had our first child on the way. I was in Dayton taking care of business, waiting for Denny to graduate so we could be married. I thought that we both were working toward our life together; however, my eyes were opened when Denny came home from school one weekend. He didn't go to his parents' home this particular weekend. He caught a bus and stayed with me at my cozy little apartment. I was excited. We were pretending to be a real family and it felt good. That was until he went back to school. I was itching severely! I had no idea what was going on and was scared to go to the doctor. I was embarrassed and panicking. Denny was the only man I had been with, and I couldn't even imagine him with someone else.

I called him and said, "Denny! What's going on? I'm itching and have little bugs on me!" I was hysterical.

He first acted as if he had no idea what I was talking about, but he finally came clean with this story: "In practice, I shared a towel with Mike. Calm down. I didn't know he had crabs! We didn't have any more towels in the locker room. All the guys on the team has them!"

Oh my God, I was crushed! I was crying and scared. I didn't know what to do. I didn't want to go to the doctor. He would think I was dirty or sleeping around and probably didn't know who the father of my baby was. Or they would think my wonderful boyfriend that I always talked about in my appointments was cheating on me and not so wonderful after all. I was too embarrassed and ashamed, so I hoped the itching would go away and the bugs would just die. I waited another two days in agony until Denny came back from school with medicine for me.

I had already told him, "You better catch the Greyhound home with some medicine from the team doctor. I can't go to the doctor like this."

I didn't want to acknowledge it, but knew in my heart from the moment Denny told me the story about the time that he had been unfaithful that he would probably never be faithful to me again. That was the first sign of his deceitfulness in our perfect, fornicating world.

Denny cried his way out of that, and I made myself believe that what he said was true when I knew it was a lie. "Rachael, I swear to you that's what happened. I would never cheat on you."

I can still hear him saying that lie. But it was just one of many issues I faced while living outside God's will. And this all was only the beginning.

Chapter 7

Breathe

"Momma," I yelled. "Come here!"

"What's wrong? Why you yellin' like that, girl?" I could hear her walking toward my bedroom real fast down the hall. "You scared me half to death! What is it, child?"

Momma had been staying with me for a while. I was reluctant to let her stay at first, but I have to admit, she was a huge help. I enjoyed her being there with me. She cooked, cleaned, and took care of me.

"Momma, I'm wet!"

"Well, then it's time to go to the hospital. Your water must have broken."

"You think so? What if I just peed?" I was scared. I wanted the baby to come, but I didn't know if I was ready for the labor pains.

Momma must have read my mind. She stood there with her hands on her skinny little hips and said, "Well, it's a little too late to be worrying about pain, child. Call Denny so he can be on his way."

"I need to take a bath first."

"You can't get in that tub. It's time to go! You don't know

when that baby is coming now. Come on here. We need to go."

She was getting on my nerves.

Momma was excited. I could hear her all the way from the bathroom, on the telephone calling Grandpa. "She going to the hospital. Her water just broke. Nah, she ain't in no pain yet. Okay, gotta go. We on our way out the door."

Momma grabbed my bags and went to get the car. I told Momma I would be down in a minute, and picked up the phone and called Denny's dorm room. No one answered, so I left him a message, letting him know my water broke and to get to Dayton as soon as he could. Columbus was about an hour from Dayton, so I was concerned when I didn't reach him. I hung up the phone and locked the door behind me.

I walked down the stairs slowly, breathing heavily. I was huge! I went from 150 pounds all the way to 240 pounds. Huge! I think I ate all of the Three Musketeers candy bars that were in Dayton at the time. I was so greedy. I liked those candy bars simply because they were bigger than all the others. Now, that's greedy!

I opened the door to go outside of the hall in the apartments and saw that it was a pretty blue sky. There wasn't a rain cloud in sight. I was so happy because I wanted my baby to be born on a beautiful day and she was.

I got to the hospital, and within the hour after I arrived, Denny came running through the door.

"Hey," I said. I was happy and relieved to see him because I really wanted him there with me. He walked over to the bed and kissed me. He was looking around the room at all the gadgets I was plugged up to.

"You all right? Why you got all this equipment on you?" He was worried.

Momma butted in and said, "Oh, she's fine. They just want to monitor the baby's heart rate."

* * *

All of the rushing we did to get to the hospital, and the baby wouldn't be born until the following day. The room I had was nice. I felt as though I was in a luxury hotel room. My doctor didn't let me go back home because my water had already broken and that meant the baby could come anytime. The hospital had a fold-out bed for the father, so Denny stayed with me all night.

Bright and early the next morning, I awoke to a nurse patting me on the leg and telling me that I was ready to deliver. "Rachael, your doctor decided to give you a Caesarean because you're not dilating."

I sat up in the bed and looked over to Denny snoring on the other side of the room. "Denny, Denny!"

He lifted his head and wiped his eyes then scratched his throat with his tongue. "Huh? Huh?"

"They're giving me a Caesarean."

"Why? What they gonna do that for, ma'am?" Denny got out of the bed with his sweats and socks still on.

The nurse couldn't even answer his question because she was so busy examining him from top to bottom. She finally said, "Oh yeah, she's not dilating. She only went to four, so we'd need to get the baby out before it goes into distress."

The nurse was older, maybe in her late thirties. I could tell she still wanted to be young. She watched Denny like he was in the room stripping and she was about to give him a dollar or something.

I was mad because he had the nerve to be flirting back with her right in front of me. "Denny! You better get over here! What you thinking?"

"Oh, baby, you know I only love you. Come on, now. She too old." He started laughing, but she had already walked out of the room when he said that.

The nurse and a couple of other people came in and prepared me for the surgery. I was scared. The doctor was shortly behind them and said, "Okay, Rachael, I'm going to give you some medicine in your back so you won't feel a thing." He smiled. "You understand me?"

I nodded. I was ready to have the baby. I wanted to know what it was and what it was going to look like. I didn't care if it was a boy or girl; I just wanted the child to be healthy. That's all I asked God was to allow my child to be healthy.

"Rachael, I need you to be very still so I can give you this shot." They turned me on my side with my back facing them, and he put the needle in my back. I felt the pain and burning of the medicine going through my body.

Then they put me on another bed and wheeled me into an operating room. In there were a couple of surgeons and Denny right by my side.

"Now, Rachael," my doctor said, looking at me from the foot of the bed, all masked up. "You're gonna feel a lot of pressure, but there won't be any pain. You understand?"

"Yes, I understand." I looked over at Denny. He was holding my hand, but watching the doctors cut my belly open. Within the next few seconds, it was over. I heard the doctor ask Denny if he wanted to cut the cord. I felt him drop my hand and go to the end of the bed to do it. Then I heard my daughter cry for the first time.

I looked over as they were checking her vitals. The moment I saw her, I cried and thought, *I have a daughter!* I couldn't say anything aloud because it was my moment to myself. I was proud to be a mother. I had somebody to watch grow and make sure she had what she needed; to see her through school and college and be with her when she did it the right way and got married. All I could do was share that moment with God, and thank Him for giving me life.

I was eighteen years old, but all I thought about were Denny's needs and my daughter's. I would do anything for my daughter's sake. I made sure she was well taken care of and happy. That was my goal in life. I wanted her to know I would do everything possible for her to have a good life. I knew I would be a good mother, and thought that Denny would be a wonderful father. I thought I couldn't have picked a better partner to have children with, but when you are living in self and not with God leading you, you get what you ask for. I didn't get the reward of what God had for me, or whom He had for me, for that matter. If I had waited for God to do complete work in me and let Him give me who and what He had ordained for my life, I would have been a lot happier.

The next couple of years, I became one of the best hair stylists in Dayton. I thought of my career as a way to make it, pay my bills and take care of my daughter and Denny. Denny was a senior now, but still had another year of football because he was red-shirted the first year there. That meant he didn't play the first year, so it would allow him to be at school on scholarship another year. I loved my family and would do anything to help his time in school go smoothly for him. I didn't want him to have to worry about us or wonder how he was going to make it at school.

I knew I had to work hard for now and do all I could do to make our lives easier. I worked at the shop all the time, striving to build a huge clientele. I didn't know it was part of my assignment from God.

Sometimes we ask God, "Why?" Why do we have to go through certain things, or why does this or that have to happen? However, if we waited and let God do His perfect work and will in our lives, all would be answered. We go through life with different life stories, and what I mean by that is our lives are broken down into different lives. As we go through things, meet different people, and have different experiences, they become different parts of our lives. Sometimes when I look back over my life, it doesn't seem like some of the things I have been through even took place. That's why I like to say that I had more than one life.

Every situation and every life experience is designed by God to push a little higher and develop us into what He wants us to be, our purpose. Getting into the hair business started out as a way out of going to the Air Force, a way to stay closer to Denny, a way to make some money. I didn't go to hair school because I wanted to be a hairdresser; I went just to say I was doing something. However, God had a plan for me. Yes, it took me years to understand that it was Him or His plan, but it all came together for His good.

All the hair salons I worked at and the different people I met, everything was a preparation for what and where I was to go and things I was to do. I had to learn how to become a leader, not through classroom or education, but through God, who has been and is my teacher. All of it was a set-up from God.

"Eye has not seen, nor ear heard, or entered into heart of man the things which God has prepared for those who love Him."—1 Corinthians 2:9.

I moved further out of Dayton to the suburbs. Momma came over frequently and stayed the night. Momma loved the baby, but our relationship was growing further and further apart. I would think to myself how I would do anything for my daughter, work healthy or sick, yet my mother didn't do anything for me. I became angry as I watched my child grow and realized how I lived to make sure she was okay, only to look at my momma and wonder why she didn't do that for us.

As the years passed, I resented her more and more, until eventually I didn't want her around. I figured I didn't have to deal with her if I didn't want to, so I didn't. I stayed away from her as the years went on. I never realized I was bitter and hurt. I never knew that I had the cure for that bitterness and hurt—forgiveness—down on the inside of me.

My new apartment was awesome! It had every modern appliance I could have wanted. I was always pushing myself for a perfect life. I wanted that more than anything; perfect husband, perfect house, car, children, career—perfect life. I paid my bills and worked hard at the salon.

My clientele was huge, and I had a wonderful fiancé that was on his way to play pro football. I thought my life was going great, but after such a thought, I was awakened by the truth.

I remember being at the hair salon when one of the girls I worked with started telling me in a subtle way that no man was faithful. Tara was always making smart remarks about Denny. I thought she was jealous because her boyfriend treated her bad, but actually, she knew what she was talking about.

Tara was a member at our church and was the same age as Denny and me. She was a tall, slender young lady with big eyes and beautiful dimples. I didn't understand at the time that she was trying to let me know that Denny was not faithful, so what she said went right over my head. I had no idea that he was a big cheat, and everybody we knew in Dayton and Columbus knew it but me.

I continued seeing him. When the weekends came, I would tell everyone good-bye in the salon and be on the way to Denny's. I couldn't wait to get there. The long walks on campus, we would take with the baby. We would walk all over that school, eating at every cozy spot we could find on the weekends. We would walk and hold hands and Denny would carry the baby. I watched him and the baby when we were together, and couldn't help but think how I was going to have a real family soon.

Denny and I would pretend we were married when I came

down for the weekends. Denny would say, "What time you gonna be here?"

"In a little while," I would say, smiling on the other end.

"Hurry up. I can't wait to see you and the baby."

I would take all the money I made from the week and spend it all at Denny's. I didn't care. I wanted to spend it and help him with groceries, and of course, when I was there, we had to party with the other players and their girls. We would cook dinner together and watch movies, and sometimes we would even go out to the movies. I was so happy. I really had someone who loved me.

After our weekends together, he went back to school, or if I was up there, I went back to Dayton. Denny's parents learned to accept me and simply tolerate the fact that I was going to be with Denny, but they loved our daughter without a doubt. They always took her and bought her nice things. They even kept her on some weekends.

About a year after our baby girl, Brandy, was born, Denny started spending quite a bit of time with some of his teammates. I didn't like it. I was jealous and knew it was going to lead to some mess. Denny hadn't been like that. Up until that point, every free moment he had was spent with me and our baby girl, but now his time became others' time.

Denny started coming back to Dayton less and less. He even started giving me excuses for why we shouldn't come up to see him on the weekends. He was smoking marijuana and drinking during the football season. He just stopped caring.

"Denny, you better stop smokin' while you playing. You gonna get caught," I would warn him.

He wouldn't listen to me. He was now the big man on campus, and I was becoming a small part of his life. He even joined a fraternity. I was in Dayton, frantic, thinking he was seeing someone else or he was growing tired of me, and decided that it wasn't me, after all, that he wanted to be with. I was losing my mind, wondering where he was all the time and what he was doing. I started talking to myself.

I wonder where he is. He's probably out with some girl. Where is he? I'm going to call one more time, and then I'm driving up there . . . Pick up the phone. Where are you? I was sitting there holding the phone and biting my nails off. Why was he doing this? What did I do?

I was such a wreck I could hardly hear the baby crying from falling down the steps. I jumped up and ran over to her, examined her and cuddled her. She was fine; just a little bump.

"You gonna be okay. Don't cry. Shh, shh. You'll be okay, angel bunny." That was my name for Brandy.

I thought for a moment, then looked around my apartment. It was beautiful; everything I wanted in a home, yet I couldn't make Denny stay with me.

What's wrong with me? I know what it is. I'm fat now. That's what's wrong. He found somebody with a better body than me.

I got up off the white leather couch and went in the bathroom to look at myself in the mirror. *I'm looking old. I do look ugly.* I was twenty years old at this time and living in torment. I had no control of my actions.

It felt as if someone else was controlling my mind and actions. I can remember one night calling him at least seventy times in a row and not receiving an answer.

I told myself, "I'm going up there. I don't care if it's late. If he's doing something, I'm going to catch him today."

I gathered Brandy's things together and put her in the car. "Come on, Brandy. We going to see your daddy. You like that, huh, you pretty little baby?" I smiled at her, rushing to pack our bags and get on the freeway.

I was wrong to have done that. I view the situation so differently now. I mean, we were kids. We both should have been somewhere in school, but I was trying to control his life and mine. I was determined to make our relationship and our lives fit together. The Bible states that he who finds a wife finds a good thing. It's not the other way around. I was out of order because I never had any order. My life with Denny should be an example to many people of what not to do. I can blame it on abandonment and no father or no love, but the truth is I knew I was out of control. I had teaching at an early age. I knew what *Thus says the Lord!* However, I chose, because of my past circumstances, to trust in myself and make it work out. I couldn't win like that. My relationship with Denny was a direct result of me doing things my own way. I can't be mad at anyone and I can't blame anybody. I can't even be mad at him for the things we went through. If only I had listened to someone.

When I arrived in Columbus that night, I pulled up to Denny's apartment and saw his car there. I left the baby in the car and went to his bedroom window. It probably was about two o'clock in the morning when I arrived. I peeked in his window, and to my surprise, he was there alone, studying. I felt like an idiot. I didn't trust the man I said I would spend the rest of my life with. I was sneaking and lurking around his apartment. I felt so bad. Nevertheless, I felt relieved. After all, he was there alone. I got the baby out of the car and walked up to the door and knocked.

"Who is it?" he said.

"It's Rachael."

He opened the door, saying, "What you doing here?" with a big smile on his face.

I knew not to tell him I didn't trust him and thought he was with somebody, so I thought quick and said, "I couldn't sleep and decided to drive up to be with you." I smiled and he smiled back and reached for the baby. He put her in his arms and gave her a kiss on the forehead as she slept.

I followed him as he walked down the stairs into his bedroom. I felt so secure.

When I woke up the next morning, Denny had already left for class. I put the baby in the bathtub, dressed her, and decided to go do Denny's laundry. I gathered up all the clothes I could find and lugged them up the stairs and out the door. I also snooped around a little to make sure there was no evidence of another woman. I packed the clothes into my little car and got Brandy.

I went to pick her up out of Denny's yard and realized how big she was getting. She was bundled up with her Ohio State snowsuit on, with mittens and matching hat. She would be two years old in less than three months. She was getting big quick.

Brandy was playing in the yard when she said, "Mommy, what's that?" She was bent over, looking at something in Denny's yard.

I stared for a moment before realizing it was a used condom. The condom was right outside of Denny's window. "No, don't touch that," I told her. "Come on, let's go." After seeing the condom, I was a little uneasy. I asked Denny about it later in the day.

"You so paranoid," he said, laughing.

"Maybe so, but it was right outside yo' window. You could have thrown it out when you knew I was here. I'm not stupid, Denny. I know you up to something."

He was smirking at me. "You know you so cute when you get jealous." He stood in front of me, put his big strong arms around me, and kissed me.

"Stop. Don't kiss me. I don't know where or who yo' lips been touchin'!"

"You, Rach. They been touchin' you. Quit trippin'!" He said it like he was tired of me. I knew in my heart he had thrown that condom out. I never mentioned it again, though.

Denny and I were still having premarital sex. I asked him frequently about getting married soon or setting a date, but he wouldn't commit.

"I want to wait. I don't have a job to take care of you and the baby yet," he responded. "Let me get out of school first."

I sadly agreed. I wanted to be married. We were living like we were married, doing things only married couples should be doing. Why shouldn't we get married? I didn't understand it and I felt guilty, like God was watching my every move. I was uncomfortable in this.

I became pregnant again. Brandy was a little more than two years old when it happened.

"You can't have this one, Rach. I can't do this. There's too much at stake. Come on now, Rach. Please don't have that baby. My parents can't handle it. Besides, we aren't married. Let's wait until we get married to have another baby. Please don't have it. If you do, I don't know what I will do. If you have this baby, you don't love me, because if you did, you would wait so that I can take care of you and the baby."

I was shocked by what he was saying. It was the first time I had seen him in a frantic state.

He put his hands on his head and said, "Baby, when I play football, we will make up for this baby." He looked so scared and so disappointed in me.

I should have taken those birth control pills, but Denny said they were making me big, so I stopped. It was my fault. I should have made sure this didn't happen again. I blamed myself.

I had never seen him this upset. It wasn't like this the first time; it was five times worse. He was gonna shut down if I didn't get the abortion. I saw it in his brown eyes. He wasn't gonna make it if I didn't agree with him.

I gave in again. "Okay, I'll do it." I did the unthinkable. I decided to have the abortion. I thought if I didn't, I would lose Denny. I would be alone to raise not one, but two kids. So, I did it. I made myself believe that I would make up for this baby and we would have plenty of kids once we got married.

Yeah, we will make up for this child, I thought.

I talked myself into doing the abortion, even though I could hear my conscience telling me this was wrong. I overrode the truth in my mind and heart to please my man when, in all actuality, it wasn't his decision to make. I was the one carrying the child. I can't blame Denny for something I ultimately did.

For years, I did blame him for many of the decisions I made and many of the things that I have done in my life. But just because someone wanted me to do something didn't mean I had to do it. I was left with the pain of some of the things I did in our relationship for years.

Denny had moved on, but I was bitter at him for a long time about some of the choices I made. I resented him and wanted him to pay for the pain I felt for years and years to come. God has now allowed me to be at peace with Denny and myself for the decisions we made as children and adults.

I was in Dayton when I went to the clinic. I was alone this time; no Denny, not even Momma. I was scared and embarrassed to go in.

I got out of the car and noticed an older, tall, slender white man holding a sign that read: DON'T KILL YOUR BABY!

I was surprised. I turned around and went back to my car. "I am not going back in there." I was rocking back and forth in the seat. "Lord, please forgive me, but I need help. Please, Lord, help me."

I pulled down the sun visor and looked at myself in the mirror. "You look a wreck. Look at you! You killing another baby! What's wrong with you? Help me, Jesus. I'm tired of this!" I screamed.

I rubbed my hand across and down my face then drove off. I began to look around for a phone booth. I found one a couple of blocks from the clinic. I called Denny's apartment, but the phone rang and rang. I was standing there, saying, "Pick up, pick up."

"Hello," he finally answered.

I was crying hysterically. "Denny! There's a man outside the clinic with a sign. It said 'don't kill your baby.' I can't go through with this! God is going to send me to hell! I don't want to kill the baby. Let's have it and get married now, please!" I begged him.

He let a deep sigh into the phone and said, "Man, come on now, Rach. I am so close to the NFL. I just need to stay focused, and this is a distraction, Rachael. We don't need another baby."

I tried to get a word in, but he kept interrupting me.

"What's everybody gonna think if we have another one now? What's wrong with you? Huh? Please, just go back to your appointment." He hung up the phone.

I kept saying, "Hello? Hello?"

I dialed his number back fast in desperation, but he never answered. I drove back to the clinic. When I pulled up, I noticed the man was gone. I wiped my eyes and ran in the clinic. Once inside the door, all I remembered was Denny saying, "Handle the situation like a lady."

I was so confused and couldn't understand why he didn't come with me. I took the $350 to the front desk and gave the blonde lady my name. She smiled and said, "Come on back."

Another nurse took me in and told me to get undressed and put on a gown, so I did. I lay on the bed and the doctor came in. I never saw his face, just the top of his head. "It will be over in three minutes. Don't worry about a thing," he assured me. "You are going to feel some cramps like your menstrual cramps, then a little pressure, and then it will be all over."

I knew it wasn't that easy, but I said, "Okay," real low, almost in a whisper. All I could think about was Denny. I knew

I was doing this for my man. I never once thought about my-self, what I was doing, or why.

The doctor looked over at me and all I saw was his eye-glasses and his blue eyes looking at me, saying, "Sweetheart, you have to open your legs wider. I can't perform the surgery if you don't cooperate."

I could feel my heart beating through my skin. I covered my eyes with my hands. I hated myself! I was hurting on the inside and had nobody to share these things with. My mind was racing; not one clear thought was going through my mind. I wouldn't dare tell anyone what I had done. It was my secret, my shame and guilt. I would keep it to myself forever. I was horrible!

Nevertheless, look at God, having me share it with the world now. Even those of us who do the unthinkable can be washed clean! At the time, I felt like I was trapped and didn't have a choice in the matter, but I was the only one with the choice. All I could think was that it would make Denny happy.

I talked to God, but couldn't even lift my head to the heav-ens from all the shame. I knew He was disappointed with me. I had promised Him I would never take a life again. But I did.

After picking up Brandy from Denny's mom's house, I came back home and held her in my arms for hours. I never took her coat off. I just held her and cried. She woke up and said, "Mommy, why you cry?" as she wiped my tears away. After that moment, I put it to the back of my head with all the other terrible memories and terrible things I did. I made myself believe it never happened.

Within two months, I was pregnant again. Denny and I never learned from anything. We just kept making the same mistakes. We went to church on Sunday, but neither one of us was listening to the pastor speak. We were busy watching the time and waiting until service got out so we could go party. We wanted to go smoke weed and drink while our daughter played in the other room with her cousins. All we were doing was having fun. That's why we made bad choices and the same mistakes, because we weren't listening.

It shouldn't have been a surprise to either one of us that I was pregnant again. We were having sex; of course, I was going to be pregnant. This time, I told Denny, "I don't care what you say; I am not having another abortion." I stood for what I wanted and didn't care about what he wanted. I didn't want to have an abortion. Yes, it was both of our faults. Both of us were careless and having sex, but I would not let another suffer for what we did. I was going to have this baby no matter what people thought or said. I was going to stand, and Denny could be with me or leave.

Of course, he told me to get an abortion, but decided we should go ahead and get married. We decided to get married after the baby was born. He was upset, but never shared with me what was really in his mind. After I told him I was having the baby, he acted as though everything was fine. However, his brother approached me and let me know just how much it bothered Denny.

"Denny don't want to get married, Rachael." He was so cold and rude to me. "He too young to be getting married. He feels like you trapped him into havin' these kids."

I couldn't believe he was talking to me like this. *This is the man who married a girl before she even graduated from high school,* I thought. *Why do he think I'm going to listen to him?*

"Denny came to me this weekend," he continued, "and told me he felt pressured into this."

I listened to him because I knew how close they were. I had no idea of any of this. I thought we were in love and we were going to be a complete family in the sight of God and man. Boy, was I wrong! I decided to call Denny and find out the truth. I didn't want to marry him if he felt like that.

"Denny, I need to talk to you immediately," I informed him.

"What's wrong, Rach? Why you sound like that?" He knew something was wrong because of the tone of my voice.

I was short with him; he could hear it in my voice. I was tired of fighting. In every way in my life I had to fight—fight to keep my children, my sanity, my happiness, and myself.

He said, "I'll be home this weekend. We can talk then."

The weekend came and I made sure I had everything in order. I got off work early, sent Brandy over to my mother's house and cooked a nice steak dinner for Denny. I wanted to find the underlying cause of this before we walked down the aisle in July. It was February now, and the baby was due in March. I didn't want to be miserable and divorcing in a few years.

I heard him turning his key, so I walked out of the kitchen, stood, and watched him go from room to room looking for Brandy. He came in the apartment looking around for his little girl.

"She's at Momma's house." I walked over to him and gave him a hug. He put his hand on my stomach and smiled. "I don't get a kiss?"

I looked at him and sat on the couch across from where he was standing. I was frustrated and at a dead-end with him. I couldn't help but think back to all the plotting I did earlier in our relationship to get him all to myself. I knew this was why it was turning out like this, but it was too late to back out now. I was in love and I was going to make sure my children knew their daddy. I was dealing with the results of being disobedient. I was really disappointed with Denny and tired of what I was starting to see in him. He was no longer the boy from high school.

"I heard you didn't want to get married. Why didn't you tell me?"

He looked surprised, stood up and walked toward me and

got on his knees. He put his hands in my lap and said, "That's a lie. I love you." He appeared to be upset.

I said, "Denny, if you don't want to get married or if you're not ready, let's wait. I'm not in a rush. I love you." I really did want to get married; I just knew it would work. I felt it in my soul that he was the one for me and we would make it. I wasn't being all the way real with him, but I needed to make sure he wanted this too.

He said that was the way his brother felt, not the way he felt. He wanted to get married. I left the matter alone, but I knew in my heart that what his brother said was true.

Over the years, I've come to the realization that our husbands are to find us. There is nothing we need to do to fast-forward it or help it along the way. If God intended for us to be with that man, then it is so.

Chapter 8

He's Cheating

I was at Denny's, seven months pregnant and hungry, making plans for the wedding with him when some of his teammates stopped by.

"Denny, what's up? Rach gonna let you go out?" one said.

Denny looked at me. I pretended I wasn't listening to them nor did I care, but I was listening.

"Man, come on to this party. There's schools coming from everywhere," Jeff said. Jeff was the running back for OSU, and he was sure to be on his way to the NFL that year. He was also going to be one of the groomsmen in the wedding. I liked him, but I knew he was a playa. He had all the chicks chasing him. We knew him before OSU because he was from Dayton too.

Jeff was laid-back, and he got everything he wanted. He already drove a brand-new Benz and lived phat even before the draft. He had a dark chocolate skin tone and was about 6'3". He wasn't real big, but was in excellent shape. I didn't trust Denny being with him because they always got into trouble when they were together.

One time, they got into a fight on campus at a bar and

broke some dude's nose. They ran from the fight because they knew they would get in trouble and be all over the news for what they did. So, I had to jump in the car in the middle of the night and pick them up in some dark alley around the corner from the bar before someone told on them. I was so mad at them because they thought it was funny. The biggest argument we would have was him spending so much time in the bars.

"Denny, that's all you want to do is party!" I rolled my eyes and walked back to his bedroom. "It's getting really old."

His friends laughed as he followed me to the bedroom. I could hear them in the living room talking about him.

"You on lockdown. Just imagine when you get married, man. You ain't gonna be able to go nowhere."

Denny turned around and went in the front room, saying, "Yeah, watch, watch me. I'll go where I want to when I want to. Marriage can't change who I am. I'm an athlete."

I sat in the room and shook my head. He made me sick. This was all a game to him.

I heard Jeff say, "You gonna be on lockdown, man." He was shaking his head and laughing with his hand up to his mouth.

Denny picked Brandy up and walked to the bedroom, where I was sitting on his bed. He told me, "I'm going with the fellas." He watched me for a few minutes then kissed the baby and me and went out the door.

I felt foolish. I sat there for a few minutes, staring and turning through a bridal magazine when Brandy and I finally fell to sleep.

I heard the phone ringing what seemed like a few minutes later, but when I looked at the alarm clock sitting on his dresser, it was almost two in the morning. I looked around the dark room and wondered where Denny was. I grabbed the phone thinking it was him.

I answered, "Hello," in a low, sleepy voice.

It was a woman on the other end, asking me, "Is Denny there?"

I said, "No," and she hung up.

About three minutes went by before it really sank in that it was a woman on the phone. I panicked, and my heart was beating double-time. I sat straight up and touched the baby in my belly.

I waited for the woman to call back. Within minutes, the phone rang again. "Hello!" I quickly answered.

"Is Denny there?"

"Who is this and why you callin' my man?" I said, frowning and looking at myself in his dresser mirror. I couldn't believe there was a chick on the phone for Denny at two in the morning! I knew what she was looking for.

"This is Kelly. Kelly Taylor." This bold chick had no problem giving her name. "And if he were yours, he wouldn't have been out all night kissing on me."

We argued for a while. She proceeded to tell me how she always knew about me, but how Denny liked her better because she looked better than me. She even went so far as to describe her features and compare them to mine, which she had seen in a picture. In the middle of the screaming, she laughed and said, "You are Rachael, right?"

I got quiet and listened.

"Yeah, I know who you are. You the baby's momma."

She was laughing and taunting me like a cat with a ball of yarn. She knew so much about me, and I had no idea who she was.

Only thing I knew was that Denny was a playa. *He kept that a secret and I was always around*, I thought. I even sneaked up on different occasions and never caught him.

"Yeah, Denny took me to his momma's house before. I met his mother and father."

She thought destroying my life and taking that knife and cutting me deeper with information was nice, but it was vicious. I was hurt. I thought I was the only one in his life. She told me how he would talk to me on the phone and she would be right there at his apartment with him, staying there for the week until Brandy and I would come up. Everything I thought I had with this man was now shattered. Thrown out the window! It was all a lie! I was so hurt; my heart was broken, beaten and stepped on, then a semi-truck came and ran it over! That is how I felt.

My eyes were full of tears and I couldn't even lift my head. Denny was the love of my life. My mind was so confused. I didn't understand what had happened. I thought if I loved him and was true, he would be the same way to me.

I argued with the female a few more minutes with her spilling the beans on Denny and his secret life, until I heard Denny and his crew pull up outside.

I hung up the phone, went up the stairs, and swung open the front door in a rage. My belly was so big that I tried to walk fast but was going slow from the extra weight. I wanted to kill him!

I went outside barefoot and in my nightgown, walking up to the car and screaming, "Get out the car!"

Denny opened the car door, saying, "What's wrong? Why you looking like that, Rach? Huh? What happened?"

"Who is Kelly?" I hit him in the chest with my fist.

His boy grabbed me and embraced me so I couldn't get loose and hurt myself.

Denny looked at me like a cat that swallowed the canary and said, "I don't know."

I knew he was lying.

"Just calm down and come inside. I'll tell you everything." He was looking at his teammates, probably wanting them to help him out of this, but nobody could help.

Denny's friends got me back inside the apartment before they left. He was walking around and pacing the floor. It was about four in the morning by now, and we were both tired.

I watched him walk into the living room, cut on the TV, and start watching rap videos. Then he went downstairs and checked on Brandy. Finally he came back up and sat across from me on the futon couch. I acted like I didn't see him. See, Denny or nobody else understood that he was my life. Him, Brandy, and this new child were all I had in the world, and to find out that he betrayed me broke my heart.

By now, it was five in the morning. We both sat up looking at each other. I couldn't help but think, *What happened? Am I the only one in love? Did I imagine the closeness I felt between us? Was it real?*

"Rach, I was gonna tell you before the wedding about her," Denny finally confessed. "She didn't mean anything to me, I swear."

I sat there silent, looking at him. Everything was out in the open. I wasn't imagining things. He was cheating.

"I was gonna tell you before the wedding, I swear." Tears were rolling down his cheeks while he talked. "She don't mean nothing to me. For real, Rach, she don't. It was just—" —He turned around, put his hands on top of his head and sat down.

All I could hear in my head were her words. They must have been close because she was staying at his house with him. He took her to Dayton, where I lived!

"You disgust me!" I was shaking my head and pointing at him. "I don't have nothing to say to you. How many times have you messed around, Denny? Huh?"

He held his head down then started crying aloud. "I'm sorry, Rach. For real, I'm sorry. I never meant to hurt you, Rach."

Denny went all the way back to when we were in high school and began telling me about the different chicks he had sex with. There were so many it was ridiculous. I was shocked. I couldn't believe my ears because we were always together, and for him to be so sneaky said a lot about Denny and his good-boy act.

I wanted to go home. I had no one I could trust this information with because everyone would think I was a fool. Everybody thought we were perfect.

I decided to pack up the car and go home that morning with no rest, never to return. It was over; the wedding, the relationship and the life with Denny. I took my daughter and tried to get out of there as fast as I could.

I cried all the way back to Dayton. All I could think about was him with other women, touching them and spending time with them like we did. How could he do this to me? I had dedicated my whole entire life to him and he crushed me.

No sooner than Brandy and I walked in the house, the phone was ringing. I looked on the wall at the phone in the kitchen then walked through my living room to answer it.

"Hello," I said.

It was Denny, crying and telling me what a terrible mistake he had made. "Rachael, I love you. I want to marry you. I don't want those other girls."

I screamed, "Why would you hurt me like this?" Then I hung up.

The phone kept ringing and ringing. Eventually, I took it off the hook. I didn't want to hear his voice, speak to him, or hear another lie from his lying mouth. Denny Calhoun was a liar!

I had to get my mind off things, so I decided to give Brandy a bath then go to the mall down the street and shop for the new baby.

"Come on, Mommy's baby." I picked Brandy up. "Let's take a bath." She was so beautiful and getting bigger and bigger by the minute. "You want a sister or brother, Brandy?"

She was so busy playing with her toys while I washed her up that she didn't answer.

I took her out of the tub and laid her on the bed to put the lotion and powder on her. I picked out the prettiest outfit in her closet and thought, *My baby has so many clothes.* I was so proud of myself. My baby had stuff I only dreamed of when I was growing up, and that right there was a big accomplishment for me. Denny's mom even bought her a white mink when she turned two.

I grabbed my purse, and we headed out to the mall. A couple hours later, we went back to the house, and when I opened my apartment door, Denny was sitting on my couch. As soon as I saw him, I started asking him all kinds of questions.

"What you doin' here?"

Before he could say a word, I was asking another one. "Where did you take her? What does she look like?" I was crying while he sat there and held Brandy. "Is it because I gained weight when I had the baby? You wanted someone smaller?" I wanted to know what I did wrong.

"Let me talk," he said, finally getting a word in edgewise. "I can't live without you. Let's go ahead and get married now, Rach. We don't have to wait."

"No, Denny, we can wait." I knew it wasn't the right time to get married. The baby was due in a couple of weeks, and besides, he was just saying what he thought I wanted to hear. He didn't want to lose me.

While he was talking, I was thinking, *When will someone wake me up from all this hell surrounding me? Just when I thought I found love and peace, when I thought someone loved me and would watch over me, here comes trouble again.*

It's funny how we look all our lives for those things, and all those things are in Christ Jesus! "Then they cry out to the Lord in their trouble, and He brings them out of their

distress. He calms the storms, so that its waves are still."
—Psalms107:28, 29.

Denny convinced me to take him back. He was the old
Denny once again, the one that loved me and cared. Unfortunately, his new changes were only temporary. There were a
few more incidents before the wedding. But he told me he
had changed. He was scared he would lose me, so he was
preparing himself for our marriage now. I was so happy and
believed that he was a changed man and had learned his lesson from cheating.

Shortly after the apology and Denny spending lots of time
with me, he started going to the bars and running around.
His change was temporary.

I remember one weekend he told me he wouldn't be
home. He said he was going to be studying for an exam. I
told him I would come up there for the weekend.

He said, "You shouldn't. You're almost nine months pregnant and need to be in Dayton."

I agreed and we hung up the phone.

I called him a couple of hours later and never got an answer. I began to call him every fifteen minutes. My mind became tormented, and I began to talk to myself, saying, "He's
probably with someone out to dinner or movies."

I got in my car at twelve midnight and drove from Dayton
to Columbus. Our daughter was in her nightgown, and I was
too. I was in my raggedy old torn-up nightgown at that!

I went to Denny's apartment, but he wasn't there. I began
to drive around the campus area. I drove up and down High
Street, where all of the students hung out from bar to bar,
drinking and laughing. I knew he was somewhere in the
area, and it would be a matter of time before I found him.

I did find him, but I wasn't expecting to see what I saw.
There was a group of football players coming down the
street, and I saw Denny right in the midst. He was walking

with two women, hugging them both and kissing on their necks right in plain view. There were so many cars and people out; it was a Saturday night, so campus was packed. I was driving, and there were maybe twenty cars behind me.

I put my moving car in park, got out in the middle of the street, and began to scream at Denny, "What are you doing?"

The females he was with ran down the street. His teammates were laughing, and he was embarrassed. He came over to the car and got in, not saying a word.

I got back in the car, screaming at him as we drove off. I had officially lost my mind! I can't believe that my mind was so messed up that I would marry him within a month of these different incidents. I was desperate and wanted Denny.

I talked myself into believing that he wouldn't be like this once we were married, but the truth was, he was showing signs that he wasn't ready to be married. I had literally gotten out of my bed at 12:00 A.M. and drove to another city with my baby in her pajamas and me in mine to see what a man who was supposed to be in love with me was doing. That's not love! Love will not have your mind tortured or confused.

"For I know the thoughts I think toward you, says the Lord, thoughts of peace and not evil, to give you a future and a hope."—Jeremiah 29:11.

Denny's excuse for everything he was doing was, "I'm getting married, so I want to enjoy everything before our wedding. I'll stop hanging out after we get married." He would get so upset every time I would say something to him about going out to the clubs.

I believed him. Well, that's not the truth. I wanted to believe him, so I settled for it. I believed I could change him, so I stayed in a dead relationship that was doomed before it even began.

Our new baby showed up two weeks late, but she was gorgeous! She had fair skin, with gray eyes like Momma and

Crystal, and she had big curls all over her head. She was beautiful. When I left the hospital, I went to stay with Denny's parents because our move to Columbus was in less than a month. I was so excited to start this new life with Denny and the kids. I was taking my babies and going to a different place for a new start. I thought that was exactly what I needed—a new life. I wondered if I could make it in Columbus. None of the old stuff would matter anymore.

I had practically been in Dayton all of my life, besides when we made a quick move to Philly when I was a teenager. I didn't know anything but Dayton, and everybody knew me. All of my family and friends were in Dayton. All of my hurt and pain was there, so I figured why not try another place, bring my daughters up in a new city? No one knew me, and I didn't know anybody.

After I came home from the hospital, I was having a continuous pain in my left side. Everybody told me it was normal and that I was exaggerating, but I wasn't. The pain was horrible! All I wanted to do was lie down.

Denny started giving me his dad's pain pills, which were Tylenol 4. I was taking them for about a week, three pills at a time, when the pills ran out.

The day I ran out of pills, Denny had decided to go out with his friends. I begged him to stay with me. The pain was terrible!

"Your father has to preach tomorrow," I told him. "I need help with the girls, your parents are 'sleep, and I don't want to disturb them. The girls are our responsibility, not theirs."

"I will be back in a little while," is all he said, and he walked out the door.

By 2:30 in the morning, I was very cold. I mean like I was in a blizzard with no clothes on! I didn't know what was going on with me. My body was shaking all over and my teeth were chattering together. I had goose bumps all over my body, and the pain on my side was excruciating. I put the blanket around me and got out of the bed. I checked on my little angels and started up the stairs.

I was so scared, but I knew I had to get some help. I knew I was going to have to wake his parents to help me. I knocked on their door.

"Yes," they replied.

I said, "I-I-I c-c-c-can't s-s-s-s-stop sh-sh-sh-sh-shaking."

They got up quickly. Before Pastor Calhoun did anything, he put his hand on my forehead and started covering me with the blood of Jesus. He started praying for me. Mrs. Calhoun called the ambulance. When the paramedic got there, they couldn't find a pulse or a heartbeat. I could hear them and see them, but I couldn't respond. They immediately gave me an IV and took me to the hospital.

We arrived at the hospital and they rushed me to the back. The doctors checked for everything possible by running tests for hours. I was so uncomfortable and I felt terrible.

Denny walked in the room a couple of hours later looking scared. "Hey, doc. She gonna be all right? She's my fiancée."

He felt so guilty. I could see it on his face. What was he thinking about coming there two hours after I had been rushed to the hospital? I was lying in the bed with IVs coming out of my arms.

I was so busy admiring how concerned Denny was that I didn't even realize he had lipstick on the collar of his shirt. He kept looking over at me and smiling. I didn't care what he did anymore at that point. I was sick and needed to get well so I could take care of my babies. Denny was a distraction.

He looked foolish, standing there talking to the doctor in front of my family as well as his own, with lipstick on his collar. He had no idea it was on his shirt. I think everybody wanted to hurt him that night. Even my doctor was distracted by his foolishness.

"Well, sir, we did a CT scan and saw fluid on the left side of her stomach. I believe after she had the baby she left the hospital with a fever, and from there infection set in," my doctor explained.

"All right, what needs to be done from here?" Denny asked.

"We're going in and draining the fluid out of her stomach because it's now toxic. We need Rachael to sign these papers stating that once we are in, if it has damaged her uterus, then we need to give you a hysterectomy."

I couldn't believe what I was hearing. I was scared. I stared into space until I finally felt the doctor tap me.

"Rachael? Do you understand?"

"Yes, I understand," I replied. I reached out, took the papers and pen, and signed.

The surgery was a success. They removed the poisonous fluid without giving me a hysterectomy. The doctor stated he had never seen that type of poison in someone's stomach before.

I was in the hospital for two weeks. Denny stayed by my side during the whole ordeal. I believe he felt so guilty because at times he would sit in the room with me and just break out in tears. But I was in so much pain I couldn't worry about that man for now. Every time I awoke, he was on his knees, praying.

There he goes gettin' all spiritual now with his silly self, I thought.

Crystal brought my daughters up to the hospital. They were so beautiful. My oldest daughter was three years old now. She was a cutie. She had wavy hair with long pigtails. She was so funny.

When Crystal walked in with Brandy, she came running over to the bed, saying, "Mommy, what's that in your nose? What's that in your belly?" She was so curious about what was going on.

The baby wasn't even a good two weeks old, but I knew she was special. She was a beautiful baby—and I'm not just saying that because she was mine. She was beautiful! Sometimes I would wonder how God gave me such beautiful girls. I love my daughters so much and I thank God for them daily.

While I was in the hospital, everyone I knew was praying for me. God answered their prayers.

"Confess your trespasses to one another, that you may be healed. The effective, fervent prayer of a righteous man avails much."—James 5:16.

Chapter 9

My Wedding Dress Was White

Denny and I married on a hot summer July day. The wedding was beautiful. Denny's dad performed the ceremony. I was finally going to have a picture-perfect life, I thought. Everyone would see I wasn't like Momma after all. I had a husband and he was the father of my children. Nobody could talk about me anymore or think I was a failure.

I was so beautiful in my white gown with white headpiece. My bridesmaids wore aqua gowns, and the groomsmen had gray tuxedos. Everyone looked nice. Denny's older brother, one of the best men, sang a Luther Vandross song—you know, the one everyone was using in the early 90s, "Here and Now."

Denny had on a white tuxedo, and he looked so handsome. When I walked down the aisle and saw him, I thought to myself, *My husband. He is really going to do it right now.*

I was only fooling myself. The night before proved that. It was horrible. I should have known it was going to be a storm from the night before the wedding. My friends decided to book us a hotel downtown and go out for a while. Just so happens that Denny's friend booked the same hotel on a different floor.

When Denny found out we were at the same hotel, he was furious. Dayton, Ohio is only so big. I told the girls in my wedding party that we wouldn't run into them. It wasn't a big deal. We got ourselves together and went to the hotel's nightclub.

Once inside, I spotted some of Denny's friends there. I walked over to one of them and said, "I thought you guys were going somewhere else."

He said, "Yeah, we did, but Denny wanted to come here too." He smiled and snapped his finger and moved toward the dance floor with a female with bright red weave in her hair.

I thought, *Oh, boy! I hope he don't start trippin'*. I turned around to see where I was going to go and who I was gonna talk to when I saw some of the wedding party sitting together at a table in the corner by the DJ's booth. I was happy to see my bridesmaids and his groomsmen all together, since everyone came from different parts of the country to be in the wedding.

I walked over to the table and said, "It's so good to see everybody gettin' along."

"Rach, you got some fine women in the wedding, that's for sure," one of the groomsmen replied. He was staring at one of my girls.

"You a mess," I said, chuckling.

I heard a song and wanted to dance, so I pulled Jeff, Denny's best man, to the dance floor. I figured if I danced with one of them, he wouldn't get upset. I was wrong.

Denny walked in seconds later and looked mad. He was wearing the cream-colored linen pants and shirt I had bought him to take on our honeymoon. He looked good. I smiled at him, but he walked up on me and pushed me back.

"What are you doin? Why you here? Huh? Get out the club, Rach!"

It was so much commotion going on. His boys were trying to stop him from coming at me, but he was so big and strong that they were even falling from his fury. He was pushing and shoving me toward the exit. I was stumbling and tripping, and a few of my girls were on Denny's back, trying to stop him. It was a mess! I was trying to keep my balance.

I was so embarrassed. All of my girls were there; the ones from high school and the new ones I had met in Columbus. The QTs were there too, and this man was out here, the night before our wedding, acting up.

"Stop, Denny. What's wrong with you?" I screamed.

The commotion caused everyone inside the club to look at us. My cousins, my friends, and his friends; everybody was there and he decided to hit me! My shirt was torn from him pulling on it. I couldn't find my shoes, and my shades were missing. I couldn't help but look at the wedding party members' faces. They were standing there in shock. Nobody could have imagined he was gonna do that.

I ran up to him once we were outside, kicked him, and started scratching him. I couldn't believe he was fighting me! Denny had never put his hands on me before. Why now? I flipped out on him. He was humiliating me in front of everybody, so I had to act crazy on him.

All I was thinking was, *I don't need to show up tomorrow, but it's too late. This is my destiny, whether it works or not. It's what I am supposed to do.* I had made my bed, and now it was time to lay in it.

The rest of the night was quiet. Me and the girls didn't laugh, cry, talk or remember old times. We just went to bed. Tears dripped down my face while I lay there. What was I supposed to do now? My husband-to-be had turned abusive! I had vowed never to let a man hit me. I had seen my mother get hit too many times to let a man do that to me.

I couldn't sleep, so I thought about everything that had happened up to this point, and the bad outweighed the good. I didn't want this future. After all the things I had been through with this man and the things I had done, I didn't want him or it anymore!

Everyone said, "Don't worry about it. He had too much to drink. It will be okay tomorrow for the wedding."

Honestly, I never prayed about that incident. I got in the hotel room, took a shower, cried, and went to bed.

When I woke up, I felt a little better and decided I was going to marry him. I loved him. I deserved him.

Grandpa walked me down the aisle. He was so handsome in his gray tuxedo, looking at me and smiling. He said, "You look beautiful."

I smiled and said, "Thank you, Grandpa."

As we walked down the aisle, everyone in the seats stood up, and different people said, "You look beautiful."

I felt like a princess. But I did have thoughts running in my mind about the night before. I wanted this fairytale so bad. I pretended everything was all right and sacrificed myself, my children, and Denny, when I should have stopped the whole thing.

The closer I got to Denny, the clearer I could see his face. He had the biggest smile on his face I had ever seen. *Everything will be fine,* I thought.

When I reached him at the altar, he whispered, "I'm so sorry." His eyes looked so serious. I really and truly believed he meant it.

Denny got so drunk at the reception that our honeymoon was spent cleaning up after him. I couldn't believe it. I was cleaning up after a grown man, messing on himself and vomiting. I always thought wedding nights were spent loving each other. But I sat up all night, wondering what my babies were doing while my husband lay in the hallway of the hotel, passed out in his own feces.

The next morning, I woke up and turned on my side in the king-sized bed and realized my husband wasn't there. I sat up in the bed and looked around the beautiful decorated hotel suite to find myself all alone. Denny hadn't been in the bed or the room all night. He was still in the hallway asleep. I was so angry and disappointed. What kind of a honeymoon was this?

I got myself together and got out of bed and jumped in the shower, put my clothes on and called my daughters. After speaking to my babies, I felt a lot better.

I went in the hallway and tried to drag Denny back inside the room. He stunk. He smelled like liquor. I hollered, "Denny! Denny! Get up!" I was so mad at him. Denny was 6'4" and 242 pounds of muscle, and I was half his size, trying to carry him into the room.

I finally got him inside and realized he needed to be cleaned up. I put him in a cold shower.

He woke up, saying, "I'm sorry. I didn't mean to get drunk. I love you."

I turned my head away from him and began to wipe the tears from my eyes.

A few days later, Denny and I packed up the girls and were on our way to our new life in Columbus, Ohio. I had a job lined up at Apogee's hair studio. The salon was top of the line. I had never seen a salon so plush. It was the first time I saw a hair salon and barber shop together in the same building. The salon was all black; black chairs, black sparkling shampoo bowls, black hair dryers, and the floor was checkered in black and white. In the waiting area, there was a white leather curvy couch and four black-and-white leather chairs. The salon was sleek, especially for a girl out of little ol' Dayton, Ohio. Dayton salons were half the size of those in Columbus.

I have to admit that I was intimidated by the appearance of everything. But I was talented and knew it. The demand for an appointment with me was high. I knew once I started working there, I could take care of my family. My clientele had gotten so big!

Denny and I lived on the north side of Columbus. Our place was a nice two-bedroom apartment with all the amenities. I had bought furniture before leaving Dayton, so we were ready. I worked and took the girls to day care while Denny went to school and played football.

For the first few months, marriage was bliss, and then Denny started doing a lot of partying, drinking and smoking much, much weed. I didn't realize that his behavior was proof of what his brother said; he really didn't want to get married. His brother was right.

A few months after the wedding, he stayed out all night long, and I didn't know what to think. I remembered him saying the night before that he was going out with Jeff, but I was asleep when he told me. I sat up in the bed and realized he hadn't come home. I looked at his pillow, unused and untouched. I couldn't understand this man's mind. Why was he deliberately trying to hurt me? I loved him.

I went to the bathroom in our bedroom, looked in the mirror and washed my face with my hands. I got a quick glimpse of my wedding ring on my left finger and smiled.

He has to be in trouble. Why else wouldn't he come home? He promised he wasn't gonna do nothing stupid anymore.

I put a pair of my Guess jeans on and one of his T-shirts and went downstairs. Brandy was playing with her Barbies on the living room floor. She had toys all over the place. The baby was sitting in her car seat on the floor, watching everything that Brandy did. They looked so cute.

"Brandy, how did the baby get down here? You brought her down here and put her in her seat?"

"Yes, Mommy," she said with her raspy little voice.

"Oh, my," I said.

Brandy was so smart, and she took care of her little sister from the time she came onto the earth. She was only three and carried the baby downstairs, fed her, changed her diaper and sat her in her car seat.

"Mommy," she said, jumping all around my legs. "She was crying."

"Okay, Brandy. Thank you for your help. You're Mommy's little helper." I smiled and bent down and gave her a kiss. "Brandy, we are going to walk to the store, okay? Put your jacket on."

"Okay, Mommy."

I put our coats on and then headed out the door. I kept looking at every car that drove up near the apartment, hoping it was Denny, but it wasn't. He was nowhere to be found. I was so worried about him. I didn't know what had happened to him. I didn't know what to think. It was 6:00 A.M., and he still wasn't home.

I was scared he had gotten hurt and we were going to be alone. We didn't have a phone at our apartment, so I had walked to the grocery store down the street to use the pay phone.

I never once thought he was somewhere he shouldn't have been or doing something he shouldn't have been doing. We were married now; all those things were behind us. I called the morgue with Brandy holding my hand and the new baby, Brea, on my hip, asking the man on the other end of the phone. "Did you have a Denny Calhoun there? Is he there?" My stomach had butterflies in it, and I was so scared and nervous. I was praying the answer would be no. I looked at Brandy, and she was beside me, looking in the mirror at the grocery store, dancing. She had no idea what was going on. Her daddy might have been dead. How could I tell her that? She wouldn't understand.

The man with the deep, rugged voice on the other end of

the phone asked, "Will you describe him, ma'am? What does he look like?"

I was terrified, almost crying as I spoke softly and weakly on the phone and began to describe Denny to him.

The man hesitated for a moment and said, "We have a Calhoun, but he doesn't fit that description."

I let out a sigh of relief. "Thank you," I said and hung up the phone.

God answered my prayer that day.

By the time we got back to the apartment, Denny was there.

"Where did you go?" he asked nonchalantly.

I was so frustrated with him. I looked at him and said, "Where have you been?"

"Oh, I passed out over my frat brother's house after we were drinking all night. I would have called, but we don't have a phone."

I walked up to him and smacked his face. I knew then he was still a liar. From that moment on, I became paranoid every time Denny took a step outside the house with me or without me. The honeymoon that never really started was definitely over!

"Husbands, love your wives and do not be bitter toward them."—Colossians 3:19.

Chapter 10

Perfect Marriage

We always looked like a perfect family; two cute kids and a beautiful mother and father. We had the barbecues, the swimming parties, and the card games. On the outside looking in, we looked happy and beautiful, but we weren't. I was miserable and Denny was too. I wanted this marriage to work, and he didn't really care. He didn't want to lose me, but he wanted to run around on me until he was ready to settle down and be a husband. I couldn't agree with that. We were young and all, but I refused to be unhappy. I had been that way for the majority of my life as a child. Why settle for it as an adult?

"Denny, I just want it to be the way it was when we were in high school. Why can't we have that?"

"Rachael, stop all the dramatics! It can't be that way, baby. We grown, and a lot has changed."

"I haven't changed, Denny. Why you treat me like this? You so cold and won't talk to me, baby. What's goin' on? Please, will you tell me somethin', Denny?"

He kept getting himself prepared for the club that night. He didn't have time to hear what I was talking about.

"I deserve better than this from you!" I stormed out of the room.

Brandy would stand there, watch, and listen to the whole argument. Neither one of us noticed her listening.

Denny became verbally abusive because he wasn't happy, and I was the target of his rampages. The disrespect got so bad that I was paranoid and scared to look at myself in the mirror without thinking I was hideous.

Denny would point to other females when we were out and say, "You should be her size. You gained too much weight. You look sloppy. You need to go on a diet." He started watching everything I ate and commented every time I took a bite of something. He would even complain about the clothes I wore. No matter what I wore, it didn't look right to him.

All the plotting and planning I did to get him when we were in high school had now backfired on me. I was so concerned about myself that I thought people were looking at me constantly. I thought I was ugly and fat. I looked in the mirror and hated what I saw.

After a year of marriage to Denny, I was pregnant again. Denny was near graduating, so I was excited to tell him. I remember cooking him a candlelit dinner with soft music. I had all of his favorite foods. I even got some champagne for the occasion.

I took the girls over to my friend's house. Shauna always took good care of the girls when I needed her to. Shauna's boyfriend was an excellent football player. He actually was the star of the OSU team.

While Shauna had the girls, I made sure everything was perfect. I did my hair real pretty and put on a real nice dress. I was looking real good.

Denny came in and shouted, "What is that cooking?"

I just smiled and I told him, "You just sit down. I got something for you."

I could tell it was a good day because he came in talking to me. I was so excited, I couldn't even let the man eat. I blurted out, "I'm pregnant!" I was thinking he was going to say, "I hope it's a boy."

He looked at me. "Oh, no. Not again. We can't have a baby."

I just kept saying, "But we're married now."

"Not yet. You got to get rid of it, and the sooner the better."

"Denny, are you for real? Why? I don't understand. We are married now. We can have babies."

He got in my face, bit his lip a little, and grabbed my face. "Naw, this is all wrong. I don't want no baby right now. Are you crazy, woman?" He pushed my head back and let it go.

I stood over by the wall for a few minutes, scared of what he was going to do, then suddenly a rage came over me and I screamed, "What's the problem? You trying to make me crazy?" I was frantic and crying. "You don't want me to take birth control pills. You keep saying I'm getting fat from them. I don't know what to do. What am I supposed to do? You keep telling me you ain't gonna get me pregnant because you have the method down, but here I am again, pregnant. God is gonna get us if we do this abortion again."

He had his back turned toward me, getting ready to leave, when I ran over to him and started hitting him in the back. "I'm tired of this. I hate you!"

"I don't care. Get rid of it! Now!" Denny grabbed the keys from the coffee table and went out the door.

I sat there for a second, gazing into space, then I decided to go get the girls. I got myself together before I knocked on Shauna's door. I didn't want anyone to think I didn't have a perfect life or marriage. I had dried my eyes and put a fake smile on my face.

"Hey, girl," I said when she opened the door. "What's up?"

She said, "Carl acting up."

I looked closer at her. She had a black eye. Carl had hit

her. I just grabbed her and gave her a big hug. I wondered if it was possible to have it worse than I did.

Shauna cried and said, "Rachael, I'm tired of fighting him. Every other day he comes in here drunk and wants to put his hands on me. I want to go back home to Cincinnati."

Shauna was tiny. Very petite, with an athletic build, she looked like she never stopped exercising. Carl thought everyone wanted her. He would break her arms, bruise her ribs, and black her eyes, bust her lips, and she would still stay with him.

We both were mixed up, but we stayed with our men.

Once again, I went to the clinic. I didn't know who I was anymore. Denny went with me this time. He rubbed my back in the waiting room, turned, and whispered in my ear, "Don't worry about nothing." He kept scanning the room, looking at the other people there. No matter what Denny did, he wanted everybody to think he was always in control and had everything together, as if he was superhuman—but he wasn't. He was a man who needed to let go and get free. Denny was uptight.

"Babe, I love you, okay?"

I turned to him and replied, "Okay." I know he was trying to see where my mind was, feel me out. But my mind was fried and had been for years. I had no control over my own life or my decisions. I did whatever I could to make him happy, and that left me downright miserable. I wasn't free. I was in prison, waiting. Nevertheless, every time it was my turn to walk the last walk, it was like the governor would call and extend my length in the prison. I was a mere shell of a person sitting in that waiting room, just waiting to have a baby ripped out of me.

"Rach? Rach, you hear me?" Denny was waving his hand in front of me.

I stopped daydreaming and said, "Huh?"

"You know I love you more than anything, and once we get ahead, we'll have more kids, okay? I promise." He grabbed my hands and kissed them.

"Rachael Calhoun."

I looked up and saw the young pretty nurse staring at me. "Here I am." I got out of my chair to go to the back. I turned and looked at Denny as I walked to the back of the clinic—alone.

The nurse said, "I can give you something for the pain."

I had one tear come down my face. I shouted, "No! I'm okay." I didn't want them to give me any comforting medication. I wanted to feel what I was doing, so I decided I wanted all the pain, to remember what I had done. I wanted to feel the pain that my baby was feeling as the doctor ripped it out of its mother.

The pain was nearly unbearable. I could hear the little baby when it went through the vacuum and landed in the container.

Thump!

I knew God was watching. I lay there for a little while, and then the doctor said, "Well, I'm done."

I hated myself. I left, and Denny was standing there waiting, looking like he threw a baseball through somebody's window. "You okay?"

My baby has been ripped out of me and you want to know if I'm okay.

I never told anyone what I'd done. I just put it with the other things. I told myself that it didn't happen.

"And not have compassion on the son of her womb? Yet I will not forget you."—Isaiah 49:15.

A Spoken word . . .
BREATHLESS

Breathless is how I felt as my unborn seed was ripped out of me, not realizing it wasn't about me. Now I know it's too late to do anything about it. I lay down and decided now wasn't the right time for a baby in my life or in the world. Every excuse would do; I was too young. Or maybe somebody talked me into laying there and killing my own flesh and blood. Bottom line, I did it. I made the choice and I felt horrible! Not for the seed that would never have a chance to grow, play, swim, go on a picnic, watch television, go to school, run a race, tie his or her shoes, color a picture, see the sunset, get married, or have a child of its own. No, I made the choices. I chose death four times over. I chose it like it was nothing.

Yeah, I cried. I wasn't happy with myself, but what about the human growing inside of me, depending on me—yeah, me— to make the right choices for his or her life? What happened to life?

As I grew and realized that God can forgive someone like me for what I felt was murder four times over, I forgave myself too. However, years after forgiving myself, the fact still remained that I had killed innocent children; their blood was on my hands. I was awakened to the truth. Four human beings did not live because of me—not the father, but because of me. I was the mother. I made the ultimate decision to have the abortion. Whether I wanted to do it or not, I did.

Be stronger than I was. Be courageous. Don't allow anyone to tell you to have an abortion. Not making the right decision will leave you . . . BREATHLESS!

Chapter 11

Alone

After the abortion, I went into a shell. I didn't talk to Denny, nor did I sleep with him. I was tired. I worked constantly. When one client left, two more were coming in. When I wasn't at work, I was with the girls.

Denny wasn't working, so I was the breadwinner, but I didn't care. After all, my husband was going to the NFL. I frequently told myself that it wouldn't be long now. I would be living the lifestyle of the rich and famous.

I was still working at Apogee's, but at a different location, when James, one of our stylists said, "Hey, girl!" to someone who came in.

"Hey," she replied to him.

"What's up with you, Miss Kelly Taylor?"

At the sound of her name, I turned my head. Kelly Taylor was the name of the chick that called Denny's house when I answered the phone a few years back. She even fit the description she'd given me of herself, never betting on the day I would ever actually meet her.

I know this woman didn't come on my job. Everybody at Ohio

State knew who I was and where I worked. I did everybody's hair. I knew she came on purpose.

I thought to myself for a minute. *But that was two years ago. What would she be coming around here for now?*

I went over to the front desk and looked at my appointment book so I could get a good look at her. She was tall, light-skinned, and pretty. She looked like she might have been mixed, and she did have nice hair, which was up in one big, puffy ball. And she was as thin as Olive Oyl from *Popeye*.

I started acting different in the shop. I was uncomfortable because I wanted to know what she wanted. I quit talking and laughing and I started thinking.

Tish, one of the hairstylists, said, "What's wrong wit' you? You so quiet. Why you so quiet all of a sudden?" Tish was kind of a tomboy. She rode a motorcycle and her hair was short and curly, tapered in the back. She always wore tennis shoes and tight jeans. Men loved her.

"Nothing's wrong. Just thinkin'."

"About what?"

"That chick that just came in used to mess with Denny. She called his apartment one day when I was there, but this was before we got married."

Tish was shaking her head. "Unh-uh. Something is going on. Why would she come up here if it wasn't? Girl, you better check her." Tish was a troublemaker, too, and always started the rah-rah in the shop. She knew how to get it going and keep it going. She only needed an opportunity and it was on.

Everybody in the shop, including the customers, had advice for me that day.

"Ask her who she think she is."

"She must still be messin' wit' him, Rachael."

"You need to show her who you are."

"Beat her down!"

I took all the comments, along with the thoughts in my

head, and decided to beat her down. She made me look silly coming up to my job. Who did she think she was? Now I had to explain to everybody in the shop exactly what type of stuff I was dealing with at home. Nobody knew up until then my husband was a cheat, but she had to come to my job and expose it. I was so wrapped up in what they thought of us. I was embarrassed.

I waited until all the customers left and I went over to her. "Do you know my husband?" I asked her.

"Why? I don't have to answer you." Every time she opened her mouth, I wanted to punch her in it. She was getting smart with me and acted as if she knew something I didn't know.

She then said, "Besides, your man is calling me. Yeah, yo' husband be asking me to come over yo' house while you up in here doin' all these heads."

She thought she was being so smart, embarrassing me in front of all my co-workers, but she didn't know who she was dealing with. I was a woman with issues. I was crushed, but everyone thought I had a perfect marriage. They didn't know it was a wreck. Now my cover was blown.

I looked at Kelly, drew my fist back, and popped her in the mouth as hard as I could. Blood was everywhere. I couldn't believe I hit her like that. I stood there and watched her grab her mouth. She was shocked. She screamed! She tried to run out of the shop, but I locked the doors. I was so angry, all I could hear were her sarcastic words going through my head.

I followed her around the shop, started picking up whatever I could, and throwing it at her. I could hear everybody who stayed for the fight screaming and laughing. There was so much going on that day.

"Stop, stop! I don't want to fight you! Please!" she pleaded.

I was hurt and I wanted her to pay for the hurt she and

Denny had caused me. I knew in my heart she wasn't the one to blame, that it was really Denny, so I called Denny. Of course, by now we had a phone, seeing that I was working and more established in the hair industry.

We just lived right up the street, so he was there in minutes. He came in with a serious look on his face.

I walked straight up to him when he came in the door. "This is what you do while I'm working? Huh? You mess around and bring her in my house? My bed?" I pointed at Kelly.

"No, Rachael. It's not like that. She lying!" He turned to her. "I should smack you, Kelly. You a liar!"

"I ain't lying, Denny. You know it's true!" She was crying and screaming hysterically. There was no way she was lying.

I watched him look at Kelly with an evil eye. He was mad. She was hurt. I didn't have anything else to say. I sat back and watched. Denny lied on her and denied everything she was blurting out. He lied right in her face. I can imagine she felt like an idiot for listening to all his false promises, because I did. All these years she played second and sat back and got sloppy seconds, only to be denied when it all blew up.

Kelly walked over to me in her four-inch stiletto heels and whispered, "Can I talk to you in private, please, Rachael?"

I never looked at her, only smelled her perfume and walked to the back of the salon with her following me. I could hear everybody whispering.

Denny looked up with those sneaky eyes and said, "Rachael, where you goin'? Don't go back there with her. She's a liar, Rach. You know that."

"He is the one who is a big liar," Kelly said to me once we were in the back. "He said he didn't love you and wished he hadn't married you. He said you didn't make him happy."

I crossed my arms over my chest and squinted my eyes up

at her. I definitely wasn't gonna let my husband's mistress see me break.

She said, "Look in my purse," and opened it up.

I looked down in it, only to see a .22 pistol. I was scared; my knees became weak and buckled. I covered my mouth with my hand and felt like I was gonna throw up.

Bam! Bam! Bam!

"What's going on in there? Let me in." Denny was standing at the door, banging hard and shouting.

"I could have shot you, but I knew you didn't know what type of man you were married to."

She was crying, and I could barely hear her. I wanted to hug her because I could feel the pain she was in.

Denny was still at the door, beating. "Kelly, get out now before I come in there and pull you out! You a trip!"

She opened the door and brushed by him without ever looking. She was terrified. Here she was with a .22 and scared. Denny was following her, calling her every name imaginable in the book.

He kept asking me, "What did she say?" Then proceeded to say, "I don't know why you went back there with her. She is a liar, Rach. You can't believe what she said. I swear she's a liar. You know what? I wasn't gonna tell you this, but she slept with half the football team. She's a slut, Rach. She's trying to break us up. Don't listen to her."

The whole time he tried to explain, I just cleaned my station, said good-bye to everybody then got in my car and drove home.

When I got home, I ran a hot bubble bath, sat in the tub, closed my eyes, and cried. I heard Denny and the girls come in the door a little while after me. The girls came to the bathroom door. I could hear Brandy and see her shadow under the bathroom door.

"Mommy, let us in. What you doing?"

I couldn't even answer them. I heard Denny walk up the stairs and say, "Let Mommy relax."

"For the Lord has called you like a woman forsaken and grieved in spirit, like a youthful wife, when you were refused, says your God."—Isaiah 54:6_

Chapter 12

Wrong Decisions

After the issue with Denny and Kelly, I didn't trust him at all, but he was trying to regain my trust. He wanted me to go everywhere with him; the clubs, movies, and plays. We went everywhere for a while. It was the first time he paid any attention to me in a long time, and I liked it. I felt special again. I still was a little unsure of his intentions, but I thought we were moving forward in our marriage.

I was cautious and decided if he did something else, I would leave, but hoped he wouldn't. I believed he loved me and didn't want to lose what we had together. Brandy was four, and Brea was one year old at this time. They were the apple of Denny's and my eye.

We were attending church and focusing on our family. Denny was in his last quarter of school at OSU and was going to football camp for the Miami Dolphins. Although he didn't get picked in the draft, we were still excited.

Week after week, we sat in the pews at church, and everything the minister preached about, we were supposed to live by. I thought as long as we went to church and heard the Word, we were safe. So when church let out at one in the afternoon, by two o'clock, Denny and I would have the grill going, with his teammates and their girls over for a little drinking and weed. We didn't see anything wrong with that.

I was wrong! I sometimes sit and wonder what if I knew Jesus then? The power of Him, the fear for Him! Can you image how many young people back then could have been on fire for Christ? Everything is for the timing of Him, and I pray that now my Father in Heaven gives everyone from my past an encounter they will never forget with Him.

After our third anniversary, I was pregnant again, and Denny said the same old thing. "It's not time for a baby. I'm graduating from school and we ain't even sure I'm gonna make it in the NFL. It's foolish, Rachael."

I sat there watching him and remembering the times he told me he had everything under control. He knew how to make love without getting me pregnant. I also remembered the times I forgot to take the birth control pills I had sneaked and got from my doctor. We were both careless. So, I didn't argue this time at all. It didn't make any sense. What would be the use? I understood if I did argue with him I would be miserable and still end up at the abortion clinic.

I did as I was told and got a fourth abortion. All the talking I did about leaving Denny was just talk. I thought I would be lost without him. Who would I be? I only existed because I was Denny Calhoun's wife. If I didn't have that title, nobody would know who I was. What would I do? I didn't have anyone else but him and the kids.

When we went to the clinic this time, I told Denny I wanted him to go to the back with me as they did the abortion.

"Are you for real? I don't wanna go in there, Rach. I'll be sitting out here reading." He looked toward the magazines that were piled in the corner of the waiting room over by the television. "Besides, they don't let people back there with you, do they?" He picked up a couple of magazines.

The receptionist was sitting there listening to the whole conversation. She took her head out of her book and said, "Sir, you can go back there with her."

Denny turned around and smiled at her. "Oh, okay. I didn't know that." He dropped the magazine and looked at me. "Is that what you really want, for me to go back there with you?"

He thought he was intimidating me to say, "Well, you don't have to." That's what usually happened when I knew he would be mad if I made him do something he didn't want to do. This time, I didn't care, though. I wanted him to see and experience this human slaughter—this sacrifice. I wanted him to know it wasn't a picnic, it was a funeral.

When we first went in, the doctor greeted us and then immediately recognized Denny from the field. "You're a Buckeye, right?"

"Yes." Denny smiled. I could tell he was embarrassed.

"Sir, you can sit right here and hold her hand."

I watched Denny during the whole procedure. His face was flushed. He trembled, and his eyes welled up and watered. He was fighting back the tears. The big football star was now a little boy. It was the first time I had ever seen him break completely down.

The procedure got worse every time. I lay on that table with my legs in those stirrups, attached to that hose that snatched out a baby who would never come into this world alive. Rather, it would be torn into pieces, all because I didn't speak up. I did the same thing every time; covered my face and closed my eyes because I knew I was killing my baby.

It never mattered how many times I was there or what reason I was there. I should have stood for what I believed! However, I let the weakness in my mind take over me and tell me silly things like, "He's gonna leave you if you don't do what he wants." So, I did it.

When we came out, Denny said, "I'm sorry, Rach. What

was I thinking telling you to do this? I wasn't thinking, Rach. I'm so sorry."

He wanted to know if I needed anything. I told him I was hungry, so he took me to get something to eat. He sat down at the restaurant we went to and cried. He told me, "I didn't know it was that bad. If I had known that, I wouldn't have told you to do it." He sniffed. "It was horrible, Rachael. I could hear everything. Man, I'm so sorry." He bent his head down and was silent. He put his arm around me and said, "I'm so sorry you had to go through that. You will never go through that again. I swear."

His arm around me felt like a rapist's arm around me. I had no feelings for Denny anymore. I was an empty shell when it came to him. I listened as he talked, and I knew it would never happen again because I wasn't going to let it.

At that moment, my heart was hardened toward Denny. I couldn't make love with him, couldn't respect him, and truly didn't like him. My way of dealing with this was to shut him out. I didn't talk to him; I didn't cook for him anymore or wash his dirty clothes. We lived together, but that was it.

He tried persistently to get in my head, but I would shut down when it came to him. I decided to worry about me and girls.

"I bet I don't worry about him anymore," I said to myself. I started concentrating on losing the extra sixty pounds I had gained from all of the pregnancies with exercise and a diet. Within four months, I had lost every pound I had gained.

I quit thinking and caring about Denny being a professional athlete. I concentrated on my career as a hairstylist. I was making money. I could take care of myself and the kids without him. I liberated myself and started going to the clubs with some of my clients. I went everywhere. I was so beautiful, and all the guys let me know it.

I went from worrying about everyone around me to worrying about my own beauty. I wasn't happy with Denny. I wanted him to pay for the things he had done to me. He was the enemy. I couldn't let him touch me; he gave me the creeps. It was as if my skin crawled whenever he came near me.

After the abortion and finding out about the different clients he slept with, I was finished with him. I just needed to figure out a way to let him know. That was the hardest thing for me was opening up my mouth and telling the truth.

"I don't want to be your wife anymore. You hurt me." I couldn't say it, so I lived with him and tormented him with silence. I knew it was over, but I was too much of a coward to tell him.

I came home from work one day, and he sat me down in the living room and said, "Rachael, it's been months since we made love."

When he touched me, I cringed. His kisses were like dead fish touching me. I pushed him away softly and blurted out, "No, I can't do this!"

He put his hand on his head and said, "Man, if you don't, I'll find somebody who will."

That's when I realized he was the same old Denny. The same one that hurt me, cheated on me and lied constantly to me. I laughed at him. "Ha, ha, ha! You a joke! I knew you would show up sooner or later."

"Whatever, Rachael. Do you know who I am? Many women want me, but I'm with you and you don't even care. Man, Rachael, I'm tired of this."

I hated him. I watched him rant and scream. Then I picked my purse up from the dresser, ran down the stairs, and went out the front door. I was furious, but relieved I wasn't having sex with him. I turned my car on and the radio up and zoomed down the street in my Camaro, not knowing where I was going. I just needed to drive.

Hours later, I came in the door. Something told me to walk slowly and be quiet. I did. I went to the steps and looked up.

I then crept up the steps slowly. I heard Denny on the phone, saying, "I had a good time with you last night." He was smiling and grinning, walking back and forth between the hallway and our bedroom. "I hope I see you tonight. I'll tell Rachael I'm going out wit' the fellas."

I ran up the stairs and stared him right in the face. He was shocked. He hung up the phone fast.

I said, "I want a separation. You got to go now!"

I don't think he ever thought I would really leave him. Not the little girl from Dayton. Denny begged and pleaded, but I didn't want to hear it anymore; it was over.

He moved out that night, and stayed with one of his friends named Ray, a Caucasian guy he used to cop weed from.

I was turning twenty-four in a couple of months and had decided to start my life. I was working during the day and clubbin' every night. I thought that was the life, but it wasn't. I had no time with the girls. It was all about me now. I was young and had never been free, I told myself. I didn't think about saving my marriage or protecting my daughters. I just wanted to have fun! I thought there was no harm, but I paid for the decision. I was a silly woman.

I decided to move on and start fresh at a new salon. I started working at Tommie's beauty and barbershop; every great stylist in Columbus was there. Tommie was a drug dealer and barber who decided to do something legit with his money. He and a friend of his put the salon together. We had barbers in the front, hairstylists in the back, and behind that there was gambling and every type of drug transaction taking place.

Everybody in Columbus would roll through Tommie's. We had professional men, professional football players, basketball players, boxers, drug dealers, and of course, plenty of women came too. We did a lot of hair, but half of the people that came and went were just hanging around. I learned the streets very fast from working there.

My marriage was over with—for me, anyway. But Denny couldn't let it go.

"Rachael, please forgive me. I made a mistake. I need you and the girls. I won't ever mistreat you or take you for granted again."

"I don't think so, Denny. You need to leave. Besides, you're upsetting the girls and I'm goin' out. I thought you said you would watch them and not come in here and trip out. Huh, Denny? You promised." I walked down the hall toward my bedroom to get dressed, with him on my heels.

"Please, Rachael, listen to me. I messed up."

All the time. He needs to quit it. If I give this fool another chance, all he gonna do is hurt me. Look at my babies. They can't go through this mess. I won't let them.

"Denny, do you understand the kind of hurt you caused me?" I turned my nose up at him and said, "And the kids?"

"Oh my God." He dropped to his knees and cried.

But I didn't believe him. I knew if he came back, he would do the same thing all over again. I wasn't falling for it this time.

The girls would stand there behind their daddy and cry. It frustrated me because he frequently used them to manipulate the situation. "Can I baby-sit them here tonight?"

I knew he just wanted to pump Brandy for information. I looked at his face. It was blood red. I couldn't say no, because he asked in front of the girls.

"Please, Mommy, can he stay?" Brandy pleaded his case.

"Yeah," I said without looking at him. I knew I was setting myself up.

Whenever he stayed over there, he would go through my things and ransack my room, but for the girls' sake, I obliged. Denny had no idea what was wrong with me or why

I was so bitter toward him. It had been over between us a long time ago. I had so much resentment in my heart for him. I couldn't forget the things he said to me or things he had done. They were painful. He would constantly talk about the new woman that he got busted talking to on the phone, like that had been the only problem. But in all honesty, it didn't have anything to do with the mysterious woman. It was everything!

Denny's parents invited me and the girls down for the holidays, so I packed up the car and we went. Denny was so happy and thought we were going to pretend that everything was going to be fine, but I was no actress. He planned for us to have dinner and go to the movies. He acted as if nothing had happened. He was wrong! I wasn't going to pretend this time.

Denny told his father about us separating, and he wanted to talk to us. We went in to talk to him. The entire time he was talking, all I heard him say was one sentence: "The next person you end up with, you still have to go through something with."

I didn't say a word. I just sat there looking at my nails and having a secret attitude about the whole thing. But I smiled gracefully.

Your son is a monster. He's off the hook. Don't you know?

He continued to talk. "I mean, if you stay with who you already have, then you will go further and work out the problems."

But I was through. I had been abused one too many times.

That Sunday, we were both called to the front of the church for prayer. I thought to myself, *His parents probably glad we're splittin' up. They never liked me anyway.* I bowed my head respectfully. *They so fake. I'm ready to get out of here.*

At the altar that day, I was so disrespectful toward God, toward my marriage and toward Denny's parents, and the sad part about that was I didn't even know it. I was being used by the enemy.

That was the last time the Calhoun family saw me for years. I was so bound with heartache and confusion that I was a category 5 hurricane. Anything that came in my path was bound for destruction.

Chapter 13

Bitterness

"Please don't go! Stay here with me. Please. I want you back. Don't go, please. Don't go, please! Rach, I got a good job now and I can take care of you and the girls."

I thought Denny was sincere, but I didn't want to take a chance. Besides, it would be a pity if I went back now. I did feel bad for him. He never got to try out for the Miami Dolphins after he injured himself playing basketball with the fellas. I knew that was his dream. He had been told he was going to the NFL ever since he was in high school, and to be so close and have it snatched away must have felt horrible.

"Rachael, please give me another chance. I'm shaking. Look at me." His whole body was trembling as he talked to me. "I can't breathe. Please stop all of this and let me move back in."

Yeah, right! I thought. *He must be out of his mind! Isn't this the guy who called me all those names? Who had affairs with my clients? Is this the guy who didn't want not one of our children?*

I never verbally expressed my anger to Denny. I guess I didn't know how, so everything I did and said, I said it to myself while he stood in front of me and begged. If Denny talked too long, he always managed to put his foot in his mouth and show the true, sneaky Denny that was laying there dormant.

"I can't be by myself," he would say, trying to make me take him back or else. "If you don't take me back . . ."

I glanced over at him.

"I'm gonna be with somebody, Rachael. I can't be by myself."

I laughed right in his stupid face! When was he gonna realize I didn't care? "Go ahead. Be with somebody else. Maybe you'll be happy." That was all I needed to tell him. It was truly over.

I smirked and walked closer to him so our eyes would meet. "I want to be free. I have been a hostage too long. Let me go."

This was a powerful statement. I had never realized what it was I wanted until hearing those words. I wanted to be free! I know the pain I went through while married to Denny was severe. It stuck with me.

Let me go. As I heard those words that God gave me, I knew I had forgiven him wholeheartedly. When I did forgive, it broke the chains in my life off me! A person never knows what or whom they are bound to until God delivers them from it. I never knew all these years that I was still in bondage to someone I thought I let go along time ago. My husband rejected me! He rejected all my children! For a long time, I hated Denny for that. Now I forgive him.

"In an acceptable time I have heard you, and in the day of salvation I have helped you; I will preserve you and give you as a covenant to the people, To restore the earth, To cause them to inherit the desolate heritages; That you may say to the prisoners, 'Go forth'; To those who *are* in darkness, 'Show yourselves.' They shall feed in their ways, and their pastures *shall be* in all high places."—Isaiah 49:8-9.

I wanted to be free; however, I was caught up in a marriage that I was no more ready for than a couple that met each other in one day and married. I made a mess of it. Going into a marriage, I was already hurt, and once inside of the marriage, we both had no idea what it was going to take to make it work. I thought it was going to be marvelous and full of love and peace. I never once thought about a future with Denny or saw him in my future. I saw him for what I thought he was going to do and be; an NFL star.

We don't look for our husbands, they find us! If we wait and be faithful unto the will of God, we will have great things and people in our lives.

After making it clear to Denny that I wanted out of the marriage, I just wanted to have a good time—dancing, smoking some weed, and flirting. That's all that was on my mind; sex, drugs and kickin' it! I wasn't thinking about him anymore.

The next couple of months were uneventful. The salon was getting ready for a hair show, so everyone but me was at practice on the other side of town, where they were having the show. I didn't go to practice because I was putting a ponytail in my hair.

"You want me to stay with you?" one of the girls asked me.

I looked at her and could see she really wanted to go, so I said, "No, I'm okay."

"Okay, girl. I'll see you in a little while. Get that head together."

We both laughed, and I hollered from the back, "Lock me in!" I never stopped what I was doing. I put the gel on my hair and smoothed it up into a ponytail then walked to the dryers. I heard the phone ring. I put the book down that I was gonna read while under the dryer, and answered the phone.

"Tommie's. May I help you?"

"Hey, Rach. What you doin'?" It was Denny.

"I'm under the dryer trying to do my hair. Everybody went

to practice for the hair show but me. What are the girls doin'?"

"They're 'sleep right now." Denny was still staying at his friend's house and he had the girls over for the weekend. "They just finished eatin' about an hour ago and after that they crashed."

"Okay, when you bringin' them home?"

"Soon. I wanna come and see you. Can I do that? I got somethin' to tell you, Rach."

I didn't think anything of it, so I said, "Okay, come on up."

Denny got to the shop as fast as the speed of light. The doors were locked, so I had to go open them for him. I went to the door smiling.

He pulled me outside and immediately began talking crazy and out of his head. "Tobias told me you been snortin' that 'caine."

I looked at him like he was crazy. "Yeah, right!" I said. I started cracking up laughing. After all, Denny knew me; he knew I didn't mess around with hardcore dope, only weed. I couldn't believe something so ridiculous was coming out of his mouth.

As I laughed at what he was saying, I started noticing his face and realized he believed those things about me. Before I could move away, he hit me with all his might in my face.

Denny grabbed me and started shaking me. We tousled for a minute, and I broke away from him. He chased me. I was scared, and my face was burning from the hit and the rocks that I had landed on. I went through the air across the rocky parking lot until I finally landed. I got up and saw people in cars, blowing their horns and watching the whole drama play out. No one helped.

All I could remember was my mother beaten in the middle of the street that day when I was a little girl, and I thought, *I know I told him if he ever hit me again, there would be no getting back together.* I ran as fast as I could to get inside the salon, with him on my heels, screaming out, "I'm gonna get you!" I hurried in and locked the door behind me.

He had never put his hands on me like that. Maybe a push or shove, but this time he closed his fist and hit me in the face with all his might.

I paced the floor back and forth and then remembered he had my daughters. I stooped down on the floor, knees balled to my chest, held myself, and cried. I had to think fast because I didn't know if he was gonna try to keep them or what. As far as I was concerned, he was a crazy man.

I sat on the floor for a minute then called Toy. She came immediately, and I told her what had happened. She couldn't believe it. Toy was the only one besides Crystal who knew that Denny wasn't an angel, but she couldn't believe he had gone this far.

Toy and I came up with a plan. I told her, "Let's go get the girls." But before we walked out of the shop, Denny called. He was crying,

"I'm sorry. Please forgive me. I know better than that. My mind is all jacked-up, Rachael. I won't ever hit you again, okay?"

"I know you won't. I have a swollen face, Denny!"

Toy was whispering to me and telling me to be nice so he would give me the girls.

"I'm really sorry, Rachael." He sniffed. "I don't know what came over me. My mind, it's—"

"I just want to come and get the girls. That's all. Okay?"

"Okay, come on. You can pick them up."

"I'm on my way." I hung up the phone, and Toy and I left to get the girls.

The house looked like it needed to be condemned. We got there fast, and I knew we had to move fast to get the girls out of the house first before I showed out. I had other plans for Denny. He had put his hands on me, and I wanted to get him for that. I didn't know what I was gonna do to him, but I was gonna get him back!

We knocked on the back door, and Ray opened the door and said, "Just a minute," and then hollered for Denny. We could hear men's voices laughing and hollering from the back porch. We could also smell the weed they were smoking.

Denny had the girls up and ready to go. When they saw me, they ran over and said, "Mommy, Mommy!" Then they saw Toy and ran to her. She hugged them both and took them outside to the car.

I looked at her and said, "I'll be right back."

I know I must have looked real crazy to her because she was trembling. I walked in the house. It was filthy. There were beer cans and doobies everywhere. I thought a mouse was going to jump out on me. I couldn't believe I let my daughters stay in that filthy place.

I got even madder after I saw the condition of how Denny was living. He was standing there between the living room and the kitchen, smoking some weed and talking to his boys. He looked so pitiful. I walked toward him and I spit in his face as hard as I could. I knew I couldn't fight him or hurt him, but I knew that would affect him.

He turned and tackled me to the nasty kitchen floor. I was furious. He hit me a few more times in the stomach and face. We scuffled. He had me in a headlock. I scratched his face, his back, and neck up as much as I could. I even tried to bite him. I wanted him to pay for putting his hands on me.

His boys came running in the kitchen to break us up. They finally got Denny off me and asked me to leave.

I cried on the way back to the salon. The girls never knew a thing. At the shop, I told Tommie what happened because he was there when I got back. He couldn't believe it. He had been the one person telling me to go home to my husband.

* * *

Denny finally graduated from OSU that summer with a degree in economics. I was proud of him, and the girls and I were at the graduation. I made it clear that wasn't nothing happening between us. I found out that summer that Denny's new girlfriend was the woman I caught him on the phone with when we separated. I couldn't wait to see the mystery woman.

Every time Denny came to the shop, all the women would look at him and say as he walked by, "Girl, you crazy. I would have stayed with that fine man."

I laughed and said, "Everything that looks good ain't good for ya!"

For a while, Denny tried to do things with our daughters. He would come and get them for the weekends and spend time with them. Eventually, the time faded to every other weekend and then every now and then. It was so sad; the girls loved their daddy so much and needed him. I didn't understand how Denny could go from being with his children all the time to doing a total disappearing act. It just wasn't right.

I was on my way out the door one morning when the phone rang. It was Denny.

"Rachael, what's up? I wanted you to know that I got a job in Chicago. I will be movin' shortly."

I was happy for him. He needed to get out of this city for a while. "I'll take care of you. You can keep the insurance that my job has provided for us. You go ahead and keep that car so you can get the girls to school. I'll make sure you guys are taken care of. You still my family."

I nodded my head and said, "Yeah, that's cool. Thanks a lot."

Within a week's time, Denny and his chick were gone. He came and took the car from me because, although I was paying the note, it was in his name. I remained calm on the outside, but on the inside, I was confused. I didn't know what I was going to do. How was I going to get the kids around?

"But did He not make them one, having a remnant of the Spirit? And why one? He seeks godly offspring. Therefore, take heed to your spirit, and let none deal treacherously with the wife of his youth."—Malachi 2:15.

Chapter 14

I Want a Divorce

Denny had been in Chicago for about two years now, but he was coming back for Brandy's sixth birthday party. We hadn't seen him, but we talked to him frequently on the phone.

I had a big party for her at the skating rink. All of her friends were there. Momma and Crystal even came up from Dayton. Denny brought his girlfriend, Indy, with him.

"Rachael, we need to get our divorce together, you know?" he said.

"Yeah, I agree, but I don't have any extra money to make that happen. You need to help me with the girls and you're not. When do you think you'll be able to do that?" I was tired of taking care of the girls by myself and him running around with his girlfriend like he was single.

"You running around with all these different women. I mean, do what you do, but you need to grow up and help me." I was tired of him, and he needed to know.

"Who even told you about the party, Denny? Yo' mom? 'Cause I sure wasn't gonna tell you jack," I said.

Crystal came over. "Ya actin' ignorant, and the kids are

watching you. Don't get that baby upset on her birthday. I don't care what he did, Rachael. You need to focus on your daughters."

I agreed with Crystal. I turned and said, "You a mess," and walked away from him.

"Rachael, can we talk about this later? Come on, you getting upset. Our daughter is six."

I shook my head and thought, *This dude thinks he is so slick.*

"You funny, Denny." I kept walking and went back to the party.

Apart from that, the party was a success. Everyone had a great time. I sat back and watched Brandy mingle with her friends. She was so beautiful and just flourishing into an awesome little girl. I watched her play for a while without her even knowing. I laughed from afar as she played and skated.

After the party, we went home. I was so tired from that day that I just wanted to sit down and watch some cable.

"Mommy, Daddy said he was getting married," Brandy said.

I couldn't believe he told her that at her birthday party. He was so stupid. I wasn't prepared to deal with that. I didn't even know what to say to her, so I said, "Yeah, I think that's awesome. You can dress up in a pretty gown and you will have another mommy." I smiled on the outside.

It made me sad because just like everybody thought Denny and I would get back together, I did too. I always thought that once he really grew up, maybe years later, we might try again. But now it was too late. The girls wanted their mommy and daddy together. They weren't happy.

The next summer, we still weren't divorced. Denny hadn't done anything to get it finalized, and I hadn't either. I had bought myself a car, fraudulently using my sister's credit. Yeah, I had gotten really scandalous. I was backed in a corner, and instead of coming out fighting, I submitted to temptation. I knew at any given time I would be found out, but for the moment, I didn't care. I wanted everyone to think I had it together; a new car, new apartment and new clothes. But it was a lie. I used other people's personal information to get what I wanted. I had been hurt, and I wanted to show Denny and everyone else that I could make it without him. I didn't care who was on the other end of my wrath. I did what I had to do to get what I wanted.

The two people in the universe who would have done anything for me, my cousin Toy, and my sister Crystal, were the ones who paid. I took Toy with me to sign Crystal's name. She had no idea what she was doing. She thought she was standing in proxy for Crystal. I had convinced Toy that Crystal couldn't get to Columbus to sign the papers even though she had agreed to do it as a favor to me, but it was all a lie. I had become a big liar! A fake! I wasn't happy with myself.

From that moment on, my life went into a spiral going straight down fast. I was evicted from my apartment. I didn't know how to get it together. It was like I was in a daze, waiting for it all to go boom!

I had a car, and now I needed an apartment, so I went into the rental office and acted as if I was my sister. I came out with a high-priced apartment that I kept telling myself I'd be able to afford.

It was like someone destroyed my life, destroyed my relationships, and I couldn't stop it. I kept going down, not realizing that the someone who was to blame was me. I was the one who was out of control and destroying and killing everything around me.

So, when Denny asked if he could keep the girls for the summer, I told him it was fine. I needed him to take them so I could try to get my head above the water. I needed to figure out a way to get out of this mess without anyone finding me out. I had dug myself into a deep hole.

When he came and picked them up, they were all ready to go. I had prepared them with everything they needed.

"Daddy," they screamed. "We ready to go."

He would always take his strong arms and scoop them both up at the same time. I leaned against the light post outside the salon, sat back quietly, and watched them. One thing was for sure, he loved his girls. His action sometimes showed different, but he loved them. I could see it in his eyes whenever he was with them.

"Yeah, I'm taking you to the park, the zoo and the beach while you're with me," Denny told the girls.

"Can we go every day, Daddy?" Brea asked.

"No, we can't go every day, Brea, but we'll go, okay?" He put them both in their seatbelts. I got in the car and kissed and hugged both of them then said good-bye.

"Denny, let me talk to you for a minute."

"Okay. What's up?"

I told him to be careful with my girls, and asked him if he was sure he could handle them for so long.

"Woman, they mine too. I ain't gonna let nothin' happen to them."

A couple of days after they were in Chicago, Denny called. "The girls wanna talk to you."

"Mommy, I want to come home. They're mean to us. Daddy wants to speak to you," Brandy whined.

"Put him on the phone, Brandy," I told her.

"Me and Indy are almost out of money," Denny said. I don't know why I was surprised. He pulled stuff like this all the time.

"I asked you if you could handle keeping the girls that long and if it was what you wanted to do. I didn't ask you to come and get them! You're stupid!" I hung up the phone. I was so mad I could have smacked him! He promised he would spend time with them this summer, and now he was only thinking about himself again.

Shortly, Brandy called back. "Mommy?"

"Yes, baby?"

"Are you mad?" she asked.

"No, Brandy, just tired," I replied.

"Is we coming home?"

"Yes, you are. Real soon."

"Okay, Mommy. See you soon. I love you!"

"I love you too. Bye."

I was so frustrated. I loved the girls, but I needed some me time. I hadn't had any time to regroup. All I ever did was go to work and take care of the girls, so him taking them for the summer was supposed to give me a chance for some time alone. But of course, it was only temporary because he was bringing them right back.

I did miss the kids, but I was able to think while they were gone. I didn't have to worry about what they were going to eat or who was gonna baby-sit them. All I had to do was get them ready for school before they came back. However, it was temporary because Denny was bringing them back in less than a week.

Chapter 15

Deceiving Looks

While the girls were still with Denny, I was out at the clubs every night. I went to every spot there was in Columbus, partying with the girls from the salon. I danced, drank and smoked weed, but didn't get what I was going after in the clubs—a man. I didn't want just any man, but one that sold large quantities of drugs. That's the one I was looking for. I thought that if I had a dope man taking care of me, all of my worries would be over.

Oh, I watched them in the clubs pull on the women and say, "Hey, let me buy you that drink." Or, "Wanna smoke a blunt?" However, none interested me. My motive was to get a paid dope man that could pay for me and what I wanted.

I woke up one morning after clubbin' to the alarm going off. I opened my eyes and realized it was 10:30 A.M., which meant I was an hour late for my first appointment. I jumped up, picked up the phone on my nightstand and called the shop.

"Hello, this is Rachael. Is my customer there?"

"Yep, she's right here," said Tracey, the stylist who had answered the phone.

I thought, *Tracey at work. I had better hurry before she does my client's hair.*

"I'll be there in a minute. Don't do her hair, either! I know you scandalous." I hung up.

I hurried in the bathroom to shower and thought, *She better not touch my client. Shoot, I know I'm late, but I need that money.* About a half hour later I walked in the salon with my wide-leg pants, my asymmetrical bob with the long piece over my left eye, and my cute, tight shirt that showed off my shape.

"Hey, Deb. I am so sorry I'm late." I said to my client. "It was a long night."

She didn't care about me being late. All she cared about was hearing about my wild night. My clients got an earful. Every time they came in, that's all I did was tell my business and run my mouth. Shoot, they lived for it.

Deb would sit, get her hair done and listen, saying, "Go 'head, girl. Then what happened?" It was as if they were watching the soaps on television. And at the end of every visit, they wanted to come back to get their hair done for the next episode.

I was standing there giving Deb a play-by-play of what happened at the club, and in walked Samantha, a co-worker of mine. She came in smiling from ear to ear, gazing into the eyes of her new boyfriend. She had been telling all of us at the shop about him all week long.

Samantha was twenty-two and appeared to have it goin' on. She was a pretty girl, very pale with freckles all over her face and red hair. She wasn't real heavy, but she wasn't skinny either. In addition, she always had a scam going on, and she sold dope in her spare time from the hair game.

She walked in with four men, all who where from New York. I didn't turn around or stop talking to Deb, but I watched them from the mirror.

"Yo, Sam, introduce me to that shorty right there," one said, pointing at me.

I thought, *I don't want to meet him.* My mouth was frowned up.

"Girl, he likes you," Deb said. "He can't take his eyes off of you."

I smiled, but thought, *He got a big ol' head.*

Samantha made her way across the salon to me. "Rachael, my friend wants to meet you. She then whispered in my ear, "He's paid, girl."

I looked at him through the mirror and he was watching, standing there, leaning. He blew me a kiss, winked his eye, and smiled. "Go out to dinner wit me, shorty." He walked over to my booth and said, "Say yes."

I looked at him through the mirror as he stood there beside me, whispering in my ear, "You won't regret it. Let me wine and dine you. I'll spoil you."

I continued watching him from the mirror, watching his mouth and lips, wondering if he was telling the truth, or was playing a game like the rest of them.

He was a big guy; about 6'2" with a bald head, and weighed in at 230 pounds. His skin was beautiful, a dark caramel color and flawless in appearance. He just had an oversized head. Maybe because it was bald, I don't know, but it was big. His eyes were big and brown. He had facial hair that he kept well-groomed, kind of a light shadow on his face. He was a real thug. I mean grimy, dirty thug! He looked as if he just stepped foot out of a rap video.

He wore Timberland boots, a Nautica jacket with Guess jeans, a white T-shirt and a button-down designer shirt. I looked at his neck and wrist and saw that he had one 14-karat huge link bracelet and a necklace around his neck. What I really liked was the way he picked his jewelry. It was expensive, but he didn't have too much. He only wore two pieces, but what he wore let you know he was paid.

I noticed all this while he talked in my ear as I curled Deb's hair. I acted as if I wasn't interested in what he was saying, but the truth is, I was very interested. After all, I just got through saying I wanted a big dope man to take care of me.

What are the chances another one is gonna come in the salon, sweep me off my feet, marry me when I get a divorce, save all his money from drug sales then go legit? Yeah, that's what I thought. I had to make a choice now. What did I have to lose? He was paid! He was one of the biggest dope men to ever come to Columbus, Ohio . . . and he wanted me.

He told me his name was Tone. He was a New York drug dealer. From the sway when he walked to the things he said out of his mouth—"Shorty this, shorty that, dime piece, up top, up North."—I liked everything about him. He was different from any other man I knew. He knew just the right things to say.

"Sweetheart," he would say, "Let me take you to dinner and get you something special at the mall." He would always touch me on my arm, leg or neck. It was all a part of a subtle seduction happening right underneath my nose. I had no idea I was being set up for one of the biggest falls in my life.

"I want you to have the best of everything, babe," he would tell me.

Everything he said, I believed. I wanted to believe. "I'm gonna marry you, move you to the suburbs, and you gonna drive the kids to the private school I pick. I'ma get you a new station wagon Benz. You like that?" And of course it all sounded good to me, so I would take it all in.

"That's a good car for a mommy. You stay at home, take care of the family and I will take care of you. That's all you need to do. I'll put a swingset in the backyard for the girls. Nothin' but the best for you and the girls."

It was all a game. I was the car in the game of Monopoly and didn't even know it. I was so blind. What he said out of his mouth was so convincing. I thought he really was telling the truth.

He would look at me with those big eyes and say, "That a'ight wit' you?"

I'd smile and say, "Yeah, that's all right wit' me."

I had never hung out with Samantha or knew much about her, but I did know that she dabbled in the drug game aside from doing hair. I never understood why. She had a huge clientele, so she made money doing hair. After a few dates and a few gifts from Tone, I was invited to Samantha's house. Tone was already there with Samantha and her dude.

I was in the area where she lived, but couldn't find the apartments. I picked up my cell and called Tone for directions.

"It's 3512. The apartment on the end, sweetheart," he told me.

"Okay, I got it. I'll be right there."

"Stop and get some blunts from the corner store, sweetheart, a'ight?"

I thought, *That's cool wit' me. I'm getting high!*

"Okay, I will." I pressed END on the cell and pulled into the corner store not far from Samantha's. After picking up the blunts, I jumped back into the car and thought, *Where is her apartment? In the woods somewhere? Dang, she lives far!*

I pulled up to the apartments. The first thing I noticed was the huge swimming pool and clubhouse. "Samantha living good out here," I said. I flipped my mirror down above the visor and looked at myself. I reached in the back seat of my car without turning around and pulled my M.A.C. foundation and eye shadow from my purse. I kept reaching because I couldn't find the lip-gloss, then I finally found it. I painted my face very fast, grabbed my Louis Vuitton purse and shut the car door.

I started walking toward the apartment, looking at my

shoes as I walked. Tone had brought me some snakeskin stilettos back from Miami last weekend, and it was the first time I had worn them. I wanted him to see me in them, so I wore a Coogie dress with the back out and the snakeskin shoes.

I had long legs and shapely body. I knew exactly how to get what I wanted from a man; after all, I was my momma's daughter.

As I walked up to the door, I thought, *I hope they don't repo my car tomorrow. Maybe Tone will pay it for me.* I had been hiding my red turbo Mitsubishi for over three months now, hoping they didn't catch up with me before I caught up on my payments. Problem was, I wasn't working too much these days. I was busy in the clubs with the girls.

I walked up to the side of this enormous apartment and rang the doorbell. "Samantha." I smiled once she answered the door. "What's up?"

"Oh, girl, nothing. Sitting in here with these knuckleheads."

I walked in the apartment and said, "Where's Tone?"

"Oh, he's downstairs watching videos." Before I could say another word, she said, "Joe's upstairs taking care of business."

I looked at her and smiled, grabbed her by the hands and whispered with a sly smile on my face, "Oh my God, after only two weeks, I think I'm in love with him. Samantha, he wants to marry me."

She looked so surprised. It bothered me a little the way she was looking, but I was so happy. I was finally in love with a man who could meet all of my needs and take care of me this time. Tone was a real man!

Samantha said, "Yeah, I hear you, but Joe got to get out of my house!" She was upset, moving around the living room and running her fingers through her red hair. "I think he's cheatin'. Can you find out from Tone?"

I was reluctant, but said I would help her. After all, she hooked me up with Tone and he was the good one.

Samantha's house was laid out! I looked around. She had white furniture and gold accessories everywhere. Nothing in her apartment looked like it had ever been touched before. Above her fireplace was a big portrait of herself with all her jewelry on. I have to admit, I was impressed with this new-found lifestyle I was embarking on. These people had everything. Samantha had every pair of shoes and designer handbag I would ever want—not to mention the designer clothes she had in her closet. It never ended.

She had two bedrooms, and both of her closets were filled with beautiful dresses, shoes, designer jeans, leather pants and short-shorts. Samantha had it going on! My eyes were so big the first trip I took to her house.

"Rach, you can have this stuff. I can't fit it anymore." She pointed to some clothes in her closet.

"Are you sure? I'm not used to people giving me stuff. What you want?"

"Girl, please. You ain't my type!" We laughed.

Tone stayed with Samantha and Joe when I first met him. I went downstairs in the basement where Tone stayed in Samantha's house whenever he was in town. The basement was nice too. She had it all decked out with black leather furniture and a big screen television that he had blasted on the rap videos.

Coming down the stairs, I heard MC Light rapping, "I need a roughneck. Gotta have a roughneck!" I loved that song. I started rapping it.

After watching a couple of videos and some small talk, I asked, "Tone, what's going on? Is Joe messing wit' somebody else?"

He grabbed me by the arms, put me on his lap, put his finger to his lips and said, "Shhh. Don't say nothing. Yeah, he dippin' out on the side a little, but don't tell Samantha. She's crazy! Joe trying to get his stuff out of her house."

Tone knew Joe was dead wrong, but went along with his friend. I felt horrible. What kind of friend would I be by not telling her the truth? I pushed away from him, using my hands on his chest, and shook my head.

I started walking up the stairs and heard Tone say, "Hey, where you going? You tellin' Samantha?"

I kept going as if I didn't hear him. I went upstairs where Samantha and Joe were. They were in her smallest bedroom that had a twin bed, a dresser and a closet full of clothes. I felt bad because she had just given me all these clothes, and here I was smiling in her face, knowing that Joe was about to do her wrong.

I sat down on the bed where she had the pile of clothes she had given me. She had given me designer clothes and hooked me up with Tone, and he was paid. All I could do was stand by and watch her get dumped. I watched her and Joe. They seemed to be so close. I started wondering as I watched them together.

He is so fake. I wonder how he can sit here and act like everything straight when he know he leaving her for somebody else. He's scandalous. I was in deep thought. *I wonder if Tone will pay my car notes and catch them up.*

I heard, "What are you thinking about? Rachael! Rachael!" Samantha said to me.

"Oh, huh? I'm trippin'. What you say?" I said.

They started laughing. "I think you getting high from smellin' all this dope in here," Joe said. He was pointing at the dope and they were both looking at me.

I was tryin' to act like it was nothin'; them sitting up there in that room packing their product up in those little plastic bags. Then I remembered I snapped out of my trance and smelled the drugs. The cocaine and heroin stunk!

I sat there quietly and watched them bag up the drugs Tone had just got off the airplane. The white powder was everywhere! I couldn't tell what was cocaine and what was heroin, though. It all looked the same to me, but the smell made me sick. I would get dizzy.

Tone walked into the bedroom and sat beside me. He whispered in my ear, "Baby, I want to marry you. That's what I want to do. Just give me little bit of time and we will have a perfect life, babe." He rubbed my back and neck, saying, "Perfect Rachael."

I heard him, but watched Samantha and Joe as they worked to put the drugs in the small baggies. Samantha watched Tone as he touched my knee. She saw me looking at her, so she smiled. I could tell she was disappointed because her and Joe didn't have what we did. I didn't give it much more thought, though. It didn't bother me what I was seeing.

With Tone always smiling at me with those white teeth and dimples, he had me hooked to his game. I was living a fairytale! Within two weeks of knowing him I hadn't eaten anywhere but at the best restaurants in town—not to mention the clothes, jewelry and gifts he bought. I thought that was what it all was about; a man spending money. Why would he spend so much on me and take me everywhere he went and cater to my every need if he wasn't serious?

"Rachael, I want to take care of you and the girls. What you need? Huh? This dope game means nothin' to me. You hear me, Rach? All I want is to stack a few more dollars, then I'm out. I'll have enough money to never have to work again.

"I didn't know you were going to come along in my life and that I would fall for you in the salon that day. I didn't know I could feel like this, you know?" He stood up, smiling, looking at Joe and shaking his hand.

"I'm a thug, baby. This doesn't happen to me."

Joe started laughing then whispered something in Tone's ear. Tone sat back down, puckered his lips up and said, "Kiss me."

I looked him in his eyes, listened to him, and believed everything that came out of his mouth. This was the one. If he said "Let's get married today," after I filed for my divorce from Denny, I would have done it. Nobody had ever spit game like that to me. I thought I had seen it all and did it all, but believe me, this was a game!

Tone grabbed me close and said, "Whatever you want, shorty, I'll do! All those knuckleheads from your past missed out."

I liked the confidence he spit out of his mouth. I thought it was sexy. I knew he talked a lot, but he was backing it up in action, and as far as the drugs, he just needed a good girl to set him on the right track. He'd thank me later for helping him see the light. Thing is, I didn't know where the light was or how I was gonna lead him into it.

The fallout between Samantha and Joe was bad. She took it real bad once I finally told her the truth about Joe.

"Samantha, Joe is seeing someone else. I'm sorry. You should move on." I put my arm around her shoulder and said, "You haven't been seeing him long."

"I know, but I think I love him, Rachael. He was so good to me when he was here. He said he loved me and was gonna take care of me. He lied to me. I want him to pay for how he treated me."

I felt terrible for her. Her face was so red like a beet, and her eyes were swollen from all the crying. I didn't know what to do besides hug her and thank God that Tone wasn't like Joe.

Before I knew it, Tone was living at my house with the girls and me. Everything was wonderful at first. We were eating out every day, and Tone was spoiling the girls rotten. I didn't work as much because Tone was taking care of it all.

"Shorty, you don't need to work today. Stay here with the girls. Okay?"

I thought I was special.

"Here, you need some money or something? Take the kids shopping today and to the movies." He pulled out of his jeans about six hundred dollars for me to spend.

You couldn't tell me nothing. I had everything, and the girls did too. Designer clothes flooded my closet. Minks, rabbits, and Coogie sweaters and dresses were all I had. He bought me a few pair of gator sandals for the summer. He even caught my car payment up for me.

I had no worries until Brandy found a box full of guns and some plastic baggies full of dope in my bedroom closet!

"Mommy! What's this?" she said, holding the box, walking down the steps with Brea behind her.

"What's what?" I said. I was in the kitchen cooking dinner. I came in the living room and looked in the box. My eyes were so big and I began to shake all over. "Put that down, Brandy, now! Go upstairs to your room!" I screamed.

"Why, Mommy, what's wrong? Are these real guns, Mommy? Did Tone bring them here?"

I didn't know what to say to her interrogating me besides, "GO UPSTAIRS!" I walked to the kitchen, took the phone off the wall next to the fridge, and dialed Tone's cell.

"Hello, Tone? What were you thinkin' leaving a box of guns and some dope in my house? Come and get them now!" I hung up the phone and began to cry.

How could I have gotten myself in this one? This was bad, real bad! And I knew it. I didn't know what to do. My baby just found the most deadly thing she could have ever gotten her hands on, and it was in her own house! Our house was supposed to be safe for my kids, not hurt them. What if she would have pulled the trigger? Or what if she had put that dope in her mouth? She could have been hurt or hurt somebody!

A few minutes later, I could hear Tone's radio in his Mercedes before I saw him pull up. The music was so loud, and I knew my neighbors hated it.

His tires screeched when he stopped. He got out of the car and ran in the house. I was furious! I wanted to smack him in the face. He was hiding criminal things in my house without my knowledge. He put my daughters and me in danger.

When he came in the door, I began screaming at him. "You put us in danger! What were you thinkin' bringing that stuff in here? Are you crazy, Tone?"

He was standing there trying to touch me and hug me, grabbing on me, but I kept pushing him back.

Brandy came down the stairs and said, "Get out, Tone! Don't touch my mommy!"

He looked at me, hid his face in his hands and said, "I'm sorry, so sorry. Listen to me, Rach. That's Joe's stuff. He asked me to hold it for a day. Just until tomorrow." His voice was low, like he had lost his best friend.

"Brandy, go upstairs." She ran up the stairs. I figured I would deal with her later.

I turned around, looked at Tone, shook my head, and said, "You have to leave. You put us in danger. I can't allow you to do that. Brandy is only nine years old and seeing all this. I can't have that, Tone."

He grabbed his bag from the closet and left.

But Tone wouldn't disappear that easy. He called and brought gifts to the house. He even sent me two dozen red roses to my job with a card attached that read: I'M SORRY.

A couple of weeks went by, and then he was calling me every night, saying, "Rachael, I miss you. You my family now, you know. I need you, shorty."

The next day, he showed up at the salon. "I miss you." He

looked so pitiful. My heart was melting for him all over again.

After all, he made a mistake. Look at how many mistakes Denny made and I took him back, I thought. He was so sexy, standing there with the right way to say something, and the right stand and body language.

I gave in. "Well, Tone, you need to apologize to the girls first."

"Okay, I'll do that."

That was all it took. He was back in my house within a couple of weeks of the incident.

Tone would carry anywhere from two to three hundred grand in cash on the airplane with him. He would leave me with five or six hundred dollars when he made his bi-weekly trips to New York to re-up. I would shop the whole time he was gone and never pay a bill. But I still wasn't happy.

"Fear and the pit and snare are upon you, O inhabitant of the earth."—Isaiah 24:17.

I was caught up with one of the biggest drug dealers in Columbus, Ohio at this time. I put my daughters, myself and any and everybody in direct contact with me in danger. I never thought about someone coming in the house to rob him or kill him. Bottom line, he was deadly! Anything could have happened. God protects us when our minds can't get clear thoughts. I praise Him for His mercy because we sit and complain about our lives when He's up day and night keeping us safe from the mistakes we make on a daily basis. And there were plenty more mistakes I would make.

Chapter 16

Spinning

My life was in total chaos. Everything was out of control when Momma called one day and decided to come up for a visit. It was so early in the morning when she called. I turned and looked at the clock; it was 6:30 in the morning. I answered the phone and in a whisper said, "Hello."

"Hey, baby, what ya doin'?"

"Sleep!"

"Oh, I'm sorry, baby. I wanted to tell you I was on my way up there. I should be there within an hour."

Momma never asked to come up; she just told me she was coming. "Okay, I'll see you in a little while. The door is unlocked. Be careful." I yawned, dropped the phone and shouted, "Ugh!"

I stretched my legs to the ceiling then jumped out of the bed to go unlock the door for Momma. After I did that, I went back to bed. I woke back up about one in the afternoon to the kids screaming and Momma yelling.

"Rachael, come down here and eat some lunch!"

"I don't want nothing," I said. "I'm trying to sleep. I'm

tired. Shoot!" I had gone to the club the night before and got in about three that morning.

"Mommy, Grandma is here," the girls called. They loved their grandmother. When she came up, all I had to do was supply them with money and she did the rest. I liked it, but Momma was so nosey, snoopin' through all my stuff all the time. It made me sick. Not only that, but she found out stuff that I didn't want her or anybody else to find out.

"Why all my papers out?" I asked her one day when I found her snooping all through my stuff.

She was standing there with a piece of paper in her hand, the other hand on her hip, looking at me. "Rachael, what did you do? Huh?" She shook the piece of paper at me. "You put that car in Crystal's name? She don't know you did that. What you do that for? You a mess." She reached down and picked up my lease. "You done put this place in her name too. What's wrong with you?"

I just stood there and looked at her. I couldn't believe she would go through my stuff. She was always into something. I knew she probably had called Crystal and told her about her findings. Everything was out in the open, and in many ways, I was relieved. It was all out; no more lying and swindling. I had to face the truth, but I was glad the charade was finally over. No more sneaking around. Who I was and what I did was no longer secret. And it was no longer a secret that I couldn't be trusted.

"But cursed be the deceiver."—Malachi 1:14.

I'd just gotten home from work with a bag full of groceries and the girls were still in the car sleeping when I heard the phone ringing inside the apartment. I rushed to open the door, thinking it was Tone making his nightly call while he was in New York. However, I was surprised to hear a woman with a strong New York accent on the other end.

"Rachael?" the female voice said.

"Yes?" I said softly, trying to figure out who she was.

"Hi. My name is Carmen. I'm Tone's wife."

I was dumbfounded. "What did you say?"

"I said this is Tone's wife in New York!"

I held the phone a minute then said, "Yeah, right. Don't call here with that mess. I ain't trying to hear it."

I didn't believe her because I could hear Tone in the background, yelling, "Rach, don't listen to her. Don't listen to her, shorty. She lying! Yo, hang up on her!" So that's what I did—hung up! Two minutes later, Tone was walking down the streets of New York on his cell, trying to explain.

"Baby, I stopped over there to do business, that's all. She's our connect to the main dope man. I don't see her no more. She's my ex. We were never married, though. She's lying."

That was all I needed to hear. Besides, he was right in her face telling me to hang up. Who would let someone talk to them like that? But I would soon find out how easy it is to let a man talk to you like that!

Tone began to butter me up and say, "Baby, when I get back from up North, I'll have somethin' nice for you."

I was excited. I couldn't wait until he came back. It didn't matter about the other woman. I just knew I wouldn't let him treat me like that. I promised myself that I would keep the upper hand in the relationship. Truth be told, I was just using him anyway.

I never knew when Tone was coming back from New York. He would just say, "Soon. I'll be back soon." He never had me pick him up from the airport because he brought dope back with him. He would come in the house and strip down. It tripped me out when I saw how he was dressed underneath his college-look disguise. Underneath his preppy jeans and shirt, he wore leggings that were close to his skin, almost like a thick pair of tights. And under there, he stuffed all types of big baggies with dope in them, taped to his arms, legs and chest. He had dope all over his body! So, one of his boys picked him up from the airport. I figured he didn't want me to get caught if he ever was stopped. But the truth is, he didn't trust me, and probably thought, *What if she brings the police with her?* I did take him, though.

What attracted me to him was that he made me feel like the only woman on the planet in his eyes. Tone knew how to make me feel special. The things he said and did, no one else had ever done for me. If I didn't want to move, I didn't have to. He made sure everything was done for me. Whether Tone was paying someone to clean up the apartment or taking my car to be serviced, I never had to ask. I didn't have to worry about food or paying a babysitter or a single bill. He took care of it all. Tone was a man. He was a few years older than I was, and I assumed that's why he was so mature. Tone appreciated me—that's what it was, appreciation.

I was at the house watching TV when the phone rang and I answered. It was Tone. "What's up beautiful?"

"Hey! What's up?" I smiled immediately and played with the phone cord.

"What you up to, beautiful?" he said.

"Watching TV and polishing my toes;" I said with a big smile on my face. He made me feel secure. I didn't have to tell him what I needed or wanted; he just provided it, and I loved that.

"When you coming back?" I said. Before I could get it out of my mouth, he was standing in my bedroom door. He scared me. I jumped up and yelled, "You play too much!" I was on the bed, but my knees were bent. "What you got for me?"

"Quit playin'. I ain't have time to stop and get nothing." He was smiling, standing there looking like a big teddy bear.

"I forgot to bring you something." He was smiling and laughing as he held on to me with a big hug.

I sat down on the bed, folded my hands, closed my eyes and pretended to be mad at him, but I knew he had something. He always brought me something.

"Quit actin' like that. You know I brought you somethin'! Quit playin' wit' me." He would dangle it in front of me, pull it out from behind his back, depending on what he had. I would take it out of his hand, put my arms around his neck, and kiss him. I really thought I had something special.

After a couple of months of pure bliss, trouble started to brew. Tone started letting his true colors show. He was filled with jealousy and control. Tone was doing so much for me and the girls that I started depending on him. That's where he got me. Everything we did, he planned. He told me when to go to work and what time I needed to be back to the house.

"Rach, you don't need to be out like that. Go get the girls from the babysitter's and come right back." He would sit in the house with the house full of his dudes from New York, smoking weed, listening to music and playing that stupid video game.

Everyone was worried about me. And because I did that stupid plot on my sister and cousin, they weren't coming around. I was completely alone, except for the girls and Tone.

After he got comfortable and knew I wasn't going anywhere, Tone started hanging out all the time. It was a lot of his dudes down here in Columbus that were from New York. They all came from such a big, fast-paced city that they thought that anyone from Columbus was slow. Tone thought he could get over on anybody, and usually did. He got over on me.

Tone started staying out later every night, and eventually he stopped coming in until morning. I woke up about 5:00 A.M. one morning and noticed he wasn't home. I looked at the clock and wiped my eyes and thought, *Here I go again. Same thing, different man.* I grabbed the phone and dialed his number.

"Tone! Where you at?"

"Beautiful . . . I'll be there in a minute," he replied as if everything was everything.

"Tone, what's up? Why you ain't here?"

He wrestled with somebody in the background, saying, "Shhh." I imagined him putting his finger over his mouth. "Hold on, Rach." I heard a lot of movement then a door shut. It was quiet.

"Rachael, shorty, I'll be there in a few, okay? I got caught up wit' Joe and them. Forgive me, babe. I'm on my way."

I had experienced this so many times before with Denny, so I already knew he was cheating. I decided I wouldn't get mad. I would just count my losses and keep it movin'. We had only been seeing each other for about five months. It wasn't a big deal. *It was good while it lasted,* is how I chopped it up to be.

I knew I was depending on Tone to keep me company, so I decided to liberate myself by going to the club.

"Are y'all goin' out tonight?" I said to the females I worked with.

Desiray turned from curling her client's hair and said, "What, you goin' out? I thought you were on lockdown. What happened to New York this and New York that?" She was trying to be funny. She was just mad she didn't have nobody, so I knew she was hatin'.

I laughed at her, turned, and said, "Anyway . . . what's up for tonight?"

"I'm wit' it," Toya said.

"All right, ladies. I'm going to the mall to get something cute to wear." I unplugged my hair stove and headed out to prepare for my night out at the club. I knew this would make Tone sweat. He went to the club every night to hustle and get money from his employees, so I knew I would run into him. I couldn't wait.

I went to the mall and brought the flyy-est little outfit I could find. It was white pants with the jacket to match, and underneath it was a pretty little rhinestone bebe tank. Tone loved the way I dressed; after all, he taught me how. I knew he was gonna like the classy, elegant-but-sexy look.

I packed the girls up and took them to the sitter's for the night then drove to the club with Toya. Ashley's was always bumpin'. It wasn't real ghetto in the club, but had ghetto folk up in there.

Toya and I went in the club and headed straight to the bar to get a drink. I didn't really like to drink. I always hated the way it tasted, but I wanted to be out of my mind, so I drank and smoked weed. The only time I didn't smoke weed was when I worked or when I was with the girls. I never thought that there was something wrong with getting high because it was "only" weed. Boy, was I wrong.

After I was feeling good, I wanted to dance. Dancing always freed me. On the floor, it was just me and the music, moving to the sound and beat. I ran into one of Denny's old teammates. I was walking by him coming off the dance floor.

"Rachael Calhoun? Dang, baby, you look nice." He was turning me around in circles like he was my dance partner twirling me.

I laughed. "Orlando Smith. Oh, my goodness. It's been a long time."

"Give me a hug, girl." We hugged.

"So, what you doing now? I heard you and Denny split."

I nodded. "Yes."

"You wanna dance, Rachael?" I agreed, so we went to the dance floor.

"Mm-mm-mm, Denny blew it. I can't believe he let you go. You should let me take you out."

Yeah right, I thought. *He's off the hook. Denny would kill us both if he ever thought I kicked it with one of his boys.* I smiled.

As we danced, Tone came in the club. I could see who was coming in from the mirror on the dance floor, and I had a perfect view of the door. I saw him looking around. He had his hands in his pockets, and his face looked like the cold wind was blowing on it. I watched him as he looked around the club, stopping in the middle and watching everyone. People were walking up to him, but he kept looking around. He saw me, and our eyes met. He came straight over to the dance floor.

"Yo, Rach, I ain't playin' wit' ya. You need to get off the floor now."

"What you mean? I can dance if I want to. You ain't my momma!" He was making me mad. Who did he think he was talking to? He walked past Orlando and came up real close to intimidate me. "You want me to bust yo' head open with this bottle?" He held his beer bottle up that his dude had handed him when he came in. "Get off the floor. I ain't playin' wit' you!"

He was on fire at me. I didn't know what he was capable of doing, so I immediately left the club and went straight to the house, thinking, *Maybe this wasn't a good idea after all.* About ten minutes later, Tone was coming through the door.

"Word, if you ever disrespect me again, on my mother, I will kill you! You understand? Yo, I ain't playin' with you. Don't leave this house until I say so!" He was so close to my face that I could smell the beer on his breath and feel his breath as he screamed at me. I closed my eyes, grabbed my head, and trembled. I was scared.

"Okay? You hear me? Answer me!" The whole time he screamed, he had me pinned to the wall, with his hand wrapped around my throat. All I could think was, *How did I get myself in this? Better yet, how am I going to get myself out of it?*

Joe would always just show up right on time. He would eventually stop Tone from killing me on several occasions. I can recall when Tone and I argued one day, probably about some chick, when Tone picked up his 9mm and pointed it at my head. Joe stepped in between the gun and my head and pulled me in the bathroom. Yeah, it was serious! I had a lunatic on my hands. I was miserable, yet I had gotten what I asked for—to be a baller's girl.

"O Lord, you brought my soul up from the grave; You kept me alive, that I should not go down to the pit."—Psalms 30:3.

Chapter 17

He's Gonna Kill You!

I started keeping the kids at the babysitter's house because I never knew what Tone was going to do next. He had guns, dope and lots and lots of money stashed at my house. He would drop me off at work, he would bring me lunch, and when it was time to get off work, he would be there to pick me up. I was in a prison once again!

Joe's new girlfriend, Tammy, and I become real cool. We would sit, smoke weed and talk about Tone and Joe all the time. It seemed like someone had sucked both of our brains out of our head or something. Who was I? Was I coming back? I thought it was cute to have a major drug lord. Everybody knew who he was, everyone knew he had money, and I was his girl. I could get shoes, boots, and outfits whenever I wanted, and in my house, I had the nicest furniture and a big screen television. I thought I had it all. See, that's what was important to me at the time—material things.

I felt as long as I dressed my daughters like little doll babies then my job as a mother was done. I was wrong! My daughters suffered, I suffered, and everything I gained from the relationship was lost or tore up before me and Tone parted ways. Material things are nothing! However, the lives of my children were so much more valuable than I could have ever imagined.

As a parent, I needed to understand the importance of who I had around my children. I needed to understand they needed spiritual knowledge about Christ, and an education. If we don't understand those things, we can lose our children to drugs, the streets, sex . . . and let's not forget violence. Someone has to lead the way for them, and if parents can't be free from their own lives that haunt them in the night, in the day, and all the time, then the devil wins! He already thinks he has us bound. He made an impression in our lives, and we can't come out of it. Now he's going after our children with the same patterns—the same self-destructive patterns that we fell victim to.

I had to wake up and let God break those chains, so my babies and me could be free! It's a vicious cycle Satan sets us up with, but the devil is a liar! God can free us from anything. He will come in and get us out of that cell! When He comes for you, you can hear Him walking. You hear the keys jingling, and the door on your prison cell flies back. You hear Him say, "Get out! You are free!" Whomever God sets free is free indeed! Remember that. Nobody can beat or battle with God. He wins every time.

"Shake yourself from the dust, arise; Sit down, loose yourself from the bonds of your neck, O captive daughter of Zion."—Isaiah 52:2.

Tone started messing around and I was mad. I wasn't mad he was seeing someone else. I was mad he wouldn't stay over there with her. Why wouldn't he leave? I would ask myself. However, in reality, I was scared. I never said a word to try to put him out.

One day, we were over at his friend's house for a cookout and he started talking about all his other females. He was trying to talk slick in front of his friends. He didn't know I was listening.

I thought to myself, *I'm leaving him here. He gets on my nerves!*

He was standing there around a crowd of dudes, being the center of attention, with his shirt tied around his head, laughing and motioning with his hands. They were all laughing at him.

I got in the rental and told him in front of everybody just how sorry he was. "You tired and lame! Find yo' own way back home." As I was talking, I was trying to put the car in reverse and take off, but he got to the car before I could do all of that. I saw him coming and knew he was gonna throw the beer bottle he had in his hand.

CRASH! went the glass in the window. I watched the bottle in slow motion hitting the glass. I closed my eyes. He yanked me out the busted window by my hair! I was screaming and shouting, "Stop! Let me go!"

He said, "Don't ever disrespect me! I'll kill you!" He picked me up by my neck and carried me over to the garage in anger.

I had my hands around his, trying to loosen his grip around my neck. My heart was beating fast and I was scared!

Joe came running over to protect me, but the other guys thought it was funny. They were saying, "Joe, forget her, man. She deserves it. She dissed him! Man, don't get in that. Yo, she deserves it, Joe. She shouldn't have done that." Joe ignored them and still came to my rescue.

When Joe reached Tone, he swung at his arms, and I was able to get loose. I ran down the street, crying and terrified. I couldn't believe this was my reality.

I remember talking to myself. "What's wrong with me? I need help!" It was late. It had to be midnight or close to it, and here I was walking in a neighborhood I knew nothing about. I looked down at my legs and saw the blood from where the glass had cut my legs. It was summer, so I had on shorts. All I was thinking about was my daughters; how I was letting them down. I couldn't bring them home. Tone had to go!

When I looked up, Tone and Joe were following me with the car. I started crying and screaming more. "Get away from me! I hate you!"

Tone got out of the car and said, "Get in the car! Yo, I ain't playin' with you! You gonna make me hurt you, Rachael! You stupid. I'll bash your head in! Get in the car, stupid!"

I was backing up, saying, "No," and crying hysterically. I tried to run, but he caught me.

"Get in the car, Rach. Don't make me chase you."

I knew he was mad. I could see it on his face. His nose was flaring out and he was breathing heavy. He had his chest sticking out and his back straight. This man was serious and I was frightened. I knew it was a possibility that he could really hurt me when he was angry. I tried to run, but he caught me. He picked me up and put me in the car. Joe drove off with me and Tone in the back seat.

Tone sat there looking over at me like I was stupid. He said, "You know I didn't hit you. I just pulled you. Don't diss me in front of my boys no more. I don't like that." He sucked his teeth and continued. "You must be crazy!"

I didn't say anything. I knew it was better to be quiet. I didn't want his rage to come back. All the way to the house, he rubbed my thigh where the glass scraped it, saying, "I'm sorry."

When I woke up the next day, he had been to the mall to buy me a pair of one-carat diamond studs. The diamonds were sitting on my nightstand, and Tone was sitting in the chair across from my bed, watching me.

"I wanna take you and the girls out tonight. Go get them." He never smiled or anything; just sat there and watched me. Finally, he spoke again. "Rachael, why you so crazy? Why you make me act like that toward you last night? I don't like doin' that to you." He pointed toward my legs.

I just looked at him, never saying a word.

"And why the girls always gone?" he mumbled.

I lay there. My body ached from the night before when he yanked me out of the window and tried to choke me to death. I put my hand under my pillow and caught a quick glimpse of the bruises on my right arm. I tucked them under the pillow to hide it even from myself. I didn't want to remember what had taken place the night before.

I couldn't tell Tone I didn't want my kids around him, so I just told him that they liked playing with the other kids over at the sitter's. But all along, my daughters were begging me to come and get them. I knew they were safer where they were than with me.

I remember waking up often in the middle of the night, wondering if they were okay. I would cry because I didn't want that for my daughters. I wanted them to be with me, but I knew I was in a bad situation and couldn't bring them home to it.

I'd sneak out of bed, watch Tone as he snored. and tiptoe to their bedroom so I wouldn't disturb him. I'd sit there on Brandy's bed and bawl my eyes out thinking about my babies and the choices I was making. I didn't know who to turn to or how to get out of this cage I was in. I felt trapped with no way out. I wanted so much to change and start over, but I didn't know how.

Eventually, I got the strength to tell Tone that I wanted him to leave. I spoke to Joe first because I knew he would try to make Tone understand. And Joe knew how to keep Tone calm, for the most part.

"Joe, I need you to make Tone understand that we need to go our separate ways. I'm scared he'll hurt me if I tell him." I had tears coming down my cheeks, and then I said, "He's crazy, Joe. Please help me."

"Okay, Rach, I will. Just don't cry. Girl, you'll be all right."
Joe grabbed me and gave me a hug. "I'll talk to him tonight,
Rach."

I felt a sense of relief. Joe kept his word. "Man, you gonna
hurt that girl," Joe told Tone. "Leave her alone, man. You
gonna end up doing somethin' to her."

Tone took heed of his friend's words and packed up his
things and left. I was so relieved, but at the same time, lonely.
Brea's birthday came and I was broke; no child support had
ever come from Denny. He always thought of his own needs
over the girls. Denny had always been like that.

As time has gone by, I realized that he treats them like that
because he fought me on having them. It's really too bad for
the people who don't see their own children. They have no
idea what they're missing!

All I had was Tone to call for help. I called him, and of
course, he was on his way. When I opened the door for him,
he had a big cake and some money in his hand for Brea. His
eyes lit up when he saw me. He said, "Let's go celebrate," as
if nothing had happened between us.

Once we broke the ice between us, Tone sat on the couch
and told me everything that had gone on at my apartment
since the day he had been gone. He knew what kind of cars
were parked in front of my apartment. He knew when I was
at work and when I left. He knew every move that my daughters and I made.

I sat there and held hands with him while he talked, thinking it was sweet and cute that he had still been so concerned
about me. However, it was crazy. In all actuality, he was stalking me!

I dropped Tone off at the airport a couple of days later.
He leaned over to kiss me and said, "Rach, Joe and Tammy
comin' up North in a few days to put Joe's car in the garage.
I want you to ride wit' them."

Tone had always talked about taking me to New York, but

we hadn't been yet. I knew this was his way to say sorry for pulling me out the window.

"Okay. I'll be ready."

"Good, I wanna take you around the city and show you a good time. Is that all right wit' you?" He poked out his lips and closed his eyes so I would kiss him.

"Yeah, that's fine," I said, giving him a kiss.

I was so excited about my first trip to New York. When we got there, Tone was waiting. He got in the car and gave me a big kiss, smiling with those dimples.

"Where we goin', Joe?" Tone asked. He sat in the back with me and put his arm around my neck. "What you been doin'? Huh?"

I smiled at him but didn't say a word.

"Man, I'm hungry. Let's go to the pizza joint," Joe said.

The pizza joint was down the street from the projects in Jamaica, Queens, where we had picked up Tone. It took us all of five minutes to get there. While Joe was dipping in and out of the traffic, I was thinking, *I thought Tone said he lived downtown in a condominium. Why we got to stay at the hotel then? Why he in the projects staying?* I wondered all of this but never uttered a word.

All of a sudden, Tone's phone started going crazy. He wouldn't answer it at first, but it kept ringing and ringing and ringing. He finally answered it while rubbing my neck.

"Yeah!"

I could hear a female on the other end; I pulled away from him.

"Yo! I'll be right back." He hung up.

I looked at him and rolled my eyes. He grabbed me and pulled me closer. I was wondering what was going on.

Ring, ring, ring! He didn't answer it.

The car stopped at the pizza place, and they hurried us in and out, trying to get us out of that hood as fast as they could.

* * *

When I met Tone, I figured out quick that he was lying about his name. I knew it wasn't Tone. One thing I had done a long time ago was go through his wallet and get his social security number, his real name and his address in New York. I told one person where I put the information. and that was Renee, my friend from Dayton. I put the information in one of my pants pockets; in some jeans that hung in my closet. Tone excited me by his lifestyle, but I knew to be certain that if he ever did something to me and I couldn't tell it, then someone would know where and who he really was.

Ring, ring, ring!

I was now getting irritated by his phone. He was too. He looked at me, put his finger to his lips and said, "Ssshhh!"

Then he answered, "Yo, babe, I'll be back in a minute. I told you I had to handle some business wit' Joe. Somethin' real quick." He hung up.

Now I knew something was going on. He called her babe. I was his babe, his shorty, his boo. What was this about? I wondered.

"Rach, I need to tell you something."

"I'm listening," I replied.

Joe and Tammy had gotten out of the car so Joe could show her downtown New York. We stayed in the car. Tone got in the driver's seat and drove around for a little while.

"Rach, the woman that called you a while back is my girl here in New York."

Oh my God, I couldn't believe it. The chick that called all those months ago and told me that she was Tone's wife really was his wife. I felt so stupid. I thought she was lying because he was telling me to hang up on her and dissin' her so hard, but she was telling the truth. I felt like a fool. I was a fool.

I asked him, "Is she your wife? You married, Tone?"

"Nah, I ain't married to her, but we been together for a long time. I'm not wit' her like that, though, Rach, for real.

I'm with you. Look at me. I need you to believe me." He pulled over, grabbed my arm and said, "She's our connect for the dope. That's all. That's why I ain't left her."

I dropped my head. "I trusted you and you lied, Tone. I let you hit me and pull guns on me and you got a woman? I'm just a fling." I hit him in the back of the head and kicked the driver's side seat with my feet.

"Okay, ma, I deserve that."

I never said a word. He kept looking back at me in the rearview mirror to see what I was going to say. "Why you mad? Huh?" Tone said. "I be with you more than her. She hooks us up with our connect."

I turned away from him and stared out the window while he continued to confess. I decided I was going to enjoy my trip. I said nothing else about her to Tone. We ended up in the middle of Times Square and I hopped out of the car.

Tone pulled over and hollered, "Wait, Rachael. You don't know these people."

I stopped and waited for him, and we walked around. I still had an attitude with him, but I felt like I was free, though. Why should I let him turn me out and I ain't even his main chick? I decided that from that moment on, no matter what he did to me, I was going to fight him and show him I who I was. He couldn't turn me out no more—at least not without a fight.

I was amazed at the buildings in New York; the Twin Towers, Times Square, the Statue of Liberty. Everything was so nice . . . just like on TV. And there were people everywhere, coming and going.

Every few minutes, Tone's phone rang. It rang constantly until he said, "Rach, you gotta go home." My mouth dropped. He called Joe on the phone and found out where they where, grabbed me by my hand and walked back toward the car.

We went and picked Joe and Tammy up, and Tone said,

"Joe, take me back to Jamaica." He was angry, and I knew he was going to do something to her.

"I'm gonna beat that witch up when I get there," Tone said to Joe.

"Man, don't do it," Joe said.

Tone turned to me before getting out of the car, and whispered in my ear, "You know I love you and only you, right?" He was holding me real tight. I didn't want to answer him, but he squeezed tighter and tighter.

"Yes, Tone." I had tears coming down my face. He scared me. I could feel the anger and was scared for the woman because I didn't know what he was really capable of doing.

"That's my girl. I'll see you tomorrow."

We dropped him off. I told Tammy and Joe that I was through with Tone when we got home. That was the last straw. They just shrugged it off, thinking I was just talking, but I was serious. I was tired of him beating on me. I was tired of him and tired of myself acting stupid.

Tone came the day after with a gift. I was very upset and the gift wouldn't work this time. I wanted out. I knew there was no future for Tone and me.

Joe, Tammy and Tone made plans for us to go to the movies when Tone returned. They swung by and picked me up after picking him up from the airport. I ran out to the car with my head covered with a jacket because it was pouring down raining.

I looked in the car and Tone said, "Rach, you drive." He was sitting in the back seat with Joe. They probably were planning their next illegal act back there. I was still furious with him for all the drama he had caused me. It wasn't just the female in New York, but it was everything. I had let this monster terrify and beat me repeatedly, and now I was fed up.

We were on the freeway when I decided to call a friend of mine. I watched the road and turned the windshield wipers up. *It's storming pretty bad*, I thought. I picked up the cell phone on the seat between me and Tammy. Toni Braxton was on the radio singing, "Seven whole days."

I was gassed up, ready to explain myself to Tone. I held the phone and listened while it rang.

Hello," a voice answered. It was an older woman on the other end.

"Hello, is Ben there?"

"He's not here. Would you like to leave a message?"

"Can you tell him Rachael called?"

"Okay, I will."

"Thank you. Good-bye," I replied. I pressed END and smiled.

Tone rose up in the back seat and said, "Yo! Who you ask for?"

"Why?" I asked him. I was hurt and wanted him to understand he wasn't the only man in the world that wanted me. Unfortunately, the next several minutes didn't go according to the way I had planned.

"Who you ask for, Rachael?" His voice was getting powerful and bold.

I chickened out. "I asked for Toya!"

He grabbed his cell phone—the one back in the day with the big battery on the back—and slapped me across the face with it as I was driving in the storm. Joe and Tammy were shocked and trying to keep him calm. The car swerved all over the freeway for a minute, but I prayed I wouldn't lose control. He was trying to come across the seat.

"I'm gonna kill you!" he screamed. There was so much commotion in the car. Joe was in the back seat trying to pin him down. He was going crazy! Tammy was helping Joe. Everyone in the car besides Tone was scared. After all, I was the one driving the car on the freeway doing about seventy-five miles per hour!

By the time I reacted and went to feel my eye, my face was swollen. I had a knot the size of a lemon above my eye. I tried to keep cool and think what my next move would be.

Tone was screaming, "Get off the freeway! I'm gonna kill you! I'm gonna kill you! Pull over! Pull over!"

I was ducking down while he was trying to hit me from the back seat. I kept saying, "Okay, okay, I will, Tone. Give me a minute to get off the road. I will, Tone."

Joe and Tammy were still holding him back, trying not to get hit by his fury. I was trying to think fast, and then it came to me. The entire time I was driving, he was screaming, "Get off the freeway! Pull over! I'm gonna kill you!"

I pulled off the freeway and went down Morse Road. When I got to Karl Road, I started driving very slowly. I went slow enough to jump out right in front of the police station. My thoughts were on saving my life, not Joe and Tammy, who were left behind in a moving vehicle that nobody was driving! I didn't think. I knew he was going to hurt me, and I had to get away no matter what.

I ran in the police station for safety. I had enough of fighting. I had been fighting all of my life in one way or another. I was tired.

I opened the door inside the police station and ran through the doors. Everyone inside stopped what they were doing and looked at me. I didn't say a word. My heart was beating fast, but I decided right then that I couldn't be a snitch. So, before I was questioned about anything, I went back outside. I walked across the street to the Kroger's store and used the phone.

I got home late in the night. My friend, Anthony, came and picked me up from the police station.

"Hey, you okay?" he asked me.

"Yeah." I didn't even want to look at him, because I knew he was staring at my swollen eye. It was out there. He could see it a mile away. It was turning black and blue underneath. I looked at my face the whole ride to my house in the mirror above the visor.

"Dang, Rach. Look at yo' eye. Why you foolin' wit' that dude?" He was upset. Anthony and I had had an on-again off-again relationship ever since Denny and I had broken up. It was some sort of horrible soul-tie I knew nothing about.

Anthony was handsome; tall, cocoa brown with curly hair. He was muscular and loved fast cars. He was pretty cool.

"You gonna be all right?" Anthony asked me, then he lifted his shirt and showed me his gun tucked in the front of his jeans.

I looked at him and said, "No, you don't need that." I was tired of this life. It wasn't for me; the playas and the dope game wasn't for me. I didn't like the violence.

"If he comes at me, Rach, I'm tellin' you right now, I'm gonna pop him! I ain't playin' wit' him!" Anthony was a good guy gone bad. He was intelligent, but used his intellect for evil.

He pulled up to the apartments and asked, "You sure you don't want to stay wit' me tonight?"

I smiled a little, looked at him and said, "No. I'll be okay here."

"All right. Call me if you need me."

I walked off, never turning around, and said, "Bye, Anthony." I heard him rev up his engine in his brand new convertible Mustang then disappear. I walked in the apartment with a surety that Tone wasn't coming. The one thing that man was terrified of was the police.

After a couple of days, he was calling me again, but I was through. I couldn't take any more of his drama. I was only twenty-five. I was too young for this mess.

I remember picking up Brandy and Brea, and Brandy touching my face softly, and looking into my eyes with her warm brown eyes. She asked me, "What happened to your face, Mommy? Who hurt your eye? Did Tone do that?"

I lied to my daughter. I looked at her and lied. I could see Brea standing behind her, and both of them were scared and concerned for their mommy, wondering who could do this to her.

I lied and said, "I hit it on the door." What a lame excuse! Why do we believe that people will believe those types of lines? A door can't give you a black, swollen eye! A fist would have to do that. I needed to face my realities and deal with them—or better yet, let Christ deal with them. We can't help ourselves out of situations like that. We might get out of them sometimes, but we really need Christ to come and heal those wounds. Truly, that's what we need.

I tried to get it together. I started back working, even with a black eye. I said to myself, "Hold your head up. You will survive this. You've survived worst." I bathed and pampered myself in all the clichés.

I needed to do what I could to take care of the girls and myself, so I kept on working, doing what I had to do. But would it ever be enough?

Chapter 18

He Had a Gun to My Back

After getting the girls home and on a stable schedule, we decided to cook dinner. We cooked spaghetti. That was my babies' favorite. We talked and played games and read for a while, but the telephone kept ringing. Brea asked me if I was going to answer it. I didn't want to, but I didn't want the girls to be scared. They had already been through so much in the past few weeks.

The next time it rang, I looked at it for a minute and then finally answered. It was Tone and some chick on the phone, playin', telling me that she was his new chick. I went upstairs with the phone so the girls wouldn't be worried or hear the conversation.

"Look, you better leave me alone or I'll call your girl in New York and tell her everything." Then I shut my bedroom door and screamed, "Leave me alone!"

He laughed and said to the chick, "Baby, she lying. That's why I left her."

I couldn't believe he was playing on my phone like this. What was he doing? I hung up the phone. About fifteen minutes later, they called back, laughing and acting silly.

"Tone, you're disturbing the girls with yo' foolishness. Please don't call here." I hung up again.

I wanted Tone to disappear, stop all this nonsense, but he wouldn't. He kept calling all night long, until finally I was forced to call New York. I had the number in the same pair of jeans I had all of his information in.

The phone rang, and I was nervous, wondering if she was gonna cuss me out or what. The woman from New York answered and said, "Hello."

When I heard her strong New York accent, I knew it was the same woman from before. I didn't know exactly what I was going to say to her, so I just said, "Hello, I'm calling from Columbus, Ohio."

She instantly said, "Rachael?"

"Yes."

"I've been trying to get in touch with you for months, ever since I called you that day."

All I could say was, "I should have listened to you."

She was so kind. She knew it was bad between Tone and me. I told her everything from beginning to end. She told me I needed to leave my apartment; that he was going to come after me. She explained that once he found out I had called her in New York, he was gonna want me dead.

I couldn't believe the mess I was in. Here I was walking around with a black eye and hiding out because Tone wanted me dead, and on top of all of that, he was already with another chick. I was losing it. And now I had his real chick on the phone, telling me to leave town. Problem was, I had nowhere to go. Where was I to go? Dayton? I couldn't go there because Tone would definitely come there looking for me. My only other option was to go to Philly or just stay in Columbus and deal with him.

I decided to stay and deal with him. I had enough with taking people's identities. I wasn't gonna take his money and run, even though I thought about it. Oh yeah, he had left three hundred thousand dollars in cash stacked at my house the night he hit me on the freeway. That just goes to show the lack of respect he had for me—he was calling me with another chick on the phone, but had three hundred thousand dollars in my possession. Believe me, I thought about taking his money and running, but I knew I would have to run for the rest of my life. I even packed my suitcase up with the money hidden underneath my clothes, but I knew I shouldn't do it. I couldn't do it.

I paced back and forth in my bedroom for hours, contemplating taking his money and starting life in a new city, but I decided in the end to return his money. Maybe that would soften him up.

I packed up my apartment and found a new place for me and my daughters. I stayed out of the way for about two weeks while I moved. I didn't communicate with anyone from work or any of my friends. I knew it was too dangerous. My daughters were scared because of all the drama that was goin' on. I had to make them stay away from the windows and get close to the ground in their bedrooms because I didn't know if Tone and his crew were coming to shoot up the place or what. I thought he was coming to get me! I knew he was coming, but I didn't know when. I didn't leave the girls at the babysitter's because he would have gone over there to get me. I had to keep the girls with me at all times. I was scared for our lives.

I spoke to Tone after the move, and sure enough, he had been looking for me. I told him I had his money. "I got your money, Tone."

"Yo, Rach, I've been lookin' for you for weeks. What's up? You playin' games?"

"No, Tone, it ain't like that. I want to meet you and give you your money."

"All right, sweetheart. Where? I'll be on my way. People

lookin' for me because I ain't gave them their dough. You trying to get me killed out here."

I knew I needed to give him his cash before he thought I ran off with it. I had taken some money out of the stacks he had. I used some of it to move, and I paid some bills. I even kept a little money so I would be ahead. I figured he would never know, and I reasoned with myself, saying, "He owes me anyway. All he put me through, I deserve this."

I went in the stacks, wrapped tight in Saran Wrap in his duffle bag in my closet and took the money out. I set it all on my bed and unwrapped four big stacks of money. I started taking the stacks and in different places, I pulled hundred-dollar bills out of the stack of money. I did this until I had about four or five thousand. I wanted to make sure I had enough to survive without ever having to call him or see him again. I wanted a fresh start with a push, just in case I even thought about going back because of his money. I didn't want him to ever get near me or my daughters again, and I felt like me taking a little of his cash would put me ahead. I knew he would never know.

Joe and Tammy were scared for me. Tone had told Joe he was gonna kill me as soon as he got his money. Joe tried to talk to him, but he said he was going to do me. For some reason, I wanted to be the one to give him his money. Joe offered to give it to him, but I told him that I'd do it myself. I didn't want it in anyone else's hands.

We met at a friend of mine's shop, Focus On U. I got there before Tone did and let everyone inside know to watch where I was at all times. "Please, do not let me out of your sight." I was so afraid, I trembled all over my body.

My friend told me, "Girl, relax. We won't let him touch you. It's almost over."

I heard her, but couldn't think of anything but the gun I knew Tone would be carrying. I had called his home in New

York and told his chick everything. I jeopardized him losing money, and now he was going to try to hurt me.

I saw him and Joe come in the door, and my heart dropped. Tone stood in the entrance of the shop with both of his hands in his hoodie pockets. I knew then he had his gun. My stomach was quivering and I felt sick, but I asked Jesus to help me.

Please! I want to live! I want to raise my kids! I don't want everybody to think they were right about my life. Please help me!

Tone looked at me with this look in his eyes and motioned me to come.

I stood up and walked toward him. I was so scared, all I could think was that I was almost out of this. It was going to be over.

When I reached Tone, he grabbed my arm and pulled me to him. He whispered in my ear and said, "I could kill you."

I backed away and he squeezed my arm tighter. I never said a word. I looked to see if anyone was watching, and they were. I felt a little better. He was behind me, talking in my ear.

"Why you call up North? Why you call her? I told you she don't mean anything! You messed up everything by calling New York. I can't get no dope. She called her connect and he won't sell to me now. I should kill you, splatter your head on one of these walls."

He was still behind me, as if he was hugging me. I could feel his hot breath in my ear as he whispered. I had my eyes shut tight, but I knew not to open my mouth.

Tone kept repeating himself, saying, "Why you call? You trying to destroy me? Huh? Answer me."

I was waiting for Joe to come and rescue me again, but he never did. He sat there this time and watched. I imagine he thought I was wrong for calling Tone's house too.

"You think you smart by having me come up in here? I'll kill you here. I don't care nothin' about these gutter rats."

He looked behind himself and then pushed me out the door.

I was now outside on the street and trying to get back to the door. I was terrified. I thought he was going to shoot me right there on Cleveland Avenue. He wouldn't let me near the door. Every time I walked over to it, he grabbed me.

"Stay away from the door, Rach. You ain't going back in there. Yeah, you stuck now." He was smiling a devious smile. "You outside now."

I started to run, but I knew he would shoot, so I stayed there and waited for him to pull the gun out and shoot. I didn't know what to do. All I knew was that he was going to kill me at any moment.

Suddenly, a couple of women inside came to the door. "You all right, girl? We called five-oh, and they'll be here in a minute!"

The one speaking was looking at Tone when she talked, to let him know she wasn't afraid of him. I nodded my head and they stood there. He was very, very upset, but I felt relief.

I told him, "Here's your money. Leave me alone!" I handed him his duffle bag.

"Baby, walk down the street with me so we can talk. You know it can't end this way. Let's talk a minute, Rach. You know I love you."

"No! I don't have anything else to say. Here's your money." I walked back in the shop and sighed. "It's over."

I just looked at him and thought, *Thank You, Lord, for getting me out of this.*

Seven years later, Tone was sentenced to prison for murdering his next live-in girlfriend here in Columbus, Ohio. I saw one of his friends and he told me that the girl stole Tone's money and so he killed her. When I couldn't see for myself how much trouble I was in, Jesus got me out of it. I feel bad for that woman that died, and her family, because I can only imagine the torture, physical abuse, and mental abuse she endured.

I thank God for saving me when I wouldn't do anything about my situation. Thank you, Jesus!

"And I have put My words in your mouth; I have covered you with the shadow of My hands, That I may plant the heavens, Lay the foundations of the earth, And say to Zion, 'You are My people.'"—Isaiah 51:16.

Interlude

Before I go any further, I must prepare some for what's to come and explain to others why I subjected myself to so much abuse. In the pages to come, the story I will tell will be the way it happened. The way I thought. There isn't very much explaining in it, and very little scripture, because that was the darkest my life had ever been. I couldn't explain it, nor could I have understood.

I didn't understand why I took the abuse when I was in the situations or wrote about them. See, I stayed because abuse was and *has been* all I have ever known. I thought I was supposed to stay. I had convinced myself things would get better sooner or later. I was wrong!

The devil had my mind in an amusement park, running through the park, getting on every ride there was, then eating and getting sick and dizzy! That's the way I look at it now. But the blood of Jesus! The mercy and grace, the love of Our Father kept me near even when I thought He was far!

Chapter 19

We Had Black Eyes in Common

My faithful customers were looking for me, while the others had moved on. When I came to work, I wore dark shades to cover my black eye, but everybody knew something was wrong. No one said anything, but I could hear them talking.

"She let Tone hit her in the eye. What's wrong with her? All for money. I wouldn't go through that for money. Can't no man put his hands on me. That's what she get . . . actin' all high and mighty."

I was embarrassed, but kept working. I wanted to stack up some money because I knew the little I had kept from Tone wasn't going to go a long way. I ignored their conversations. Besides, they all had been through something or other themselves. That's what gets me—everybody wants to talk and laugh, but we all had a time when we went through one thing or another that we aren't proud of.

Tammy stopped by to see if I was okay. "Girl, Tone's crazy. Don't talk to him when he starts calling again. Mm-mm-mm, I can't believe he did that to you. He needs to be ashamed of himself. That's jacked up what he did. Look at yo' face, Rachael."

Then she turned her head and looked at the others that were working. "I know they had a lot to say." Now her nose was frowned up. "He shouldn't have done that. Stay away from him. He's a sorry excuse for a man. I told Joe he better not ever try that crap on me."

I thought back as Tammy was still going on and on about Tone blacking my eye. I remembered him being on the bed with a gun in his hand one time. I was kneeling on the floor with my arms and hands folded on the bed, watching him play with his new toy. He was so intrigued by his weapon, holding it and pulling it out like the police do when they are in hot pursuit of a criminal. I watched him take the gun off safety, but realized he thought he had put it on safety.

I was gonna yell, "Be careful! You took it off the safety," but as my mouth was ready to say it, something told me not to say a word. I didn't, and right after that, he pulled the trigger and it busted my bedroom window out.

I was dumbfounded. All I could think of is if I had opened my mouth, he would have told me, "No, it's not. See . . ." and pointed it at me and pulled the trigger. God kept me silent!

"Do you hear me?" Tammy said.

I looked up, staring at her mocha-brown skin and her sparkling diamond ring that sat on her ring finger. Tammy had a beautiful pair of diamond stud earrings and a matching bracelet that sat on the opposite wrist from her Cartier watch. She was so lucky, I thought to myself, looking her up and down for a quick second.

I snapped back and said, "Yeah, I hear ya."

I was so troubled that water was getting on the floor and on my client's back as I washed her hair. "Oh, no. Lean back. You're getting wet!" The client was all in our conversation, and she didn't even realize she was getting wet.

Tammy ran her fingers through her layered hair, looked at herself in the mirror, pulled out her M.A.C. glaze lip-gloss, put it on, gave herself the once-over then said, "Girl, I'll see you later. Let me get home before Joe come lookin' for me."

"All right, girl. I'll see ya later." I said. As I watched Tammy saunter out the door, I wondered, *Did I make a mistake by leaving Tone and not giving him a second chance? Should I call him?*

I paused for a moment. "You must be out of your mind," I said aloud.

My client, Ms. Rose, sat up and asked what happened to my eye. Ms. Rose was a delight. She was a principal at one of the high schools, but was excited to be retiring that summer. She had a shoulder-length bob with layers cut throughout. Her hair was graying, but she kept sparkling wine hair color over the top to hide it. Ms. Rose had a wide nose and always was jazzy in dressing. Everything she wore, and her makeup, was done to perfection. She was around sixty-five, but you wouldn't know unless she shared it with you.

She grabbed my wrist and said, "You too young and beautiful to let some sorry man hit on your face. You understand me? Baby, you get yourself out of that."

I couldn't believe she called me beautiful because I didn't see myself like that.

"You hear me?" she continued. "Get away from him."

"Yes, ma'am. I did. I left him alone." I put my head down as I talked to her. If she would have said one more thing, I would have burst into tears right there in the salon in front of everyone.

"Rachael, line one," I heard someone say.

Ms. Rose paid and tipped me, and then I took the call. "Rachael speaking." It was Crystal. I hadn't spoken to her in months, since she'd found out about me stealing her identity.

"Hey, Rachael. What's up with you?"

"Oh, hey, Crystal." I closed my eyes, just happy to hear her voice. I loved her so much and missed her terribly. I regretted what I did and wished I could have done that whole day over.

"I just wanted to tell you I forgive you for putting the car and apartment in my name, and I won't be pressing any charges on you. Just pay for it, okay? I gotta go. Talk to you later."

I held the phone a few seconds and hung up, wishing she could help me out of my situation.

I sat at the desk for a few more minutes, counting the money I had made from the day and realizing money wasn't going to help me solve my many problems. I sat there with my elbow on the table and hands over my eyes, thinking about what Crystal said, but I didn't have the heart to tell her the car had been repossessed already, which destroyed her perfect credit. I was in over my head. When you do dirt, you bury yourself in it. All the evil things I had done were coming out.

I heard loud music outside the shop and looked up to see Peaches getting out of the champagne-colored Caddy truck with the rims still spinning. She went to the driver's side, gave the man a big kiss, reached for the wad of money he was dangling, smiled, and came into the salon.

Peaches was a young girl in the game. She was sweet, but slick, and learned a lot from the dudes in her hood. Peaches was about seventeen, but one would never know just by looking at her.

She came into the lobby. "Hi, Rachael. Is Samantha here? She supposed to do my hair today."

"Yeah, she's back there." I smiled. I couldn't help but watch her. She wore her house shoes in the shop with short-shorts and a tank top that showed her belly ring. Peaches had glitter coming from everywhere—on her shorts and tank, even in her layered ponytail holder. I guess you could say Peaches was an around-the-way girl. She was always in the salon getting her hair and nails done. When she came in the shop, you knew she had arrived, with all the loud talking and plenty of friends behind her.

Peaches was 4'9" and 120 pounds. The dudes in her neighborhood called her "tight fat," which meant her big curves didn't shake. She had a squeaky voice and a heart of gold. Her boyfriend was an older dope man that she had met in the neighborhood. She was bubbly, always smiling and happy. Her mother and her boyfriend would buy her everything she wanted, like shoes, clothes, jewelry, and purses. She was spoiled.

I walked to the back of the salon to clean my work area when she came over, saying, "Are you okay?"

I looked up at her while I was sweeping and said, "Yeah, I'll be all right."

I was tired and ready to go home, so I didn't feel like talking to her or anyone else. I wanted to go home and try to figure out my next move, but I noticed her left eye was black. It looked as if it was healing, but I could tell it was a black eye.

She saw me look at it and said, "Well, I walked into my door at home. That's what happened to my eye," she joked.

I looked at her, took my shades off, and said, "Yeah, right. Girl, you better face your reality. Just don't let it happen again. I don't intend on it happening to me again."

She shook her head up and down. "I'm not, I'm not."

That was the beginning of our friendship.

Over the years, Peaches and I did a lot of partying and talking about our continuous bad relationships with men. We leaned on each other and depended on each other for strength. We were more like sisters than anything else. We didn't have any of the answers, but walked through our storms together, and I know that made them a little easier to walk through. She was truly a friend for life!

The projects she lived in were one of the roughest neigh-

borhoods in Columbus, "The Short North." There was a lot
of dope boys and drug-selling going on. Every corner was
filled with dope boys hustling and pushing their product.
The females in the neighborhood would be outside looking
for and hoping for one of the dope boys on the corner to
take them home and maybe even rescue them out of their
situations and nightmares. I'm sure they imagined sitting in
their cars and flossin' the diamonds that they would have received if they were one of the dope boys' girls. Their circumstances and way of life was so hard that that was probably the
only way some of those chicks could even imagine getting
out of that hood.

I tried to pick up the pieces in my life and move forward.
I didn't get seriously involved with any men for a while. I didn't
see anything wrong with playing with men, though. I started
treating them like they had treated me—like an object. I had
no love for a man. Shoot, I had been through hell! Men I
had married and dated did me in, so I decided to do a few of
them in now.

I started going through men one after another. Whatever
anger and hurt I experienced, I passed it to someone else,
and I'm sure they did the same. All I wanted was a temporary
fix. I wanted a man to wrap his arms around me and love me
even if it was for a moment. Even if it was a lie.

I was now a female mac. All of my friends thought it was
cute. They thought I was the one to look up to and admire,
but in fact, they all should have been running in the opposite direction of where I was heading. In everyone's opinion,
I had it going on, but I wasn't happy with myself or what I
was doing with my life.

I used men. I used them to buy me cars, pay my bills and
feed me. I just wanted to have fun. That was my way to deal
with my situation. I would go to bars, drink and smoke somebody else's weed.

I tried to protect my heart from hurt, but after a year or so of this type of behavior, I was tired. I didn't like who I saw in the mirror. I didn't like using men to get what I wanted. All I wanted was a good man to share my life with.

I decided it was time to try again with love, but this time I would have a younger man, someone I could teach how to be a good man. Back then, I thought I had enough experiences with men to train one. *How hard could it really be?* I thought.

I now know that a woman can't teach a man how to be a man. That's control and manipulation, which is a jezebel spirit and a form of witchcraft. (2 Kings 9:22) The only way I could get rid of that spirit was to get in my right place and do what God wanted me to do, which was line up with Christ.

I was looking for someone I could tell what to do. I thought it was about control. I thought that would make me happy in a relationship. I had no idea what I really was working in or any idea that it was witchcraft.

You know we really have to get serious about the Word of God. People have no idea what type of demonic draws we are dealing with. I would manipulate men for years to get what I wanted, and I didn't know I was working in those spirits. We really do perish for lack of knowledge.

After making that statement about wanting a younger man, one was introduced to me.

"Rach, my brother wants to meet you," Peaches said to me while I was doing her hair at her house, getting ready for the club.

"Who, Peaches?" I had seen Peaches fix her friends up with her so-called "brothers," and I didn't know if I really wanted to be bothered with one of them. Yeah, I had fun around them, smoking their weed and playing pool at the Eight Ball, but to date one was a completely different thing.

Peaches had that sly smile on her face. "Come on, Rachael. He's so nice and he's cute."

"Whatever. I know your 'brothers' ain't no good. What I wanna get involved with one for?" I never dated the dudes that actually stood on the corner selling eight balls of crack cocaine. I dated the ones that supplied them and had them on the corners.

Most of Peaches' "brothers" were corner boys. I knew this would be a step down for me, but I thought for a second while she was going on and on, *He probably makes about a grand every two or three days. That's not too bad.*

"Are you gonna do it?"

I didn't know at the time that he had given her a hundred bucks and the weed we were smoking on to convince me to say yes.

"You gonna meet him or what?"

I put my finger to my chin. "Hmm . . . yep, I'll meet him."

"Good. He's so nice. When you finish my hair, we can go to the store around the corner and find him."

I finished Peaches' hair and we got in the car. She had rolled a blunt for us to smoke. Peaches lit the blunt and passed it to me. "Drive around the corner to Kelly's," she said.

I took two hard puffs of the weed, passed it to Peaches, and started the car.

I had bought this white mini-van from Jason at the car wash next to the salon. The van stuck out like a sore thumb, with 20-inch chromed-out rims, tinted windows, and a boomin' stereo to match. I didn't care. I needed transportation, and Jason sold it to me for seven hundred dollars. The van impressed men; at least the ones in Peaches' hood.

Kelly's corner store was where all the dope boys stood and gathered. They were out there all day and night. It was the hangout. They stood outside the place smoking their blunts back to back, with their baggy pants and white T-shirts, waiting for somebody to pull up and buy their product.

There were so many flyy cars in the parking lot that one

would swear the store was crowded, but it never was. SUVs and Hummers with the chromed-out 22s , Lexus and Mercedes cars were sitting at this tiny corner store waiting for five-oh to pull up, then everybody would take off one by one, hoping they didn't fit the description of whoever the po-po said they were looking for.

Peaches lived a street over from Kelly's. We pulled up, and she hollered, "Billy! Billy!" Then she turned and said, "Now, Rach, he is cute, but he has a slight acne problem. It's not really that bad." Then she smiled.

I sat in the van while all the dope boys ran up to the car one by one, flirting and trying to get a quick hit of the weed we were smoking. I watched in the rearview mirror as this dude with a black hoodie appeared behind the van, walking around to Peaches' side.

"Hi, Billy. I know you heard me callin' you," she said.

"I was comin'. I needed to take care of somethin' real quick." His voice was soft, not all the way mature like the other men I knew. He wasn't that tall, maybe 5'9", and he was skinny. I mean skinny! He probably weighed in at 125 pounds, if that.

"Billy, this is Rachael. Rachael, this is Billy," she introduced.

He looked through her window and said to me, "How you doin'?"

I couldn't quit staring at him. He had acne really bad, but even through the acne, his features were nice. His eyes were light brown. He had a wide nose that pointed at the end, his lips were full, and his eyebrows were thin. His skin was a dirty red color, and he had a well-groomed afro with facial hair that was cut so accurate. He was clean.

He walked over to my side of the car and smiled. I couldn't help but notice his eyes were red. I looked out the window, down at his shoes. They were Timbs, and his pants were Sean John. I thought, *He may be all right.*

We started spending a lot of time together, going to the movies and out to dinner. He was so different than any other man I dated, probably because of his outward appearance. I was used to dating the athletic type, and Billy was far from that, plus he was a lot younger. However, I wanted someone different inside and out. I really thought if I dated someone totally different than what I was used to, then maybe he would be different. After all, what could it hurt?

Of course, the relationship, like the others, started good. He was everything I wanted. He listened to me and catered to my every need. I was totally in control. I decided what we did and when we did it. If I wanted to go out to the movies, that's what we did. I ran the whole show and liked it. I thought it was because he loved me and wanted me to be happy. So, after a few months, I invited Billy to move in with me and the kids.

"I think we should stay together. After all, you're always here," I stated.

He looked surprised. "Rach, I never lived with a woman besides my sister." Then he hesitated and said, "Don't be putting me out every other day; that's all I ask. I need to know this is for real and we gonna make a family together—me, you and the girls. If not, I don't want to do it."

I couldn't help but smile. He was saying exactly what I'd been waiting to hear all this time, and the answer was in a younger man. Why couldn't it work? I thought. He lived in some condo way out in Dublin, Ohio on his own. Therefore, helping each other couldn't be anything but gravy.

I couldn't believe it. This dude was nineteen and was taking care of his business. He had his own place and his own money. He had it going on. But hadn't I told someone once that everything that looks good ain't good for you? I should have taken my own advice.

I didn't see anything wrong with moving Billy in. I guess I hadn't learned from my past experiences. I wasn't divorced, and I didn't think about my daughters, and I didn't think at all about the stuff that went on between me and Tone. I didn't think at all, or use my God-given sense! I wanted him there so I wouldn't feel like I was alone. I wanted someone to depend on me. For some reason, I had it in my head if a man needed me, then he would love me. I wanted to cook and clean for a man, be loved by a man and adored. However, it was all a figment of my imagination.

"Casting down imaginations and every high thing that exalts itself against the knowledge of God bringing into captivity every thought to the obedience of Christ."—2 Corinthians 10:5.

Denny and I had been separated for a few years now. We both were living with other people, and still hadn't gotten a divorce. I never once considered that we were both adulterous, but that's exactly what we were.

"Rach, we need to get this divorce finalized. Indy wants to marry me this spring."

"Okay, when do you wanna end this?" I was holding the phone with my shoulder and neck, watching Brandy try on her cheerleading uniform.

She was standing in the mirror, saying her cheers aloud. She was so beautiful. It amazed me that me and Denny made such beautiful children and had such an ugly relationship. Brandy's pigtails were hanging past her shoulders now, and she was so tall for eight. I listened to Denny but watched Brandy, and that allowed me to keep a smile on my face as he told me he filed the divorce earlier that day.

After hearing Denny out, we worked out an agreement to finally set everything in the past in order. After walking out of the courthouse when we went for the divorce, we shook hands and said our good-byes. As I turned and walked away, Denny screamed out with a bellowing sound, "Rachael!" It scared me. I thought he had been hurt. I turned around suddenly and he said, "I still love you." He was looking at me with sad, puppy-dog eyes, standing there all by himself.

I wondered, *Where is his fiancée?* I turned back around and left the courthouse, never saying a word to him. I wondered how things between us had gotten so bad.

"Live joyfully with the wife whom you love all the days of your vain life, which He has given you under the sun, all your days of vanity; for that is your portion in life, and in labor, which you perform under the sun."—Ecclesiastes 9:9.

Billy and I were lying in the bed asleep when the phone rang. "Hello," I softly whispered into the receiver, looking over at Billy balled up, the covers off his feet.

I slid out the bed, walked past the dresser, and turned and looked on the nightstand at the clock. I couldn't believe it was only 5:00 A.M.

This better be good, I thought.

I went to the bathroom in our bedroom and looked back at Billy to make sure he was still sleeping. I then shut the door behind me. The light from the bathroom disappeared from the bedroom and the shadows it made on the walls.

"Who is this?" I said softly.

"Rach, it's me, Denny."

"Why you callin' here at this hour? Isn't it your wedding day? What's wrong?" I was still a little upset with Denny because we had only been divorced for four months, which meant he and his girlfriend had already planned their entire wedding. Denny was scandalous!

"I-I-I just wanted to talk to you."

"Are the girls all right, Denny? Did they get there okay?" I started worrying. I sent them up to Chicago for his wedding earlier that week. They caught an airplane by themselves. The airline assured me they would keep their eyes on them.

But now that he was calling at five in the morning, I was thinking sending them may not have been a good idea after all.

"No, no, no, Rach. The girls are fine. They are right here with me, sleeping. They so beautiful, Rach. I'm sorry for what I did to you, Rach," he whispered.

I opened the bathroom door a little to see if Billy was still 'sleep. I watched him sleep in peace as if he never felt so comfortable before. I closed the door back quietly and said, "It's okay. That was in the past. We're twenty-seven now. Let it go."

"No, it wasn't right, Rach." He was crying. "Rachael, do you think I'm making a mistake?"

I know you're making a mistake.

I said to him, "I think you should be alone for a while. You need to spend time with Brandy and Brea before adding someone else in the picture."

"Do you want me back? Just say it, Rach, and I'll call all this off."

I thought for a moment and said, "No." I knew it hurt him, but he hurt me so many times, and now he was marrying somebody not even six months after our divorce was final. A part of me wanted to hurt him.

Over the next several years, Denny would get married twice and have four more children.

After two years of Billy and me living together, we decided to get married. I condemned what Denny was doing, yet I was living with another man. How could I possibly think God was going to bless my relationship with Billy? He wasn't.

For a long time, I didn't want to get married again because of the past experience I had, but one day at work, Billy's friend, Will, called, sounding frantic. "Rach, Rach, you need to get up to Grant Hospital right away. Billy's been shot!"

I started trembling then dropped the phone and ran out of the salon. I didn't tell my clients anything. I just left.

There was a security guard and a short white lady sitting at the desk in the ER with a sheet of paper and pen. They were both watching the news on TV. When the lady saw me, her facial expression changed. She looked nervous.

"Do you know where my boyfriend is?" I still had my smock from work on and probably smelled like hair products.

"What's his name, sweetie?" she asked.

"Um, his name is"—I couldn't think—"He was rushed here with gunshot wounds about twenty minutes ago." I said to myself, *Think, Rach, think,* while holding my head with my hands.

She was busy trying to find out who this mysterious man was when I shouted, "Oh, Billy Carson! His name is Billy Carson." I was relieved to have come to my senses.

"Okay, I see him. He's on the ninth floor in intensive care."

I stumbled back. I was breaking down. Intensive care meant this was serious. I was scared.

"Ma'am, ma'am, are you gonna be all right?" the security guard said, now standing, waiting for my reply.

"Yes." I wiped my eyes. "I'm all right."

"Go around the corner and down the corridor to the left set of elevators, past the gift shop. Then take it to the ninth floor and tell the nurses at the station who you are and who you're here for." She smiled sympathetically.

"Okay, I will. Thank you." I never thought about what would happen if Billy died in the streets. I began to cry while people walked by, some used to the tears in these hallways, others wondering if someone had died.

The shooting made me change my mind. I knew I loved him after that and thought he would slow down his lifestyle.

*   *   *

We planned the wedding and decided not to have a big one, but would go to the courts and do it. We invited his family and mine. However, no one from my side except the kids showed up. His mother, sister and a few of his relatives came to show us their support.

The girls were nine and six when we married. Brandy didn't want me to get married. She still loved her daddy and thought one day we were going to be together.

Before the wedding, Billy made sure he came in at a reasonable hour and we went places as a family. If the girls cheered or had events at school, he was there. We went as a family. Billy didn't have a car, so he kept mine when I worked. He picked the girls up from school and brought them to the salon until I called him to come and get us.

He wasn't much of a father figure to the girls; usually not even speaking to them at all. He didn't interact with them at all after the marriage. It started bothering me, so I questioned him.

"What's up with you? Why you don't talk to the girls?"

He sat there on the side of the bed, watching *SportsCenter*, twirling a piece of his untrimmed beard that was growing in.

"You hear me, Billy?" I stood over him with my hands on my hips, waiting for his reply. "Hello?"

"Rachael, get out my face. Ask their daddy why he don't do nothin' with 'em. That's who you need to be askin'. They ain't my kids." He stood up in my face so close that I could smell the Black and Mild cigarette on his nasty, stank breath.

"Shoot, it ain't my responsibility to take care of another man's kids." He walked off mumbling.

I stood there looking stupid. I knew I was getting into a mess, but I kept going further and further in it.

Our honeymoon night was spent with Billy's back turned toward me. Never once did he touch me or say, "I love you. You're my wife, and I'm going to take care of you."

I lay looking at his back all night long in tears. I now believe one of the reasons I married him was because of pride.
Denny was married, and I didn't want to be alone. I wanted
him to know someone wanted me, even if it was all make-
believe.

I knew before I married Billy that he had issues he was
dealing with, but I married him anyway. I didn't care that he
was out on his own from the age of twelve. I never questioned him about his mom being addicted to crack cocaine,
or the molestations that he experienced when he was a child
himself. I didn't think about that stuff. I didn't think about
the future with him or anything else; just the moment.

Billy had a hard life, just as I did. He had no education
and no trade. He worked for himself on the streets as a drug
dealer. Would I ever learn my lesson?

Chapter 20

In My Own Hands

Here I was, back in the same boat. Denny and Billy were one and the same. Yeah, one worked a legitimate job and one sold drugs, but I was going around in circles.

"As a dog returns to his own vomit, so a fool repeats his folly."—Proverbs 26:11.

I needed something of substance to hold on to. Something that would let me know why this was my life, my destiny. I decided to go back to church. "Yeah, that's what I'll do," I said to myself. "Go back to church, so God will talk to me again."

After all, I hadn't heard from Him since the abortions. The Lord had stopped talking to me after I lied and told Him I wouldn't abort my babies. He wasn't listening to my lies anymore, but I needed Him now. I needed to know what to do. Was I making the wrong decisions? I knew I was, but I wanted God to fix it.

I had grown up in church, and knew that's where I needed to be for things to be turned around. I always knew God was with me, and I talked to Him constantly growing up. No matter what I did in life or where I was, I talked to my God.

"But the very hairs on your head are all numbered. Do not fear therefore you are more value than many sparrows." —Matthew 10:30-31.

I started attending one of the largest churches in the Columbus area, World Harvest. The first time I walked in, I was amazed at all the people shouting and praising the Lord. The atmosphere was so peaceful and warm, filled with the presence of the Holy Ghost. I exhaled.

"This is the church, babies," I said to the girls. I remember holding their little hands all the way down the front of the church to join after the anointed service. They both were smiling, and I knew they felt protected and secure like never before. I had made such a mess of things, and the girls had no real stability. I walked down the aisle to salvation, redemption, and forgiveness, thinking this would make us stable.

Joining church was the best decision I had made in a long time. We loved getting up on Sundays, but we couldn't get Billy to go for nothing.

"Billy, Billy," I said to him, putting on my makeup in the mirror. "Come on, get up and go to church with us."

"No, man. Leave me alone. I keep telling you I don't want to go. Quit asking me that. You getting on my nerves." He put the pillow over his head.

I mumbled, "It's eleven and he still ain't out of bed. He's so sorry." I walked back in the bedroom and said, "You know what? After the shooting and you being left for dead, I would think you would want to be in somebody's church. You should be giving God praise that you still here."

He hastily took the pillow off his face and looked at me with those beady little eyes as if he hated me, and said, "Shut up!" He put the pillow back over his face.

I went to the church off and on. I felt the move of God in the place, but I didn't believe God had forgiven me for all I had done. I was tormented with the abortions I had, along with everything else I had done and was doing, and I hadn't forgiven anyone for what I'd been through.

However, I heard a message from Pastor Rod Parsley, which let me know that God has indeed forgiven me for my past. It was just something about the way he explained God's forgiving power, and for the first time, I could let some things go that I previously couldn't forgive.

"Do not remember the former things, nor consider the things of old."— Isaiah 43:18.

So, for the first time in fourteen years, I felt like God could love me. I knew that Jesus died for my sins. It didn't matter how big or small, but all of them. I was excited about Christ. While in Christ, I started believing in life, in me, in God.

As I went to church, I was looking for Jesus to do a miracle within me because I was truly sinking inside. I wasn't happy at all. I knew Billy wasn't faithful to me—not to mention he sold drugs. Billy was going deeper and farther in the streets, and I was holding on by a string to the Lord, hoping for a change in both of our lives, maybe even salvage of our marriage.

We were married for about a year when things got even worse. Billy started hanging out in the streets day in and day out.

"Billy, what are you doing? You can't be out there like this. You're married to me and I need you here. I thought you were gonna get a job when we got married. You promised you would leave the streets alone. I'm sick of this!"

He listened to me for a moment without leaving the room, then jumped up toward me and said, "So leave! I ain't changing nothin'. I like what I do. Either you gonna stay, or you can leave, Rach. But to tell you the truth, I don't care what you do."

I was scared he was gonna hit me. I drew back and covered my face with my arms, thinking, *Where did my nice, controllable little boyfriend go? This is the man I gave money to and helped get his street business going, and now he turns on the one that fed him.*

"I ain't gonna hit you! I'm out here tryin' to take care of business and you complaining." He looked at me as if I was a stranger, not his wife.

Billy had an excuse for every time he wouldn't be around. He was busy, he was trying to make some money, or he was out somewhere with his boys. It was always something, and always a reason not to come home.

I tried everything to keep my man at home. I even went to Bed Bath & Beyond and bought a fancy cookbook because I heard the way to a man's heart was good cooking. But nothing worked. The house had everything he needed to stay home—PlayStation, Nintendo 64, whatever. I had come to grips with the fact that he just didn't want to be there. It was out of my hands, and my husband wasn't interested in me or anything I had to offer.

I started looking at my life, and I had nothing but Brandy and Brea. Everything else was a failure. Brandy and Brea were two decisions I knew were the right choices I never had to question.

I wanted to do something with my life that would make me a success and at the same time attract Billy. I decided it was time to get my own hair salon. I started planning. I went to the State Board of Cosmetology to get all the facts. Once I had it all in order, I found a nice small building that had been a salon before. I told a few of the girls I worked with what I was doing and when I was leaving. They asked if they could come with me.

"Sure, I would love to have you," I told them. I was excited because going in with workers was a plus, I thought.

After months of owning my own salon, business was booming. I bought a brand-new money-green 2000 Dodge Intrepid with only four miles on it. I believed this would make my husband love me and want me, but instead of wanting me, he took my car, dropped me off at work, and drove around all day, selling dope and chasing chicks.

As for the salon and Billy being proud of my success, it didn't happen like that. Instead, he told everyone it was his salon and he had me there working and running it for him.

I also bought my first home. It was in the hood, but on a quiet street tucked away in a corner on Taylor Avenue. Newly remodeled for me and my family, the yellow aluminum-sided cottage was so warm.

I can still remember the first time I walked in after the closing. The walls were so clean and freshly painted white. I could smell the new carpet. It had two bedrooms downstairs and one up. I had one bathroom that I decorated in black and silver, with the hall leading to the girls' rooms painted gold like the living room. The hardwood floor in the kitchen was painted red.

Brandy and Brea had their own bedrooms, with new furniture throughout the place. I had a white two-piece couch and loveseat in the front room and a wooden dinette set with six chairs to match the wood on the kitchen cabinets in the eat-in kitchen that was loaded with new appliances. It had a full basement with a brand-new washer and dryer.

I was happy. I had done it! I finally had the picture-perfect life, so it seemed. I was excited and proud of my achievements. Things were really turning around for me. I was learning about Christ and what He could do in our lives. I was on the right track.

After a few years of letting God lead my life and bless my family and me, I gave up on God. All the praying and crying I did regarding my husband, and nothing had changed. I felt guilty for the things I sat by and watched Billy do. Guilt started backing me into a corner and farther away from God. I decided to get out of the church before God put His wrath and judgment on me.

I couldn't stop Billy from his drug activities, or anything else, for that matter, so I gave up. I kept saying I was gonna leave him, but instead, I left Jesus. I quit going to church. I felt like a hypocrite. My husband was selling drugs. How could I possibly be in God's will? I was telling him to stop. I was praying that he would stop. But I didn't do anything about it. I was still in the same house with a drug dealer. I couldn't go to church, speak to God and worship Him like it was nothing, knowing my husband was a dope man. I wasn't lined up with God in marriage, and my husband didn't want my God at all. I hate to say it, but that meant that he was serving the devil, whether he knew it or not.

In the Word of God, it states: "For many deceivers have gone out into the world who do not confess Jesus Christ as the coming in the flesh. This is a deceiver and an antichrist."—2 John: 7.

Bam, bam, bam!

"Billy, somebody at the door," I called out.

It was 7:30 in the morning and I just lay back down after putting the girls on their buses. Who could this be?

Billy jumped up, grabbed his Nextel and chirped somebody. I could hear whispering as he walked downstairs. "Here I come."

I followed behind him quietly and sat on the stairs.

"Hey, Billy, sorry for disturbin' you this early, but I needed to get that. Man, that's fire what you got. Fire," a female said softly.

"Shhh, keep yo' voice down. My wife's 'sleep." He had his fingers over his lips, looking back at the steps to see if I was coming.

I jumped up and went back up the stairs and lay back

down before he saw me. I covered my mouth and said, "Oh my God. This idiot is selling dope out of my house. I have kids and he don't even care."

"Hey, babe. What you still doin' awake?"

"Billy, what's up? You got crackheads comin' to my door. I didn't buy this house for that. This is where my daughters lay their heads. That's not cool." I threw my hands in the air and rolled my eyes at him. How stupid could he be, having dope fiends coming over my house? *He's an imbecile.*

"Wait a minute, Rachael. I live here too. I'll have whoever I want come up in here."

"All I know is you better not do that again." I walked over to the bedroom window and saw the old red Fiesta still parked in my driveway. I was tripping that the fiends were still in front of my house.

I continued, "That's wrong. It's bad enough you out there selling it on the streets, but I refuse to watch you do it in my house. I would think crack was the last thing you wanted to be a part of." Then I walked over to Billy and touched his shoulder. "After all, your mother is on drugs. Don't you ever wonder or care about people and what they're doing to themselves? It should bother you."

He moved away from me. He jumped up and began walking around the room, breathing hard and huffin' and puffin'. Then he punched a hole in my bedroom wall.

"Aw, shut up. You so dramatic. Ain't nobody comin' in here doin' nothing." He was waving the gun he had bought off the streets from one of his customers.

I didn't say anything else because I knew I was in over my head. I was sitting there in my purple silk PJs, my hand across my mouth in total disbelief.

"I don't need this, all this naggin'. Leave me alone. I do what I want when I want. Don't question that, Rachael."

"Okay, Billy, I'm sorry. I don't want you to get mad." I

hated myself and who I had become. I couldn't believe I'd just said that to him. What was I thinking? I never let a man talk to me like that or do those things. Even when I was with Tone, I didn't back down to his threats, and now I was taking all this lip and threats from a man that didn't pay one of my bills or speak to my children. What was wrong with this picture?

Billy came and went whenever he was ready, and not to mention we never made love. He wouldn't touch me. I found out later he was just too tired. He was having sex with so many other women that he didn't have time for me.

He had me wondering, *Is he gay? Maybe he don't like women. Maybe this marriage is a cover-up.* It all started to make sense. I was in a full-blown abusive marriage. I was going crazy. If it hadn't been for Vicky, Peaches, and the kids, I probably would have been in an institution. They kept my mind off Billy.

Vicky was another friend of mind that I met years before when I was married to Denny. She was our babysitter. I was her hairdresser and we hung out. Vicky was so funny that she could have been a stand-up comedian. She was 5'8" with a medium-built frame. She was dark chocolate with smooth skin and looked as if she wore makeup all the time, but never did. Her nose was pointed and went up at the end. She wore contacts, which made her appear to have light brown eyes. Her hair was short, fine, and curly. Vicky always dressed like a diva; high heels and matching designer bags and scarves. Vicky was very busty and made sure she showed it off with low-cut blouses and short- short skirts, but managed to pull off her style without looking easy.

On one occasion, there was a lady that came to the house to buy dope from Billy. I felt horrible for her and wondered if she had children. I wanted to pull her to the side and tell her she needed to get away from these drugs, but I never said a word to her. I did say to Billy, "You shouldn't sell her drugs. Go get a trade or a job. How can you live with yourself? What if it was your sister or brother somebody was selling crack to?"

"Please . . . if that be the case, that would be their fault for getting hooked on drugs. Leave me alone."

I knew his anger was within himself, but I didn't know how to help him. He had a wall up, and I couldn't climb over it. I knew his pain with drugs stemmed from the fact that his mom was using them, but I couldn't get him to talk about it, nor go around her. Billy hadn't seen her in years. We saw her at the wedding and at his grandmother's funeral, but in between that, he wouldn't go see her. He was bitter and angry. Oftentimes, I was scared he was going to hurt me to take his anger out. He would get in such a rage when he got upset.

"Leave me alone, Rachael. Don't start that stuff right now. I don't feel like hearin' it."

I looked at him with tears in my eyes. *I made a mistake.*

Billy had hooked up with one of the biggest drug dealers in Columbus, Ohio. Tyson was peanut butter brown with braids to the back of his head and stood 6'3" and appeared to have zero body fat, all muscles. He drove a brand-new black Range Rover truck with tinted windows and chrome rims.

I knew once Billy started hanging around Tyson and his crew, it would be nothing but more trouble. I was right. Tyson's name was all over the city because he was doing crazy stuff, like making somebody who owed him money strip. Then he would beat them with guns, or shoot them in the hand. Females would fight over him in the clubs.

Funny thing about him was that I had known him to hang with many different crews, but when they went down, he always managed to move on. I wondered to myself if he was five-oh. We didn't like each other but spoke to be polite. I told Billy to keep him away from my house because I didn't trust him.

Once Billy was in that crew, his status in the streets went up. What I mean by that is he was popular to everyone—the females, the dope boys, and the police. He had respect in the streets now. He wasn't making the kind of money Tone did, but he had his own crew. He was the one with the weight now and the dope houses.

He made about $7,000 a week and thought he was invincible. I sat back and watched him go from a young dope boy who thought he had to survive the streets by any means necessary to a dope man wanting this as a lifelong career. He was in the streets daily, watching his workers get his money. He had become a monster with no respect for anyone.

I worked one day and listened to a customer say, "Rachael, girl, I seen your husband in front of the CNS today. He's always there. Every time I ride by, I see his car." She smirked.

I knew people wanted to get a rise out of me when they told me half the story. I also knew that the story they told me went much deeper. For instance, "Girl, I seen yo' husband today," meant really they'd seen my husband with another chick. I read between the lines.

He was driving me crazy. Eventually, Billy got a new car. He asked me to put the car in my name for him. I did. I thought if I did that he would surely love me. It didn't work. Nothing I did worked.

The car was a new teal green Cadillac with the spinning rims that looked like bones and the windows tinted to look like mirrors. Everyone in the city knew what that car looked like and whose it was, bringing even more attention to us.

I was so embarrassed and felt very much alone, because everybody knew Billy was unfaithful to me. That was the word on the street. I couldn't tell anyone all the pain I was feeling and about all of the betrayal.

I answered the phone one afternoon in the shop, "Flava Hair Design, may I help you?"

"This Rachael?"

"Yes. Would you like to make an appointment?"

"No, I wanted you to know I was sleeping wit' yo' husband." Then she began to laugh.

I held the phone and said, "Hold on." I went in the bathroom to get more privacy. I still remember that first call and the two chicks on the other end sounding so young and playful, like all of this was a joke or something. They didn't have any regard that my heart was being ripped out of me as they told me the awful details of what went on with my husband and them.

There would be so many different chicks calling my salon, telling me they were sleeping with Billy. I couldn't even begin to count them all over the years. My husband wasn't my husband. He was coming in at five or six in the morning.

Billy made me feel like I had the plague or something. He would come in, take a shower, lie down, go to sleep, get up the next morning, change his clothes, and do the same thing over again. He never said a word to me. It was as if I didn't exist.

I never knew how much money he had or what he was doing with it. All I knew was that I was starting to struggle. The bills from the new home, my car note and taking care of my daughters was straining me, and I was struggling to pay the salon bills. I was in over my head and had no help from him. He didn't feel like he was supposed to. It was my salon, he would say. Then he would tell me how he didn't even want that house.

"You bought it, so you need to pay for it." Billy would argue with me whenever I asked him to help me with a bill. He would give me a hundred bucks every now and then because he stayed there, but he said, "You go to work all the time. Why you don't have nothin'?"

I hated asking him for anything. At one point, I'd rather lose it all than ask him for money. He made me feel like I was begging him. I never knew why I couldn't leave Billy. It was as if I wanted to be dogged by him. I knew it had to be a woman that made him feel like this about me. The lack of respect he had, he had to be comparing me to somebody else. That was the only thing that made sense to me.

I can remember desperately going through his messages daily, sometimes fifty times a day, hearing female after female calling him and telling him how they wanted to see him today. It would rip my heart apart. I had no control.

I was in the salon one day and followed the same routine, which was listening to Billy's messages in the morning before he got up and deleting them. I took the cordless phone to the back of the shop where I kept the supplies, closed the door behind myself, and dialed the code.

Hey, Billy. This is Vanessa. What's up for the night? You didn't forget my birthday, did you? Call me back. I'm going to get some cigarettes real quick. Bye.

Before I finished listening to it, I was bent over in the chair, crying quietly. Why did I keep taking this? I was doing this to myself, because I knew he didn't love me.

I remember thinking, *Why would Billy want somebody who smokes nasty cigarettes?* I was in so much torment that all I could think about was the fact that she smoked, not that my husband was cheating or had a woman calling him. I couldn't let my mind concentrate on the real problem.

I was angry with the women, thinking it was their fault that my husband was out with them. I wouldn't admit or accept the fact that he was wrong.

The female left her phone number, so I decided to give her a call. I called the number and asked, "Can I speak to Vanessa?"

She said, "This is her."

Her voice was deep, and she sounded as if she had some sense. I wondered what she looked like.

"Hello, my name is Rachael, Billy's wife."

The phone was silent.

"Did you hear me?

"Oh, yes, I heard you."

I told her nicely I wasn't trying to get a confrontation going, but I prayed and asked God to show me what was going on in my marriage, how I listened to his message and found her number. I wanted to remain calm talking to her. so she would feel comfortable enough to share the truth with me, but it didn't work.

"Oh, that's fine. Me and Billy are friends. I grew up with him. We ran into each other at the CNS and exchanged numbers so he could come to my party, that's all. He told me he was married."

I knew she was telling a story because she stuttered through the whole conversation and tried to convince me she was innocent. I wanted to believe her, but I knew it was probably a lie. The same story with a different man—first Denny, then Tone, and now Billy. What did I do to deserve such a horrible relationship? Of course, I accepted the treatment I was getting, so the roller coaster never ended. I needed to get off the ride. It was my fault, my bad choices that I was living with again.

Every relationship with a man got a little bit worse than the previous one. I questioned myself as to why. What made me get to the point that I let a man tear me all the way down? All I knew was that it hurt. I was scared to be alone, and I wanted a man to love me.

For a minute there, Billy tried to do right. He started coming home earlier, but it didn't last. He was back in the streets within weeks, and I was paranoid and obsessed with him being with different females.

I didn't trust him. I called him every three minutes. "Billy, what you doin'? Who's that I hear in the background? I know I hear a female. Where you at?"

I couldn't eat or sleep. I was miserable. After one incident died out, there would come others. Females would call the salon, ask for me, and begin telling me stories of their life with my husband.

Chapter 21

Why You Dogging Me?

I started following Billy around, driving three and four cars behind without him noticing, singing along with Jill Scott on the radio. I was so depressed. "If I catch him with somebody, I'm leaving. That's it, I promise."

Ring, ring, ring!

My cell phone rang during one of my excursions. "Hello?"

"Mommy, where you at?" Brandy asked from the other end.

"I'll be there in a minute, Brandy. Okay? Go back to bed."

"I had a nightmare. Mommy, something was wrong with you."

"I'm okay, silly girl. Get back in bed. I'm out at the store getting milk for your cereal in the morning, okay?"

"Okay, Ma."

I watched the drops of rain hit the windshield softly as I drove. *She's so mature because of all the choices I made for them. It has made her grow up fast.*

I closed my cell and watched Billy turn his Caddy into the CNS. He only sold in one particular area off of Fifth Avenue in Columbus, and that was at the CNS Bar and Grill, one of the local hangouts for everyone that wanted to get into something that would get them in trouble. Nothing good came out of that bar.

Billy hollered, startling me. "Stop following me!"

I didn't even know he had seen me until he was beating on my hood and kicking the chrome rims he had put on my car.

"Go home. I don't want you here!" The whole time he yelled at me, he was looking around to see who was watching him. Billy worried about his reputation on the street, and when I came around, it reminded him that he was married.

I got out of the car and grabbed his wrist. "Come home and let's make this right!"

I noticed he was wearing Cartier cologne. It smelled so sweet. His face was deranged as if he was going to commit murder, and I was without a doubt the victim.

"I love you. Please stop this and come home. Please?" I begged him.

Billy looked at me with one of the coldest glares I'd ever seen. He walked up real close to me and looked me in the eye. "Go home!"

I couldn't stop this bad rollercoaster ride. I felt like he could be a good husband if I could just get the female to leave him alone. He would see that I was still there. I had tried everything. I went on an extreme diet and even lost seventy pounds. I started dressing more like the younger ladies. I changed my hair. I smoked the weed more. I gave him money, bought him clothes and whatever else I could for him, but nothing worked.

I had formed a pattern. I would work all day and hunt for Billy all night, with nobody suspecting that I was losing my mind. If it hadn't been for Jesus holding me and protecting me, I would have very well done something I would regret.

As I drove around stalking my husband, I listened to the voices in my head that told me where he was.

Go down the street. That's probably where he is.

Then another: *He's with somebody making love to them and laughing at you.*

All I wanted to do was to catch him, and then I would be through. I meant it.

My eyes would glance back and forth down the street as I drove with the lights out to try to catch him, not knowing where he was. Some nights I would see his car parked at the CNS.

One particular night, I called Peaches and Vicky to see if they wanted to do something, maybe take in a movie or get a drink, but they were nowhere to be found. I decided to dress up and show Billy how good I really looked, now that the weight was off. I put on my pair of red Gucci sandals to show off my pedicure.

It was so hot out that day. It was at least 11:30, but the sun had baked us that day and the heat was still lingering in the air. I wore a soft gold-and-red Gucci dress that was cut out in the back and form-fitting in the front, showing off my new curves. I had purchased the dress from a booster that came in the shop earlier that day, selling clothes. My hair was shoulder-length and was dyed "warm brown" with golden highlights throughout. I had one of the girls from the salon braid it and let it loose before we left, so it was wild-looking, but in a good way. I was pleased with the new me. I looked in-credible. I put my Very Sexy perfume from Victoria's Secret on and went out the door, leaving the girls at home by them-selves.

Everywhere I went, I was noticed, but my husband didn't see me. I went to the CNS because I knew he would be there. That was guaranteed to be his location until 2:30 in the morning.

I saw his car parked and stopped. I went to the car, opened the door, and there he was, sitting in a smoke-filled car with some chick. I startled them.

He jumped out of the car with weed in his hand and shouted, "What you doin'?" He ran over to me and pushed me down. He was trying to fight me too. "Why you out here? Go home, Rachael! Quit following me!"

Some dude in the parking lot ran over to my aid and said, "Man, don't hit yo' wife. You wrong, Billy."

"I'm sitting with my friends smoking. Leave me alone!" His face was frowning and he looked as if he hated my very guts.

I cried, "Billy, don't do this. Come home. I love you." I hurried up off the parking lot from his push and wiped the little pebbles out of my hands from the fall.

Billy walked away from me and signaled for the female to get back in the car. Then he pulled off. I felt so stupid standing there watching the back end of his Caddy make a left in traffic. I heard the onlookers laughing and whispering as I picked my purse off the rocky parking lot and got in my car to leave. I looked over at some dudes talking and could hear one say, "Now, that was cold."

This behavior and pattern went on for years with no peace. In addition, my daughters suffered the consequences for my bad decisions and behavior. Brandy was in the seventh grade and having sex, and I had no clue. I came in one night, and my neighbor stopped me and told me how when I pulled up, a boy would jump out my back window. I was so wrapped up in Billy I didn't even know what was going on with my daughters. I had to get it together because they were suffering and had been for a while now. I thought my daughter was a virgin. In addition, I had no idea she was stealing Billy's weed, taking it to school and selling it, until she confided in Vicky, who told me one day.

I lay on my floor in our bedroom and cried. I cried even when there were no more tears in my eyes. I went into my marriage with the attitude that I was the ruler and queen.

When I married Billy, I bought the wedding rings and planned everything. He was never interested in anything I was doing. I knew then he wasn't ready to get married, but I was selfish and I wanted to say to everybody I was married. I definitely reaped what I sowed regarding the decisions I made.

I was desperate when it came to Billy; so desperate that I lied and told him I was pregnant just to try to keep him interested in me. I figured if I told him that, he would surely straighten himself up, get a job, and leave everyone else behind. I went on with this lie for months, dressing like a pregnant woman and eating like one too. All I wanted was him to love me, but the problem was, I didn't even love myself.

Billy's problem was that he had his own deliverance he needed to be worked out. He didn't care if I was pregnant or not. It didn't change him. He still stayed out in the streets, and he still messed around. Every night, I went to bed alone, feeling disgusted, worthless, and a liar. I didn't feel very good about myself.

"Let the husband render to his wife the affection due her, and likewise also the wife to her husband."—1 Corinthians 7:3.

A few days after I found out Brandy was selling weed at school, I decided to take her and Brea to the state fair and spend some time with them. I thought maybe she was acting out to get some attention. I also felt bad because I beat her down after finding out about the boy coming over and the weed she was selling.

Vicky went to the fair with us. While Vicky and I were walking around and stuffing our faces, my cell phone began to ring. The girls had run off, going toward the rides.

"Hello," I said.

"Hey, Rach, this is yo' Uncle Al."

I was wondering, *Why is he calling? He never calls me.*

I was laughing at Vicky when I answered the phone because she was talking about somebody walking by. "Hey, what's up?" I asked.

Uncle Al's voice sounded so serious. He always joked and played, so his tone concerned me. "Your momma wanted me to tell you that your grandpa ain't doin' too good. He's in the hospital."

"Is he gonna be all right?" My smile had now turned into a cry. I didn't know what I would do without him. I loved him and hadn't seen him in almost a year.

When I met Billy, he never wanted company or family over, and he definitely wouldn't go to Dayton with me to meet my family. He never wanted to mingle, just wanted to be isolated. I went for it, allowed him to do it. I isolated myself from everyone I loved, including Grandpa.

I had quit going to Dayton altogether when I plotted against my sister and cousin. Though they forgave all, I hadn't forgiven myself. I would send the girls down for holidays and summers, but I stayed behind with Billy. I was so afraid of leaving him home because I knew he would cheat.

"Rachael, you there?" Uncle Al asked.

"Yeah, I'm here."

"He's in Kettering Hospital. His doctor said he has a brain tumor and there's nothing they can do for him. They've given him ten weeks to live."

I dropped the phone and began to scream out, "NOOO!"

Vicky picked up my cell off the ground and started talking to my uncle. She put her arm around me and said quietly, "It's gonna be all right, Rach." She took down the information from Uncle Al and hung up the phone.

I didn't know what to do. I called Billy and told him what was going on. "Billy, I just got a call from Dayton telling me that Grandpa is dying."

"Aw, that's too bad," Billy said.

* * *

I left for Dayton the next day. I asked my husband to go with me, but he said, "I need to take care of some business here."

I didn't care if he went. All I could think about was getting to Dayton and how my mother, aunts, and uncles were doing.

I had to decide what was important. I couldn't wait any longer for Billy to get it together. I had been praying to God to wake this brother up or release me, but God wasn't listening to me. I was totally in the dark, maybe because I was living in sin.

I walked in the hospital, and Grandpa started smiling.

"Where's yo' husband?"

I didn't know what to say. "Um, he's at work."

Brandy and Brea looked at me, knowing I was lying.

I kissed Grandpa on the cheek, chatted with Angel and Lisa for a moment, then ran out of the room to call Billy. "Billy, what you doin'?"

"Nothin'. Sittin' in front of the CNS. Call me back."

"Hello . . . ?" I stood outside the room for a minute, closed my eyes, took a deep breath, and walked back in the room.

Grandpa died exactly ten weeks later. I traveled back and forth to Dayton every weekend to see him before he died, and Billy never came with me. Grandpa was a strong man of God. I watched him take his last breath and die peacefully with all his children and grandchildren around him.

I went back to Columbus to prepare for the funeral. I watched my daughters while we drove up the windy freeway that September day. They sat in the back seat, leaned over on each other, sleeping. They were upset about Grandpa's passing. He had them spoiled rotten.

Billy had said he would go to the funeral, but when it was time, he backed out, saying, "I need to stay here and take care of my business."

I knew he was up to no good, but I didn't want to get into

an argument with him, so I said nothing. I did notice he had brand-new clothes laid out on his side of the room, new shoes and new hats, but I couldn't concentrate on him right then. I had to prepare the girls and myself for one of the saddest days I would face. I didn't have time for all that drama I was in. I had to put away all that mess, forget about it for a moment.

I packed up and then told Billy we were leaving. He stayed in the bed and mumbled something. He never moved. He acted as if I said I was going downstairs to get a drink of water. His attitude amazed me. It was as if he were sent here by Satan himself.

I stood there with my Gucci suitcases in my hand and the girls yelling from downstairs, "Come on, Mom. Forget him! He won't even go with us!"

They were mad that I tried to make excuses for Billy, but I had no more. It was what it was, and my daughters knew it stunk.

"Billy, Billy," I said to him.

He turned over and looked at me, removing the pillows from his face.

I looked at the hair on top of his head, which was fading away from spreading acne. He wouldn't go to the doctor to get it treated, so it got worse all over his face and head, until his scalp opened in areas and caused an ever-present odor around him. I believed it was an infection.

"What? Why you callin' me like that? I heard you say you were leavin'. Call me later. I'm tired, Rachael." He put the pillow back over his face and went back to sleep.

When I walked up to Grandpa's porch, I remembered that it was my haven, the safest place in the world for me as a little girl. I became overwhelmed.

I could see my sister and myself as little girls, and hear my Grandma telling us, "Grandpa's home from work."

We would run and hide in the closet. I could hear him open the front door and my Grandma whispering to him, "They're in the closet." Then we'd hear his shoes on the floor, walking over to the closet.

Crystal and I would be in the closet laughing, the coats not even reaching our heads. He would open the door and start tickling us.

I can remember when my grandparents would take us on vacations with them. We would get in their camper and be so excited just traveling across the Midwest with them, fishing and camping.

All of the Christmas dinners and Thanksgiving dinners were held there at my grandparents' house. The whole family would gather. They knew how to keep us close. I can remember that like it had just happened. I thanked God for those memories.

After the funeral, the girls and I went to our hotel. Although different family members wanted us to stay with them, I said no. I wanted to be near the freeway, so I could get up early and go home. Besides, there were so many relatives there from out of town, it would have been stacked. I was tired, and it had been an extremely long day.

I made sure the girls were situated then I called Billy. I wanted to see what he was doing. I heard loud music and people yelling in the background when he answered the phone.

"Yeah, what's up?"

"We just left the funeral. I was just checking on you." I smiled, thinking we could get close and talk tonight until I went to sleep. I knew if nothing else, he would feel bad for my loss and talk to me, but he wasn't interested in what happened or in me. Billy was at the bar. He didn't have anything to say to me—never asked if I was okay or if the girls were fine or anything.

I was just holding the phone because we were both sitting in silence. I heard his friend holler, "She said she had to get her keys, man."

"Who got to get her keys, Billy?"

Click!

I called back, but he never answered.

Chapter 22

Reality

I just buried my granddad, and my husband was in another city messing around. I couldn't sleep. I wanted to drive home, but it was late, and I was tired. I stayed up all night, calling my house and my husband's cell phone. Crying, I left him at least twenty messages, telling him to please answer the phone.

"Why are you doing this to me? My grandpa is dead. I need to talk to you."

I never heard from him that night. I imagined him being with another woman. I knew it. He didn't care what I went through.

When his grandmother passed, I bought him something nice to wear and held his hand through it. What gave him the right to treat me this way?

"It's over when I get back," I told myself. I cried all night long in that room.

Brandy woke up one time and asked me if I was okay.

"Yes, go back to bed." I was uneasy and mean. I had a conversation with myself all night that night.

"How could he stoop so low? I knew he was vicious, but I never thought he would do this at a time like this."

When daylight hit, I called Vicky. She lived around the corner from our house. It was around 6:00 A.M. when I called her.

"Vicky, can you please go to my house and see if you see Billy's car there? I'm sorry I woke you up, but I can't find him. He won't answer the phones."

"Okay, I'm on my way." She sounded so sleepy.

About twenty minutes went by, and she called back. "Rachael, his car is there."

"Thanks, Vicky. I'll tell you what's goin' on later."

"Mm-hmm." She yawned.

I called the house one more time before we got on the freeway. When he answered, I screamed, "Where have you been?"

"I was 'sleep, Rach. Why? What's wrong?"

"I've been calling you all night long. I called your cell and the house and you ain't answer."

"I didn't hear you calling."

"Billy, the truth will come out. Whether it's today or next year, it's gonna surface. If you want someone else, I beg you to tell me now."

"You talkin' crazy, Rachael. I don't want nobody but you. You know that. When you coming home?"

As he talked, my heart melted. I realized I was stressed and imagining things. I accepted what he was telling me as the truth. I wasn't ready to let go, even though I knew it was time. I didn't want to be alone, but I was already alone. We had nothing between us; just lies.

I started praying more and more. Every time I would pray, God would reveal something that Billy was doing. I mean, there were women coming from everywhere. He had ten to fifteen affairs when we were married; maybe even more.

I was so paranoid and confused, I didn't concentrate on anything else. I didn't pay any bills, didn't watch what my daughters were doing, didn't listen to the employees at my salon. I'd lost so much weight that people began to think I was on drugs. I was miserable.

I eventually lost my salon. All I wanted to do was escape my life, so I would spend all of my money. I lived in a fantasy world of shopping, going out to dinner and the movies or to the bars with friends. No one knew how I really felt or what I was really going through, since I hid my feelings with fake smiles.

"Oh, I'm fine," I would say. "Everything is okay."

People in the salon used to talk about me. "Girl, she so stupid. He ain't worth it. I don't know why she takes his crap. He treats her like a dog."

I would hear them, smile, and just hope they never were faced with what I was going through. All the weight I lost left me looking good on the outside, even though I was ugly on the inside.

The one person I wanted to notice me didn't pay a bit of attention to me. Billy didn't care about the weight loss. All he cared about was the streets. Billy wasn't coming home at all now except to change clothes.

I was so depressed. It was only a few months after we buried Grandpa, and I had never dealt with his death. It was hard for me at this time in my life. I wanted a good life with a strong husband in it. That's all I ever wanted. It was such a simple thing to ask for, but it didn't happen. It didn't happen because I lived in sin with Billy. We started a relationship while I was still in a marriage, to begin with. You can't be blessed in a mess like that.

After Grandpa died and it had sunk in how low Billy really was, I wanted to pay him back. I figured I might as well hang out with my girls. Peaches, Vicky, and I went everywhere. We started shutting Columbus down every night for a couple of years. He was out so much that he didn't even know I wasn't at home—or he didn't care.

I cooked dinner before I left and made sure I was in the house before he came in in the morning. He came in about 6:00 A.M., so I came in at 3:00 A.M. I was so sneaky with what I was doing. I would call him and ask questions about what he was doing and when he would be home, then made plans based on whatever he said. It always worked. I thought I was getting away with something. I wanted him to pay for all the women that called me at the salons and let me know they had my husband for that night. I didn't care that he didn't know what I was doing. It just felt good because I knew what I was doing and was smart enough to get away with it, unlike Billy. That was enough for me.

Billy had so much weed stashed at the house. It was inside the hole he'd made in the wall when he was angry at me and hit the wall instead of my face. I started taking it and smoking it with Peaches and Vicky. Me, Peaches, and Vicky met and smoked every night before we went to the clubs.

I never went to any clubs I knew Billy was at, but I still had time to stalk him. The majority of the time, I was high, weed being the only fix that took me out of my reality. I didn't know how else to deal with it besides smokin' weed.

I called Billy, asking him the same question repeatedly: "Are you cheating on me?"

He got so upset with me and screamed on the other end of the cell. "I'm tired of you asking me if I'm cheating and you always accusing me. It's annoying and unattractive."

I could tell in his voice he was angry. He threatened to leave me if I kept it up. I begged him not to leave and promised him I wouldn't say anything about another woman again.

I started working in a small salon right next to the CNS. It wasn't a good idea to work next to where Billy hung out. In fact, it was a horrible idea. I was like a private eye looking for clues to solve a case. We had a huge picture window in the front of the salon that allowed me to see everything that went on outside the bar. I would see his car going up and down the street all day long, and females walking over to his car, leaning in the window.

"Are you bound to a wife? Do not seek to be loosed. Are you loosed from a wife? Do not seek a wife."—1 Corinthians 7:27_

"Rachael speaking. May I help you?"

"Hi, Rachael. It's Lesha," one of my customers said on the phone. "What you doin?"

"I'm doin' hair. You wanna come in today?"

She hesitated. "Rach, I'm callin' you because somebody put somethin' in my ear today, and you need to hear it."

"What's up, Lesha?" I was curious. I knew whatever she was about to say was true because she didn't bring mess to people. She wasn't like that.

"I know this female named Vanessa."

My heart dropped, and my stomach felt like I was on a rollercoaster ride going down a hill. I listened to Lesha tell me the story. She told me all about this chick Vanessa that Billy was supposed to be messing with. Vanessa was the same chick that I spoke to on the phone about nine or ten months earlier, who said Billy and her were friends and she was just calling to invite him to celebrate her birthday. I knew exactly who she was.

"She works as a clerk at a gas station. Speedway. Now, Rachael, the girl has ten kids, but none of them live with her."

All I could think was, *What would he want with her?*

I went home and went in my bedroom and pulled the bill box out from under the bed to find the receipt from the

Nextel bill. I sat on the floor in my room with my dog, MJ, pushing me, trying to get me to pet him so I wouldn't cry.

"Move, MJ. Not right now, okay?"

He looked at me, turned away, and lay down in the corner by my television set.

I felt bad and called him back over. "Come here, MJ. I'm sorry."

He got up, came over, and licked me on the hand.

I looked through the phone records, petting MJ at the same time. I closed my eyes and said, "Lord, I know I keep asking You this, but I need You, Jesus. Please, let me find what I'm looking for."

I got up and looked out my bedroom window to see if Billy was anywhere in the area. He wasn't. The neighborhood was quiet and beautiful, with all the trees blowing softly on the warm August day. The kids were on the front porch, talking to their friends from the neighborhood.

"Lord, show me what numbers to call, please." The first number I called out of two long pages of phone numbers was one of my old clients. I was shocked.

"Hey, what's goin' on, Sherry?" I said.

"Oh, hey, Rachael. What's up?"

I could tell from her tone that she wasn't expecting to hear from me. She didn't know what I knew. She was trying to act innocent, but it was too late for that.

"I'm trying to find out why your number is in Billy's phone. What's that about?"

"Um, um, I think you need to ask him."

I know she ain't getting fly with me.

"I'm asking you. What's up?"

She breathed heavily and then hung up.

I stormed through the house, grabbing up his clothes to throw out the window. I started to call him and tell him what I knew, but first I wanted to check some more numbers.

My phone rang, and it was Sherry calling me back. "Rachael,"she said, "I'm Billy's friend, that's all. I'm sorry I hung up on you, but he's out of control."

Shoot, she was my client. I fixed her nappy hair and made her beautiful, and that was how she repaid me? Sleeping with my husband?

"So, Sherry, what you and him have to talk about? Why you talking to my husband, huh?"

She really couldn't explain it to me.

After I got off the phone with her, I tried to figure out the next number to dial. I went through the pages of numbers. I just picked one and dialed. I asked for Vanessa.

The female on the other end said, "She's not here, but I'm looking for her too. She owes me money."

I knew then I could get any info I wanted out of her. I told her who I was and played on her sympathy. I cried and told her how Billy was doing me.

She was a country girl talking with an accent from down South somewhere. "I think I know where you can find her." She said they grew up together and also let me know that Billy had been to her house to see Vanessa before.

I was angry. I wanted both of them to pay and pay big. I took the gun Billy left behind and put it in my purse.

Enraged, I walked back and forth in my bedroom, talking to myself about what I wanted to do.

She knew he was married. I told her myself. She had no excuse. I was gonna make her pay. I got in my car and went to her job.

"And that they may come to their senses and escape the snare of the devil, having been taken captive by him to do his will."—2 Timothy 2:26.

The devil thought he had control over my mind to the point where I went up to the gas station to shoot that woman, but God knew there would come a day when someone else was going to hear about my story and it would change their situation and their plan for another.

I drove up to the Speedway she worked at on Cleveland Avenue and 161st. I knew exactly who she was. I put the gun in my purse and went in the gas station.

Vanessa and a couple of employees were standing around laughing when I walked in. I looked her up and down to see what it was he liked. She had a caramel skin color, almost as if she was tanned, but she wasn't. Her hair, a sassy little bob cut with blonde streaks, was medium length with a lot of body in it. Vanessa was short, about five feet tall, and was medium-built. She was an average chick, but looking at her, you would think she had it all together.

"Vanessa, I'm Rachael. I know you're sleeping with my husband, and I want to know why you lied to me. You told me he was just your friend."

She was shocked, and her co-workers stepped away from her, leaving her standing there by the coolers of beers by herself. She said, "Let's go to the back."

I followed her, and when we got to the break room, I could tell she was scared. She didn't know what I was going to do, or capable of doing. I didn't either.

Before I knew it, I grabbed the gun out of my purse and put it to her head. "Look, I came up here so you can tell me the truth. I'm tired of hearing about you braggin' about you and my husband. You disrespecting me, and I need some answers." I looked her in her eyes. "I ain't playin' wit' you either!"

I didn't care about her being at work or all the crying and trembling she was doing. She was wrecking my life, and she was gonna tell me something.

She was bending down, trying to duck, and her hands were shaking as she attempted to cover her head.

"Okay, okay, I'll tell you. Just don't shoot." She started telling me about how they ran into each other at the CNS when I went to Dayton for a funeral. She said, "We went to a couple of hotels, but he decided to go on Brice Road to the Red Roof Inn."

She described everything he had on. It was the same clothes I remembered on his side of the room before I left to go to Dayton. As she talked, my eyes swelled up from the knife being jabbed in my heart. This was the first time any of the women that I suspected Billy of being with told me the truth. It hurt bad. I wanted to crawl on the floor and die.

She told me that he left her at the hotel early in the morning but returned at 11:30 A.M. to pick her up. But he wasn't in his car. He was riding with a friend.

I remember when I came home from my grandpa's funeral, Billy was 'sleep, but woke up early in the morning and left with his friends. He didn't drive his car but rode with them. I knew she was telling the truth. It just hurt so badly. Billy, my husband, was back home when I was burying my grandfather, and he was sleeping with another woman. I didn't deserve that. No one deserves that.

Vanessa looked at me. She examined me, my two-carat diamond rings on both of my fingers, and my twisted hair back in a bun. She looked at my designer heels and my designer jeans and said, "Why did he do that to you? You're beautiful."

I stood there on alert, with the gun still in my hand, pointed down at the right side of my body, never saying a word.

"I'm so sorry. I don't have an excuse for what I did, but I'm sorry, Rachael."

I put the gun in my purse and watched Vanessa sit in the break room and cry. I stared at her for a few more seconds then opened the door and left, never looking behind me. I left there looking for Billy, contemplating my next move with him.

Vanessa eventually left her job because I was obsessed with calling there daily and asking her questions about what happened that night. One time I told her, "Sorry to bother you, Vanessa, but I need to know—Did Billy wear a condom when you were sleeping with him?" I was obsessed with the affair, trying to figure it out in my head and wanting her to explain to me what it was she had that kept Billy around.

After plenty of days and nights of pure agony and defeat, Vanessa was forgotten about when a new chick came into his life. This one worked at the CNS bar he ran his drug dealings out of. Things had already gone from bad to worse. What was next?

Chapter 23

Street Pharmacy

Billy's next affair was with a crack cocaine dealer named Shyann. Shyann drank and smoked weed with Billy and his crew. She was also a part-time cook at CNS. They even sold dope out of her apartment.

When I found out about her, Billy denied it, saying, "Yeah, right! I wouldn't mess with that rat for nothing. Get out my face! All you do is accuse me. You're crazy!" He flung his hands in the air, and I ducked. "Go get yo' head check!"

Just then, his phone rang. He reached for his cell and answered it. "Hello." He smiled. "I'll be there in a minute."

Then he said to me, "You think I mess with everybody. I ain't messin' with nobody." He laughed.

I drew back and took cover when I saw him ball his fists. I felt like nothing after that confrontation. The way he spoke and hollered at me left me feeling belittled, standing there against the wall with tears streaming down my face once again. I stood there smelling the seductive fragrance of the Burberry cologne I'd bought him.

Billy sat there on the edge of the bed and put on his Timberland boots as if I wasn't even there. He sprang up, rubbed his hands back and forth, looked in the mirror over the dresser at himself, and threw on his fitted baseball cap. Then he grabbed his keys and headed down the steps and out the front door.

I knew he was lying, but I wasn't strong enough to deal with him. He had emotionally and mentally beat me to death. I sat against the wall and listened to him whistle as he walked to his car in the driveway, his cell phone ringing.

I could hear his car start because the window was open, allowing the soft summer breeze into my bedroom against the right side of my face, reminding me of the many times I lay in the grass and dreamed on the hot summer days in Dayton. I came back to reality as soon as I heard Billy's music blasting down the street.

I went over to the Shyann's house one night with another female that I'd found out about by checking Billy's messages. When I called her, she began to tell me that he was having an affair with Shyann from the bar. I was so desperate that I asked her to take me to where she lived, and she did. I was so confused. Here I was riding with—no, picking up—a woman that was messing around with my husband to take me to another one's house. Now, that made no sense.

I pulled up to the projects Shyann lived in, straight in front of her house. The outside of these apartments was a mess, filthy diapers in the dirt-filled yard and trash everywhere. Someone pulled the sheet back from the window, and then she came running straight toward me with a butcher knife.

I closed my eyes. *Jesus, please don't let her cut me.* My heart was beating fast.

She was screaming and hollering in my face, "Don't come to my house. Why you out here?"

I couldn't believe it. She was tiny, like a nine- or ten-year-old girl, but her eyes had heavy bags underneath them, which told me she had to be in her late twenties or early thirties. She had blue weave in her hair, standing straight up.

I was shocked, and my mouth was wide open as I gazed into the eyes of this rowdy little street pharmacist that was sleeping with my husband. I went back in the car and called Billy as she argued with Celeste, the chick that rode with me and showed me where Shyann lived.

"Billy, come around here. I want to get everything out in the open."

"I'm not coming around there, and don't call me. You don't have no business at that girl's house. If she hurt you, don't be mad." He hung up on me.

Shyann just kept saying, "Why you out here? What you want?" She was wired up, wanting to cut somebody with the knife, swinging back and forth, excited from the attention she was getting from her neighbors.

"You messin' with my husband?"

She instantly began shouting and screaming in my face. "No, I don't want yo' husband. We do business, that's all."

"Please, I don't know you. Just tell me the truth." I reached for her and touched her arm softly so we could connect and she could feel the hurt and turmoil I was going through.

She pulled back and put the knife away. I knew she was feeling what I was saying. After all, we were both women here, and one man was playing both of us like fools.

Billy never came around to take me home or see if I was hurt. Nothing.

I started sleeping away the majority of the day, not getting up for my daughters' school bus or anything, and I worked in the evening, wanting to disappear for the rest of my life but not knowing how.

I started writing everything I felt on paper. I was able to relieve pressure when I wrote.

"My brethren count it all joy when you fall into various trails."—James 1:2.

God prepared me to tell my story. When I went through the mess I was in, He put in me to write everything down so I would not forget it. He was preparing me to help bring others out of what I was in.

"You will show me the path of life; In Your presence is fullness and joy; at Your right hand are pleasures forevermore."—Psalm 16:11.

Peaches tried to get me to leave Billy. Vicky tried too. They didn't know how to get through to me, but truly nobody knew how bad it really was. They saw Billy cheat and dog me, but they really didn't know how bad it was. They didn't know about the voices that kept me up until morning, or the thoughts I carried around daily. I was stuck, trapped, couldn't get out. Why couldn't I leave this man? What was it going to take? I'd drive around all night, anywhere I thought he would be, talking to myself and looking for his car.

The devil thought he had me. He thought I was going to kill someone or either kill myself, but the devil is a liar. I tell you, I thank God for renewing my mind.

I stopped asking Billy questions altogether when he would come in. I would turn my back to him and cry myself to sleep, smelling the residue of the club, food, and weed. It got to the point that whenever I even thought he would be cheating, it was true. I was busting out females' car windows and harassing every female I found out about, not realizing that I could have been hurt or someone else could have. I was out of control.

Shyann told me about her affair with Billy about two years and about six chicks after our confrontation. One day, I was driving to work and she was in an old, raggedy Cadillac beside me. We started arguing on the road.

She said, "I hate you! You stupid!"

I said something silly back to her and then thought about how we had both let a man make us act like animals. We were ready to kill each other over a man that was messing around on his wife.

After the argument, I went in the salon, wanting to beat her down for being alive and breathing the same air I breathed. I decided to call over to the CNS where she worked. I knew the only way I could get her to talk was to provoke her, and I did just that.

"Yep, I been messin' wit' Billy for years," she finally confessed. "Ha, ha, ha! What you gonna do?"

I was relieved she finally admitted it.

"When you call him, he's usually laying in the bed with me. Yeah, I be hearing you begging him to come home." She laughed. "You a dummy, taking care of him and he hates you. He said if he could kill you and get away with it, he would. Billy can't stand you."

I looked at Vicky sitting there in the salon with me as I talked on the phone. We were the only two in the salon. Vicky could tell Shyann had said something foul, because it broke me right then and there. I couldn't hide it.

"He sits up at night when you call, thinking of ways to kill you. He thinks you're disgusting. Now, you want to know the truth, I'm telling you the truth—Yo' husband hates you. You can't do nothin' for him." She giggled. "He told me he don't even sleep wit' you. You pitiful!" She laughed more.

Vicky walked over to me and took the phone. "What happened, Rach? What did she say? You all right?"

I couldn't answer her. I sat there looking across the salon at the gold walls and beautiful mirrors that hung on them. I couldn't even look at Vicky. I was too ashamed.

I dialed his number. "Billy, what's going on?" I said, crying and screaming on the cell phone.

He began to shout. "I don't want to hear that. I told you to leave the chick alone. That's what you get. Quit calling me wit' that nonsense. I told you, Rach, before, I don't have time for this mess. You just stupid!" He hung up.

I didn't want Vicky to know he hung up. "Billy, Billy." I hung up.

Vicky was standing there shaking her head back and forth, her arm on my shoulder. "It's got to get better, Rach. Leave him alone. You got yo' answer now."

I didn't listen. I wanted to be right. After all, he was my husband, not Shyann's. I decided to go over to the bar where she worked.

When I went in, she was in the kitchen. The CNS was small. It went straight back with a dance floor to the right, pool tables in the back, and the bar and kitchen was to the left. There weren't many people there because it was day-time, but there were at least nine in the whole place.

My heart was racing because I really didn't know what I was going to do. I wanted to hit her dead in her face, maybe scratch her eyes out or something. I wanted her to pay for her vicious words. She was standing behind the bar near the kitchen, smirking when she saw me.

We started arguing and I said, "I'm gonna get you. Come from behind the bar!"

"Come and get me." She smiled. "What? You mad because Billy don't want you?"

Her co-worker was holding her back, and the security guard came over to me and asked me to leave.

Shyann laughed, looking me right in my face. "I got your man."

Vicky tapped me on the shoulder and said, "Look."

I turned around to see what she was talking about and saw Billy sitting down. He was in the bar the whole time this was happening and never said a word.

He finally got up and rushed over to me and said, "Leave! You so stupid!"

Shyann thought it was funny.

Billy then said, "You gonna get me kicked out of here, acting stupid!" He grabbed me by the arms and pulled me out of the bar while I continued to argue and shout with Shyann. I was sliding and falling on the ground when one of my heels broke.

He pushed me out the door and said, "You get on my nerves, actin' stupid!" He turned around and left me outside.

I watched him walk back in there through the glass doors, smoking his Black and Mild on the bar stool and talking to an older man, waving his hands and laughing. I was banned from CNS after that.

I went back to work and continued doing hair. My mind was on what had happened, but I couldn't do anything about it right then. I was gonna make Billy know I was right. It was wrong for him to treat me like this. I kept thinking about what Shyann said. I called Billy's phone to talk to him, but he never answered it.

When I got home from work that evening, Billy was there packing his clothes. He seemed to be angry. He had veins sticking out the side of his neck and he was breathing heavily. I couldn't believe that he thought all of this was my fault. It didn't make any sense.

"Billy, please don't leave. We need to talk. I won't act like that again, but I need you to talk to me. Tell me the truth, and maybe we can work it out from there."

"Get away from me, Rachael. I told you, the next time you start actin' all crazy I was out."

I tried holding on to him, but he was smacking me away with his hands.

"Get off of me!" he screamed. "I'm out!"

"I won't ask any more questions about where you goin' or where you been, I swear. Just don't leave like this, please. We need to talk. I just want the truth, Billy."

"You crazy, Rachael. I told you the next time you did something like this, I was leaving."

After he said that, something in me snapped. *Who does he think he's talking to? He think he can walk all over me and I keep taking this mess. He's cheating on me. Let him go!*

I blurted out, "Go ahead and leave!"

Usually when he packed up and pretended to leave, I would cry and beg and then he would stay, but not this day. I was tired and didn't want to be in this a day longer. I picked up some strength from within.

His eyes got big when I said that. He probably thought I was going to beg him then everything would be back to the way it was until the next time.

"You can't take nothin' out of this house," I added. "Not the big screen, not that Caddy you drivin', nothing!" I was following him around room to room to see what he was taking. He didn't deserve to have anything. All the money I spent on us to live nice, I bet I wasn't gon' let him take it.

He came back up the stairs from taking his stuff to the car. "What you mean, Rachael? I can't take the big screen and my car? I'll take whatever I want. I paid for it."

"You don't do nothing around here but buy yourself tennis shoes and clothes. All you do is spend yo' money on yourself and dope. You ain't takin' nothin' out of here." I was in his face, probably spitting all on him. I was so mad. Billy was a sorry excuse for a man. He didn't care about nothing but himself, and I was tired of him.

I could hear the girls downstairs saying, "Let him go, Mom. We don't need him. Let him take what he wants."

We fought in our bedroom that day.

I could hear my daughters coming up the stairs. "Stop, Billy, before you hurt her!" They were both crying and screaming. They knew what I was going through and they never said anything about it until now.

I couldn't hide the abuse I endured from this relationship, and even though I thought I kept it out of the sight of my daughters, they knew. My mind was lost, and they were old enough to understand I was being mistreated. They heard and saw the conversations that I had with Billy. Even though they never opened their mouths, they could hear the conversations when I called him. They sat back like flowers on the walls and listened. They saw and heard it all. I had never protected them, even though I thought I had.

Billy had me by the throat, so I couldn't breathe. I could hear my babies getting closer up the stairs. I screamed, "Go outside and wait for me!"

Billy and I were eye to eye, looking into each other's brown eyes as he attempted to choke the very life out of me.

After I got away from him, I tried to flush the dope down the toilet, but he grabbed me and threw me on the bed. He was on top of me with his hands wrapped tightly around my neck. I surely thought I was going to die. I couldn't see anything, and I couldn't breathe. I screamed in my head, knowing I was going to die in my bedroom, on my own bed, with my daughters standing outside on the front porch. I was lying there thinking the one I trusted is the one that was going to take my life.

I screamed in my head, *God, come and help me! Please, Jesus, I repent. I repent!*

Suddenly, the room got dark and I couldn't see or hear anything. I blacked out.

"Let her go! Let her go! BILLY, LET HER GO!"

I opened my eyes and felt the pressure loosening around my neck. I could hear Billy's mother screaming for him to let me go. All of a sudden, I felt the weight of Billy double on top of me. She had jumped on his back and was fighting him, beating him in the back with her fist to let my neck go. I could hear the thumping of her fist against his back.

I don't know how she got to our house or when she came up the stairs. She was just there. When she finally got him out of the house, I had two broken fingers he'd twisted to get the dope out of my hand, broken bones in my shoulder, and marks and bruises around my throat.

"Then they cry out to the Lord in their trouble, and He brings them out of their distress."— Psalms 107:28_

Billy went to live with his mother and her boyfriend, and I stayed in the house. That day he strangled me, his eyes were black, and the expression on his face was blank. He looked demonic. I'd never been so scared of losing my life, not even when Tone tried to kill me.

Five or six months after the separation from Billy, Vicky convinced me to go out with her. I hadn't been anywhere in months. I was depressed and only went to work and back home. Vicky and Peaches called every day and checked on me and stopped by some days with some weed to relax my nerves.

"Girl, you got to get out of this house," Vicky said. Her eyes glanced around my messy room. "Rachael, you hear me? It ain't good to be stuck in this room. What about the girls? You need to get it together. You need to be glad he's gone, for real." She puffed her cigarette then exhaled.

I sat at the end of my bed and looked out the window, wondering where Billy was. *Who is he with?* I wondered if he was with Shyann. I was sinking in depression, but I knew going out was a way to get my mind off Billy.

"Yeah, I'll go out tonight." I jumped up off the bed and grabbed my cell to call Dee-Dee to do my nails. I wanted to look nice for the night.

I reached out to Vicky and took the weed she was puffing on. I put it to my mouth and began to inhale. I closed my eyes and decided this weed was going to take me out of my reality.

I was sinking fast and far into something. I didn't want to come out of. I would get my hands on weed and escape from everything around me. I didn't even care who knew I smoked or who was in the room when I did it. I'd convinced myself that it was a sure way to keep my mind off my husband; to keep my sanity. I smoked constantly. I mean more than ever, if that was possible, and I still had the same problems. I was high more than not. At work, in the car, it didn't matter; my mind was altered with drugs.

I started dating different men for their money, prestige, and weed. I knew the big dope men and the athletes kept it, so I targeted them and surrounded myself with those types of men. At the clubs, they were the only ones I would give attention to. All I wanted to do was have a little fun and smoke their weed up. I wanted to be in the light and go places that I'd never been before. I wanted to feel special. However, if I kept on living the life I was living, I was surely going to hell. (Isaiah 54:11-17)

Chapter 24

Mental Abuse

I appeared to have it all together to the average person looking in at my story, but the truth be told, I was a hot mess. I was playing a role maybe from a movie I had seen or something, but it was all an act. I never told anyone what I really was feeling or going through because all my life I knew when bad came before me, I was to act as though it wasn't. I had been doing it for years. What was the big deal now? I would hurt in silence.

One day while I was in the shop, Billy called. "Hey, Rachael, how you doin'?"

I didn't expect the call, so I was caught off guard. "Hey, Billy. What's up?" My response was dry. I wanted him to know it wasn't okay to put his hands on me.

"I just called to say I was sorry. I didn't mean to hurt you that day, but you be trippin'."

"I be trippin', Billy? No, you—" I took my cell and went in another room after realizing the other girls in the shop were watching. I went up the stairs into the bathroom and shut the door. "Billy, you hurt me."

"No, I didn't. You okay?"

"I had to go to the hospital. You broke two of my fingers, and I had broken bones in my shoulder."

"You lying? I didn't do all that."

I heard the music playing behind him and knew he was sitting in his car. He inhaled the smoke from the weed and blew it in the phone. His voice got low and he said, with the smoke going through his lungs and penetrating his vocals cords, "I'm sorry if I hurt you."

I went out the bathroom to the front window of the salon and saw his car pulling off. "Where you at?"

"Don't worry about it. I'll call you later, Rachael." He hung up.

I looked at the phone and dialed his cell but then hung up. "It ain't gonna be that easy," I said to myself.

After speaking to him that day in the salon, he started calling me more and more, until we were talking daily. I couldn't shake everything that had happened between us, though. It stayed in my heart and on my mind. Billy wanted to act as though everything was okay, but I couldn't. I needed some answers from him.

"Billy, why did you want Shyann? What made you cheat on me with her and the rest of the women?"

"I don't want to talk about them. Come on, Rachael. Let's forget about that stuff. Move on."

"I can't. I need to know."

He breathed out over the phone as if I was getting on his nerves. "I told you I was only friends with those women. I never slept with any of them, Rach."

I couldn't believe he was still lying after all the facts. He was busted and needed to face it, but he would never admit to having any affairs. I wanted to know if Billy was still cheating, so I decided to set him up. I should have just walked away from the marriage, but I didn't. The way I saw it, he was *my* husband. I couldn't shake the affairs, especially this last one with Shyann.

I knew he wasn't telling the truth, and I suspected he was still seeing her. I was so confused. Why wouldn't he just leave me alone? I was doing fine until he started calling.

I sat on my bed and talked to myself. "Why would he call me if he didn't want me? He was out clean. He didn't have to start calling me again if he wasn't serious. I'm his wife, not Shyann."

I decided when I went to the shop that I would have my first customer for the day, Stacey, call his phone and act as if she was Shyann's sister. I couldn't wait until Stacey came in that morning.

I heard the salon's doorbell ring as Stacey came in. I was sitting in my styling chair, looking in the mirror at myself, wondering why Billy had cheated on me. I was beautiful, and I knew it. I had lost all that weight, and my skin and face was so pretty. So what made him want other women? I even treated him good. And I was smart. It baffled me.

I spun around in the styling chair with my feet and said, "I've been waiting for you." I was the only one there. No one else was scheduled to come in until later in the day.

She smiled. "What?" Stacey knew something had happened because every time she came in, it was something else. Another episode of my life.

Stacey was tall, probably 6 feet. She kept her hair done, sometimes even getting it done twice a week. Her husband stayed in trouble with the law and in and out of prison for drug-related charges, and when he was away, she took care of all his business. She was intelligent, but used her intellect to deal in the dope game.

She came in talking on the phone and making moves for the day. She was in charge of her husband's crew while he was in prison. She was wearing a chocolate-brown mink that touched the ground as she walked. Her fingers were covered in expensive diamonds, and her neck was decorated with a diamond choker. Stacey drove a brand-spankin'-new Benz truck. She was beautiful too. She got her hair done the same way every time and didn't want a piece out of place.

Looking back on her now, you would think she had it goin' on, but the truth is, she didn't. She was a shell all dressed up and miserable on the inside.

Stacey took care of me. She paid above the price, and if she came back in the same week, she paid all over again without a problem. She was paid. These days, she was coming in maybe once a month, and her husband was waiting in a halfway house to come home.

"Hey." I smiled. "Do me a quick favor.".

She smiled, trying to figure out what scheme I had going on now. "Okay, what you need?"

Stacey called Billy and pretended to be Shyann's sister looking for her. She said, "It's an emergency. If you know where she is, can you tell me?"

She watched me and smiled. She liked busting him.

"Yeah, she's at Bingo with Nina," Billy said.

After Stacey left, I looked around disoriented, grabbed my purse and left the salon. I got in my car and knew at that very moment that he must love her. I screamed from the top of my lungs, "I can't believe this! He knows where she is! All this stuff Shyann did, telling me about her and him, and he's still seeing her! I hate her! I hate her!"

I could hardly breathe, and my dress was wet in the front from all the tears. I didn't know where I was driving. I was just driving around the neighborhood, wondering what I did to deserve such a treacherous husband. He was plain evil, flaunting his affairs in front of my face.

Somebody's gonna pay for this.

"They must think I'm a chump, taking all this drama. I'll show them who they dealin' wit'."

I went to her house and waited for her to get home from Bingo. She pulled up about ten minutes after I did, not noticing my car or me. I watched her as I slid down in my seat. I put the small gun in my back on the inside of my jeans, with my shirt over top of it. I got out of the car slowly, watching her every move. I walked over to the door of her car, smiling, took the gun out of my back, and tapped it against the window.

She turned around and grabbed her chest.

"I just want to talk to you."

She began to cry and took off in her car, driving like a mad woman out of control, swerving back and forth in the parking lot.

I ran behind the car with the gun pointed at the back of Shyann's head through the glass. I closed my eyes and pulled the trigger.

Pop! Pop! Pop!

I heard her tires screeching all the way down the street. I ran back to my car, holding the smoking gun in my right hand. I had adrenaline running through my veins, feeling empowered by something that was overpowering me.

I started the car and drove off quickly. I drove with my right hand and felt for the small hole in the door with my left hand. Billy had the gun in there and had forgotten about it. He put it there for when he drove my car and had to deal with somebody.

I heard the sirens coming after me and had to think fast. *What am I going to do? Think, Rach. What you gonna do?* I pulled in front of the shop and ran in. I didn't feel like me. I felt like someone had taken over and was leading me to my total destruction.

I knew the police were outside the shop because I could hear the sirens in the neighborhood. I was scared. All the power I felt went right out the window.

I went outside like I didn't know what they wanted. The police officer was standing there with his 9mm drawn.

"Put your hands where I can see them!" he ordered.

I started to cry immediately, realizing I was in some serious trouble. "Okay," I said in a sad, scared voice, my hands raised to high heaven.

The policeman came toward me and patted me down. "Turn around!" He put handcuffs on my wrists.

I can't believe this. I have handcuffs on. They're tight and hurting my wrists. I'm going to prison.

He sat me in the back of his car. "Where's the gun?"

"What gun?"

"The gun you shot off around the corner. Don't play games with me! We know everything! We're gonna find it. If it's in that car, we will find it, young lady, so you might as well tell us where it is."

I knew not to do that.

The tall, blond, blue-eyed policeman went to the car and searched, but couldn't find the gun.

I started to pray. *God, if you get me out of this, I quit. No more silliness. I quit.*

I could see the officer talking to two more officers who had pulled up in their cruisers. He pointed toward Shyann's apartment, then back toward the shop, then at me. The other officers looked at me.

Then I heard on his police radio what was going on.

"She doesn't have any warrants or anything. I don't think she had a gun," one officer said.

"Copy that. Let her go."

The officer came over to me and said, "You don't have a gun, but we talked to the other female involved and she admitted that she had an affair with your husband. Leave him."

By this time, Billy was pulling up. He jumped out of his car with the music still blasting, screaming, "What's goin' on? That's my wife! What she do?"

I was crying. "Billy, I don't know."

"You all right, Rach? Huh? Let her go, man. She ain't do nothin'."

The officer grabbed him and put him in the back of the other cruiser. They blamed him for everything and decided to run a fifty on him, to see if he had any outstanding warrants.

"Yeah, you sit back there," the officer told him. "You a sorry man, putting your wife through all this mess. What's wrong with you?"

The police officer turned to me. "Lady, I don't know you, but I'm telling you, you don't belong in this situation. Let them have each other." He was serious, looking at me with those spectacular sky-blue eyes. "They look like they belong in this mess. They talk like it. But he is not worth it."

I was daydreaming, wondering what had happened. How did things get like this?

The officer continued his lecture. "You listen to me. Get yourself out of this now."

I wanted to do what he was advising me to do, but I knew I wasn't going to leave my husband. After all, for the first time, he had come to my rescue.

Billy had an old warrant for not going to court for a traffic violation, so the officers took him downtown. I went downtown to get him out of jail, but when I arrived, he was leaving. His friends had been there to bail him out. I ran into him when he was leaving.

"Man, Rachael, get out of my face!" He was huffing and puffing, walking around with his shoulders out, ready to fight me. He was cussing and pushing me. "You stupid, out there shooting at that girl. You got me locked up!

"Where's my gun, Rachael? Stay away from me. If you don't, I swear I'll kill you!"

I stood there paralyzed. He had driven me to a place that I would have trouble coming back from. I realized then that this marriage had been done for a long time. I was holding on to nothing.

* * *

I changed salons again. I wanted a new start away from Billy and all the trouble that came along with him. I knew as long as I worked so close to where he frequented, it would drive me crazy.

The girls were out of town visiting my mother, and I was home alone. I had moved my bedroom to the living room. I didn't like sleeping in my bed anymore. When Billy was there, I was alone mentally, but I could still feel the heat from his body, and somehow I convinced myself that that was good enough. It was now MJ and me.

One night, I was awakened by MJ standing between the living room and the hall, toward Brandy's room, looking in her room like someone was standing in there. I was nervous. I knew I was the only one there besides the dog.

I turned on the living room light and realized he was wagging his tail and the light in Brandy's room had mysteriously come on. I hadn't turned it on, and I knew the dog didn't do it. As I went toward her bedroom, someone went out the window. I knew it had to be Billy because MJ wasn't barking. I was scared. I didn't know what he was thinking.

I didn't know if he was planning on hurting me or what, so I decided to stay at a hotel. I was moving out of the house anyway because it was going into foreclosure from lack of payment. It was only a matter of time before the bank was coming to take the house. So, I packed everything up, put it in storage, and moved into the Marriott on Busch Boulevard. I was moving my kids around all the time it seemed. Was I Momma? Was I worse?

Chapter 25

Trying to Escape

I was staying in the hotel until I knew what my next move would be. I had lost my clients from changing salons without notice, so it would be a while before I would be making decent money. I was deep in debt, but it was my fault because I let this man get away with so much—so many lies and so much deceit. I took whatever he dished out and settled for less for me and my daughters. Thing is, I got just that—less. All I wanted to do was be somewhere else, escape my reality, start over. Problem was, I didn't know how to start over; without doing wrong, that is.

I refused to dig myself into a hole. I decided whatever it was going to take to live right, I was gonna do it.

"Rachael, line one. Rachael, line one."

"Okay, thank you." Smiling, I walked to the phone. My new workplace was awesome. Everything in the place was wood-grain and red, not to mention the barbershop on the other side with all the gorgeous men I could look at all day.

* * *

Rachael, concentrate. That's what got you into this mess in the first place—men. "Hello. Rachael speaking." I was still smiling from the thought.

"Hey, Rach, how you?"

"Who is this?"

"You don't know what yo' husband sounds like no more?"

My heart dropped, but he couldn't worm his way back into my life this time. I was fed up with Billy. "What do you want, Billy? How you get this number?"

He laughed. "You think you can get away from me, Rach? Come on, you know me better than that. I own these streets. I can find you, babe."

I wanted to hang up on him, but I couldn't.

"Rachael, let me take you out this weekend. What the girls been up to?"

He didn't know anything. He didn't know where I lived or where the girls were. I hadn't spoken to him in months. And now he wanted to do what Billy did often—pretend nothing had happened.

What do I do? I wanted so badly to hang up and walk away from him and this so-called marriage, but I couldn't. Like I hadn't had enough of this nightmare.

"Rachael, come on, baby. I miss you. You know I love you, don't you?"

That's all it took for me to let him back into my life.

Billy stayed with me in the hotel for two weeks, but continued to do the same thing he always did. His phone rang constantly, and he wouldn't come in until morning. Nothing had changed.

I said to myself, "I can't go back in this. I'm not strong enough."

I knew if I went back to him like this, I would either die or lose my mind. So, before I moved into my apartment, I sat down with him and told him if he wasn't ready to give up the streets, then he couldn't come with me.

That night after our heart-to-heart, Billy never came back to the hotel. I realized I needed to move on. The kids were coming back, and I needed to have them ready for school and focused. Perhaps this time I really could start over.

Chapter 26

Me and the Girls

The new apartment was for new beginnings. It was me and the girls. Our new home was nice. The apartment sat on a ravine overlooking a small brook with water flowing down it. I could sit on my patio and look at the view.

Crystal sent money to help me with the move. We had talked and solved everything from the past and became close again. Brandy was starting high school, and Brea was starting middle school.

My clientele was now back to where it was in the old days. I was on demand. The salon I was at was awesome. The woman who owned it was one of the women that stood in the door when Tone wanted me dead. Darla now had her own salon, and it was beautiful, one of the classiest salons in town, chandeliers and mirrors everywhere. Darla was a classy woman.

I had worked at Darla's shop for a year when the State Board of Cosmetology came through to check everyone's licenses. It was a Friday and it was crowded. I knew that I hadn't renewed my license, but I didn't think it was a big deal. I thought I would get fined and that would be that.

The woman typed up my information on the computer with her long, slender fingers. "You haven't renewed your licenses yet?"

"Um, I don't know. I thought I did."

"No. It says right here you haven't." She was serious and she never took her head out of the computer in her lap while she talked. "Yeah, it says right here you didn't renew, sweetie. Let me make some calls to see what they want me to do. You go ahead and finish the client you have, then pack up your things when you finish her."

"Are you serious?" I asked.

"Yes, very serious." She turned and looked at me with her green eyes. Her badge was on her red blazer, like she was the police.

I was devastated. What was I going to do? How was I going to make money now? Not to mention I felt terrible for Darla. She had taken me in and trusted me. I had lost her trust. I agreed that when I got everything taken care of I would come back, but I knew I couldn't face anyone in there. I was a big fake.

I started working at home, and I had to go to the library and study so I could be ready to take the state board test again. I knew I got what I deserved. I worked there irresponsibly and didn't think about the consequences. I hadn't taken the test in over seventeen years, and the last time I had taken it, I had teachers to prepare me. This time, I was truly on my own.

I'd always thought it wasn't a good enough career, but God showed me to quit complaining. Hair was exactly what I wanted to do. I loved making women feel good about themselves and showing them how beautiful they were. I really enjoyed it. I'd worked from the time my daughters were born up until the time I was told to go home. I didn't take vacations or time off except when I dated Tone.

I worked straight for seventeen years, and it was time for a break. I stayed home watching movies, and cooked, cleaned, and spent plenty of time with my daughters.

My clients started leaving once I was out of the salon. Only a few would come to the house. God provided, though. It was a hard four months, but He provided. I had to pay over $700 worth of fines.

I got my license back and went to work with a female I had worked with at Tommie's. Nicky was the manager of Royalty hair salon. She knew about my mishap at Darla's shop. She wanted me to come over to the salon she was managing. I agreed and went. It was a good move for me and the girls because I was able to make good money to support us.

After a few months, Billy found me and started calling again, this time telling me he was ready to change, start over and treat me and the girls like a family. He would call and leave all sorts of messages. He sounded so sad, but I had no sympathy for him. My attitude had changed, and I didn't want him back. He hurt me and the girls so much in the past. Billy wanted to come back like nothing had happened.

I started listening to him and thinking maybe he had changed. Maybe he really did want to be right. I started letting him come over while the girls were asleep or gone for the weekend, but two incidents occurred during this time.

First one, I left Billy at my apartment one morning when I went to work. I had calls to my phone forwarded to my cell. He didn't know this, but decided to use my phone and call a woman. The female's boyfriend called the number back, and it went to my cell. Her boyfriend told me Billy had just called for his woman seconds ago. Of course, when I called Billy, he denied ever using my phone. He was still a liar, but it was too late.

The second incident was already in motion by the time the first took place and left me devastated. Billy had given me a sexually transmitted disease.

"Rachael, I don't feel so good. Let me stay here a few days," he begged.

He stayed in my bedroom, and I catered to his every need. Every need he had, I was there. I thought he had the flu or a virus, so I took off work, cooked dinner for him, and gave him aspirin, hoping he would feel better, not realizing that within a few days I too would have the same exact symptoms.

"Billy, you need to go to the doctor. I don't know what's wrong with you. It's scaring me," I told him.

"I'm all right. I'm gonna leave today. I need to take care of some business, but I'll be back later."

I didn't want him to come back because the girls were coming back later that day from visiting Denny, and I didn't want them to see him there. I said, "I'll call you."

He got up and slowly put on his shirt and shoes and walked out the door as if he was in pain. I watched him out of my window, limping to his car.

Within a few hours, my symptoms overtook me, and I called Peaches. "Peaches, I need you to drive me to the emergency room. I don't know what's wrong with me." I began to cry softly. I knew something was wrong, but had no idea what it was.

"Girl, I'm on my way."

I called Billy while I waited on Peaches. I could tell he was in the club from the background noise. "I'm going to the hospital. Something is wrong wit' me."

"Okay, call me later."

We walked in the hospital to the front desk, where a woman sat. "May I help you?" She smiled.

"Yes, I think. Well, I don't know what's wrong with me."

"Okay, let me get your temperature, and then I'll bring you back."

"Peaches, I'll be right back."

"Okay." She grabbed a magazine from the rack and sat down.

"Okay, Rachael, is it?"

"Yes, it's Rachael."

The foreign-born doctor looked at my chart. "Have you had sex over the past two weeks?"

"Yes, sir, with my husband."

"Well, let me do a pap anyway. Your symptoms look like an STD."

I got real quiet, and my heart was pounding, I could hear it. I covered my eyes during the exam.

"I'm finished," he said. "Now put your clothes back on. I'll be back in a few to give you the results." He smiled and walked out of the room.

I sat there on the table, trying to figure out what I was going to do. I thought, *Oh my God! Please don't let me have nothin'. I know Billy didn't give me anything.*

The nurse came in the room and took some blood. Then the doctor came back in and said, "Ma'am, I need to tell you that you do have a sexually transmitted disease and need antibiotics, in fact."

My mouth was hung open in disbelief. "How? I only been with my husband, sir."

He looked at me and said, "I'm sorry."

I cried and cried and cried. I looked at the doctor. He was rubbing his forehead. I was so embarrassed and betrayed. Billy was a disgusting, nasty, dirty dog, and this right here was the end of me and him. I could never go back to him or trust him again. What was I thinking, letting him back in my life? I knew who he was and the things he was doing.

When I left the hospital, I called Billy.

"Billy, you gave me something. You a dirty dog. What were you thinking, out there sleepin' around wit' God knows who? Man, I ain't got nothing for you. It's over! I hate you!"

He sat on the other end of the phone like he didn't know

what I was talking about, but I knew he knew exactly what I was saying. I was so stupid.

All day I lay on my bed in shock, with Peaches telling me everything was gonna be all right. I wondered if she was gonna share my secret with anyone else. I stared at the ceiling, lifeless and pitiful. Why was this happening to me?

As soon as Peaches left, I heard someone knocking at the door. I knew it wasn't Denny and the kids because he'd called and said he was going to keep them with him a few more days. I went to the living room and looked out the peephole. It was Billy standing there, trying to peek through my living room blinds.

I opened the door, and he was standing there, smoking weed and staring at me. I looked at him this time, not like before. I looked at the residue on his face from the skin problems, all the scars from him not taking care of himself, his head covered up with a 'do-rag, so no one could see his scarred, bald scalp. He was a walking infection that could have been prevented if he'd just cared about himself.

"What do you want? Huh? I ain't got nothin' to say to you, Billy. You off the hook!" I turned away from the door and walked back toward my bedroom, with the front door still open.

"Wait a minute, Rach. Let me explain." He shut the front door and came in.

"Explain what? How? You gave me a disease. You nasty! I don't have anything to say to you."

He reached for my arm. "Rachael, I'm sorry."

I pulled back. "Don't touch me!" I walked toward my white leather sectional in my living room.

"Oh, man." When he covered his face with his hands, I noticed his long fingernails that he wouldn't cut.

"I'm sorry, Rachael. I'm sorry."

I sat there watching him with my legs crossed. I hated him. I wanted him out of my life. I never wanted to see him again.

I didn't care anymore. I did everything I could do to show this man I loved him and wanted him, but he didn't care. If he did, he would never have let himself get in a position like this.

"You need to go to the doctor as soon as possible. You need medicine so this can go away."

He couldn't look at me.

I was so angry with myself for having sex with him and not protecting myself. Deep within, I knew that he was sleeping around, but I wanted to believe otherwise. I slipped up and had to pay for it, but what if I had to pay for it with my life?

Chapter 27

Did My Husband Give Me HIV?

Istarted thinking that if Billy was out there sleeping around like that, perhaps I needed to get an HIV test. I didn't want to, because I was afraid, but I needed to know. All the time this was going on, I never shared it with anyone. Not even Peaches or Vicky. I went to work and spent time with the girls like everything was fine, but down on the inside of me, it felt like someone was turning me inside out. I knew I needed the Lord now, so I prayed and asked God to help me as I went to the lab by myself.

After I had taken the test, I found out I was fine. I had no disease, no sickness, and the STD was gone. I knew God did it. The whole time I waited for these test results to come back, all I could do was wonder, What if the test came back positive? How would I tell my daughters or my family? I didn't want to die. I wanted to live, and I wanted out of this mess.

Billy never once called or came to my rescue. He didn't help me at all with what I was going through. He stayed away, hiding in the shadows of his mistakes. I called him and told him that he needed to protect himself on the streets then I hung up. I couldn't understand why he wouldn't protect himself when he was out there. He didn't even care enough about himself to make sure he would live.

I moved on.

Brandy was the captain of the cheerleading squad at Brookhaven High School. We were trying to live a normal life and go forward with our lives. I kept the girls in my view at all times. We were at the salon or the house. Our relationship had gotten close. They were my best friends.

I became friends with my barber, Michelle. She kept my hair tapered in the back of my head. I always had a sassy, short hairstyle, except when I decided to rock some weave. Michelle was the only one that knew how to cut right. She was short, maybe five feet or so, bleached-blonde hair and cocoa skin. Her hair was cut close to her head and was curly from the chemicals she put in it. She was very curvy and worked with men all day. She flirted all day long and flaunted her shapely body in their faces, knowing exactly what she was doing. But she was sweet.

Michelle was a hard worker. She had four kids, ranging from twelve to seventeen. We had a lot in common. We both had been married, and now we were raising our children by ourselves. We shared stories about our past relationships with men and talked about our kids, and on the weekends, we would have cookouts.

Another thing we had in common was marijuana. Now, Michelle and I were weedheads. We smoked the whole day. It wasn't about anything else but weed. We even smoked in front of our kids. It didn't matter; we had to be high.

After leaving Michelle's house one night, I pulled up to my apartment, tired and high, when I saw Billy sitting outside in his car. I saw him before he saw me, so I didn't pull in the parking lot. He had been blowing up my cell all day, and I ignored it, so I guess he decided to just come over.

"Dang! Why did I tell him where I lived?" I was mad at myself. "What do he want?" I was agitated. I didn't want to be bothered with his mess. I also was nervous because I didn't know what he wanted. What was he gonna try to do? I had told him that I was through and filing for divorce this weekend.

I went off the deep end with my thoughts. *Maybe he's thinking if he can't have me, nobody else will!*

I drove past the apartments and down the street to Peaches' house. I had been through hell and back because of him, and I had enough. I didn't owe him anything. He had destroyed everything between us.

The thing is, as much as I wanted to, I couldn't treat him the way he had treated me. I didn't want to hurt him. I wasn't like that. I cared for him and didn't want to be mean. Yes, I had gone on with my life, but I refused to be mean to him. That was a mistake because I wasn't ever firm or direct with him long enough for him to take what I said seriously. I was working at a nice salon and taking care of my children. I didn't need any drama in our lives anymore.

Ring, ring, ring!

"Yeah."

"Rachael, why you pull off?" Billy asked.

"What? When?" I said, pretending not to know what he was talking about.

"I seen you. You pulled up to the apartment then pulled off when you saw me."

"I'm at Peaches' house. I'll call you tomorrow."

"It will be too late by then. If you don't meet me now"—he began to cry—"I'll kill myself right outside of here. I swear, Rachael, I swear!"

I didn't know if he was bluffing or telling the truth, but I knew my daughters were in that apartment. I had to think fast and get him away from there. "Okay, okay. Come down to Peaches' house. I'll talk to you." I didn't want to put my babies in any danger, just in case he started acting a fool. My problem was trying to tell him that I didn't love him or want him anymore. That has always been a weak point for me.

I pulled up and waited for Billy to get there. I sat in my car, trying to figure out what I was gonna say to him.

"Billy, you did too much," I told him on the phone before he pulled up. "Let's just go our separate ways." I knew he wasn't gonna agree.

As he pulled up in the Caddy and parked next to me, my stomach turned and I felt sick. I looked over at him and signaled for him to get into my car. I didn't trust getting in his because I knew he carried a gun in his car. I didn't want him to hear me say something that he didn't agree with and reach for it.

He said as soon as he got in the passenger's side, "Rach, I'm so sorry. I-I didn't mean to—"

"It's all right, Billy. I'm over it. I just want to move on."

"Without me, Rach? You want to move on without me, huh?" His eyes were red and filled with tears, and his nose was wet. He took his arm and wiped his nose. "Huh, Rachael? You through with me?"

Yep, you bet. I'm through with you.

I didn't say a word. I just listened to him all night sit there and talk. I was looking at this man cry as he was pouring out to me, but I didn't care. All I wanted to do was go home and get in the bed. It was too late for his apology, and I knew I had to go to work in the morning and get the kids ready for school. As far as I was concerned, he was a snake. Besides, all the different times I had cried to him, he told me to get out his face.

Billy sat there saying, "I can't live without you and the girls. You the best thing in my life. I didn't know that then. I'm sorry, Rach. Please give me another chance. You don't have to worry about nothing. I promise. I know I been a terrible man to you. I'll do better. Please . . . give me another chance."

I sat there as close as I could to the window and my door without falling out. I didn't want him to touch me. I kept looking at Peaches' apartment, measuring the distance, just in case I had to run. It wasn't that far, but could I beat his gun shooting off? I wondered.

"Rachael, I don't have nothin' else to live for. My momma is strung out on crack, and I ain't seen my dad since she shot him years ago. What I got left? Huh?"

He was crying hysterically. I had never seen him like this. He had lost so much weight and looked like he hadn't slept in days. I felt bad for him, but I made myself remember some of the things he'd done over the years, to keep me strong that night. I was thinking about how he told me he wanted a divorce and didn't want me anymore. I was thinking how harsh it was when it came off his lips and tongue. But now he loved me and couldn't live without me. I wasn't buying what he was selling.

As Billy talked, I watched the clock. It was 4:37 A.M. I knew I needed to be home before the time the school bus came.

Billy was upset. He realized that he wanted his family back and there wasn't anything else out there in the streets. I, on the other hand, was hurt. He had cut me so deep, and I didn't trust him, or any other man, for that matter. All I ever got was taking care of a man and giving him the most precious thing I ever had—me.

I believe God has answers to our problems, and sometimes we have to go through our mess so we can come out stronger. I am a pioneer. I went through my mess for others, to tell them there is a better way: His name is Christ Jesus! He and only He can turn your entire life upside down and right way up!

Chapter 28

More Tricks

After another seven months, I gave in to Billy's pleas and apologies and let him move in. He came back on the terms that he would quit selling drugs, get a job, and stop running the streets. I battled with the idea of him coming for a while, because I knew in my heart he was gonna mess up again, and I didn't want to go through anything else. Besides that, I didn't love him anymore. I cared about him, but anything else would just be obligation.

I now understand I had a problem with myself because there is no way I should have been anywhere near this man, let alone have him around my kids after the way he treated us. I needed deliverance, but first I needed the Lord.

"I don't want him here, but he has no place to go," I had cried and reasoned. I decided to quit asking God what to do. He wasn't giving me the answer I wanted—or rather I just wasn't listening—so I took matters into my own hands. I figured Billy was going to mess up eventually, and within a few months, things would be back to the way they used to be and he'd be gone again anyway.

Over the next few months, he never got a job, and continued to sell drugs. It was all a game. When Billy and I had separated, he had full control of my mind. He could have told me to sit and I would have done it, but now he had been gone almost a year and it wasn't that easy to control me. I dealt with his games long enough, and I wasn't taking it anymore.

We argued constantly. I was always mad because Billy would sell drugs and get caught telling lies. He had no ambitions, no dreams.

I resented Billy and despised him with every breath I took. I was bitter and blamed him for everything when, truthfully, I had the power to just walk away. Instead, I just kept letting him back in only to put up with the same mess.

"You said you were going to get a job and you were gonna spend more time with us!" I fussed at Billy as I watched him move through the house, smoking on his weed.

"Rachael, why you don't cook no more? Or wash my clothes? Why I got to do everything myself?"

I looked at him, my hands on my hips. "You don't deserve nothing I can do. Are you crazy? Last time I did all that, you took it out to another woman."

Billy turned his head and walked away, smoking his Black and Mild.

I hated him. Everything he did irritated my very soul. I started believing in my head that I really wasn't married to him anymore. I had myself fooled anyway. I figured that Billy would be caught cheating and I would divorce him for real this time. He was hanging around on borrowed time, was how I looked at it. I knew in my heart he was gonna mess up. I couldn't believe anything else. I was too scared to, so I went around acting like I wasn't married.

I had an affair with Marcus, a man that I had known for years. It started when one day I went to pick Brea up from the recreational center in our neighborhood. I ran into him. Turned out he was the basketball coach there.

He watched me enter the center then ran out of the gym over to me. "Hey, Rachael. How you doin'? I haven't seen you in a long time." He smiled.

Marcus was the overall nice guy who had not ever encountered a woman like me. He was nice-looking, but what really made him attractive was his sense of humor and the love he had for kids. He had no problem working, while most men I ran across were in the streets selling drugs.

"So, Rachael, what's goin on wit' you these days?"

I watched him as he looked at me and admired everything about me. I'd heard he had a big crush on me back in the day. I was in control again. He was a slave to my appeal. He was so much bigger than he was back in the day, I guess from being in the gym all day. He looked pretty nice.

"Oh, nothin'. Just taking care of these girls." I smiled.

"I know what you mean. I have three kids myself, and it's hard out here." He ran his fingers through his long braids that stopped on his back.

"Yeah, it is." I was wondering if he was married. "So, you married?" I looked at his ring finger and saw it was empty.

"Nah, nah." He shook his head. "Not me. I'm lookin' for the right one." He smiled and looked at me with his slanted little eyes.

I smiled, not wanting to be married to the idiot I was married to. I waved good-bye to this chocolate six-footer and wondered, *What if?* I decided not to go back in the center again because I knew this man was too good for me and I would corrupt him. I knew I was still married and if I got mixed up with him, I would eventually hurt him. I decided it was best to walk away.

"Brea, when you get out of basketball practice, come out to the car."

"Why, Mom? You can come in and get me. All the other parents do," she said with that thirteen-year-old attitude.

No, I can't. I knew I needed to stay away from Marcus. Billy might have been a jerk, but he was still my husband.

Like I said, Billy would definitely do something else to mess up, and lo and behold, he did. One of my clients, Lashell, saw him at a restaurant on the east side of town with some unidentified chick. Lashell called me at the salon and shared the details.

"Hey, Rachael, I'm sorry to bother you at work, but I'm out here on Main Street and who do I see? Yo' husband, Billy, standing out here in front of the Golden Griddle with some floozie! He out here hugged all up with her, Rachael, and kissin' on her."

I couldn't get a word in. I just listened and thought, *This is exactly what I need to get rid of him once and for all.*

"Girl, I told him I was calling you. I even asked for yo' cell number, but he gave me the wrong one."

I started laughing to myself on the other end of the phone because Billy was sure 'nough a piece a work.

"He's scandalous!"

"Okay, Lashell, thanks for telling me. I'll handle it."

"Yeah, you do that, 'cause he out here makin' you look like a fool, girl."

After we said our good-byes, I stood by the desk, staring into space, wondering what was wrong with him. He just couldn't leave well enough alone. He was busted.

Before I could call him, my cell was ringing. I looked at the number, and it was him.

"What's up, Rach?" I heard his friends in the background over the music he was listening to.

"Hey, Billy. What's up?"

"Nothin'. Just sittin' out here at the CNS waiting for my money to come through."

I couldn't believe it. He acted like nothing had happened.

I lost it. "Billy, you out there at the restaurant with a chick? You must think I'm a joke, huh?" I screamed out. "I want a divorce!"

I hung up the phone and turned my cell off. I looked around the salon only to find everything had stopped and everyone was staring at me. I didn't care. I was through.

He kept calling the salon, but I wouldn't talk. I wanted him out of my house and out of my life. I was better off by myself.

When I got home, he was sitting there on the side of the bed, staring out the window. I acted as if I didn't see him, but he stopped me as I gathered my dirty clothes to go in the basement to wash.

He grabbed me by the wrist. "Rachael, I'm sorry. It was nothin'. I was playin' with her. We went to school together."

I looked down at my wrist and twisted it away from his grip. "I'm tired, Billy. I want you to leave." I wasn't playing with him, nor did I stutter, or make him feel like I didn't mean what I'd just said out of my mouth.

"Rachael, I'm not leavin'. I love you, and I pay rent here too. I can't let you go. We been through too much."

"You got to get out of here! You have brought me nothing but grief. Throughout this whole marriage, it's been pain and grief, and I don't love you anymore. I want you out of here now!"

He began to cry and tell me how my client was lying on him to sabotage our marriage. I thought, *What marriage?*

Billy never left. He said he had nowhere to go. I didn't know what to do, so I just stopped talking to him. I decided if he wouldn't leave, cool. But I didn't have to talk to him, I didn't have to touch him, and I sure didn't have to love him. I knew he thought he deserved it.

* * *

I was no better than Billy. I went back in the center a few days after finding out about Billy and his new affair. I decided I was going to date Marcus.

"Can I have your number, maybe take you out to dinner sometime?" he offered one time.

I smiled and said, "Sure. Why not?" I knew I was playing with fire, but I didn't care about nothin'. I was tired of what I was in. I needed an escape, and Marcus was going to be it.

About six or seven months into the affair with Marcus, Brea started acting up at school, fighting constantly and arguing with everyone. Her school would call me daily, saying, "Brea did this," or "Brea did that." It was driving me crazy. I didn't know what to do with her.

My answer to her problem was sending her to live with Denny in Dayton. I don't know what I was thinking about. He never spent any time with the girls, almost pretended that he never had them at all. Now I was going to let her go live with him. I did lose my mind.

I told Brea that if she didn't get it together, she would have to stay with her father forever. Neither one of the girls wanted that. Denny wasn't right, and even the girls knew that. Denny did what he wanted. He would come and get them when he wanted, which was rare. But I thought, for some stupid reason, that he was the answer.

Chapter 29

Chains Falling Off

Brea was staying with her dad. The arrangement was that she would stay just for the first part of the year then come back home to me. She was still acting up in school, and I didn't have time to deal with one more problem, and the weed wasn't helping anymore. I figured that if she stayed away from home for a while, she would get it together and want to come home and do right. Thing is, the problem wasn't her. I was the problem and I didn't want to face it.

Denny had other plans, figuring if he took her, he didn't have to pay child support. He tried to convince me to sign legal custody over to him, but I knew he couldn't be trusted. I told him I would put her in school down there and we would see how it went, but all he wanted to know was if I was going to sign her over. I knew then that his heart wasn't for the right thing.

Brea was already down there staying with Denny for about four days when I had to go down and enroll her in school. I didn't know what to do about her. I really didn't want to be away from my baby, but at the same time, I wanted her to grow into a successful woman. I didn't think I could raise her to be successful. I was nothing, and was making terrible decisions in my own life. What could I do to help her? Nothing.

Denny was now a minister, and I thought he would raise her well. I convinced myself, thinking it would only be for a little while, and hopefully he could get her on the right track.

However, it didn't sit right with me. I didn't feel comfortable with her being down there because I was responsible for her. Now I was trying to give that responsibility to others. I felt guilty for bringing her to Dayton.

While I was driving, I talked to the Lord, asking Him to help me, to show me what I needed to do. I screamed as I drove an hour to Dayton. I cried out to the Lord like never before.

"Jesus, can you hear me? Please, Jesus, show me now. Please, Jesus, show me what direction You want for me and my children. I need You!"

As I talked to God, my cell phone rang. It was my friend Michelle.

"Girl, we went to church Sunday. Mm-mm, it was awesome!"

Michelle had asked me to go to church with her a week beforehand. She was tired of the streets and wanted to get her children into a church. I had told her yes, but in the back of my mind, I wasn't serious. I knew that I wasn't living right, and I knew that I didn't want to play with the Almighty God. I knew when she asked, I wasn't going.

"Girl, it was powerful how the Lord moved through the place. You need to go! I mean, Rach, you need to get the girls together and get there."

I drove and listened to her. I heard the excitement of the Lord coming into her life, and I wanted that.

She went on to tell me how her and her kids got up and accepted Jesus as Savior.

I wanted to have Jesus back in my life. "What's the name of the church?" I asked.

"It's called Power and Glory," she screamed with excitement.

"Hey, let me call you back. I think that's the church Tanya told me about."

Tanya had been telling me about this church for the past two years. She was my friend and my hairstylist. Whenever I got my hair done, she would always talk about her church. I sat there listening to her talk about Jesus, and I would be high. She just continued to smile and tell me about her church and God.

After I hung up with Michelle, I immediately called Tanya. She didn't answer, so I left her a voice message, asking her what was the name of her church.

As I drove down the freeway, she called me back. She was so excited.

"The name of my church is Power and Glory Ministries, and the presence of God is in the church."

Immediately, I felt chill bumps go all over my body. "I will be there Sunday."

From that day, my life has never been the same! I knew God had answered me on that freeway.

When I reached Denny's house, I knew I was taking Brea home with me. I knew that God was going to change our lives. I didn't have any idea how He was going to change it; I just knew life as we knew it was over.

I told Brea to pack up her things, and I put her in the car. Denny watched and never said a word. God had a plan!

When we reached Columbus, I told the girls we were going to go to church. I told them we were going to change some things in our lives.

"Brandy, Brea, we gonna change everything in our lives. You hear me?" I grabbed them and hugged them. "We going to church from here on out and giving everything to the Lord." I really didn't know what I was saying out of my mouth and just how God was going to really come in like a flood and change everything.

One thing I know now is that the Lord has those He loves set aside for a time to come unto Him, for His purpose. And what's so awesome about that is that He will allow anyone through obedience in Him to be a part of Him.

I kept my word and woke the girls up first thing Sunday morning, and we went to church. I asked Billy to come also, but he declined.

As I sat in the pew and cried, I felt like I had just put down everything in my life and laid it at the feet of Jesus. The heaviness was gone. I knew that God was there. I could feel His presence like never before. I listened to the man of God speak, and the power of the Lord was upon him. By the time he called for salvation and those who wanted to join the ministry, my daughters were already at the altar. I had to catch up with them.

Over the next few months, I still saw Marcus while married to Billy. I had issues that only God could work out.

One thing I kept doing was going to church. No matter what I was wrapped up in, I stayed in church and knew somehow that God was gonna work it out for me. I went every Sunday, and the messages started hitting me harder and harder. Eventually, I would be convicted of different things in my life. Life couldn't go on as usual. It was impossible for me to hear the Word of God and receive it then continue to live in sin. God was looking upon my life, and it wasn't a very clean thing to look upon.

I started wanting to know more and more about this Jesus, and the way my Apostle explained the events in the Bible, it just came to life. I started writing down everything he said in services, the scriptures and all, word for word, and eventually I found myself talking more and more about Jesus Christ. The more I heard, the more I had to know.

Whatever my Apostle would talk about on Sunday, I would write it down and go home and look up the scriptures and read. I was so excited about the Word. I would sit and read the Bible for hours at a time. I took it wherever I went—to work, to the store. It didn't matter; all I wanted do was read. I wanted Jesus more and more. I now knew why Grandpa loved the Bible so. I realized life was in the Word. Everything we do and breathe is in the Word.

One Sunday, my Apostle called everyone that had been battling addictions to the altar. He said, "If anyone has an addiction to anything, run to this altar because God is going to deliver you today!"

I believed him. Moreover, I believed God. As I ran to the altar, I couldn't stop crying. All I wanted to do was please God. I didn't want anything that was unlike Him in my life anymore.

I kneeled on the altar and began to pray. "Father, take it away! The feeling, Lord, everything! You help me. I want to be free. Let me use You to help me face my problems, my fears, my everything. You help me. Let me not ever put marijuana to my mouth to smoke again."

When I got off the altar, I never touched weed again. Praise God. And I know that I will never again. Through Christ that strengthens me.

"Who Himself bore our sins in His own body on the tree, that we, having died to sins, might live for righteousness by Whose stripes you were healed."— 1 Peter 2:24.

Before that day, I let the enemy trick my mind and tell me things like, "I just won't do it on Sundays," or "It's natural. It's from the earth!" Truth is, it is a drug and it alters the mind; therefore, it is harmful. Thank God for deliverance!

God can get a person out of any situation, any addiction, anything! You must trust Him and believe He can do all things.

Deliverance from marijuana was an easier battle to win than some of the others. The next one was a lot tougher. I didn't know what to do about Marcus. My feelings were wrapped up in him. I mean, I never had a relationship with a man like him before. I knew it wasn't right because I was married. However, no matter how bad it was, I didn't divorce Billy, so Marcus should have been off limits. Meanwhile, Billy hadn't changed anything. He was still selling dope and running around. We needed to come to a resolution.

Chapter 30

No Better Than He Is

Cheating on Billy was making me no better than he was. I was so confused, and I wasn't making the right decisions. I wanted someone to care for me and love me. That's all I wanted. I wanted to feel secure, so I selfishly took it where I was getting it from. The need of wanting to be loved and noticed.

I'd messed around on Billy before, when we were separated, but I never had gotten attached to any of those men. I did it to fulfill needs, which were companionship, attention, and of course, sex. But the relationship with Marcus was more.

I felt guilty. And the only reason I was feeling this way was because of God. If I hadn't given my life over to Christ, I would have thought it was okay to stay in the relationship with Marcus. It would have been justified by the doggin'-out Billy had done to me.

Here I was saved and having an affair. What was I thinking? I asked myself that question time and time again, but the truth is, I enjoyed Marcus's company. I couldn't understand how it could be wrong because when I was with him, it felt so right.

Now, Marcus truly was unlike any other man. He was authentic. I hated that I was going to have to stop seeing him, but I knew it would only be for a little while, just until I got my divorce.

I pulled up to his apartment, and he buzzed me in.

He was standing outside the door, waiting for me with his FedEx uniform on, ready to go to work. "Hey, why you lookin' like that? What's so important you couldn't wait until I got off work, Rach?" He was smiling and pulling my hair softly. He studied my expressions.

Marcus knew me in a different way, not like the others that had thrown me away. He cared about me, my heart. I knew I couldn't hide my thoughts from him.

I couldn't go on this way, and I knew that only God in Heaven was going to get me free and keep me that way. Not Marcus. Not anybody. I figured if we were meant to be, then it would have to be a different time and a different season for us, not like this.

I looked at him, put his face in my hands and felt his smooth, soft hair against my skin. I closed my eyes, took a deep breath. "Marcus, we have to stop seeing each other."

I opened my eyes and saw that his were closed. He didn't respond. "Did you hear me?" I said softly.

"Yeah, I heard you." He pulled back, put his jacket on, and started for the door.

I couldn't look at him. I kept my eyes closed tight. "I can't do this because I know it's—"

He interrupted, "Oh, it's cool. Don't worry about it. I'm a big boy, baby." He tried to act as if it didn't bother him, but I knew it did. I could see it all over his face. He opened the door as I stood in his one-bedroom apartment and said, "Come on, girl. I gotta go. I'm gonna be late," he said jokingly.

I walked out the door feeling terrible. But I knew it was the only way to get completely clean. We said our good-byes, and I stopped talking to him. My heart wanted him around all the more, with frequent thoughts of us being together, but I knew I had to do the right thing. All I went through, and I was no better than what the different men had put me through. I didn't want to be a cheater anymore.

Marcus would come around every now and then asking me why I wouldn't see him anymore. He called me phony on several occasions because he didn't understand what was going on with me. He wasn't living for Christ, so to him, as long as we cared for each other, he thought that should have been enough. But it wasn't. I needed more in my life, and I knew that Jesus was what I was missing.

I didn't have an answer for Marcus. I just knew us being together wasn't right. My mind was so tricked by the devil and blinded from the truth, thinking I was supposed to be with him. I didn't realize God wasn't going to ordain my mess.

I was the one who was sending myself straight to hell. That's why I tell women now_not to have affairs. It will cause you to lose your soul. You get deeper and deeper into a relationship that you can't see your way out of.

I wasn't seeing Marcus anymore, but things with Billy weren't good. He was now saying I was getting on his nerves with this church mess.

"You act like you all holy. Don't forget you smoked weed too."

"Billy, I don't care what I used to do. God has made me new."

I sat on the bed and read while he blew weed smoke in my face. Billy would offer me the blunt every time he smoked marijuana.

"No, thank you." I smiled because God had delivered me from it, and it felt good to say no and truly mean it. God is amazing! He put a standard in me. I wouldn't go back to the drugs.

Billy and I had a problem connecting. Our marriage and life at home was a mess. He never showed any affection toward me. I wanted a man's love. Problem was, I was looking for it in the wrong places. I now know that I have a Father's love, which is my Father in Heaven.

"A father of the fatherless, and a judge of the widows, is God in His holy habitation."—Psalm 68:5.

I am not making an excuse for any of my actions because I was dead wrong for some of the things I was doing back then.

Billy and I would lay in bed beside each other, but we didn't have a physical relationship. I would pray and ask God to keep me at peace, my mind, and my body. Just keep me at peace. It's real hard to be with someone and they don't touch you, talk to you, and care what goes on with you. It could have driven me back in the arms of Marcus, if it hadn't been for the Lord.

I began to understand that all I did was talk about Billy and what he did to me, but what did I do? I thought about all the times he was in the streets before I was saved, and how I would lay on the floor in our bedroom and cry out to God to do something. But then I would get up off the floor and I didn't let God fix it. I tried to fix it myself by getting back at Billy. Moreover, jumping into bed with different men, going to the clubs and talking about how stupid and grimy he was to my friends, I was doing the same thing he was doing. I was doing it in the dark.

Nobody knew how sneaky I was. Was I going to divorce him and not even give him a chance to learn about Jesus? Was I not going to tell him anything about Christ? I had to find out what God really wanted for me. For us. Maybe through prayer Billy's will would change and he would surrender to Christ. I didn't know, but I had to at least try before ending the marriage altogether. I didn't want to try, but I knew me. And what I mean by that is only God could have changed me, so who was I to say that Billy couldn't change and fall in love with Jesus too? I had to try.

I decided to start praying for him, and I asked God to stop his clientele, stop people from buying his dope. Eventually, after praying that prayer, no one bought drugs from him anymore. He couldn't understand why, but I knew God removed them.

I wanted him to know that Christ was over his life, so I told him everything that I learned. Whatever my Apostle told me and whatever I read in the Word, I shared it with him. Billy witnessed God move in my life in a tremendous way and a quick way. He knew it was the power of God, without a doubt.

Billy started talking different and went and found a job after that. I couldn't believe it. He hadn't ever had a job. I was amazed.

He said he was going to come to church with me, but after six years of me being in the church, he didn't come. He told me repeatedly that he just wasn't ready to give his life to Christ. I stayed in the marriage for almost eleven years.

After the few changes in our lives, he went back to the drugs and the mental cruelty. I did everything I could have done to make it work, but he just didn't want it. Before I went through with the divorce, we lived in the house together for one whole year with him sleeping on the floor and me in a completely different bedroom. It was as if we were roommates. What he cried about to get in the house became a lie in front of my face.

I prayed, I cried, I went up for prayer at church. I even repented, because I couldn't pray for him anymore. I despised him so much. The thing is, the devil wants us to hang on to those feelings of hate, anger, bitterness, and holding grudges, because if he can cause us to hold on to people right where they hurt us and never let them go, then we would send ourselves right to hell. You cannot get to Heaven by being unforgiving.

I wasn't happy, he wasn't happy, and my daughters weren't happy. I thought by taking him back that I had to take the treatment he dished out. I thought a sanctified wife sanctifies her husband. I went around quoting that scripture. I'd learned that a wife does sanctify her husband, but if he is not willing to change his will to God's will, it won't happen.

I thought I was free from all the pain I went through with him; the affairs, the STD, the cruelty, but it still hurt.

As I walked with God, I learned through the Holy Spirit that I couldn't make someone want my God. I also couldn't make someone love me and be faithful to me. Billy didn't want Christ, so he couldn't be the husband I desired. He thought it was all right to treat me like I was nothing. Don't get me wrong; I was guilty too. Just like with Denny, I didn't handle anything the right way.

I prayed for three years on the matter and lived two of those years in separate houses from Billy. I didn't see anyone else; I just concentrated on the things of God.

After doing that, I realized I could leave Billy. Billy hadn't changed and wasn't going to change. I decided I'd rather be alone and serve the Lord, allow Him to take His place as my husband.

It was time to get out of this. I refused to spend the rest of my life miserable.

Today, I don't have a problem with Billy. I'm his friend. I just knew he wasn't supposed to be my husband. I believe he was miserable too. I also believe I hindered him from becoming a man. For so long, I was a momma to him, catering to his needs. I frequently pray that God saves him and he marries again and has children. That's my desire for him. I forgive him for everything we went through and hope he forgives me.

* * *

Keep talking and don't lose faith. Be obedient and know that God is watching and listening. God has truly shown His amazing power in my life. I now realize that throughout my entire life, He has been with me. I have totally given my life to Christ. Sold out. There is no turning back. I decided the day I was on the freeway and the Holy Spirit let me know that I was being called, that I wouldn't leave my God.

Before now, I had no type of enthusiasm to share my struggles or tell the truth. When the Lord showed me that my story would help others, it was no longer about me. Anything I can do to show the Lord that I can be used for His victory, I will do it. That is the least I can do for what He does for me. The Lord has washed my sins away, and He has made me a new woman.

I never thought or imagined the things that God has placed in my life. Everything I did was based on what someone else thought or wanted done. It was never what I truly wanted to do. God came in like a flood and gave me the ability and confidence to use my own mind. He freed my mind from bondage. But I'd never tried to please God, and the thing that is so amazing about God is that no matter what I did, He remained faithful.

"For His anger is but for a moment, His favor is for life; Weeping may endure for a moment, but joy comes in the morning."—Psalm 30:5_

It's never too late to find Christ. When all seems lost and hopeless, it's not. I found Him and He turned my life around. I went from the extreme into God's glory. And if He can do it for me, He can do it for you.

Altar Call

Jesus, come into my life. I want to be free. No more chains, no prisons, no darkness.

Jesus, I ask You to shine the light of Glory on my life, my situations, on me. Save me. Make me new. Forgive me of my sins. I believe You are the Son of God. I confess with my mouth that You died for my sins on the cross, and I believe in my heart that God has raised You from the dead. Romans 10:9 says that if you confess with your mouth the Lord Jesus and believe in your heart that God raised Him from the dead, you shall be saved.

Reader's Group Guide

1. How did Rachael deal with the sexual molestation that she experienced as a child? How did the molestation contribute to her promiscuity as a teenager? As an adult?

2. We often hear the term "word curse" to describe the negative, destructive words spoken by others that may help to bring about mischief and mayhem in the spiritual or physical realms. Were any such "word curses" spoken into Rachael's life as a child? If so, by whom? If so, how were they fulfilled?

3. What role did foolish curiosity and peer pressure play in Rachael's life as a teenager with respect to drug use?

4. To what extent did Rachael's rebellious attitude lead to pregnancy? What does the Bible say about rebellion?

5. How did the invisible chains of darkness guide Rachael's actions as a teenager? As an adult?

6. Define self-ignorance and how it contributed to Rachael's choices in key relationships.

7. How did being raped affect Rachael's search for God?

8. What circumstances led up to Rachael's divorce to Denny? Were those problems resolved prior to her second marriage? If so, how? If not, what could have been done to bring resolution?

9. What part does forgiveness have in Rachael's life in relation to herself, family, past relationships, and her spirituality with God?

10. Identify seven key events in Rachael's life that ultimately allowed God's divine purpose to be realized.